D0946066

Venus Envy

Shannon McKelden

TOR®

A TOM DOHERTY ASSOCIATES BOOK

NEW YORK

This is a work of fiction. All of the characters, organizations, and events portrayed in this novel are either products of the author's imagination or are used fictitiously.

VENUS ENVY

Copyright © 2006 by Shannon McKelden Cave

All rights reserved, including the right to reproduce this book, or portions thereof, in any form.

A Tor Book
Published by Tom Doherty Associates, LLC
175 Fifth Avenue
New York, NY 10010

www.tor.com

Tor® is a registered trademark of Tom Doherty Associates, LLC.

ISBN-13: 978-0-7653-5497-6
ISBN-10: 0-7653-5497-7

First Edition: January 2007
First Mass Market Edition: January 2008

Printed in the United States of America

0 9 8 7 6 5 4 3 2 1

To Jon...my love, my life,
my future chauffeur. 1-4-3!
To Jessie and John Michael...the best kids ever.

Acknowledgments

Books (mine anyway) aren't written in solitude. I want to give my special thanks to the following people:

To Deidre Knight for her unshakable faith in me, even when I get a little shaky myself. You are the Best Agent Ever!

To Natasha Panza for loving Venus enough to take a chance on her and on a brand-new author. And for "getting" Venus even better than I got her myself sometimes.

To the Goalkeepers: Christina Arbini, Serena Robar, Erin Eisenberg, Kelli Estes, Barb Roberts, and Cara Kean—I could never do it without all of you!

To my parents for raising me to follow my dream. Love you!

And, last but not least, to my husband's boss, Darryl Scott, for assuring Jon's schedule accommodates my writing career. Bet you didn't think I'd do it, did you?

Venus Envy

Venus Cronus

It's not every day a fairy godmother gets to pick her next victim . . . er . . . godchild.

Actually, today's not good for me, either. I'm so bored with the whole thing, I could just spit. It's the same every single time. Pick a loser human female from the crowd, try to convince her she can "be all she can be," and then wait until she gets it through her thick skull. Then, you move on to another vict— er, godchild—and go through the same process again.

Ad nauseam.

So, in an effort to keep from flinging myself to my death from the next skyscraper I come across (an impossibility, since fairy godmothers can't die—unfortunately), I've decided to liven things up by using a different method for choosing my next godchild. Something more interesting. No, "interesting" isn't the right word. *Entertaining*. Definitely entertaining.

I just haven't figured out how yet.

I'm off to my favorite pastime . . . creative retailing. "Retailing" being shopping . . . for basics like Jimmy Choos, microminis, and that incredible Prada bag that is *so* on my must-have list. "Creative" because fairy godmothers don't have a clothing budget. And, no, I don't shoplift. That would be unethical, and I am ethical if nothing else—although occasionally that depends on who's defining the word "ethical." All that counts is that I uphold the standards of my position.

Even if I *hate* my position.

But, back to shopping. I do not steal to supply my fashion needs. They're given to me. Usually by wealthy (read: horny) men who are only too happy to supply little old me (and by "old," I in no way mean to imply that I *look* old) with the very items that will bring me the most joy. They're *grateful* to hand over that American Express for me. Really. That glimpse I give them of cleavage—that their aged, saggy wives no longer possess (or won't share)—makes it all worth their while.

Well, that and the little mental ego-stroking I provide.

It's just one of my many skills. I "tell" them how wonderful they are, how virile, how overwhelmingly *hot*. Never underestimate the power of a well-placed psychic suggestion. I may walk out of that boutique with a shopping bag full of my favorite designers, but the men who fill those bags for me walk out feeling stroked and stoked and larger than life. And after that, I'd bet they're so *fantastic* in bed that their wives/girlfriends don't even notice the five-hundred-dollar women's clothing charge on the credit card.

So anyway, today, in an effort to assuage my boredom, I'm heading to a darling boutique that's been calling my name. I think I'll pop in there and see what I can do to lift my spirits and those of some unsuspecting, er, *grateful* male. And, perhaps I'll also find the next contestant for the Venus Cronus Extreme Love Life Makeover.

Or perhaps not, and I'll just get a momentary reprieve from the tedium.

Rachel Greer

Geez! Get out of the line of fire." I pulled the horny little Chihuahua out of the way of the stream coming from under the slobbery Saint Bernard's lifted leg just in time. "When will you learn? You're both male. Besides, he's twenty times your size and you aren't really doing anything productive grinding on his leg." Well, he wasn't doing anything for Junior, the Saint Bernard, but was probably accomplishing a lot for himself.

"Anyway," I continued speaking to my mother who was on the cell phone haranguing me as usual, "I know I haven't made it to dinner in a month. I'll try, I promise. How about if I pencil you in for next week?" I gave the leads another jerk, as Junior tried to take a bite out of the nameless Chihuahua who was trying to hump his leg again. "Stop it! No, Mom, not you. The dogs. I'm walking the shelter dogs. Yes, I do own a pen. No, I don't want a Montblanc pen set for Christmas, because I still won't use ink in my planner. Pencil is neater." For when I erase the things I pencil in—never intending to do them in the first place—just to appease whoever was trying to get another piece of my time.

Really, don't get the wrong impression. I love my mother. I love my entire family. They're fun and boisterous and loud. They're loving and caring and interesting.

They were also a reminder of everything that I would never have in my own life.

"I really need to go, Mom. The border collie is trying to herd the others into traffic, I've already spent two hours at the senior center balancing checkbooks, and three hours with Habitat for Humanity today. I'm wiped. I really just want to go home and take a hot bath." This last part was a lie. But if I told her that I planned on going to swim laps, too, before I crashed into bed later, she'd probably stage an intervention. "I'll talk to you soon. I promise."

I snapped my phone closed and groaned aloud to the dogs, who were exhausting me more than usual today. "It's not your fault, I know," I reassured them, as we continued down the boardwalk to the little stretch of beachfront that butted Cameron Creek up against the Puget Sound. "I'm not blaming you. It's just that everyone is on me today. My mother. My grandmother even. And she usually minds her own business."

But not this morning. Grammy had been in fine form, telling me how worried my mother was about me avoiding the family. How worried she was about my lack of social life. About how busy I was all the time.

Unfortunately, it wasn't the nagging itself that bothered me. It was how much it made me miss what I was missing. My older brother's twin boys growing up. The new baby they were looking forward to in the next few months. The planning of my younger sister's wedding. It was all too much for me to deal with.

But it was all too apparent that I missed it.

"Maybe I should stop volunteering at the senior center," I commented as I paused for a small unnamed mutt to sniff around in the bushes at the edge of the sand. "It's too much of an opportunity for Grammy to talk to me about how much I'll regret leaving my dreams behind. As if. Just because I was a naïve little girl once, dreaming of Prince Charming sweeping me off my feet and carrying me off to his castle, doesn't mean that's still my dream now. I'm thirty years old, for God's sake. It would be a little silly to cling to that fairy-tale fantasy, wouldn't it? I mean, really, the divorce rate is enough to turn any potential Cinderella's stomach."

Junior, the Saint Bernard, watched me with soulful—or was it rheumy?—eyes, wisely listening to my whining.

Which was interrupted by my cell phone chiming "Yesterday" by the Beatles, reminding me yet again that my troubles had once been far away.

"Rachel. Hannah." My best friend spoke in short, staccato sentences when she wanted people to listen up.

"Hannah. Busy." It doesn't have the same effect when I do it. She never listens to me no matter how I talk.

"I know. Always are. But, listen, Griff and I are going to check out that new club in Pioneer Square tonight. You have to come."

"I don't have to do anything but pay taxes and die. And, anyway, I have plans."

"Plans? Rachel, plans are dates. Plans are dancing. Plans are dinner and a movie. Plans are not reorganizing your Franklin Covey planner for the tenth time this week."

"Hannah. I don't do clubs. You know that. Give up."

"It's been two *years*. Seven hundred and thirty days since Eddie—"

"Stop! Do not go there. It won't help your case."

"Okay, fine," Hannah snapped, knowing she would have really been pushing her luck to drag Eddie into any conversation she wanted to win. "But, you are meeting me at Vintage and Vogue this afternoon for the Half-Yearly Sale, right? You are *not* blowing me off for that, right?"

"I'm not blowing you off."

There was a pause. "But, you're not coming." I could hear her pout. Hannah was very good at pouting.

Hannah Weeks and I have been friends since high school. I'd lived my whole life in Cameron Creek, a "quaintly old-fashioned town, nestled alongside the Puget Sound, near enough to Seattle for a fantastic night life, and far enough away to seem a world apart from the bustling city" (according to the Chamber of Commerce brochures). Hannah moved here at age sixteen with her wealthy parents (on whom she perfected her pout), when they decided that Seattle might be a little rough for their precious only child and that the small-town atmosphere of Cameron Creek would be safer. Hannah hated it . . . and me . . . from day one. Until I used the 1965 Mustang I drove (before sensibility led me to my current Subaru wagon) to pull her Beamer out of a ditch one Saturday midnight. However lenient and un-parentlike her folks were, even carefully choreographed pouting wouldn't have gotten her out of trouble had she been caught drinking and driving.

She was so grateful, she decided to be my best friend.

We'd been friends ever since.

"I can't come today, Hannah. I have too much to do. And buying new clothes will not make the world a better place."

"It might," Hannah replied, barely bothering to hide her sarcasm. "Some of the things you've been wearing lately—"

"Good-bye, Hannah. The dogs are waiting."

"Of course they are. And Lord knows that cast-off canines are more important than your best friend."

"They are not," I said. "Stop being melodramatic."

"Melodramatic would be if I pointed out that you spend every waking moment paying attention to everyone but me. Like, what were you doing this morning? Instead of having coffee with me like we used to on Saturday mornings? Habitats for Humans?"

"Humanity," I corrected.

"Whatever. The point is, I haven't seen you except at work,

for, like, months. I'm thinking about putting up flyers for a new best friend. You know what I'm looking for . . . the kind who actually *acts* like a friend."

"Hannah," I pleaded. "Don't be like this. You know my volunteer work is important to me."

"I know that it's *all* that's important to you anymore. And, I'm not the only one who thinks so."

Without giving me a moment to defend myself, she hung up.

With sagging shoulders, I put my phone away. When had this become so hard? I was just trying to make the world a better place, to help out, to contribute to the betterment of the community. If it meant walking shelter dogs who had no families to love them, that's what I did. If it meant hanging Sheetrock in the houses of people who would otherwise not have a home, so be it. If it meant that I had to skip my mother's pot roast and green-bean casserole in order to serve pot roast and green-bean casserole to the homeless at the Gospel Mission, why couldn't anyone understand that?

Why couldn't my family and friends understand that just because I wanted to give my time and talents to helping others, it didn't mean I loved them less?

Shaking my head, I sighed and straightened up. There was no time to bemoan my misunderstood status right now. I had things to do. Dogs relying on me. Dogs who didn't accuse me of neglect and were appreciative of my effort to help out.

"Come on, ladies and gentlemen," I said, tugging at the leads as I trudged back toward the road. "It's almost time to go back. Not that I haven't enjoyed your company." I was just too tired, physically and mentally, to put a great deal of effort into anything at the moment. "God, what I wouldn't do for a cup of coffee about now."

As if by divine intervention, a Starbucks appeared across the street. Okay, it had always been there, but it felt like it just appeared before my ever more weary eyes. However, it didn't do me much good, as I couldn't very well take five dogs in with me.

"Maybe some stranger will take pity on me, seeing as how I'm being dragged around by all of you."

We crossed the street, Pepper, the border collie, dashing around behind me to ensure that everyone made it safely to the other side. It resulted in a tangled mess of leads and legs—mine to be specific.

"Pepper, stop. Just hold still." I stepped over the lead wrapped around my knees, and tried to untangle the ropes at the same time Buck, a spaniel mix with sad eyes, decided he needed to relieve himself in the middle of the sidewalk. "Oh, please. What? Are you so acclimated to the kennel that you can only poop on cement?"

He stared at me with those pathetic eyes until I sighed. "Okay, I'm sorry I snapped. I've had a rough day."

Digging in my pocket, I stuck my hand in a plastic baggy and picked up the steaming mess. As I struggled to juggle five leads attached to tugging dogs and with turning the baggy inside out so it could be disposed of, I caught sight of someone heading into Starbucks weighted down with shopping bags.

"Oh. Oh, excuse me!"

I didn't recognize the woman who turned around in response to my heartfelt cry. I quickly flipped the bag the rest of the way out, intending to dig some money from my pocket, but realizing that I couldn't exactly do that while holding a bag of dog poop in one hand and a pack of animals in the other.

"Could you hold these for just a minute, please?" I shoved the leads in her direction—ignoring her look of abject horror as she stared alternately between the leashes in her hand and the smelly brown muck in my hand—and then dashed to the green garbage can at the corner where I disposed of Buck's "prize." "Thank you so much," I continued, jogging back to take the dogs from her. "Can I ask you one more favor, please? Here." I shoved a ten dollar bill at her. "I would give *anything*

for a vanilla latte right now. You can even keep the change. Buy
your own coffee with it. Please?"

The woman, who had as yet not opened her mouth to
speak, but did hold it a little open in what could only be described as disgust and distaste, gave me a glaring once-over,
unmistakably noting my dirt-stained jeans, paint-splattered
T-shirt and Mariners baseball cap and wondering whether I
was homeless and, if so, what I was doing with five dogs.

Well, I could give once-overs with the best of them, so I did.
She was stunning. Her makeup was impeccably applied
to high cheekbones and a perfectly proportioned mouth.
No Botox necessary for this gal, I'd have wagered. Masses
of blond, spiral-permed curls cascaded down her shoulders,
which were encased in a see-through, zebra-striped blouse,
under which I wasn't sure she had much more than a black
bra or camisole. She was probably just shy of a size two, had
gravity-defying breasts that may or may not have been real,
and her legs made mine look like tree stumps. She appeared
a few inches taller than my five foot six, except that I had on
sneakers and she had on four-inch stilettos, so she looked
positively Amazonian compared to me. I might have been in-
timidated by the look she was giving me down her nose; however, Hannah used that same look on me occasionally and it
didn't scare me anymore.

"Please," I repeated. "Just a vanilla latte, a small one, and
then I will never bother you again, I promise. I have to get
these dogs back to the shelter in one piece, and I'm afraid that
without caffeine that just might not be possible."

With a barely concealed scowl, the woman took my money
and disappeared quickly into Starbucks.

The dogs and I waited as patiently as possible on the sidewalk, the only incident being when someone tried to get past
us on the sidewalk and Junior refused to budge. He stuck his
nose into the bag the man was carrying.

"Hey!"

"Junior! Leave it." I tugged on his lead to no avail. Junior appeared not to be predisposed to leaving it. When I noticed that the bag carried the logo of Red Max Meats on it, I deduced why. "You might want to lift the bag out of his reach, sir. I'm not sure I have the strength to stop him if he decides he really wants it."

Luckily, the man had more of a sense of humor than the woman buying my latte, and he clutched the bag to his chest and pushed past Junior, with a pleasant smile in my direction.

"Walking the dogs from the shelter?" he asked, once out of Junior's reach. I nodded. "Good work, young lady. Not enough people making sacrifices to help out these days."

"Thank you," I answered, standing a little taller, feeling a little better. This was why I volunteered. Because it was appreciated and because compliments like that made me feel I was giving back to the world and making a difference, no matter how small a difference it seemed. Or how little those closest to me understood.

The door to Starbucks opened and my savior appeared, her expression no more pleasant than it had been before. She silently handed me my white cup and change.

"Nothing for yourself?" I asked. "I really didn't mean to keep you from your own coffee."

"You didn't," she said, her curled-lip look at the dogs letting me know that she was most definitely not a hound lover, and that that had probably been what put her off her latte.

"Well, I'm sorry if I ruined your coffee break anyway," I said, smiling pleasantly. "I really, really appreciate this." I tried to think of something to say to make up for the favor. Finally, I focused on the red leather tote she was carrying. "Great bag," I commented.

She looked positively stunned and made a sound in the back of her throat that was an odd combination of choke and sob. She shifted her gaze heavenward before grinding out between brilliant white, clenched teeth, "You have *got* to be kidding."

Geez. You'd think I'd said something wrong. Most women (especially women who clearly devoted more time to their appearance each day than I did in a month) would have been flattered to receive a compliment about an obviously pricey handbag. Wasn't that the only reason they carried them? To elicit comments from other people who were awed that they spent so much money on a purse?

"Well, sorry, again," I said, with a wave of my coffee cup. "I'd better get these dogs back to the shelter. Thanks."

I turned to move down the sidewalk again, pulling on the dogs, who were still sniffing intently around the strange woman's feet. "Come on, boys and girls."

We got across the street, while I gulped down my coffee, scalding my throat and tongue in the process, but knowing that as soon as that caffeine hit my system, I'd be good to go for another few hours. I didn't worry too much about falling asleep tonight, as I'd be beyond exhaustion by that time, as usual, and would be in dreamland as soon as I hit the pillow. Dropping my now-empty cup off in another conveniently placed trash can (no one could accuse Cameron Creek residents of being litterbugs), the dogs and I were heading back toward the shelter when I heard the voice calling me.

"Wait!"

Turning, I found the woman from Starbucks had followed us—apparently reluctantly, judging from the continued unpleasant look on her face.

"Can I help you with something?" I asked, trying not to be alarmed at the vaguely maniacal look on her face. Her brow was furrowed deeply over wild-looking eyes, and she was breathing hard, not from exertion, but almost like she was about to have a panic attack.

"Not hardly," she choked out.

At her cautious glance toward the dogs—whose range she had stopped well out of—I thought I finally understood. "Oh, do you want to adopt one of the dogs? That would be great!

I'm on my way back to the shelter now. Which one do you like? Personally, I like that one there." I pointed at the digni-fied, curly-haired pooch sitting patiently away from the oth-ers, waiting for permission to move again. "She's a little sweetie. I'd take her home if I—"

"I don't want a dog," she interrupted. "I want you."

My mouth dropped open. This had to be the weirdest pickup situation ever. "I . . . uh," I stammered when I finally got my ability to speak back. "I'm sorry, I don't . . . I date men. Well, I don't date men . . . or women, right now, because, well, I'm just not in the market to date now. Or, ever. Really." I realized I was babbling, a nervous habit, and I clamped my mouth shut. Now that the woman knew that I wasn't a lesbian, she would probably just thank me for my time, sorry for the bother, and leave.

"Let me rephrase," she said slowly, as if she were talking to a small child. I was just freaked out enough by the situation not to take offense. "I *need* you."

"But, I just told you, I don't swing that way," I replied, get-ting a bit irritated.

"I don't believe I mentioned swinging," she snapped, toss-ing a handful of hair over her shoulder. "What are you talking about?"

"You just said you wanted me . . . or *needed* me," I said. "I'm talking about the fact that I'm not a lesbian, and wouldn't date you even if I was accepting dates right now, which I'm not. I'm not looking for a man. And I'm *really* not looking for a woman."

"I wasn't asking you out!" If possible, her look of repulsion got stronger. "I'm telling you that I'm . . . oh, upon Zeus, why does this have to be so difficult?" When I continued to stare, she finally squared her shoulders and looked me straight in the eye, and said with the seriousness of a comedic straight man. "I'm your fairy godmother."

Venus

Upon Zeus, this was not what I had in mind when I said "entertaining." Deciding that the next person who complimented my new Gucci handbag would be my next godchild was clearly not a well thought out plan.

I mean, look what I've gotten for my foolishness.

Rachel—her name came instantly to me the moment she was "chosen"—is wearing jeans (and not even designer jeans!) and a T-shirt sporting some corporate logo (not a cute one, like DATING DIVA or PAMPERED PRINCESS), which appears to be covered with dust and paint splotches. Her blond hair is pulled back into a taut band, which sticks out the back of her ball cap like the tail of a chariot horse.

And she said—out loud, I might add—that she "*wasn't* looking for a man."

Could I have made it any harder on myself?

Right now, she's staring at me with her mouth agape and her body jerking around at the tug of the impatient animals trying to get her back on task.

If I could back out now, I would. I'd turn around, walk away, and choose a different project. Only I've been given rules. Fairy Godmother Rule #245 states that, "Once a god-child is chosen, no matter the method used for choosing, she is 'it' until the project is completed."

Which means I'm stuck with her.

"I can't leave you alone," I say, much to my regret. "I am your fairy godmother now, hopefully for as short a time as possible."

"Right. And, I'm the Easter Bunny. Or," she continues, with a laughing gesture at the mutts, "the Pied Piper. I just forgot my pipe today and decided to use leads." She turns to leave, the dogs falling into step behind her.

She's going to be difficult, I can tell.

"Wait!" I shout, getting her attention. She turns around to watch me through narrowed, suspicious eyes. "You really do need to take me seriously," I say, making eye contact. "This is very important."

"Important?" she asks, her resolve faltering under my pointedly convincing gaze.

"Yes. I take being a fairy godmother very seriously." Okay, I don't really, but she doesn't have to know that. "You need to listen very carefully and take it seriously, too, *Rachel*." I stepped closer, still staying out of reach of the grungy dogs, but making sure we don't break eye contact.

Rachel blinks dazedly, belatedly processing that I've used her name when there is really no way I should know what her name is. I have relatively few powers at my disposal, but this particular one comes in handy—the ability to know what I need to know about my chosen godchild at the appropriate time.

"How do you know—?" Rachel begins.

I smile my most endearing smile and give my eyelashes a few flutters. Works every time. Mortals are so easy, it's pathetic.

"I know about you what is necessary to do my job."

Again, Rachel nods, completely at my mercy. Inwardly, I sigh. This won't last. As soon as I let go of her, she'll be back to her normal self, and if that happens before I convince her,

there's no telling how long it will take me to get her cooperation. I'd be helpless to do anything but persuade her to cooperate the normal way. Fairy Godmother Rule #419: "Mental
influence may be used once and only once on the subject."
Mental influence is kind of like the mental ego-stroking I use
to get my fashion needs met, only there are limits when it
comes to my godchildren. Apparently, being able to just psy-
chically bend them to my will in order to get it over with and
move on is too much to ask. I have to work at it.

Usually mental influence isn't necessary until much later
in the project, so I'm a little miffed to be using up this wild
card so early.

"We're going to have a little talk," I say. "About how I'm going to help you."

I'm feeling pretty proud of myself, as Rachel again nods in
compliance with my wishes. Maybe it will all work out in the
long run. Usually, I have no problem at all with my godchildren. Mortal women are so eager to find their Prince Charming, that my offer of help is usually accepted with open arms.
I suppose that every once in a while, I should be glad of a
challenge.

Except that I'm not.

Suddenly, I feel something on my leg. I'm forced to break
eye contact, as I glance down in horror to find a little ratlike
dog going at it on my leg. "Ugh! Get him off!"

Still somewhat under my "spell" Rachel is slow to respond.

"Now! Upon Zeus, remove him!" I shake him off and resist
the urge to kick at the now growling little bugger. Apparently
he doesn't like being interrupted mid-screw.

"No-Name, stop it." Rachel finally recovers enough to control the tiny varmint. Rubbing her eyes, she looks over at me
again. Her eyes widen when she recognizes me and remem-
bers that just a few minutes ago she was afraid of me.

As she turns to leave again, I apply my most convincing
charm. "Don't go. I just want to talk to you."

Rachel relaxes a fraction, after a brief glance around to assure herself maybe that the dogs are between us, so what harm could there be in talking to me. "Who are you? Really."

"As I said before. I'm your fairy godmother. Much as it pains me to admit."

Without waiting for a response, I juggle my shopping bags and the same damn Gucci bag that got me into this fix in the first place. I just wanted to spice up the process, and assumed that only a classy, fashionable woman—someone with whom I would have something in common—would even *know* to compliment a Gucci handbag.

This was an obviously faulty assumption.

But, nothing can be changed now. I'm stuck for the duration.

"So, let's get down to business," I suggest, wanting to get it over with. Maybe this partnership won't have to last long. All I need to do is hook her up with her Prince Charming, make sure they fall in love, and then move on.

"Wait! No *business* until you tell me who you are. And what's going on."

"Venus Cronus. Your fairy godmother. Now, we have a lot of work to do . . . obviously." I give a pointed look at her filthy shirt. "I will formulate a plan that we can begin implementing right away."

"A plan?"

Really, she is totally clueless, isn't she? "A plan to reinvent you. To make you irresistible to your soul mate."

"Wait!"

I heave an exasperated sigh. "This is going to take forever if you continue to interrupt me."

"You're my . . . fairy godmother," she states, giving a sharp jerk on the leash of the largest dog in the group, who appears to be heading for home despite the fact that no one else is.

"Yes."

"And, you are going to . . . fix me."

"Exactly." I grace her with one of my most winning smiles. She deserves it, if she's going to pick up on this stuff so quickly.

"Nice to meet you, Venus. But, I need to go now."

I gape at her retreating back. She can't just dismiss me like that!

I leap to follow her, dodging dogs and a big blue mailbox in an effort to catch up.

"Now, wait just a damn minute," I call after the little twit, who has the advantage because she's wearing . . . upon Zeus, *sneakers* of all things. My Manolos, on the other hand, may be the most perfect shoe invented by mortals, but they aren't running shoes. "I'm not through talking to you. We have things to discuss."

She stops and turns so quickly that I run smack into her, the breath expelling from my lungs. All the dogs stop, and the black and white shaggy thing dashes around me, wrapping Rachel and me up in his leash.

"Stop that!" I gasp, pushing away from her.

"Stop following me and Pepper will stop thinking you're part of the herd," Rachel snaps, struggling to untangle us.

"Stop running from me and I won't have to chase you," I argue, before I'm finally released from the rope's grasp. I take a few steps back, staying far enough away that I won't be ensnared, should the dog decide I'm a damned sheep again.

"Stop . . ." Rachel pauses, looking a little confused by the exchange. "Just stop. I really don't want to call the police, but I will if I have to."

Again she turns away from me, heading along the waterfront, probably back toward wherever the dogs came from. I try to keep up, despite having my toes pinched off.

"You don't understand. I'm your fairy godmother. You don't have a choice. It's in the contract."

At first she slows almost imperceptibly, but then finally stops and turns.

"Contract?" she asks.

"The fairy godmother contract."

"The fairy godmother contract?"

I nod as patiently as I can. She obviously isn't very bright if I have to continue repeating myself. "Yes. Like it or not, you are my godchild. The contract cannot be broken."

"I don't want a fairy godmother," she says.

"Well, I don't particularly want a godchild," I reply sarcastically, "but we can't always have what we want, can we?"

"You're going to have to find another Cinderella," she says, then lowers her voice to mutter to herself, "Might want to get your meds refilled while you're at it."

"I heard that. You don't understand. I've already done Cinderella—"

"There's no such thing as fairy godmothers—except in Disney movies."

I shudder. "Don't even mention that contemptible company. Everything they said about me is a complete lie."

Rachel's eyebrows lift a fraction.

I run my fingers down the sides of my perfectly attired— and toned—figure. Then lift the ends of my exquisitely salon-styled tresses. "Do I *look* like a gray-haired old lady in a bonnet and hoop skirt? And, I'll tell you right now, I wouldn't be caught dead singing 'Bibbidi-Bobbidi-Boo.' Besides," I continue, "frumpy fairy godmothers have no credibility. Rule #79: 'Image is everything. Clothes make the fairy godmother.' I mean, would *you* take love life advice from someone who looks like your grandmother?"

For a minute, Rachel just stares. Then she throws back her head and laughs, which sets the tan and white, sad-looking dog to howling. When she finishes her guffawing—something I will have to nip in the bud pretty quickly if she has a prayer of keeping a man's attention—she peers around to see if anyone is watching. "I'm on *Candid Camera,* right? Did my mom set this up? Or Grammy? That would be so like them."

"I know nothing about any camera," I snap, starting to get really annoyed that she isn't taking this seriously. "All I know is that I'm your fairy fucking godmother, and I'm going to fix your seriously screwed up love life, whether you like it or not."

She still doesn't believe me. I can tell by the little quirk of her lips as she tries not to smile. "Prove it."

"Prove what?"

"Prove that you're my fairy godmother. Because truthfully, I'd be more inclined to believe you if you did sing 'Bibbidi-Bobbidi-Boo.'"

"Fine," I huff. "Follow me."

I stalk back down the boardwalk toward a stretch of sandy public beach. Rachel and the dogs—who probably realize that they just came from this direction—drag their feet, but do follow. When we finally halt in what I guess to be as good a spot as any, Rachel stops next to me, arms folded across her chest, lips pursed in challenge.

I don't really want an audience for this. I gave some old man a heart attack a century or so back, while proving I am who I am to a godchild. A quick glance around now shows only a few teenage delinquents loitering a hundred feet down the boardwalk, smoking and listening to music on headphones. They probably don't count, as I'm sure they won't notice a thing, so lost are they in whatever crap they have blaring into their skulls.

Satisfied, I frown at my disbelieving godchild. "Are you ready?"

"For what?"

"Proof."

She shrugs. "Sure, *Fairy Godmother.* Give me the best you've got."

"Fine."

I take a deep breath and turn my eyes heavenward, steeling myself for the show to come.

"Zeus is a pompous windbag who couldn't find his dick with a map and a magnifying glass."

Rachel

A single thunderbolt split the clear blue sky and slashed a skid mark in the sand not fifty feet away.

I screamed as Pepper and Junior tried to take off down the road. At the same time, Buck fell over in an apparent heart attack.

I swallowed down my stomach and struggled to get the dogs under control before turning to Venus. "What the *hell* was that?"

"Zeus," Venus said, examining her manicure and trying to appear bored.

Her hands were shaking.

"Zeus?" I repeated. "As in king of the Greek gods, Zeus?"

"How many Zeuses *are* there?"

Right. How many Zeuses were there? None that I knew of. At least not in Cameron Creek.

"And . . . he doesn't like his genitals insulted?"

"Obviously," Venus said, with a sidelong glance at the still smoldering sand.

Still not sure I could believe my eyes, I shoved the leads at Venus and jumped down onto the beach and tentatively approached the blackened ground. Poking at it with the toe of my shoe, I found that the sand had solidified where it was struck by the lightning, like in the movie *Sweet Home Alabama*. Except that, unlike in the movie, where the lighting came as a result of a wild southern storm, the Pacific Northwest sky above us was completely cloudless . . . from horizon to horizon.

When I turned back, Venus was casting wary glances at the sky, as if half-expecting another light show.

"So. How about you start at the beginning."

A haughty smile appeared on Venus's perfectly made-up face. "You've decided to cooperate."

"I've decided that maybe I should listen to your explanation before I tell you to get lost. I might want to write my memoirs someday."

"I already told you. I'm your—"

"Fairy godmother. I got that part. I want to know about the Zeus-with-the-small-dick thing." I waved a hand in the direction of the heavens.

Venus cringed, handing me back the dogs. "We should probably not mention that again."

I shrugged and took a seat on the edge of a bench obviously used as a resting place for the town seagulls, judging by the white streaks down the backrest. Junior and the now-recovered Buck lay down, with the little curly-haired mutt standing quietly to the side. Pepper fought against the lead to circle around the group, just in case any of them should try to escape. No-Name, the Chihuahua, obviously still satiated from humping Venus's leg, merely yipped and jumped around on his hind legs trying to get Junior's attention.

"So, spill it. How does a fairy godmother like you get to be insult buddies with a Greek god?"

"He's my father."

I blinked. "Your father."

"Yes. I am the goddess Aphrodite."

"Aphrodite."

Venus/Aphrodite stomped her stiletto. "Do you *have* to repeat everything I say?"

"Until you say something that doesn't sound like it's coming from a mental patient, yeah."

"What is *mental*," snapped Venus, "is the fact that I, a born goddess, am stuck here on this godforsaken Earth, trying to fix what obviously cannot be fixed."

"I thought you said you were a fairy godmother." If a person was going to be psychotic, the least they could do was stick with one psychotic story at a time. A quick glance at my watch told me I was late getting back to the shelter and that I was risking missing out on my swim session, but I found myself so curious, I couldn't let it go.

"Zeus *makes* me call myself a fairy godmother," Venus practically spat out. "It's a complete insult to *me*, but supposedly it's easier for humans to believe in ghosts, goblins, and fairy godmothers than it is for them to believe in the reality of my true identity. So, I start out with the fairy godmother routine, and if I don't make any progress, I get down to facts."

"And the facts are?"

"That I am Aphrodite—"

"Goddess of Love?"

"Yes. Goddess of Love. And Beauty. Naturally," she added, with another vague wave in the direction of a body most women would kill to have. "And Fertility. I am all those things. Or was."

"Was? You mean it's not 'Once a goddess, always a goddess'?"

"Not when your father is a pig-headed, egotistical—"

At a rumble of not-so-far-off thunder, Venus abruptly shut her mouth.

"Not when your father is Zeus?" I said hastily, really kind of hoping to stave off any more shows of force from Mount

Olympus—not that I really believed that's where the thunder-bolt came from, but just in case. "So, why are you a so-called fairy godmother?"

"So-called nothing," Venus bit off. "I *am* a goddess. Unfortunately, I'm a goddess trapped in fairy godmother hell for over two thousand years. Two thousand, one hundred, and twelve years to be exact. And I think I've been punished long enough now, thank you. Very. Much." The last statement was directed upward.

There was no response, so she continued. "Zeus, my father, doesn't understand my need for . . . passion. He married me off to a god with no passion, no fire. I don't know how he expected me to survive like that. Personally, I think he found my free spirit threatening." Venus sank down onto the opposite end of the bench, curling her lip at the bird droppings. "It was an entirely unfair punishment. He was just trying to stifle my true nature. He can't expect me to ignore all the attention I get. I'm beautiful for a reason. I'm to *share* my beauty."

Not *too* full of herself, I thought. "And he didn't agree with that?" I found this all a little bit hard to swallow. I mean, really. A goddess in Cameron Creek? Well, more like a diva, actually, with all this "share my beauty" stuff.

"No. He didn't agree with that. Apparently, he felt threatened enough that he decided to . . . demote me."

I couldn't help but laugh. "Goddesses can be demoted?"

"It's not funny," she snapped. "Being a fairy godmother, after being a *goddess*, is like . . . is like being a trash collector after being a fashion model."

"And you're here to collect my trash?"

"Not by *my* choice."

"Well." I stood up and offered Venus my hand, as I tried to hold back the laughter bubbling up inside me. This was sooo going to be a story to share around the lunch table at work on Monday. "I'm sorry I can't help you out. But, as I mentioned before, my life is just fine the way it is."

As I walked away, the dogs quickly getting the idea that I was heading home and jumping up to follow, I heard a frustrated growl, and turned just in time to see Venus flop back on the bench.

Right into the bird poop.

"Come on, Rachel," Hannah whined Monday morning, as she continued her campaign to get me to go dancing with her and her boyfriend, Griffin. She had apparently forgotten, or decided not to pursue the "you're a bad best friend" line of accusations, for which I was grateful, because I still hadn't figured out how to get past that little guilt trip. "It was so much fun. You'd love it. And one night of fun will not taint your otherwise nunnish life."

"I don't *need* that kind of fun," I replied, heels rapping smartly down the hallway from the supply room, where we'd just stocked up on Post-its and undoubtedly defective pens. "I get my fun elsewhere."

"Okay, I get where putting on a bikini and flashing some skin for the lifeguard at the Y before you swim laps might loosely be described as fun—"

"I wear a one-piece."

"—but hanging out with the Ben-Gay crowd at the nursing home? That is not exactly f-u-n, if you ask me." Hannah waved a heavily bling-laden hand in my direction. "And, don't even get me started on what you get out of chilling with the high school delinquents."

"They are not delinquents. They're underprivileged girls in need of a little guidance. Something you of the million dollar mansion would know nothing about."

Hannah and I are an odd couple of friends. Her family is upper-*upper* class, with a mansion on the hill above Cameron Creek proper. My family is mid-middle class, with two working parents, living in a ranch-style house off Main Street. Hannah is an only child, a born diva, with the proverbial silver spoon in her delicate little African-American mouth. I'm the second oldest of four blond-haired, blue-eyed Caucasian siblings, and have had a job since I was fifteen. As friends, we could bring up differences like that to each other.

"And you," Hannah lashed back, "as an under*serviced* woman, are in need of a little sex."

That, however, was uncalled for. "I don't need sex."

"Everybody needs sex."

"Not me. Besides you aren't asking me to have sex. You're asking me to go dancing. Not the same thing, last I heard."

"Just because of what happened the last time you danced—"

My head snapped in the direction of my best friend, who, if she pursued *that* line of topic was *seriously* going to lose that position of honor. "Don't even go there," I warned, before continuing down the hall toward the refuge of my desk.

"Look, Rach, just because you were dancing when you found out Eddie—"

"It has *nothing* to do with that." I stopped again, waiting while one of our coworkers hurried past us, probably fearing bloodshed because of the maniacal gleam in my narrowed eyes and my decidedly aggressive stance. "My life choices have nothing to do with Eddie. Or Aaron. Or Mick." Too late, I realized I'd been duped into listing my failed relationships— the Loser List I had vowed never to utter aloud again because doing so did nothing to perk up my mood. However, it did firm up my resolve that I was doing the right thing in not pursuing the misbegotten fantasy of happily every after. "It has to do with me. With being fulfilled as a human being. With giving back to my community. With . . . with—"

"Filling the emptiness in your sad and pathetic life?"

"Bitch," I muttered and headed for my desk.

"Call me what you like, but you know I'm right."

"If you think you're right about that, then you have obviously not paid any attention to me at all in the last fifteen years."

"Oh, I pay attention all right." Hannah lowered her voice as we reached the lobby. She was going to the teller line, where she was head teller—a perfect job for her, because she got to boss people around, and I was bound for my customer service desk near the front door, where I got to *help* people, something I'd spent a lot of time trying to convince Hannah I *liked* to do. "*I* remember when you used to have fun and took chances and weren't a chickenshit."

I attempted to melt her with a fiery look, but her attention was already elsewhere. She whistled softly under her breath.

There was a customer seated at my desk.

"Damn," she whispered. "Speaking of sex. If it weren't for Griffin, I'd be on that man like pitch on bark."

I groaned. "Ever since Griffin made you plant that tree for Arbor Day, your analogies have gotten seriously weird."

"Don't change the subject. I expect a full, juicy report," Hannah said, without taking her eyes off my customer.

Aka, Mr. March.

Again.

Squaring my shoulders, I turned to face the inevitable. I really was going to have to put a stop to this nonsense.

Hannah snaked out a hand and yanked me back, nearly pulling me off my feet.

"Make me proud," she begged.

"If by 'proud,' you mean helping him with whatever his banking needs are, then I'm all over it."

The customer, Mr. March, er, Luke Stanton, was seriously the best-looking guy I'd ever seen. Apparently, I wasn't the only one who thought so, because he was one of the local fire-fighters highlighted in the firefighter calendar for the month of March—hence *Mr. March*—put out to benefit burn victims.

He seemed to think I needed *my* fire put out.

I, of course, chose not to even have my fire lit in the first place, thus had no need to have it put out.

No matter how fine the holder of the hose.

He's no big deal, I told myself as I crossed the lobby, a pleasant smile pasted on my face. He's a guy, with as many faults as every other guy in this world—he's just packaged better than most.

I used the long walk across the lobby to prepare my turn-down line.

I almost had it perfected when I heard a sound.

"*Psst.*"

Wha . . . ?

"*Pssst.* Rachel."

Venus, the delusional fairy godmother, was parked on the lobby couch, a few feet behind my desk.

With a "One second, please," to Mr. March, I juggled office supplies, yanked Venus off the couch by her arm, and dragged her behind an overgrown potted palm on the other side of the lobby.

"What are you doing here?" I chewed out between clenched teeth.

"Hey! Hands off the Versace." She gave me the brush-off and then spent a full thirty seconds checking for damage to the black sleeve of a dress that may or may not have actually been Versace at all to my untrained eye.

"Why are you here?" I repeated, crouching to pick up some Post-its that had fallen out of my arms. "I'm working. I thought I made it very clear that I don't need a"—God, I couldn't believe I was saying this out loud—"fairy godmother."

She shrugged, flinging a cascade of golden hair back over her shoulder and peering through the palm fronds toward my desk. "You can stop calling me fairy godmother. You know I'm a goddess now, so no need to keep up the pretense of thinking otherwise. And it doesn't *matter* what you want. You're my godchild and I can't take that back, much to our *mutual* disappointment." She turned her attention back to me, giving my navy wrap dress a once-over. "You do clean up pretty well, though. He seems to like it, which is all that counts."

"He?"

"The guy at your desk. That's him."

"Him who?" I did my own peering through the branches and noted Luke had kicked back in one of the chairs provided for my customers, posing much like his photo in the fire-fighter calendar Hannah had shown me a few months ago when we had first figured out who he was. "Luke?"

"Oooh, is that his name? Very sexy." Venus brushed aside some branches and all but stuck her whole head through the bush to get a better look. "If I was mortal, I'd be tempted—"

I smacked her on the arm. "Will you just go away? Please?"

Venus pulled out of the palm tree and flashed me some teeth. "Can't do that."

"Why not?"

"Fairy Godmother Rule #245."

"You have fairy godmother rules?"

"Of course. It's my job. You don't think I'm allowed to wreak havoc without rules, do you?"

Admittedly, the idea of a fairy godmother wreaking havoc seemed a bit out of character from what I knew about fairy godmothers. "I guess. So what's Rule #245?"

" 'Once a godchild is chosen, no matter the method used for choosing, she is 'it' until the project is completed.' You've been chosen."

"So, *un*choose me," I instructed. "Because I have no intention of being set up with Prince Charming."

Venus huffed impatiently. "I told you, you can't be *un*chosen. You complimented my great red Gucci bag, and now we're stuck with each other. I have mentioned that this is a *mutual* disappointment, haven't I?"

I stared at her with my mouth hanging open for a minute before I could formulate any words whatsoever. "I became your godchild because I complimented your handbag? You're kidding, right?"

Venus shook her head, looking a bit like she'd swallowed something nasty.

"So, I take it back," I said, throwing up the hand that wasn't still loaded down with office supplies. "I didn't even know it *was* Gucci. It's just a handbag. And not one I'd even want to carry if it were the last bag on Earth. There. I'm going now."

I turned to walk away. I did, after all, have a job to do. And a customer to do it to. With. Whatever. Seeing as how I was definitely not doing anything with or to Luke Stanton except maybe balancing his checkbook or stopping payment on an errant check, there was no point in carrying on this conversation with Venus, whoever she really was.

"Hey! Don't walk away from me!"

"Don't hold your breath," I muttered as I walked away from her.

Squaring my shoulders, attempting to put myself back into customer service mode, I approached my desk.

"So sorry to keep you waiting, Mr. Stanton," I said in my most professional voice, as I dropped my stockroom loot into a desk drawer. Closing the drawer, I took a fortifying breath before standing upright again. "Is there something I can help you with?"

"I thought you were going to call me *Luke*." Luke stood up at my approach.

Mannerly, I noted. Obviously a front to cover up whatever was really wrong with him. Because anyone pursuing me *had* to have something wrong with him.

"You're right, I was. Sorry. So, what can I do for you, Luke?" I sat down in my chair, preparing for the inevitable.

Luke also sat down. In the chair reserved for customers. Which he was, so I really couldn't ask him to vacate it. No matter how much I wanted to.

"How about dinner?"

Most girls, when receiving an invitation like that, especially when it's delivered by Mr. March Firefighter—or any other month for that matter—would say, "*Now*. Take me *now*, Luke Stanton. Put out the burning fire within my loins."

I was not most girls.

Instead, I made a dramatic gesture of looking at my watch. "A little early for that, isn't it?" A gentle put-down was what I was going for. It failed.

He laughed.

He had a nice laugh. I'd admit that. It was one of those infectious kinds of laughs that made you want to join in.

However, it still didn't sway me into going out with him. I took a moment to log in to my computer before turning back to him.

He continued without missing a beat. "If I open a savings account will you go out with me?"

I smiled my polite-customer-service-representative smile when what I really wanted to do was growl in frustration. I couldn't be impolite. Impoliteness to customers was frowned upon at Cascade National. But, I wasn't going to date the man—no matter how good-looking he was.

And he was *really* good-looking. Neatly trimmed dark blond hair. Eyes warm and blue and crinkly at the edges when he smiled. A jaw that always looked a little stubbly and touchable.

Not that I wanted to touch.

There would be *no* touching.

I had to be firm. As much for his benefit as Venus's, because I noticed that she hadn't walked past my desk yet. Which meant she was somewhere still behind me, watching me carefully for signs of cracking under the barrage of testosterone.

"You have three savings accounts with Cascade National, Luke. A vacation account, a Christmas Club account and a, uh, Ferrari account, I believe. You don't *really* need another one, do you?" My supervisor would have killed me if she knew I was actually trying to *discourage* a customer from opening more accounts with Cascade National.

"Stop being difficult!"

The stage whisper came from behind me, and I jerked around to find Venus back on the couch, her nose buried in *Money* magazine.

"Go. Away," I snapped, in my own stage whisper.

She just smiled and flicked her fingers to indicate that I should get back to my waiting customer.

I brought out the customer service smile again. "Sorry."

Luke leaned sideways and glanced in Venus's direction. "Problem?"

"Nope. Don't pay any attention to her," I said firmly, then raised my voice just enough for Venus to hear also. "She's. Just. *Leaving*."

Of course she didn't leave. I couldn't be so lucky.

"So, anyway, back to your multitude of savings accounts, and the fact that I'm not going to go out with you . . ."

Luke grinned. "You've memorized my savings accounts."

"You're in here every week. Sometimes twice a week," I reminded him. "Besides, that's my job."

"How about a CD? If I open a CD will you go out with me? Or maybe a second checking account?"

I shook my head. "Sorry. Maybe if I worked on commission."

Luke threw back his head and laughed again.

I sighed. Why didn't he get it? Did I need to spell it out? Obviously Venus needed me to spell it out—and I certainly had no qualms about being rude to her—but I *couldn't* be rude to a bank customer.

I tried for professionalism again. "So, can I *really* do something for you? Cash in a CD? Verify that a check has cleared?"

Luke's returning smile gave new definition to sexy, and the twinkle in his ocean blue eyes provided the stars with competition.

I didn't notice.

"You asked me all that yesterday," he reminded me. "And the day before."

"And I'll ask you again tomorrow if you sit in that chair. It's my job. Customer service." I pointed out the plaque on my desk embossed with my name and job title. "Just like, if I light a match and toss it in my in-box, starting a fire, you'll put it out. Because that's your job."

"It's the chair, isn't it?" Luke asked. "The chair triggers the automatic banking questions."

I simply arched an eyebrow.

"So, if I *wasn't* sitting in the customer service chair when I asked you out . . ." He stood and came around to the side of my desk, looking exceptionally . . . *decent* . . . in his button-flies and navy T-shirt with the CAMERON CREEK FIRE DEPARTMENT emblem on it, which clung to a very nicely muscled chest.

I didn't notice.

Again.

"If I come around here," he continued, "and, say, lean over like this . . ." He leaned over me, bracing his hands on the arms of my chair, slowly spinning me around to face him. "And *then* I ask you 'Will you go out with me, Rachel?' Then you won't ask me all those questions about CDs and savings accounts, right?"

Good grief. Just because most girls fell for lines like those, didn't mean I was so gullible.

"Look, I'm sure you're a really nice guy—"

"I am."

I actually rolled my eyes. I couldn't help it. After multiple failed relationships, I had come to the conclusion that men will tell you whatever they think you want to hear, in order to get you into bed. Once the bedding is done—give or take a few weeks or a year—all bets are off. Their reassurances of honesty are forgotten in the dust of discovery that they weren't *really* working late, they were holding down a barstool at a local strip club with their friends. Their pledge to be loyal is eclipsed by the unearthing of the red lace thong in their glove compartment—too small for you, but just the right fit for the new girl they've been nailing on their lunch hour. And your belief that they're worth every moment of your time and attention is dashed to the ground by the discovery they're already mar—

Well, it doesn't matter. All that matters is that discovering all those hidden faults is enough to make any girl question her judgment.

I, for one, was completely incapable of making sound decisions about men. Thus, I had given up even trying.

"I don't date," I told Luke. "And I'd still ask you if I could help you, even if you weren't in that chair. That's my job."

Luke grinned, his face close enough that I noticed for the first time a tiny pale scar down the left side of his nose. "I hate your job."

"Excuse me a minute," Venus piped up, from where she had appeared beside us. Thrusting her hand out, she glared at me before turning a seductive smile in Luke's direction. "Hello. *Luke*, is it?" She said his name like she had her mouth wrapped around an exquisite piece of imported chocolate.

With a nod, Luke took Venus's hand.

Feeling suddenly a bit green, I searched for signs of testosterone elevation. Venus, was, after all, a stunning woman.

Luke displayed nothing but politeness. He must be gay.

"Luke Stanton."

I held my breath waiting for—

"I'm Venus. Rachel's cousin."

I shot her a startled look.

"Very nice to meet you, Venus, Rachel's cousin. Maybe *you* can talk her into going out with me."

"Precisely what I was thinking."

I started to growl at her, but quickly turned it into throat-clearing when Luke turned his attention back to me.

"I'll leave you to it, then. Let me know how it goes," he said, winking. With a salute, he vanished through the front door, measuring in at a precise six foot on the yellow marker used to determine the height of escaping bank robbers.

I had no intention of letting Luke Stanton rob *me* of my resolve. Even if he was hotter than a four-alarm fire.

Venus

My own brilliance nearly blinds me at times.

After Rachel threw me out of the bank this morning (we're going to have to work on her gratitude), I picked up the latest issue of *Cosmo* and sat at Starbucks the rest of the day.

I came up with the most incredible plan.

Okay, *Cosmo* came up with it, but I'm using it. If it works for Rachel, I'll put it into regular practice.

What am I saying? Of course, it will work for Rachel.

It *has* to work for Rachel. Because there's no failure allowed for in the Fairy Godmother Rule Book. Rule #521: "Commitment to a godchild shall be maintained until she is firmly dedicated to her Prince Charming."

So, in keeping with my forced obligation to see this through to the bitter end, I also spent the afternoon studying up on Rachel's issues. "Issues" are those life details from their pasts that mortals dredge up over and over again in order to prevent themselves from getting what they really want out of life. Rachel has issues with past relationship failures. I'm not sure how she figures these relationships to be failures. She got sex out of them, didn't she? She had men worshiping her (however briefly), didn't she? So what's the problem? I don't have "issues" with my past lovers, even the ones who were only momentarily part of my life because they became tedious or stopped affording me the time and dedication I deserve. When it was time to move on, I moved on. No dredging up their faults or my faults (which would really have been a waste of time, considering I don't have any) or trying to analyze and decipher the whys and wherefores of relationship dynamics.

Rachel, however, has turned them into "issues."

I'll take care of that.

I just have to get her to agree to let me do my job and fix her.

To that end, I'm waiting outside her apartment when she arrives home from work—three hours after the bank closed! To say that I'm cranky about being left out in the cold fall air—which damages my skin like you wouldn't believe by looking at me—is an understatement. Chapped lips are not attractive on a goddess.

"Where have you been?" I demand.

Rachel drops the treasure-chest–sized bag she's carrying and stops in the middle of the sidewalk.

"And what are you wearing?" I demand again. "The dress you wore at work today was acceptable under the circumstances. But this?" I take a tour around my godchild, examining her from every angle. She's in sloppy sweatpants (has she never heard of spandex?!) and another one of those completely boring T-shirts. Maybe I should team up with Trinny and Susannah on *What Not to Wear*.

On top of the fashion disaster that is Rachel, her shoulder-length blond waves are damp and unstyled. And, I swear, she doesn't have any makeup on. "This I just can't deal with. You have to at least *try* to work with me here, Rachel."

"What are you doing here?" she demands, looking uneasy. "How do you know where I live?"

I tap my temple. "It's all up here. Every detail of your life. As soon as you agreed to be my godchild—"

"I didn't agree to anything." She grabs her bag and stalks toward her door. "How many times do I have to tell you, I don't want to work with you? I don't *want* a handsome prince, *Fairy Godmother*."

"You know, you don't have to say it with such contempt."

"Why not?" She shoves her key into the lock and throws open the door, following it swiftly with her bag, which must contain bricks for the thud it makes hitting the floor. "You do."

"I'm allowed."

"Look, Venus. I'm tired. I don't have the energy to argue with you tonight."

"That will greatly simplify things."

Rachel just shakes her head, then turns to close the door, but I'm fast on my footwear and make it inside before it shuts all the way.

"Hey! You can't just barge in like that."

"Once you hear what I have to say, you'll be only too glad for my help."

"Nothing you say could change my mind about needing your help." She picks up her bag again from the floor. "With anything."

Even though the eye contact/mental coercion thing has expired, I use it for emphasis when I drop the bomb.

"I know about Eddie."

The lead-weight bag lands on my toes.

Rachel

You what?"

I seriously didn't care if I did drop my very heavy gym bag on Venus's designer shoes. Or her toes for that matter.

"Who told you about Eddie?"

"*Pfft*. I don't need anyone to tell me anything. I told you, I know everything I need to know about you." Venus pushed past me and limped into my living room, dragging, I notice, a Louis Vuitton suitcase (even *I* recognize Louis Vuitton because of the logo). First Versace and then Louis Vuitton? Where did fairy godmothers get the means to buy all these designers? Olympian Express? Don't leave the Mount without it?

She threw herself rather ungracefully onto my couch with a dramatic sigh. "Get me some ice, will you? I'm starting to swell."

My sigh wasn't so much dramatic as peeved, but I went to the kitchen to make her an ice bag for her foot. No sense inviting a lawsuit from this obvious lunatic.

I probably should have made one for her swelled head while I was at it. Where did she get off thinking she knew anything about me?

"So," Venus piped up when I came back in the room. Her feet were propped up on pillows, her never-ending man-magnet legs taking up the whole couch. I was really surprised—and mildly impressed—that Luke hadn't forgotten all about me the minute he laid eyes on the Goddess of Love/Beauty/Fertility who now graced me with her unwanted presence.

"So, what?" I asked, handing her the bag of ice, which she set on the coffee table instead of on her foot.

"Ready to get to work?"

"I'm not doing *anything* with you. Why don't you get that?"

"Oh, I get it," she replied, then busied herself pulling files and notebooks and pens from her bag. Not the red Gucci this time, but another bag whose designer I didn't recognize. It matched her shoes, naturally. "It's no picnic for me, either. Trying to find the perfect mortal matches and then having to babysit you all through them, until you finally come to your senses. Besides being so far beneath me that I can feel the heat from the core of the Earth—"

"Then, why do you insist on doing it?" I asked. "You don't want it. I don't want it. What's the point?"

"Quota."

"Quota?"

Venus nodded. "I have a quota."

"Like how cops have a certain number of tickets they have to write a month?"

"Like how many Extreme Love Life Makeovers I have to do before I get to go back to being a goddess."

I laughed. "Extreme Love Life Makeovers? Sounds like a bad reality TV show."

Venus sent me a long-suffering look. "It *is* a bad reality TV show. One in which I seem to be eternally stuck."

"So how many makeovers until you can return to being a goddess?" I was so humoring her. I mean, really, there was no way I was buying all this nonsense about her really being a goddess demoted to fairy godmother. Intelligent people do *not* believe things like that. Even with a lightning show for effect.

Apparently, Venus wasn't all that intelligent, because she totally believed she was a grounded goddess.

"I don't know how many. Zeus didn't bother to share *that* with me." She slapped a stack of papers down into her lap. "And I'm *still* a goddess. I just don't get to be treated like one. Have you ever heard of someone being punished with an open-ended time limit? It is *so* not fair."

"Well, fair or not, I'm not going to be part of it. I don't want Prince Charming. I believe I've mentioned that before." Despite my protestations, she didn't appear to be going anywhere soon, so I sank into the camel-colored armchair across from the couch.

"Right. No Prince Charming for you." Venus went back to shuffling papers and what looked like a *Cosmo* magazine. "So, this is my plan. Your issue is that you've made mistakes and don't trust yourself—"

"Excuse me? My *issue*?"

"Yes," she said, looking quite a bit like a schoolteacher relaying some pertinent fact to a student. Except for the whole perfectly-coifed hair thing. None of my teachers ever looked like Venus. "Mortals have issues. It's a proven fact. Your issue is your lack of trust in yourself to make sound judgments about men."

How the hell did *she* know that? I mean, that wasn't something I went around telling people. Even Hannah didn't know the half of it. Unusual, I guess, given that most girlfriends gossip about bad dates and the shortcomings of their significant others. I didn't. Somehow, it always felt like their even *having* shortcomings was more reflective of me and my lack of man-picking savvy.

"More specifically," Venus continued, "you don't trust your own actions with regard to relationships. You choose losers—"

"Hey!" Okay, so I *did* choose losers. The Loser List proved that. But, it sounded so harsh coming from someone else's mouth.

"You choose losers," Venus persisted with a frown at my outburst, "and then, as evidenced by your most recent relationship, behave in a manner inconsistent with your moral values."

I glared at her. "You don't know anything about my moral values."

"Rachel, Rachel, Rachel," Venus *tsked*. "I am your fairy godmother. It's my job to know it all. I know about the Eddie Incident. I even know what came *after* the Eddie Incident."

I froze.

And then vaulted out of my seat.

"How can you know about that?" How could she know enough about that to know that I *called* it the Eddie Incident? I'd *never* said those words aloud, although that's how I thought of that whole fiasco.

And the *other* thing . . .

No one knew about the other thing except the two parties involved. Me and . . . him.

"How did you find out about that?"

"Once more for the dim-witted," Venus muttered sarcastically. "I. Am. Your. Fairy. Godmother."

And she really must have been.

Because there is no possible way she could have known about the two most horrible events of my life otherwise.

SEVEN

Venus

Have I mentioned recently my extraordinary brilliance, legendary beauty, and supreme intelligence?

It took only common sense for Rachel to see the truth of my status. I know things that I couldn't possibly know but for the ability I have to know everything I need to know about my godchild. I have to give Zeus points for leaving me with that, at least. If I had to pry all the details from reluctant mortals, like psychiatrist from patient, I'd get nowhere fast.

"It's quite simple," I say. "Your issue is that you don't trust your judgment of men. You are afraid—"

"I'm not afraid," she protests, with a very unattractive creasing of her brow and wrinkle-inducing pursing of her lips.

"You are *afraid*," I repeat, more firmly, "of being unable to make a sound decision when it comes to men. Completely understandable, of course, as men are, in fact, very untrustworthy creatures."

"And yet you persist in trying to pair me with one." Rachel frowns and leaves the room.

When she returns, she slams a Diet Coke—as if I need to worry about calorie content—onto the table in front of me and then opens one for herself, its release of air sounding much like the sigh she lets out.

"Being paired is part of the natural order of things," I explain.

"Are you *paired*?" she asks. "I'm not really up on Greek mythology."

I raise an eyebrow. "That is sooo un-PC. Do I *look* like a myth to you?"

"Sorry," she mumbles, not sounding sorry at all.

"Anyway," I continue, "I've been paired many times. By choice *and* by force. I have a husband, such as he is. Hephaestus. That was Zeus's first attempt to control me."

"And you weren't to be controlled?" Rachel asks before wandering across the room, where she begins unloading the bag she brought in with her. "That's why you got thrown out of heaven? Or off Mount Olympus or whatever?"

"Something like that," I mutter. "I need passion in my life. Hephaestus doesn't exactly do it for me, if you know what I mean. So, of necessity, I sought passion elsewhere. Zeus disagreed, despite being a cheating philanderer himse—" With a glance out the window, I think better of pursuing that train of thought. No sense pushing my luck. I once let my feelings about Zeus's two-faced condemnation of *my* romantic practices get the better of me . . . and caused the near destruction of a small Ohio town in a flash flood. "Anyway. Mortals have a rather antiquated idea of passion and usually choose only one paramour. Yours will be Luke Stanton."

"Now wait a minute!" Rachel drops what looks suspiciously like a hard hat back into her bag and whirls around. "Luke Stanton is *not* going to be my paramour. Or my anything else."

I close my eyes and count to ten. Why does this have to be so difficult? Why do I have to convince mortals that coupling is natural? Eros ("Cupid" to those who insist on envisioning my very masculine hunk of a son as a pudgy cherub) was given a simple bow and arrow with which to prompt mortals into making the matches that should have come naturally. Why couldn't *I* have been given a bow and arrow? Or better yet, just have the love potion in the heel of my stilettos? One kickbox shot to the solar plexus and Rachel would fall in love with Luke Stanton instantaneously.

Or, too bad my Golden Girdle doesn't work on anyone but me.

I sigh at the thought. It was the one gift Hephaestus ever gave me that was worth anything (not that he didn't realize his error within moments of my putting it on). Wearing the girdle, with the little thread of magic gold filigree that my husband so kindly wove throughout it, no male could resist me—like I wasn't irresistible enough already. But a goddess can never have too much adoration. Now, I mainly pulled it out for special occasions . . . like when it is time to par-*tay*.

Or when I'm so depressed that only a little male adoration will pick me up.

Sometimes, now, I can't resist taking the girdle out of its box (safely in my suitcase at the moment) and remembering what it used to be like. When I was still the goddess I was meant to be.

But, anyway, it's worthless when it comes to mortals. It works *on* them, but not *for* them. So I'm stuck convincing them of their need for relationships the old-fashioned way. If only it were as easy as using the girdle. I'd be saved the inconvenience of having to convince Rachel of something she'll do in the end anyway. Instead, I have only my powers of persuasion.

"Luke has also been chosen."

"Chosen schmosen! What, did he compliment your perfectly pert breasts?"

"You really like them?" I ask with a smile and a quick boost of my favorite assets. "They *are* pretty terrific."

"Argghh! I don't want or need a man in my life," Rachel objects, without breaking from unpacking her bag and putting things in their proper places. "I have my volunteer work with the nursing home and with the girls at the high school. I read to sick kids at the hospital. I make a difference in the world. I help people. And, I'm going to help myself . . . maybe go back to school to be a high school counselor. Or take a Thai cooking class."

"Filler," I declare, examining my perfect manicure, as watching her busy-ness is wearing me out, and she doesn't appear to wish to discuss the perfect state of my breasts any longer.

"It's not filler," Rachel insists. "It's meaningful. Fulfilling."

"And what about your dreams?"

Rachel stills, then examines the fibers of the carpet at her feet. "Dreams are just that. Dreams. Fairy wishes of childhood."

"And, yet, strangely important to you mortals."

She narrows her eyes stubbornly at me. "And goddesses don't have dreams? Like going back to Mount Olympus maybe?"

"That," I shoot back, "is not a dream. That is a reality that will come to be as soon as mortals like you stop being so stubborn and mulish and help me rack up the brownie points."

"Look, Venus, I just can't help you." Rachel again picks up the hard hat and heads for the back of the apartment.

Grrr. Launching off the couch, I start to follow her—no longer bothering to fake the hurt foot that gained me five seconds of sympathy—then go back for the suitcase I left by the front door. Seeing as I have to do all the work around here, I will obviously be taking the more comfortable lodging.

"Fine," I snap, quickly catching up to my highly aggravating godchild and entering what appears to be her bedroom. There is a bed, a bureau, a nightstand, and a rather comfortable-looking easy chair by the window. All decorated in a rather subdued sky blue. It smells vaguely of oranges and baby powder. Though certainly not the elegant bedchambers I am accustomed to on Mount Olympus, it will suffice. "You don't want to cooperate, so I do believe I don't want to keep my knowledge of the Eddie Incident quiet. Or the other thing."

Rachel rounds on me, eyes flashing. "What?"

I shrug, oozing nonchalance. "You have secrets you want kept quiet, correct? *I* have a quota I need to achieve." I heave my suitcase onto the bed and open it. "We can either work together, or I can blackmail you."

EIGHT

Rachel

Blackmail?

For a minute, all I could do was gape at this woman who professed to be my fairy godmother. You can damn well bet Cinderella's fairy godmother didn't resort to extortion.

Oh, wait. Venus claimed *she* was Cinderella's fairy godmother. Apparently Disney never personally met with Venus Cronus before developing the part of Cinderella's kindly elderly helper.

"You would really tell someone?" I finally asked incredulously, then realized that she was carrying stacks of expensive-looking garments to my closet and hanging them up, shoving everything *I* owned aside in the process. "What are you doing?"

"Unpacking," Venus replied. "And, no, I wouldn't tell someone. I would tell *everyone*. At least the people you most wish *not* to know." She ticked them off with her fingers. "Your parents, siblings, Hannah. Perhaps even your coworkers. Never underestimate the power of peer pressure."

"But that's blackmail!"

"We've already established that, haven't we?" Venus carried a long flat gold box and what looked suspiciously like underwear—well, lingerie, given that they didn't appear to be the Hanes prepackaged underwear *I* bought these days—to my dresser. She opened the top drawer, pushed aside my stuff, set the box down in the center of the drawer, and then dumped her lingerie in the empty space on the other side of the box. "You can move your things later," she offered.

"Why are you unpacking?"

"I need a place to stay."

"What, you don't get travel expenses for this job?"

"Not when Zeus holds the checkbook. How much floor space is in your closet? I cannot have my shoes touching each other or the leather gets scratched."

"You can't stay here," I stated.

Venus began precisely lining up what appeared to be twenty pairs of shoes—most being of the four-hundred-dollars-a-pair variety—in my closet. Shoving aside my own shoes in the process. Apparently the leather used to make *my* shoes was too low quality to worry about scratches.

" 'Can't stay here.' 'Can't set me up with a gorgeous, hunky firefighter.' 'Can't give away my secrets.' You aren't a very agreeable person, are you?"

Once Venus had ensured that her suitcase was empty, she snapped it closed, and handed it to me. "Find someplace safe for that, would you? Oh, and don't let it touch anything else. It might get—"

"I know. Scratched."

Needing a moment to collect my thoughts, I took my apparently new roommate's luggage to the front closet. Pissed off as I was, I didn't worry too much about what it might be rubbing against as I shoved it in between the vacuum cleaner and the sewing machine I hadn't touched since high school. Then I made my way back to "my" bedroom to find the woman calling herself my fairy godmother lounging back on "my" bed.

"I suppose I should set up the couch for myself?" I asked, layering on the sarcasm as thickly as I could.

"That would be great," Venus said, brightly. "So, you've decided to cooperate." It wasn't a question.

"Apparently, I don't have a choice if I don't want you to—"

"Spill your dirty little secrets?" Venus offered, *more* brightly if that was possible.

I gritted my teeth. "I wouldn't call it that."

"What would you call it, then?"

I chose not to answer. "You realize whatever your plan is to get Luke and me together won't work?"

"Of course it will. It always works."

"Not this time."

"Just wait until you hear my plan. It will amaze and thrill you with its genius."

"I doubt it. I'm leaving. I'm going to serve at the soup kitchen at the Gospel Mission. I'll be back in a few hours. I'd prefer it if you were gone by then." Wishful thinking, I was sure, but I had to try.

"Oh! Soup! I love soup," Venus declared. "Can I come?"

"You don't *eat* soup there. You serve food to the homeless and less fortunate."

Venus stared at me uncomprehendingly. "That's the dumbest thing I ever heard . . . not eating soup in a soup kitchen. I'll never understand you humans."

With a shake of my head, I turned to leave the space formerly known as my bedroom, sure that if I stayed a minute more, I'd be the prime suspect in a homicide. I stopped in the doorway and turned back to Venus, as a thought occurred to me. "If you're really the goddess Aphrodite, why do you go by Venus?"

Venus smiled wickedly. "Because it irritates Zeus that I refuse to go by my given name." She flopped back on my pillows and placed her arms comfortably behind her head. "And because *Venus* rhymes with my favorite male body part."

* * *

Venus's plan had to be the single dumbest idea I'd ever heard.

"You want me to what?" I practically shouted at her in the car on the way to work the next day.

The morning had not been good as far as mornings go. As far as anything goes. I was now in the car with a crazed supposed deity who had spent two hours in the bathroom this morning, leaving me with an entire fifteen minutes to get ready. Shouldn't she should have just been able to wave her magic wand and make herself beautiful?

Said maniacal fairy godmother also insisted on my changing clothes *four* times before she was satisfied with the kilt skirt and deeply V-necked cotton sweater I was now wearing, instead of the typical tailored suit or conservative dress I usually wore. Consequently my hair was still wet as I drove to work. Real good look for me. When I pointed out to Venus that *I* needed time to get ready for work in the morning, she told me that if I managed *my* time better, *her* time in the bathroom wouldn't be a problem.

My time management classes had mentioned nothing about planning your life around deranged goddesses.

"You are going to interview Luke Stanton's ex-girlfriends," Venus repeated, applying lipstick while peering into the passenger side visor mirror.

I purposely swerved, hitting a large pothole in the middle of Main Street, causing Venus to slash a bloodred stripe across her cheek.

She shot me a withering look and reached for a tissue. "Your issue is trust. You don't trust that you can judge what kind of person Luke really is, so you'll interview the exes, get their opinions, and realize, by the time you're done, that Luke is your perfect match."

"And what if they tell me he's a serial killer with a secret longing to lick the inside of women's shoes?"

"They won't."

"What if they do?"

"They *won't*."

I rolled my eyes. "It didn't occur to you that *Cosmo* publishes these articles for entertainment? Without really meaning that you should try them?"

"Of course you should try them. You should do anything necessary to get over your hang-up."

I slammed my Subaru into park in the lot behind the bank. "Have you ever thought that it's not a hang-up? Maybe I really want to be who I am. I'm happy. I don't need a man to be happier."

"Of course you do." With that, Venus jumped out of the car, slamming the door behind her and striding toward the employee entrance of the bank.

I hustled to catch up with her, not an easy feat in the three-inch heels she'd forced me into—Nine West slides that I owned from a few years ago, since my closet didn't currently contain any Beverly Feldman, much to her chagrin. "Where are you going?"

"To my couch."

"You're not—"

"Rachel!"

Hannah hurried across the parking lot toward us. Upon reaching us, she gave me a once-over. "Wow. Since when do you dress like that for work? Gotta admit, it'll bring in customers when it gets around town, but—"

"Shut up," I warned.

"*I* dressed her this morning," Venus offered, throwing her shoulders back.

Hannah finally noticed I had someone with me and raised a perfectly arched eyebrow in Venus's direction. "And, who would you be?"

"Nobod—"

"I'm her long-lost cousin Venus."

"Rachel doesn't have a long-lost cousin Venus," Hannah said, eyes narrowing further in suspicion.

"Actually, she's—"

"Of course she does," Venus corrected. "Since I'm her, I ought to know. And since I'm 'long lost' it would suffice to say that people wouldn't know about me. Especially people like you."

"Hey!"

"Hannah," I warned, as she raised herself to her full ominous height and leaned toward Venus. They were about equally matched in height and build, but I'd seen Hannah mad, and I was pretty sure she could whip a starving lion in that state. "Hannah, calm down."

Hannah relaxed a fraction. "Long-lost cousin? Rachel? What's going on? Didn't I see her sitting on the lobby couch for a while yesterday?"

Dammit. I obvious couldn't tell Hannah the truth . . . not unless I wanted her hauling me to the nearest mental institution. Which, I realized, might not be such a bad idea as I was clearly completely losing my mind.

Because, amazingly, I appeared to be buying into the whole "fairy godmother" thing.

"I . . . she . . . she's right. Venus *is* my long lost cousin," I stammered. "On my father's mother's side of the family."

Hannah stared suspiciously from the faux sincere look on my face to the gloating triumph on Venus's face. "Is that right? What did you say your name was? Cousin . . . *Virus*, was it?"

"Venus," I corrected, then grabbed her by the arm and pulled her through the door with me. I released the door behind us, hoping it would perhaps knock Venus unconscious and discourage her from following.

No such luck. She came in behind us, bypassed the employee cloakroom and headed straight for the couch, parking her behind, while I carried on a whispered conversation with Hannah.

"She's not well," I confided, with a look of mock concern shot in Venus's direction. "Something's not quite right."

"Like what?" Hannah asked.

"Um, like . . . she thinks she's my fairy godmother." I smiled as genuinely as I could under the circumstances. "It's the weirdest thing. But, I feel, kind of, you know, *obligated* to humor her. Being related and all."

Hannah directed a narrow-eyed glance around the corner at Venus again. "And she's going to sit there all day? Millie is definitely not going to go for that."

Millie—Millicent, to those of us who didn't want to be fired instantly—was my boss.

"I couldn't talk her into staying at home. She'll be fine, though. I'll make sure she doesn't do anything."

How successful that would be remained to be seen. I left Hannah in the back hallway and headed for my desk, trying to pretend nothing was amiss. Already I was getting odd looks from my coworkers getting ready for their day. Millicent Bernard, the loan officer, assistant branch manager—and my supervisor—glowered in my direction. She was in her late fifties, but looked a hundred if she was a day. Her bitter attitude matched the brittle makeup she wore on her face, lips outlined five shades darker—and in a completely conflicting hue—than her lipstick, shockingly thick blue fluorescent shadow covering all skin beneath her thick eyebrows, which were penciled on in an exaggerated arch with what looked like barbecue charcoal.

If I had to make a comparison based on the current metaphor that was my life, I'd have to say, if Venus was Cinderella's fairy godmother, Millicent was Cinderella's wicked stepmother.

"Rachel, may I speak to you for a moment?"

And that really meant "at me."

"Yes, Millicent. Just a moment."

As I passed Venus, who appeared to be deeply engrossed in *Investor's Business Daily,* I leaned down to whisper, "If you have a magic wand in that bag of yours, now might be a great time to whip it out and turn my boss into a pumpkin."

Millicent sat behind her desk like it was a throne. "Rachel, who is that woman? We don't allow customers in before the bank opens, and I do believe she came in with you."

"Yes, she did," I admitted, trying to keep my expression benign, when what I really wanted to do was tell her to shove her superior attitude up her— "She's my, uh, cousin. She's staying with me and really doesn't have anyplace to go during the day. And she's—" I snuck a quick look at Venus, hoping for inspiration. Venus smiled and raised the newspaper a few inches. Ah-ha! I turned back to Millicent, knowing exactly what would work . . . and probably save my behind. "She's interested in banking. She's really wealthy and wants to learn more about investing."

Millicent's mud brown eyes gleamed. "She's wealthy?"

I nodded. "Disgustingly. She doesn't like to talk about it. However," I leaned toward her conspiratorially, wincing at the odor of garlic coming off her, even before 9:00 A.M. "I bet, if you play your cards right, and give her some time, she may just choose Cascade National Bank as the new home for her millions."

Millicent looked like a starving woman who'd just had a buffet rolled out in front of her. "Millions? Well, then, certainly, if there aren't any problems, Rachel, she's most welcome." She rose from her seat and craned her neck to get a better look at her potential favorite new customer. "Perhaps you should offer her coffee and a doughnut from the lunchroom."

Now wait a minute. I had no intention of becoming Venus's personal maid while she was here. I'd nearly forgotten I didn't want her around at all.

But, with a sigh, deciding it was better to keep everyone content, I got the damn doughnut and coffee.

Venus

A day on the bank couch, with an endless supply of coffee and doughnuts provided by my serv— my *adoring* godchild, gave me ample time to plot and plan. (You didn't really think I was actually reading *Investor's Business Daily,* did you?) I'm pressed for time, so I decided the best plan is to be proactive and make sure Rachel takes this first, all-important step.

"Phone's for you!" I holler through the bathroom door.

"It didn't ring," Rachel replies. Apparently it doesn't occur to her that it could have rung while she was in the shower.

It didn't, but it *could* have.

"It's still for you," I say, as I push open the bathroom door.

"Hey!" Rachel tugs the towel tighter around her breasts. "I'm naked."

"He'll be thrilled to hear it, I'm sure."

"He?"

I give the phone a little shimmy and thrust it into the hand she tentatively sticks out.

"Hello?"

"Rachel?" Luke says, and I watch her eyes narrow in my direction.

My presence isn't needed at the moment, so I step out of the bathroom to give them some privacy. After that "I'm naked" comment, the opportunity is wide open for a little steamy phone sex. Not that Rachel would recognize that opportunity if it bit her in the ass.

Actually, I just want to get away from all the hostility she's directing at me. I'm not used to so much animosity. I'm more of an all-love-all-the-time kind of goddess.

Doesn't matter whether I'm in the bathroom or not, anyway. I can "hear" their whole conversation in my mind. Rachel doesn't know about this little talent of mine or I'm sure she wouldn't mention to Luke that her cousin Venus really shouldn't be "butting her nose in where it doesn't belong."

I lean back around the corner and shoot her a glare of my own.

Thankfully, with a bit of sweet-talking, Luke manages to get her to agree to coffee the next evening. I might have mentioned to him that I was pretty sure she'd agree to go out with him if he was persistent enough. I just didn't tell him that she would only agree to it in order to avoid having her mistakes outed to the world.

"Are you out of your mind?" Rachel practically shouts when she comes out of the bathroom a few minutes later. She slams the phone onto its charger and whirls around to face me, fighting mad and still clutching the towel around her chest. She's wrapped it so tight, it's got to be cutting off the blood supply to her brain. Which would explain the completely unjustifiable anger she's projecting.

"How could you call him and tell him to ask me on a date? Especially after I've told him 'no' so many times. That was humiliating—"

"Oh, give it a rest." I wave my hand at her and drop onto the couch. "I'm here to help. So, I'm helping."

"This isn't helping. It's . . . it's coercing. Arm-twisting. Railroading."

"Just getting the party started. I don't see what you're so bent out of shape about. Have you *looked* at him? He's like . . . smokin'. Get it? *Smokin'*? Firefighter?"

At first she just gapes at me. She wants to laugh, I can tell. Okay, maybe she doesn't. But, she should, because it's funny.

"Seriously, Rachel. Have you taken even one second to check him out? He's Mr. Hot Body. He's got shoulders out to here. He practically oozes testosterone. And his hands . . . have you *seen* his hands? Do you *know* what having hands that big means?" I stop to fan myself before continuing. Rachel isn't making eye contact, and she's fiddling with the towel. *She* knows what I'm talking about. She just won't admit it. "Most importantly, he wants you. And while I may not entirely understand the reasoning behind that, since there are probably a bazillion perfectly *willing* females out there—"

"What. Am I. Supposed. To say. To him?" She grinds out, finally interrupting me. "I can't tell him we're destined to hook up because my *fairy godmother* says so."

"Uh-uh." I interrupt her with a stab of my finger. "You know full well that I'm a *goddess*, there's no reason to continue poking at me with the 'fairy godmother' shit. It's one thing when I call *myself* that—"

She throws up her hands, almost loses the towel and makes a grab for it as it slips. This does not improve her mood. "Are you or are you not my fairy godmother?"

"It's my *job*, not my *identity*. I bet when you converse with your garbage collector, you don't remind him every other sentence that his sole purpose in life is to collect your trash."

Rachel opens her mouth to speak, then closes her eyes and her mouth and stands there. She suddenly looks very tired. Must not be sleeping well for some reason.

"Back to Luke," she finally says, opening her eyes again. "It was unfair to make him call me. I'm not going to tell him I suddenly have a burning desire to go out with him, because you know full well that I don't."

"But you will."

"Not if I can help it."

"You can't help it. Because we all know what's going to happen if you don't follow through, right?"

Her face drains a little of its color.

I look away. I'm not a *complete* bitch. I don't get off on putting the fear of Venus in her. But I'll have my way about this, there's no question. I'll do whatever it takes. And if she thinks she can stand sneaker-to-Manolo with the Goddess of Love and come out the winner, she has another think coming.

"You'll think of something to tell Luke," I reassure her. "And once you come to realize that you two are made for each other, you'll be thanking me for all the trouble I'm going through."

TEN

Rachel

Stop shoving me!" I snapped at Venus, who seemed to think that if she didn't bodily propel me down the street I wouldn't go.

She had a point.

"Come on. You're going to be late." She readjusted her grip on my elbow. "Didn't you put this in your frantic planner? Wouldn't want to mess up that impeccably timed schedule now, would you?"

"*Franklin* Covey planner," I corrected. "And yes, I put this farce of a meeting in it last night when you told me to." And was mightily sorry that I hadn't been able to erase that particular penciled-in entry.

"Well." Venus paused in front of Starbucks—through whose windows I could see Luke waiting patiently at a table—and began straightening my blouse. "Try to at least look like you want to do this."

I slapped her hand away when she tried to unbutton the blouse one more button. It was mortifying enough to remember that he'd heard me *say* I was naked last night. He certainly wasn't going to *see* me naked today. Or ever. "I *don't* want to do this."

"You will sooo thank me for this when all is said and done. You'll be begging to write me a recommendation."

"Dream on."

Venus opened the door and started to step into the store.

"Wait!" I halted her with a fistful of hair.

"Hey! Hands off!" Venus bent forward and squinted at her reflection in the window, turning this way and that to ensure I hadn't damaged the hairstyle that had taken up another large chunk of *my* bathroom time this morning.

"You aren't going in there with me," I said when she finally finished checking herself out and had apparently decided the damage wasn't fatal.

"Why not?" Venus asked indignantly. "I *am* your fairy godmother."

"Did you go with Cinderella to the ball?"

Venus pursed her flawlessly outlined lips. "No. I wasn't *invited* to the ball."

"Well you aren't invited to Starbucks, either," I said, refusing to feel sorry for her. However, it was kinda pathetic to hear her say she hadn't been invited to the ball. "If I'm going to make a complete ass out of myself, I don't need any more audience members than necessary."

I pushed past her into the warm coffee smell of the shop, but was halted by Venus, this time with a fistful of *my* hair. Since I hadn't had time to style my own hair because *her* hair took so much time in the bathroom this morning, I knew she couldn't do much damage.

"Wait yourself," she said, narrowing her eyes at me. "How do I know you're really going to do what we agreed on?"

"You mean what you *told* me I would do or you would blab my sins to the world?"

"Well, yeah." For a moment I thought she might have the decency to look sheepish . . . but the moment passed.

"I penciled it in my planner," I pointed out. "I canceled my mentoring this afternoon for this. I guess you'll just have to trust me."

Venus sniffed. "That's exactly what Zeus said to me before banishing me." The now very ticked off fairy godmother/goddess turned and stalked away down the street.

A few minutes later, Luke had purchased our coffees and settled us on a cozy couch in the corner. Starbucks was pretty busy with the after-work crowd, but everyone seemed bent on grabbing their caffeine to go, heading home for a busy evening of family time. I didn't have *that* to do, but since Venus had made me cancel my evening at the high school, I did have a few minutes to actually sit with my coffee.

And Mr. March.

"So, what made you change your mind about going out with me?" Luke asked, sitting sideways on the couch, which was much too small for my liking. His knee brushed the side of my hip every time I took a breath.

I shook off any thoughts about what it felt like to be sitting close to a man for the first time in more than two years and focused on what was more important.

I *felt* like an idiot.

I really didn't want to lead him on, to make him think he had a snowball's chance in hell of creating any kind of "thing" with me. But, I also couldn't tell him that my "fairy godmother made me" go out with him.

"Look," I began, then stalled for time by taking a sip of my decaf latte (even exhausted from my extracurricular activities, sleeping on the couch made it difficult enough to fall asleep without being kept awake by caffeine). "I'm really just doing this to prove you wrong."

Luke's eyes lit with amusement. "Prove me wrong?"

I sighed and examined him. Most of the time, when he was

stalking me at work, I avoided spending *too* much time looking at him. It would have made it harder to turn him down over and over again—which was just a necessity. He really was quite . . . hot. His closely-cropped, dark blond hair had that messed-up look that was so popular with guys—and girls—these days. Serious after-sex hair, Hannah called it. Underneath the black form-fitting T-shirt and jean jacket he wore, I knew he was all smooth skin and buff muscle—because Hannah had forced me to look at his photo in the calendar once. Not that I had memorized what he looked like or anything.

I started drifting off into fantasy land—you know, that place where you can imagine what it might be like to be hosed down naked by a firefighter hot enough to have his own *month*.

"Rachel?" Luke touched my shoulder and I snapped to attention.

"Sorry. I was just . . ." Think of *Mick,* I mentally slapped myself.

Mick—of Loser List fame—had had a smile like Luke's. One that reached into you and stroked all those soft places inside that turned a girl to mush. Mick, the embezzler. Mick, the career criminal. Mick whom I had once thought might make a great husband and father. He was handsome and fun, treated me like a queen, taking me out, spending money on me. For a while anyway. It turned out that what money he was spending came from his company's treasury. Money he appropriated by cooking the books in his spare time. McNeil Island Penitentiary was his current place of residence.

I had to focus on Luke being a *man*—not in the sense of a man I wouldn't mind being bed pals with, but a man, like my ex-boyfriend, Mick, who had to have some glaring fault (or faults) hidden deep inside somewhere. They all did.

"I need to be honest with you," I finally began firmly. "I fully intend to prove that we shouldn't go out. And, it's not just you I won't go out with. It's men in general."

"Oh." He looked a bit crestfallen. "You date women. I guess I missed the signs."

"What signs?" I glanced quickly down at my outfit, with the nearly indecent neckline. Maybe I should have let Venus unbutton another button. "I'm not . . . I don't date women, either. I'm an equal opportunity non-dater."

"Good. So, why do you need to prove me wrong?"

"I don't *need* to," I said, frankly. "I just know that I will. It's quite simple really. I don't trust men. I've been burned too many times."

Luke's eyes softened, which wasn't what I was going for. "You think I'll hurt you," he said.

"You're a man," I replied, with a shrug. "Of course you will. Look, I'll be honest with you—"

"I thought that's what you'd been doing already," Luke interrupted.

I laughed. "Right. Sorry. Anyway, I've had three big relationships in my life, and lots of . . . lesser relationships. And what I've learned is that every one of those guys appeared to be one type of guy when I met him and an entirely different type of guy after I fell in love with him. One of the 'Big Three' turned out to be a criminal. The other had an Internet sex addiction."

Aaron. He was my first serious relationship after the typical high school crushes and business college boyfriends. Aaron and I had a great time together and enjoyed an active sex life. Which hadn't been the case with Mick, who, on the surface, was kind of prudish and overly moral. At least from a sexual standpoint. Apparently, theft didn't contradict his moral values. This was okay with me, though, because, after the Aaron fiasco, I was pretty turned off by sex in general.

Anyway, my sex life with Aaron had been active. And good, from what I could tell from my limited experience. He, however, subscribed to the Bill Clinton sex philosophy. If it didn't involve actual penetration, it wasn't sex. So, while he and I had a good sex life, he was also having "sex" (in my book anyway) with anyone else he could find to have sex with—online. To me, that's the same as cheating offline.

While watering his plants for him when he was on a business trip, I decided to boot up his computer to check my e-mail. Imagine my surprise when an instant message popped up inviting Aaron to "fuck like a duck." (Apparently, ducks were something of a turn-on for my boyfriend. I was unaware of this, thankfully, although it did explain some of the odd positions he wanted to try.)

Five minutes and a half dozen IM sexual propositions later, and his little sex secret was excruciatingly obvious. I broke off that relationship by telephone before he even returned home from his trip. I'm sure his plants died, because there was no way I was going back to that den of filth to water anything.

Good thing he hadn't had a dog.

Luke cringed at my mention of Aaron's little "problem." "And the third?"

I stared at the white plastic lid on my coffee cup. "I don't talk about the third." And I would sit through this hideously embarrassing meeting with Luke to ensure that Venus didn't, either.

"Fair enough. So what do your past relationships have to do with me? I don't have any outstanding warrants. And I prefer my sex with live, warm women."

I sucked in air and met Luke's eyes. His mouth was turned up at the corners, eyes dancing. "You're teasing me."

He shook his head. "No, really, it's true." He leaned toward me and lowered his voice. "Making love is much, *much* better that way."

I gulped and quickly hid behind my coffee cup. Dammit! I was supposed to be convincing Luke that we were all wrong for each other, not getting turned on by him.

Think of Mick. Think of Aaron. Think of Eddie . . . okay, don't think of Eddie because that was just *too* depressing. But thinking of Mick and Aaron reminded me yet again—like I needed reminding over and over again (apparently I did!)—that the guys who appeared great on the outside all turned out to be terrible mistakes in the end.

I'd been hurt.

I'd had my feelings crushed beneath the soles of their uncaring shoes.

And Luke would do the same thing—if I let him. He would become yet another entry on Rachel's Loser List.

This was not something I would subject myself to again.

"Rachel?"

I raised my head, squaring my shoulders, and prepared to tell him Venus's plan as I had promised. With any luck, he would laugh hysterically and tell me to take a flying leap. It would save us all a lot of trouble.

"All right," I said. "I promised my . . . cousin Venus that I would try something. To see if we might be compatible. I have no expectation that it will work. In fact, I'm completely sure it will only prove my point, and then we can go our separate ways and forget all about it."

"What's the plan?"

"It's so stupid. The dumbest thing I ever heard. It's certainly not going to prove anything, and it'll probably be completely embarrassing for you. In fact, feel free to tell me no, if you don't want to go along with it."

Luke chuckled. "What's the plan? Stop trying to talk me out of it already."

I took a deep breath. "I . . . Venus thinks I should interview your ex-girlfriends."

He raised his eyebrows. "Interview my ex-girlfriends?"

"See, isn't that stupid? Like it would make any difference what they said about you. I mean they could make up anything they wanted to. Or . . . or you could call them and tell them what to say to me. If you were, like, on speaking terms with them, I mean." I was babbling. God, I was so embarrassed. I was so going to kill Venus for putting me through this. "It's not like most exes say flattering things about their, um, exes. I mean, when couples break up, it's not usually because they still *like* each other, you know—"

"Okay."

I stared. "What? *Okay?* Why would you let me do that?"

"Because I don't have anything to hide."

"Everyone has something to hide."

"Not me."

I narrowed my eyes at him. "You honestly believe none of your ex-girlfriends will say anything bad about you?"

"If they do, I probably deserve it, and you'll be proven correct. But I don't think they will." He grinned. "At least nothing too damaging."

I shook my head. "Are you taking medication for that delusional state you live in?"

ELEVEN

Venus

Ah, this is a prince after my own heart. I couldn't have asked for better cooperation. At least one of them is cooperating. Rachel, on the other hand, has been in a serious rant ever since she got back from her meeting with Luke.

She's decided that the fact that he agreed to such a "lame-brained plan"—her words, not mine—is proof that he's a few rungs short of a full ladder. It's obvious to me that it means he's willing to go for what he wants with confidence and determination.

Not unlike yours truly.

Maybe with Luke's assistance, this love life makeover will actually work out better than it first appeared it would. While stubbornness can be an admirable quality, I want it to be *for* me not *against* me. The thing is that, in the end, Rachel will totally see that I was right and she was wrong. So why can't she just accept that I'm right in the first place and get it over with? I don't have time to waste trying to cheerlead mortals into winning the game of love.

If I can just get rid of nosy Hannah—who apparently has no concept of the word "teamwork"—I'll be three steps ahead.

She's like a shadow. Every time I move, she moves, just to see what I'm doing. She's been prancing around Rachel like her own personal bodyguard, like I'm going to *do* something to her. Upon Zeus! Hannah's been trying to get Rachel to go out with Luke ever since he showed up. She's just pissed because *I* got Rachel to have coffee with him, which she couldn't do.

Oh, and she was *sooo* eyeing that new paisley cami I wore today. If she even *tries* to copy me, she is so going down. Not that I don't completely get why she would want to emulate my impeccable taste in fashion. I just don't buy into that imitation being the sincerest form of flattery thing.

But forget her. I am. I'm here to do a job, and I'm going to do it, whether I get cooperation from Hannah or not. Hell, I'll even do it without *Rachel's* cooperation. I'm sick of the earthly realm and want to go home already.

I'll just have to make sure I continue to get Luke Stanton's cooperation in the seduction of Rachel Greer. He's really the only one who *has* to cooperate. There's no way Rachel can resist Mr. Alpha Male Firefighter forever.

Especially with me doing a little creative prodding from the background.

Rachel

Everything was quiet for the next four days. Hannah and Venus circled each other like equally-matched boxers in a ring, or princesses at the ball, vying for the attention of the lone prince. The fact that the prince was hypothetical didn't matter to the two of them. It only mattered that, had there been a man present, they would have been on equal footing. And it irked them both.

Knowing Hannah like I did—and having been on the receiving end of her suspicion and contempt fifteen years ago when I first met her in high school—I recognized the signs. She thought something wasn't quite right with Venus—just as she had suspected in high school that my being nice to her was some kind of ploy to "get at" the new rich girl. The only difference was that she had reason to be suspicious of Venus.

Fortunately, they had come to an uneasy truce when I finally told them I wouldn't speak to either of them if they didn't stop making my life a living hell with their bickering and sniping at each other.

*Un*fortunately, Luke agreed to bring me the list of names and phone numbers of his ex-girlfriends. However, he couldn't do it until his next day off, which gave me four days of reprieve. "Reprieve," in this case, is another word for sit and reflect on what kind of trouble I'd gotten myself into, all because I couldn't stand up for myself. Because I didn't say no. Because I didn't say, "I don't want a fairy flippin' godmother." Or better yet "I don't *believe* in fairy godmothers."

So my four days of reprieve were spent doing what I've done for the last two years . . . fending off my mother's ever more forceful insistence that if I didn't show up at the next Greer family Sunday dinner, I was going to be cut out of the will. And, in between that, filling my life with what was meaningful and fulfilling . . . the things I intended to do every day for the rest of my life. The things that had saved me and made me feel whole again after Eddie.

When things ended with Eddie (who wasn't just a boyfriend, but my fiancé) my life felt like one huge failure. Like when you tell a lie that will hurt the feelings of someone you care about, which you never intended them to find out, but you hear that they did find out, and you know you're going to have to face them. That twisting knot of failure in your stomach. That bile-flavored taste of knowing you have some sort of deficiency . . . from which you will probably never recover, based on your current track record of oh for three.

These feelings were left behind when I finally made the decision to move on with my life. In an effort to do something to fill the time, I volunteered to work with Habitat for Humanity. It saved my life. It gave me something I knew I could accomplish without fear of screwing up. Not much chance of getting your heart broken while painting siding.

And besides, people appreciated my help. Soon, I found myself volunteering more and more. It was like an adrenaline rush. After such a pronounced failure with Eddie—heaped upon the other failures that made up the Loser List—I needed those pats on the back. I needed the appreciation. So, I'd rededicated my life to the service of others.

And it had been working perfectly until Venus arrived.

The problem now, even as busy as I was, was that the next four days weren't really a reprieve considering I was stuck with a prima donna fairy godmother—oh, excuse me, *goddess*—who seemed to take the idea of me as Cinderella just a bit too far.

"I could use some more iced tea," Venus called from the living room couch, which served as her throne when it wasn't my bed.

"You know where the refrigerator is, your high-ass," I called back from the bedroom where I was changing out of my work clothes. "Sorry. High*ness*."

I was headed for my mentoring group at the high school, but had been forced to come home first to change clothes, since there was no way I could show up in the ridiculously sexy clothes Venus continued to insist I wear to work, just in case Luke showed up. However, I have to say that I'd managed to open new accounts for more men this week than I had in the last month. They were probably passing around the word that Rachel Greer's cleavage was on display over at Cascade National for the price of taking out a CD or opening a money market account.

Double-checking my image in the mirror, and finding that I was at least presentable in jeans, a camisole, and a short tweed blazer, I headed for the living room.

"I'm leaving now," I told Venus, as she came out of the kitchen, carrying a glass of iced tea that she had miraculously been able to get for herself. Cinderella might have been surprised to find herself not treated in such slavelike fashion had she only refused her evil stepmother's commands a few times.

"How late will you be?" Venus asked with a pout. "I get bored by myself."

"A few hours. Watch TV."

I refused to feel sorry for her. I also refused to give in to her demands that I stop all this "extraneous" activity that I would be—according to Venus—quitting anyway after discovering that Luke was the perfect guy for me.

That wasn't going to happen.

The quitting *or* the discovering.

Venus

"Venus?"

I turn to find the hunky object of Rachel's eventual affection standing beside me. I've been stationed outside the bank as an unofficial greeter, mentally prompting Cameron Creek citizens—well, the men—in to Rachel's desk to open new accounts. It's my duty to keep her busy, so she doesn't have any time to spend devising ways to get out of following our plan. My encouragement—and her low-cut sweater—have been getting Cascade National Bank more business this morning than they've probably ever seen before in a week.

"Why, Luke. How nice to see you."

Damn this man is fine.

Why again am I doing this for an ungrateful godchild instead of myself? Used to be I snagged men like this for *me*. I was—*am*—after all, the Goddess of Love. I had plenty of playmates on Mount Olympus. Men. Gods. Didn't matter. I was an equal opportunity lover.

Apparently this was a goddess faux pas, according to Zeus.

Considering *his* love life, you'd think mine would've been of little consequence. But, *nooo*. I was supposed to be the dutiful goddess wife. I was supposed to ignore that every male within a hundred miles—within the entire *kingdom*—wanted me. I was supposed to be the good little goddess, helping others make *their* love lives better—

"Venus?"

Luke is staring at me curiously.

"Sorry," I say hastily. "Just . . . dreaming."

"Rachel here?" He glances through the lightly tinted glass of the bank doors.

Rachel's at her desk with a *very* happy customer. Mr. Atkinson will be leaving in a few moments with a new checking account, courtesy of Rachel—and a new libido, courtesy of me.

"Of course, she is." I reach out and lay my hands on his arm. I resist the urge to give it a little squeeze just to see if it's as muscular as it looks. "She was really excited to hear about my plan to interview your ex-girlfriends."

Luke raises a skeptical eyebrow.

Okay, so he's not stupid enough to believe that.

"Well, she *will* be excited, once she recognizes that it's a great idea. Don't you think it's a great idea?"

"It's an interesting idea. I'm not exactly sure how it will help, but if it gets Rachel talking to me—"

"It'll work," I promise, leaning in and batting my eyelashes a bit. "You'll have to trust me on this. I know what I'm talking about. I'm a bit of an expert when it comes to . . . matchmaking."

Luke's laugh is delightful.

"Well, I brought the list." Luke pats his back pocket, where I hear the crinkle of paper.

I lean sideways to peer at his lovely ass— I mean, at the piece of paper sticking out of his pocket.

"Perfect." In more ways than one. "So, go give it to her. It's her lunchtime anyway. I'll make sure she gets going on it tonight. *If* I can get her not to dog-walk, house-build, teen-sit, or soup-feed." I roll my eyes.

"Soup-feed?"

I wave my hand dismissively. "Don't worry about it. Just dumb stuff Rachel wastes time on." I give his shoulder a little nudge. "She'd be much better off wasting time with a hot fireman like you."

"We'll see if I can get her to think more like you," Luke says, as he heads for the door. "So, I forgot the list in my truck, okay?"

I take the opening to give his very fine jean-encased ass another look-see. "If you say so."

"I have a little surprise for Rachel, so just play along."

FOURTEEN

Rachel

Venus was outside the bank hanging all over Luke. Despite not caring what was going on—heck, if she got him interested in *her*, I'd be off the hook—I couldn't help but peer around the new customer I was opening an account for, just to see what they were doing. Her high-pitched girly giggles filtered through the not-quite-sealed-tight front doors, grating on my nerves.

"Thanks so much, Mr. Atkinson. Have a terrific day." I stood and shook my customer's hand when we'd finished our transaction, trying to focus on him and not be distracted by the exchange between Luke and Venus on the sidewalk. "Please come see me if you have any further questions."

Mr. Atkinson said good-bye, gave my too-visible cleavage one last glance, and then pushed out one of the doors, just as Luke held the other door for Venus to step through. I quickly sat down and pretended to be busy straightening my desk. It wasn't like I was interested in anything they had to say anyway.

"Rachel, look who's here," Venus gushed, as she dragged Luke toward my desk by his not unimpressive bicep.

I put on my most casual face before looking up. "Oh, hello. What brings you here, Luke?"

Lame, lame, lame, I thought. Could I sound like I was trying any harder?

"I have the list for you." He smiled and I lowered my gaze back to my desk, shoveling papers into a pile, so he'd know I didn't care.

"List?"

"The Ex List," Venus said pointedly. "The one you haven't stopped talking about for the last four days."

I shot her a glare. Of course she didn't point out that I'd been *complaining* about the list for the last four days, not *anticipating* it.

"That list?" I asked. "Oh, yes. I suppose I should get started on that, shouldn't I? The sooner we get it over with, the sooner we can *all*"—I narrowed my eyes at Venus—"stop giving it another moment of our time."

Luke's mouth was twitching, which was kind of irritating, as I was not trying to be funny in the least. I was completely serious.

"So, Venus tells me that it's just about your lunchtime."

I glanced at my watch, even though I knew full well what time it was. "Oh, I guess it is."

"Well, Luke left the list in his truck," Venus said. "By accident, of course. You'll have to go out with him to get it."

I stared at Luke, suddenly a little alarmed. What if his fault was that he was a serial killer? What if he wanted me to go with him to his truck to kidnap me and hold me for ransom? My parents didn't have that kind of money. Besides the fact that they had probably forgotten they even had an eldest daughter, since I rarely put in an appearance any more.

I instantly vowed to myself to drop by and say hi to my family soon. If for no other reason than that they needed to be able to remember what I looked like should I be kidnapped and held for ransom by a psychopathic killer.

"Um, where are you parked?" I asked, trying for nonchalance.

"Around the corner on Sixth," Luke said.

Was that a deranged gleam in his eyes?

As much as I hated to rely on her, Venus was my only hope for rescue should I not return. "Did you hear that, Venus? Luke has his . . . what kind of truck is it?"

Luke chuckled. "A red Dodge Ram. Do you need the license number?"

I flushed, caught. "Of course not." I retrieved my purse from my desk drawer and reluctantly stood. "I just have to go grab my coat. I'll be right back.

I dashed back to the alcove by the lunchroom that held the employees' coats. Hannah was just coming out, since we usually had lunch together.

"Where's the fire?" she asked, when I ran into her coming around the corner.

"At my desk," I replied wryly.

Hannah peeked around the corner into the lobby. "Damn. How can a chick who hates men have one that hot hanging all over her?"

"I don't hate men," I snapped, yanking my coat off its hanger and shoving my arms into the sleeves. "I just don't want to have relationships with them."

"Sickness. Pure and simple sickness." Hannah shook her head and started to follow me.

"Wait." I grabbed her arm and dragged her back to the cloakroom. "I'm not . . . I'm not going to lunch with you." God, I did not want to tell her this. She'd never let me hear the end of it.

"You're not?"

"I'm . . . Luke has—"

"Holy shit, Batman! The girl has come to her senses." Hannah nearly whooped, and I smacked her arm.

"Shut up. I have not come to my senses." I groaned. "I mean, I came to my senses a long time ago, when I decided not to date anymore. This has nothing to do with senses."

"If you think going out with *that* guy won't involve any of the five senses, it has seriously been too long since you got laid, Rach."

"I'm going to his truck to get a list, Hannah, not to get laid. God."

"What list?"

"Just . . ." I wracked my brain to think of an appropriate lie. I really didn't want to get into Venus's plan with Hannah.

"Are you coming or what?" Venus appeared from around the corner. "He's waiting."

"Waiting for what?" Hannah asked. "What list?"

"Noth—" I started.

"The list of his exes," Venus finished, choosing this particular moment to decide to be more open and sharing with Hannah. "The ones that Rachel's going to interview, to see what kind of prize Luke Stanton really is, so she can get over her phobia."

I opened my mouth to protest—that Luke wasn't going to be a prize, that I didn't have a phobia, that Venus was fucking nuts—but nothing came out.

Hannah was staring between Venus and me like we'd both lost our minds. In truth, I think we both had. Venus had started out nuts, and I was quickly following suit.

"I can't talk about this right now," I finally said. "Luke's waiting and I'm just going to get this over with."

"You . . . go, girl," Hannah said, sounding completely bewildered. As I walked away, I heard her begin drilling Venus. "So what the hell have you cooked up, Vegas?"

"*Venus.*"

I shook my head as I crossed the lobby to meet up with Luke, who was waiting patiently by the front door. Stepping up to him, I was sure I was making the biggest mistake of my life.

Luke politely held the door open for me, and I stepped out onto the sidewalk. After an involuntary glance around for patrol cars, in case I needed to call for help, I fell into step beside him. Despite my resolve, I couldn't help but notice how nicely our heights matched. He was tall enough that I felt feminine beside him, but not so tall that I had to strain my neck to look at him.

Not that I was looking at him . . . but, if I'd wanted to.

"This was all planned, wasn't it?" I finally asked, as I spotted the monstrous red truck in the distance. Was it one of those overcompensating things? He drove a big red fire engine at work, but couldn't compete at home, so bought the biggest, reddest truck he could find, to compensate for what he was lacking?

"Yes, it was."

I glanced sharply at him, a current of fear that I'd actually been correct about the kidnapping thing shivering through me. "You planned that I was to come to your truck to get the list?"

"Yep." With a grin and a sideways glance, Luke stepped out into the street at the back of the truck and lowered the tailgate.

In the bed of the truck was a big plaid wool blanket on which sat a picnic basket, a bottle of sparkling grape juice, and two glasses.

I looked at Luke questioningly. "What's this?"

He shrugged. "A transparent ruse to get you to have lunch with me. Because there's no way you can turn this down without looking completely rude. Or paranoid."

I laughed despite myself. "Sneaky."

"You can use that to head up the list of my faults that you're making."

Shaking my head, I gestured to the picnic, which was really . . . *really* sweet, but was in no way going to sway me. I couldn't let it. "I'm not exactly dressed to be jumping into the bed of a pickup." Miniskirts didn't allow for much high-stepping.

With a gesture of flourish, Luke produced a stepladder that had been tucked up against the side of the truck bed. Then he hopped—without help of the ladder—into the truck and held out a steadying hand for me.

Slipping my hand into his, I tried—without much luck—to ignore the strong warmth of Luke's fingers. There was something very sensuous about one palm brushing against another. I tried to conjure up the memory of holding hands with my ex-boyfriends, the rat finks. No matter how great it had felt to hold their hands, they'd still been creeps in the long run.

Still, I had to admit that I missed the intimacy of having a boyfriend . . . the hand-holding, the warm, stubbly cheek pressed against mine, the bodies entwined . . .

I quickly pulled my hand away from Luke's and sat down on the wheel well, on which a cushion had been placed. He apparently thought of everything when he was trying to make a point. "You really didn't have to do this."

"It's not going to change your mind, is it?"

He was also very perceptive.

"No. I'm afraid not." Although, I admitted to myself, if I *was* going to change my mind and let a man into my life . . . I might let in a man who was thoughtful enough to surprise me with a picnic lunch in the back of his pickup truck.

Luke sat down across from me, tugging his khakis up his muscular-appearing thighs, in that way men have. I slapped down that little bit of thrill I got at being alone with a man for the first time in a very long time.

"Didn't think so."

"Then why did you do it?" I accepted the glass of sparkling grape juice Luke handed me, and took a sip to wet my suddenly dry throat.

"You have to eat. I have to eat." He shrugged, blue eyes shining. "I have you alone. All to myself."

At just that moment, a group of preschoolers ambled by, apparently part of a day care group, the children holding on to a rope held taut by a teacher at each end. They chattered away, pointing out downed maple leaves washed up against the curb by a rain shower a few days ago, some of the boys exclaiming at Luke's big red truck, all looking happy to be out in the fresh air.

"Not sure this counts as being alone," I laughed.

"Works for me. Turkey, ham, or tuna?" Luke produced an array of wrapped sandwiches and I selected the tuna. "Goodman's Deli, I'm afraid. This was a kind of spur of the moment ruse."

"I like Goodman's Deli. Thanks."

"So," Luke started, after taking a few bites of his turkey sandwich and washing it down with the bubbly grape juice. He chewed with his mouth shut and didn't belch out loud, so I crossed those two possible flaws off my mental list. "What gave you the idea to interview my exes?"

"Well, like I said the other day, this isn't my idea. This is Venus's. I'm basically doing it to—"

"Shut her up?" Luke asked.

I raised an eyebrow. "Know her that well already, do you?"

He laughed. It was infectious and I found myself laughing, too.

"But you don't think it will work."

"No."

"So we ought to get right to this doomed-to-fail trial, I guess."

While I tried hard not to be amused, Luke dug the list out of his back pocket.

I was shocked. "You had it with you all the time?"

He looked at the list like he hadn't even really noticed it before. "Wow. Guess I did."

I leaned over and swiped it out of his hand, then set the rest of my sandwich down on the napkin I'd placed across my lap and unfolded the list. "Raven Wolf." That was the first name on the list. Odd name. I almost darted an alarmed look at Luke. But I realized in time that that would be rude.

"My most recent ex," Luke explained. "She works in Pike Place Market. She's a psychic. And a tarot card reader."

I shot him the look of alarm anyway. "Tarot card reader?"

He nodded. "She's pretty good at it. Well-respected anyway. She's the sister of a guy who works with me."

"Okay." I went back to the list. "Gwen Steele, MD?"

"An OB/GYN."

"That's quite a difference from a . . . a psychic," I commented, then took up my sandwich again and stuffed a bite in my mouth before I said something I shouldn't.

"Gwen and I met at a party." He hesitated and then finally continued. "I don't think I should comment on any of them. I don't want to bias your scientific results."

"Funny." The next name on the list had me dropping my sandwich back into my lap. "Harry Middleton. *Harry?*"

Luke shrugged and took another bite of his sandwich.

I blinked and caught my breath. When I suspected a major flaw in Luke, this hadn't been it. It was said that all the good-looking guys were gay, but . . . Luke?

I thrust the paper back in his direction. "I can't . . . I mean, it's not that I don't completely respect your choices . . . but, I can't—"

"Stands for Harriet." Luke grinned.

"What?"

"Harry." He gestured toward the page still clutched in my hand. "Stands for Harriet. However, to prevent bodily harm, I would suggest you don't call her Harriet. She's been Harry since college, and I sincerely doubt she's changed her mind about that."

"Harriet." I let out the breath I'd apparently been holding. Not that it really upset me or anything to think that Luke was . . . you know. Because, really, it would have made this whole thing easier to find out that he straddled that particular hose. I could have turned him down on that fact alone. So,

I wasn't relieved at all. Really. "Harry. Okay. I'll remember that, I guess."

The last name on the list was Sarah Henderson.

Luke finished the last bite of his lunch and wadded up the paper wrapper. "I went to high school with Sarah. Guess you could call her my first love."

I smiled at the obvious emotion in Luke's voice, but when I looked up at him, there was a shadow in his eyes. It disappeared quickly as he met my gaze, though.

"Do you keep in touch with any of them?" I asked, for lack of anything else to say.

"Raven," Luke answered. "None of the others. We're all busy with our own lives now."

He picked up the bottle and offered me a refill, which I accepted. "So, where did Venus get this idea?"

"*Cosmo*. A women's magazine," I added, not knowing whether *Cosmo* was part of the male vocabulary.

"I know what *Cosmo* is. I have two sisters."

"Ah," I answered noncommittally. I didn't want to get all chummy, when I had no intention of taking this relationship any further than . . . well, interrogating his ex-girlfriends for information about him.

"I need you to know something, Rachel."

"What's that?" I asked, then finished off the last bite of my sandwich, glad of a subject change.

He leaned forward, bracing his elbows on his bent knees. "I'm not planning on backing off while you're doing the interviews."

Slowly, I looked up at him. "What do you mean?"

"I mean, that I don't plan on just stepping back and waiting for you to finish talking to everyone on that list."

"Why not?"

"Because this isn't a game for me. I'm serious about you."

Something in my chest constricted and forced out a little

laugh. "You can't be serious about me. You don't know anything about me."

He shrugged. "I know enough to know what I want."

It was a little uncomfortable to realize how decided he was about this. Heck, I wasn't usually that sure about something I'd been thinking about for a long time. That *Venus* claimed Luke was The One further added to my confusion.

In fact . . .

I looked sharply at Luke, searching his face for clues. "Have you felt . . . have you been feeling . . . coerced lately?"

"Coerced?" His serious look changed to one of surprise.

"Yeah, like, not yourself. Pushed into something you didn't want before?"

Luke started to shake his head.

"Rachel!"

I blinked at my name being called. Luke hadn't said it. I peered around, but other than a few of Cameron Creek's residents meandering the streets, there was no one around to have called my name. I guessed I was imagining things, and when I turned back to Luke I couldn't remember what I'd been saying. I just knew that I had what I'd come for and I needed to get back to work before Luke got all serious on me again. Dealing with him when he was flirtatious was far easier than in his present mood.

I pointedly glanced at my watch. "I need to get back."

"I'll walk you." Luke stood and hopped off the tailgate. He reached up a hand and helped me step off the truck.

"No, thanks. I could use a few minutes alone."

"Sure?"

I nodded. "Thanks for lunch. It was really . . . nice."

He leaned in close to me, and when my breath caught involuntarily, I smelled his cologne. Something fresh and masculine. "There's more nice where that came from."

FIFTEEN

Venus

This is going to be a breeze!

A few interviews, a bit of personal reference gathering, and bingo! Rachel will have no choice but to admit that I am completely right about her and Luke being meant for each other.

I mean, really, how could she not totally melt when he brought her that picnic the other day? That was so sweet.

Reminds me of that lovely spring day with Ares, God of War (and Most. Fantastic. Lover. Ever.). We picnicked overlooking the valley, dining on ambrosia and sipping sweet nectar. Ares whispered love poetry in my ear, nibbled my neck, licked his way down . . .

Who'd have thought someone who made war for a living would make *love* even better?

But, I'm getting distracted. Thinking about my past won't serve any purpose but to depress me. I really must concentrate on Rachel and Luke. After all, if Rachel turns out to be my final godchild before I'm released from my hellish punishment, I'd hate to look back and see that I'd dragged my feet, postponing my return to civilized goddess-dom.

So, phase two of the plan starts today. The first interview.

It's a step in the right direction. If only I could convince Rachel to stop all the other nonsense. Why does she want to build houses for other people? Especially when she has a *life* to build for herself? She obviously needs a nudge.

"What are you doing?" Rachel asks when she comes out of the bathroom, where she has been for a half hour—hiding out, I suspect, so she won't have to go to the interview, because truthfully, she doesn't look like she's spent a great deal of time doing anything else in there.

"Helping you remember what you're working toward," I say, stepping aside so she may fully appreciate my handiwork.

"Oh no you don't!" Rachel stalks across the room with malicious intent in her eyes.

But, I am not to be stopped. I slap one hand across the calendar—the date part, not the picture part, as that would just be a waste of good man-flesh viewing—and hold it firmly to the wall, while shoving at my willful godchild with the other hand. "Leave it alone. It stays."

"It goes!" Rachel snarls—yes, *snarls*.

Upon Zeus, she is more trouble than she's worth just to get one more homework assignment closer to freedom.

"It stays," I insist. "You need a reminder."

"I don't need a reminder. I've seen this before. I don't want it on my wall."

The truth hits me. "Ah. I *understand*. You don't think you'll be able to resist." At Rachel's widening gaze, I know I've hit the right nerve and continue the subtle, but necessary, manipulation. I run a fingertip along Luke's well-toned abs. The image of them anyway. "Kind of like putting a picture of chocolate on the wall of a diabetic, I suppose. I can see where the temptation might become too much if you have to stare at the nearly-naked image of Mr. March day after day after day. Your resolve to abandon your dreams may not be so easy to keep up, in light of the constant reminder of what you're missing—"

"Enough!" Rachel snaps. "I can resist temptation just fine. In fact, it's no temptation at all."

"No?" I ask, smiling so sweetly my teeth almost hurt. "Then you'll be okay with it here?" I gaze back at what really is a fine specimen of the male body. He's stretched out on the fender of a fire engine, half in his fire gear, half out—of course, it's the half-out parts that will keep Rachel's attention if she starts to lose focus.

"Fine," she says firmly. "It'll be fine."

I have again amazed myself with my ingenuity.

She, on the other hand, is slightly pissed off. Okay, more than slightly. In fact, so much so that she stalks out of the house to go to her interview way ahead of schedule, as if to punish *me*.

It's amazing how little it takes to manipulate humans.

Now, I just need to sit back and watch what happens. Rachel still hasn't caught on to my little secret about getting into her head where I can watch what happens at her interviews.

She'd probably kill me if she knew.

SIXTEEN

Rachel

How could this not be a disaster?

Having agreed to this insanely ludicrous plan, I treated it like every other unwanted interruption in my life. I made an appointment and penciled it in my planner between swimming laps, walking dogs, and paying bills, in hopes that by the time the actual time of the appointment came, I'd be able to erase it because some miracle had occurred.

Unfortunately, there was no miracle, so here I was. Faced with no other choice, I would just follow through, file the report of the plan's dismal failure with Venus (aka, the debit in my otherwise credit-filled existence), and then return to my regularly scheduled life.

As I made my way through the faintly musty smelling underground hallways of Pike Place Market, to the office of RAVEN WOLF, SPIRITUAL SEER, I tried to be open-minded. But Raven Wolf was *sooo* not her real name. And "seer"? What could she see, other than what everyone else could see?

Surely it hadn't taken special powers for her to come to the same conclusion that every woman eventually came to: that, as a man, Luke Stanton was nothing but a disappointment.

According to Luke, Raven was his latest girlfriend, with whom he'd split about a year ago. He hadn't provided details when he'd stopped by the bank to find out when I was scheduled to meet with her, telling me again that he didn't want to "taint the evidence."

"Are you a cop or a firefighter?" I had asked.

"I'm a guy who really wants to have something with a girl who needs to decide for herself whether I'm worth it or not."

Geez. Could he really be any nicer? It was like God (or should I say, Goddess?) was throwing this really great guy in my face thinking I couldn't keep myself from falling for him.

Except that I *would* keep myself from falling for him.

Despite having to stare at his totally hot body over my Frosted Flakes every morning.

I fully intended to prove Venus wrong, I told myself, stopping outside the purple-velvet–curtained doorway. And Raven Wolf, Luke's *ex*-girlfriend (who had to be his ex for some very good reason), was just the person to help me accomplish that.

I stepped through the curtains into the requisite—I guessed, being unfamiliar with seer decor requirements—dimly lit foyer. A small, spiky-haired girl sat behind a desk, reading a novel with a bare-breasted woman on the cover. I couldn't see the title, but the words "An Erotic Novel" were printed beneath said bosom.

"Raven Wolf?"

The girl glanced up and I tried not to flinch away from the light glinting off the dozen or so safety pins impaled in the skin of her face.

"You're here to see Raven?" she asked, folding over a corner of the page she was on.

I nodded. "I called for an appointment. Rachel Greer."

The girl giggled, which sounded kind of odd . . . such a soft sound coming from what amounted to a human pin cushion. I wondered if she had to take all the pins out of her eyebrows to pluck them, or if she just plucked around them.

"That was pretty funny. Making an appointment. No one makes an appointment here."

"Oh, well, I just didn't want to make the trip down here and have to . . ." I glanced around the foyer, which was empty of anything except for me, the desk, and the girl watching me in amusement. "Uh, wait in line."

"No lines, as you can see," she said. "That'll be twenty-five."

"Twenty-five?"

"Dollars. For your reading."

"Oh, I don't want a reading," I corrected. "I just want to talk to Raven."

"About what?" The girl narrowed her eyes suspiciously while flicking at her tongue stud with her upper incisors.

I cringed and tried to focus on her eyes, which were far too close to the safety pin line to make them any less cringeworthy than the tongue piercing. "It's personal."

"It always is. That'll be twenty-five."

Wasting time arguing is not my forte. Except maybe when it came to arguing that dating Luke Stanton would be just as big a mistake as dating, say . . . anyone else I've ever dated. The only way to avoid the arguments was to gather the evidence necessary to prove that it would be a huge waste of my time to pursue a relationship that would take me exactly nowhere.

So, for the sake of time, I handed over the contents of my wallet for a minute of the All-Seeing Raven Wolf's time. I was shown into a small back room, which was just as dimly lit as the foyer, but with small white votives burning in each of the four corners of the room and all along one wall, the wafts of smoke coming from the wicks making the air in the room slightly stifling. Pin Cushion Girl directed me to take a seat at the tiny square table in the center of the room and wait for "Madam Raven." Okay, the fact the Luke dated someone who called herself Madam Raven? That in itself put his taste into question.

"Hi. I'm Raven."

The woman who stepped into the room was gorgeous. I instantly took back Luke's taste in women. In fact, I had to wonder, in looking at her, why he wanted to slum around with me.

She was Venus's dark twin . . . volumes of black curls pillowed around her face and shoulders, accenting chiseled cheekbones and full lips. Her beautiful midnight blue velvet dress was embroidered with red and gold dragons, laced up the front, pushing up two—obviously—perfectly-formed breasts, which I was pretty sure weren't surgically or Wonderbra-enhanced. Flared bell sleeves floated gently around delicate wrists as she reached out to shake my hand.

"You're Rachel," she said with a wide smile.

I stared at her in shock. "How did you—"

"You made an appointment," she said with a chuckle.

"Oh, yeah. Right." I quickly sat down before I offered any more proof of my idiocy.

Raven lowered herself gracefully into the seat across from me and picked up a deck of cards and began absently shuffling them and smoothing them with her hands. Finally, she handed them to me.

"Shuffle the cards, please."

"Oh, I don't want a reading." I, however, accepted the cards she handed me, as it would have been impolite not to. "I just have a few questions about—"

"Don't tell me yet. Just shuffle."

So, I shuffled.

"Now, cut the deck."

So, I cut.

Then, Raven picked up the colorful cards—tarot, I guessed—and began laying them out on the table. "Think of your question."

So I thought. *Why shouldn't I date Luke Stanton?*

"You know, you really don't need to go through all this," I said, gesturing at the arrangement of cards taking shape on the table. "You should be able to answer the questions without the help of the cards."

"So can you."

"What?"

"You can answer the questions, too."

"No, you see, this has to do with—"

"Ah, look."

I looked and saw a naked couple with what looked like a colorful angel above them. "What does that mean?" I asked, curiosity getting the better of me. I'd never had my cards read and, even though I really couldn't say whether I believed in all that stuff or not, it was intriguing to think that maybe it meant something.

"It means your true love is near." She smiled at my obvious surprise. "Not 'in this room' near, but 'out there' near. You are soon to enter a romance."

"I don't think so," I laughed. "I don't even date anymore."

Again, she just smiled her serenely lovely smile, and turned over another card, this time a blindfolded and bound woman standing among some swords impaled in the ground. "This card shows that your view of things is clouded by something. You need to research carefully."

"Not bad," I said. "I'm actually here to do a little research about—"

"Ah, this card further explains your difficulty. The Hanged Man," she pointed out. He was upside down. "Your logic tells you there is only one solution, but you must be willing to try the unorthodox."

Nothing could possibly be more unorthodox in the twenty-first century than accepting that a fairy godmother and *Cosmo* could repair a nonexistent love life.

"Well, what I'm trying to do *is* very unorthodox," I said, hoping to move quickly into the question-and-answer portion of this evening's entertainment. "I need to ask you a few personal questions."

"Oh?" Raven asked, without looking up from the cards.

"It's about Luke Stanton—"

"Oh, look! The King of Cups."

I sighed. "What does the King of Cups mean?"

"He indicates a male under forty entering your life."

"That's just it," I replied. "Luke Stanton wants to enter my life, and I want to ask you a few questions about that."

Raven tapped her lips with her index finger and examined me until I felt like squirming. She didn't seem altogether surprised that I had come asking questions about her ex-boyfriend. Maybe she *was* psychic. "Why do you need me to answer your questions about Luke? Why don't you answer your own questions?"

"Well. Because . . . I don't know the answers."

Raven stroked the King of Cups card again, smiling fondly at it. "This card tells me the man entering your life is a romantic. He thinks with his heart. He's generous and thoughtful."

"Wait," I put my hand down on Raven's to get her to quit stroking the card. It was unnervingly like Venus stroking Luke's calendar photo. "Are you talking about the card or Luke?"

"The card speaks of the man you are to become romantically involved with. If that's Luke . . ."

"Well, I wouldn't go that far—"

"He loves kids."

"The King of Cups?"

"Luke. I'm a single mom with a daughter. He was very good to her. And to me."

"But?"

"But, what?"

"What was wrong with him?"

"Nothing."

I sighed. "Look, we're both women here. There's no need to protect men. There's always something wrong with them—"

"If you look for it, there is."

"What do you mean?"

Raven smiled. "Whatever you look for in life is what you'll find. If you look for things to go wrong, the Universe will accommodate you. If you look for things to go right, the Universe, in turn, opens up windows and doors to wonderful things. I try to see only the best in people, and that is almost always what I get."

This was all little too philosophical for my taste. Plus, it didn't help my case. "But if you only saw the best in Luke, why did you break up with him? Or, did he break up with you?" I didn't know who did the breaking.

Raven shrugged. "When you don't have it, you don't have it."

Now we were getting somewhere. "What didn't Luke have? What are his faults? Does he snore? Scratch himself in public?" Okay, not really devastating faults, but there had to be something.

Raven's chuckle melted into a wistful smile. "He works too hard. He doesn't play enough."

I frowned. That was kind of subjective, wasn't it? I mean, people thought I did too much, but *I* knew that I didn't. Besides, being dedicated to firefighting was pretty noble if you asked me . . . putting his life on the line day after day, working harder at his job daily than most people did their entire lives.

Not that I was defending him or anything.

"Didn't he, like, take advantage of you or anything? Maybe forget your birthday or buy you really lame gifts?"

Raven shook her head and turned over the last card. "The Hermit. You have much distrust."

How can you tell? I thought sarcastically.

"You need to learn to trust the judgment of others. And yourself."

I squirmed in my chair. It was little uncomfortable having a total stranger—and a deck of cards—nail me so firmly on the head.

"You know the saying 'Do what you've always done, and you'll get what you've always got'?"

I nodded. "I guess."

"Do something different, Rachel, and you'll get something different."

Riddles have never been my strong suit. "Well, thanks for your time," I said, rising. "The reading was . . . interesting."

Raven smiled back and rose with me. "Gave you lots to think about, didn't it?"

"Sure."

When I reached the door, Raven called out to me. "Oh, one other thing." She looked a little pained. "Luke didn't do much for me in bed." She shrugged. "Just thought you should know."

SEVENTEEN

Venus

Ha!" Rachel gloats as she stomps around her bedroom (my bedroom), throwing things in her gym bag. She's just returned from her first interview, and I must say, she's in quite a snit.

"What did I tell you?" Rachel continues. "Something had to be wrong with him. And, I'm not dating someone who's bad in bed."

"Oh, like not getting it at all is so much better," Hannah says, as she lounges back on Rachel's bed (my bed!).

"Do you mind? You're unfluffing my pillows," I snap, yanking the pillow from beneath her heavy human head, which then slams solidly against the wall.

"Ow!" Hannah yelps, rubbing her skull.

"*Whose* pillows?" Rachel snaps back, stuffing a clean towel into her bag. "Last time I checked, this was *my* bed. *My* bedroom. *My* apartment. Not that I have any say around here anymore."

"Back to the 'bad in bed' comment," I redirect. "That could mean many things. We need further clarification."

"I agree," Hannah says, but I can tell she doesn't want to.

Which is fine with me. I don't much want to find myself on the same side as her, either. "What *is* bad?"

"Bad is . . ." Rachel begins. "Bad is . . . well, something I don't want in a man, that's for sure. That's all that's important."

"No, it's not," I say, firmly, but not unkindly. We're making our first bit of progress here and if I must coddle her to keep her from having to start all over, then that's what I'll do. It's imperative that she continue forward. Time's a wastin'. I have a two thousand year overdue date with Ares. "Bad in bed can be fixed, depending upon what it means. If he's too fast, he can be directed to slow down. If he's too slow . . ." I shake my head. "Well, there's just no such thing as too slow."

"If he can't get it up," Hannah says, "there's Viagra."

Rachel glares at her as I launch the pillow in her direction, hitting her squarely in the face.

"Not helping. Either of you."

"Again, I insist we get further clarification," I say.

And, of course, when I insist on something . . . it is simply done.

EIGHTEEN

Rachel

I cannot believe you two are making me do this," I said, negotiating my way back through the busy Seattle streets for the second time in two days, with life's two most annoying people in the car with me.

"You're not getting away with half-assed research," Venus said from the backseat, where she had been pouting most of the way. When Hannah called "shotgun," Venus considered producing one and putting it to good use. Apparently the backseat was beneath her.

"It doesn't matter," I said, scoping out a parking space as we neared Pike Place Market. "It's not going to make a bit of difference no matter how carefully I 'research.'"

A space was free in a nearby open lot, and I pulled in and parked next to a Mercedes.

"Why don't you have a car like that?" Venus asked, slamming the door to my two-year-old Subaru wagon with as much disdain as you could put into a slam. "That is a much cooler car. Men would be far more attracted to you—"

"She *has* a better car," Hannah offered, and I shot her a look of annoyance. "In her parents' garage."

"Really?" Venus looked completely surprised. "What is it? A Beamer? A Porsche?"

"I work in a bank," I snapped. "Those cars aren't exactly within my budget."

I stalked off down the sidewalk, leaving the two of them to follow behind, our heels clattering on the concrete like a herd of well-shod horses.

"Well, what kind of car is it, then?" Venus demanded.

"A Mustang," Hannah replied. For days she'd barely spoken two words to Venus. But now that they were ganging up on me, she was *all* talk. "A cherry-red, classic 1965 convertible Mustang she and her older brother, Matt, restored when she was in high school. That car got her dates all the time. She once used it to date thirty guys in thirty days after deciding she wanted to get married."

"You can shut up anytime," I demanded. Thirty guys in thirty days had been an idea born of a bottle of really cheap wine one dateless Saturday night many years ago. The Mustang had merely been the bait to get that many guys to look at me.

"The car is gorgeous," Hannah continued, thankfully getting my message and not picking back up on the marathon-dating subject. "And so much cooler than the Subaru. Guys were drawn to it like flies."

"Get it out of the garage," Venus said. "You need to improve your image. And mine."

I whirled around so quickly, Hannah plowed into me. "I do not need to improve my image. And I don't care about yours," I said. "I'm not interested in attracting anyone. I drive the Subaru because it's practical."

"Bo-ring," Venus mouthed, then pushed past me and into the crowded market.

Hannah wisely kept from commenting further, but flashed me a look of concern mixed with pity that made me want to throw something. What the heck was going on? Now I had the two of them ganging up on me. Three if you counted Luke, who at least was nice about pressuring me to change my ways. Venus and Hannah were brutal.

Imagine . . . turning the kind of car I drive into a relationship issue. It had nothing to do with anything! I just decided that it was silly to drive it, is all. There was no practicality behind the Mustang that Matt and I had rebuilt. All the dumb thing seemed to do was attract unwanted male attention. I was constantly getting stopped and asked about the car . . . by buyers, sellers, guys who just thought it was cool. Guys who thought it was even cooler when they found out I'd had a hand in rebuilding it, and wanted to get under the hood . . . the car's or mine, I never knew.

The car became a liability to my newly altruistic world. I couldn't give of myself if I was fending off admirers. And, since I'd sworn off men after Eddie, driving a man-magnet car was stupid.

Leaving it behind was the best thing I'd done.

I glared at the backs of Venus's and Hannah's heads. Damn them for making me feel like there was something wrong with me! There was nothing wrong with me that having the two of them jump off the seventy-third floor observation deck of the Columbia Tower wouldn't cure.

"This is it," I practically growled, as we approached Raven Wolf's curtained storefront. "I don't know what you think you're going to say to this woman that won't be completely and utterly embarrassing to all of us."

"We'll just ask her to explain herself," Venus said. "Surely there's no crime in that?"

"Most people in polite society don't ask other people about their sex lives."

Venus flashed her broadest smile. "I never professed to be part of polite society."

With that she spun on her Ferragamo heels and brushed the curtain aside. And immediately halted. Hannah and I slammed into the back of her and knocked her into the foyer, the three of us tumbling in like the Three Stooges.

Raven lifted her dark head. From where she had been in the middle of a lip-lock with her much-pierced receptionist.

"That would explain it," Venus muttered, and I slugged her in the shoulder blade.

"Sorry to bother you," I said to Raven. "My . . . friends here. They were just, uh, curious."

"Yeah, curious," Hannah said. "I think we've had our major question answered, but do you mind if we ask you a few more?"

"What?" I stared at her in shock.

"Of course," Raven said with a broad smile. The woman was apparently unflappable. "Come right back."

She directed us to the same room I'd been shown to the night before. I followed reluctantly, wishing I could just melt into the wallpaper.

"So, what can I do for the three of you?" Raven asked, once she had closed the door behind us. "Were there questions about Rachel's reading yesterday?"

"More like questions about the man who's going to break Rachel's two years of celibacy."

"Hannah!" Oh, God. I sank down into the chair I'd been in yesterday and buried my head in the crook of my elbow. Could it possibly get worse?

I should not have asked.

"Obviously you're a lesbian," Venus stated.

Raven chuckled at the same time I groaned aloud.

"Yes," she admitted. "I am. Kate and I are partners."

"So that's why Luke sucked in the sack?" Hannah asked, without any sense of embarrassment at all. What was it with these people? Did they know no shame?

"Well, yes. I guess that's why. When Luke and I were together . . . I was very happy with him. He's a great guy. He loved my daughter, and I think he loved me, too. I just . . . didn't think of him in that way."

I lifted my head, unable to resist. "Why did you go out with him if you're a lesbian?"

"Good question," Raven laughed. "I'd been fighting my feelings about my sexuality for a long time. I was attracted to Kate, and had been attracted to other women in the past, but felt that it wasn't . . . right, I guess. I wasn't sure I should pursue it, since I had a young child."

"What changed your mind?"

"Luke."

"See," I said, directing my narrow-eyed gaze at Venus and Hannah. "I told you. He drove her to being a lesbian. Something is definitely wrong with him."

Raven tossed her hair back and laughed. "Nothing's *wrong* with Luke. He's a terrific guy. We just didn't have chemistry. In fact, Luke helped me come to grips with my sexual preferences. He talked me into being true to my feelings."

Venus looked troubled. "A *man* talked a woman into being a lesbian? Usually they don't do that unless they're allowed to watch."

I frowned at her. "Just because he isn't completely focused on his penis, doesn't make him odd."

"Defending him?"

"No! I just don't think you should judge him because he was sensitive enough—" I ground to a halt when I realized I was, indeed, defending him.

"Look, Rachel," Raven said, drawing my attention away from Venus's gloating look. "If Luke is pursuing you, no matter what your hang-ups about men—"

"I don't have hang-ups about men," I interrupted.

"You should at least give him a chance. He really is a great guy."

"Aren't they all? At first," I muttered. Standing, I headed

for the door. "Thanks for your time, and sorry for all the personal questions, Raven."

"No problem."

"See, 'bad in bed' was an entirely subjective thing," Hannah said, as we made our way out of the market.

"Right," Venus agreed. "Luke is obviously a sensitive guy, if he could set aside his own hormonal needs to help Raven feel comfortable with herself. I think that's score one for Venus."

"Agreed," Hannah agreed.

"I like it better when you two hate each other," I mumbled. "Besides, I don't think that proves anything. Luke may have helped Raven out of the closet, but that doesn't mean he was okay with being rejected. Hell, now he's probably suffering from raging insecurity about having his manhood questioned, because Raven didn't find him attractive."

"You're drawing straws, Rach," Hannah replied, paying for an hour's worth of parking. I let her, since she'd traitorously agreed with Venus's idea to come back here, showing complete lack of support for me.

"Well, I'm not interested in being his sex therapist or repairing his bruised ego. He probably just wants to hook up with me to prove that he's still a man."

"Oh, like you're making it sooo easy on him," Venus said, wryly. "I think there are probably a thousand other girls out there who would be more than willing to make Mr. March feel like a man again if that were the case."

She was probably right. So why didn't Luke pursue one of those thousands of other women?

"Where is my damn planner?" I muttered the next afternoon, as I searched the top of my desk, the desk drawers, and finally my purse. No luck. Maybe I'd left it in the lunchroom.

I didn't have a customer, so I got up to go check. Venus was in her usual spot on the couch, within eyesight of Millicent, who spent most of her days practically salivating over Venus's imaginary "millions." I'd had to stop her from approaching Venus on several occasions, telling her what a mistake that would be and making up some story about the last banker being too pushy. I'd told Millicent that Venus had not only *not* put her money into that bank, but had protested outside the bank, using her stunning beauty to get wealthy male customers to pull *their* money out of the bank. So Millicent refrained—barely—from bothering Venus, who just kept the couch warm and people-watched day after day, making the occasional jaunt to Starbucks or shopping.

This afternoon she appeared engrossed in a leather-bound book, which she was attacking with the eraser end of a pencil.

"Hey!" I dashed over to her when I realized the book under assault was my missing Franklin Covey planner. I snatched it from her hands. "What are you doing?" There was eraser dust all over the pages and far fewer entries than I remembered.

"Just lightening your load," Venus said, all mock innocence. "You need to make room for your soon-to-be-blossoming social life."

"There will be no blossoming," I said. "And you have no right to erase things from my planner."

Venus just shrugged and retrieved a tattered financial magazine from the coffee table. "I wouldn't need to erase things from that stupid book if it had more interesting things in it."

"What I find interesting is none of your business." I went back to my desk, removed my purse, and dropped the planner into the bottom—lockable—drawer, and locked it. "I'm taking my break. I don't want to see you for the next fifteen minutes."

Like that would ever be long enough to put my world back in order, I thought, pushing through the front door into the chilly fall air.

Where I ran directly into the solid chest of Luke Stanton.

"Sorry," I apologized, quickly trying to sidestep from where he grasped my elbows to steady me.

"I was coming to see you anyway."

I attempted a half-hearted smile. "I'm not in the best of moods, so now might not be the time to ask me out yet again."

"Okay." Luke fell into silent step beside me.

After a moment, I gave him a sidelong glance. "What are you doing?"

"Walking with you."

"You don't even know where I'm going."

He shrugged. "Doesn't matter."

A small laugh pushed its way out of me. "You're strange, you know that."

"I've been called worse."

"Starbucks," I said. "That's where I'm going."

"Starbucks it is, then."

We walked the few more blocks to the Cameron Creek Starbucks in silence. I was surprised to find that I didn't feel it necessary to fill in that silence. I've never been one for empty spaces. At least not for the last few years. Empty spaces tended to be filled with thinking time. I wasn't big on thinking time. Probably because my thoughts were rarely of the cheerful variety, but tended toward the depressing, woe-is-me variety. Not that I understood this at all. Because, really, my life was totally fulfilling. I did good things for people. I helped out, made the world a better place. People looked forward to seeing me. I mean, geez, Twila at the animal shelter, *hugged* me whenever I showed up to take the dogs for their daily constitutional. I made a difference in the world. So, why did I so often feel like something was missing?

But walking silently with Luke wasn't like that. It was comfortable. I appreciated that.

When we got to Starbucks, Luke opened the door, motioning me to enter with a mock bow.

"Cinderella," he said.

I stopped and stared at him. "Why did you call me that?"

"Cinderella?"

I nodded.

He shrugged. "No particular reason. Just popped into my mind."

I slowly moved up to the counter to place my order, an uneasiness settling over me. It seemed too coincidental that Luke would call me Cinderella. Not the typical thing a modern guy might call a girl he was interested in.

Especially not when said girl had recently had a fairy godmother appear in her life.

Shaking my head, I tried to relax. I was treating everything suspiciously these days. It was just that Luke seemed too good to be true, in too many ways. There had to be something wrong. And chances were, if there was, Venus was behind it.

The barista asked Luke for his order, to start along with mine.

"I'll get this," I said, casually testing the waters for hints of problems to come.

"Great. Thanks," Luke replied with a smile.

"Really?" I turned quickly to judge his reaction to my offer to use *my* money to pay for *his* coffee. "You don't have a problem with me paying?"

He shrugged. "Should I? It is the new millennium. Wouldn't it be sexist to assume that I can't accept a cup of coffee from a woman?"

I narrowed my eyes as if looking through a smaller field of vision would make it easier to see if he was lying to me. "That's the only reason you said yes? Not because you're secretly broke or . . . or suffering severe financial fallout from something?"

He laughed. "No. I can truthfully say that I could afford to pay for my own coffee. And yours, if you like."

"No. No," I said, now feeling kind of idiotic for suspecting him of some kind of huge conspiracy to deceive me just because he accepted my offer for a cup of coffee. "I'll get them. This time."

"So," Luke finally said, after we'd ordered and were back on the street headed for the bank again. "Did that little outburst about who was paying have to do with some past relationship?"

"I guess," I said, flushing. "The ex-boyfriend I mentioned was a criminal? He was embezzling from his company, and when he finally stopped—because he was worried about being caught—he suddenly expected me to pay for everything. From the most expensive restaurants down to the tiniest cup of coffee."

"So, I basically agreed to let you pay too quickly, making you suspicious that my budget was somehow suffering?"

I shrugged, catching the little smirk on his face and trying not to smile back. I was supposed to be embarrassed.

"Well," Luke continued, as he stepped around a blue mailbox in the middle of the sidewalk, "you could always check my bank balance when you get back to work. It might ease your mind."

"That's unethical," I protested.

"Oh, all right. I'll bring last year's tax return in then, if that'll work."

I punched him in the arm. "Stop teasing. I made a fool out of myself. I admit it."

"A beautiful fool."

Again, I flushed, and simultaneously realized that the past fifteen minutes with Luke, despite my complete social faux pas, had greatly improved my mood.

"So, how's the interview process going?"

"I've only spoken to Raven," I said, blowing on my steaming coffee, and glad for the change of subject.

"Ah, Raven. She's great." Luke smiled. He smiled a lot, I'd noticed. Kind of made you want to smile back, even when you didn't really feel like smiling.

"Are you still friends with her?"

"Sure. Why not?"

"I don't know." It seemed odd, in a way, I guess.

"Aren't you still friends with any of your ex-boyfriends?"

I laughed a little incredulously. "Uh, no." Then I realized that might say more about me than about them. "Just hasn't come up."

Luke let it drop. "So, when's the next interview?"

"I haven't set it up yet," I admitted. "Isn't this weird for you? I mean, I can't imagine most guys letting someone interview their old girlfriends."

"I find it more odd that you want to interview *them* and not *me*."

"Huh?"

Luke paused at the corner across from the bank and I stopped in front of him. "Isn't it unusual for the person applying for the job not to be interviewed? Wouldn't it make more sense to ask *me* what kind of person I am, than to rely on what others say about me?"

I pushed back the slight sense of embarrassment that crept in. "But you could say whatever you wanted to me. Tell me what you think I want to hear."

"You mean lie?"

"No. Well, yes. Maybe." I swallowed uncomfortably. "It's just that . . . in my experience, men either see themselves differently or they just plain lie to get women into bed."

Again, with a smile that could have turned me into mush if I was susceptible to that sort of thing, Luke started walking backward away from me. "What if I'm not trying to get you into bed?"

"You're not?" I blurted out, before thinking. Blood flooded my face. "I mean—"

"Bye, Rachel." Luke winked and waved, then turned and walked away, leaving me alone with my mortification.

I swam like a thousand laps that night, all to the mantra "I am so stupid. I am so, so stupid."

I couldn't believe I'd actually said that to Luke. How desperate for attention had I sounded? Especially after I'd already implied that letting me pay for the coffee was a bad thing, and that the male of the species were all basically liars.

I berated myself further as I showered and redressed in the locker room. This was such a bad plan all the way around. I was finding Luke too nice, which told me I was clearly missing something—probably something glaringly obvious, but it was being fogged over by my unfortunate attraction to him. I wasn't being objective and impersonal. I was letting Venus push me into something I knew was a bad, bad idea.

And I was starting to have marriage fantasies again. The ones where I was happily living out my dream the way everyone in my family seemed to be doing.

I had to get rid of them. The dreams, not my family.

Not wanting to go home and face Venus's nagging—or analyzing—I was kind of lost. My high school mentoring group had been canceled because school was out for some reason. It was too late to head up to the hospital to read to the kids. The shelter dogs were being walked by a different volunteer tonight. Dinner hour had come and gone, so I wasn't needed at the soup kitchen. I wasn't used to having nothing to do.

I finally decided a guilt visit to my parents' house was in order. I hadn't been to see them in so long, they had probably forgotten who I was. Or so my mother would mention a few times during the visit to attempt to shorten the length of time before the next visit. Besides I had vowed to show my face to my family again soon so they'd remember what I looked like in case Luke turned out to be a kidnapper.

Of course, if he was, in fact, a kidnapper, he didn't seem to be very good at it.

I should have appreciated the fact that I could drop by my childhood home any time. Hannah practically needed an engraved invitation—or at least an appointment—to visit the icy mansion on the hill that her parents treated less like a home than an entertainment tool. The mid-sized ranch house just off Main Street, where my parents had lived for thirty-five years, was always open to us kids. Something I had always wanted to re-create with my own kids some day.

Something I was *not* going to think about anymore.

The garage was open, and I could see my dad at his workbench as I pulled into the driveway.

"Hey, Dad," I called as I stepped into the warmth of the garage. Dad had installed a small woodstove in the back corner, which kept the room toasty warm, even in the winter, making it more comfortable to work on whatever project was keeping him busy at the time.

"Hey, Greasy." Dad called me by the nickname he'd given me in high school when my brother Matt and I had spent so much time working on my old Mustang. He looked surprised to see me. "What brings you around?"

I stood on tiptoes and kissed his cheek. "Can't I drop by for a visit with my family?"

He shrugged and turned back to where he was working on some car part. "Sure. Just don't do it that often anymore."

"I've been busy. With work and stuff." I ignored the tightness in my throat and leaned back against the bench to watch him checking out a couple of spark plugs. "Whatcha working on?"

"Joe's car." He jerked his thumb toward the side of the garage where my seventeen-year-old brother's Jeep was parked. "Needed a tune-up, but he's too busy studying to do it himself."

"Probably wouldn't want to even if he wasn't studying," I pointed out. My little brother was a senior at Cameron Creek High, and clearly setting out to prove himself the brains of the family. He dreamed of medical school and eventually becoming a surgeon. He preferred blood to grease.

Between Joe and me was Roxanne, a senior at the University of Washington, getting her degree in some obscure psychology something or other, and planning for the wedding she and her fiancé Davis would have after they graduated. *She* had scrimped and saved all her babysitting and birthday money for years prior to getting her license, so she could buy a new car which "didn't require daily prayer" to keep running.

On the other hand, Matt and I spent much of our high school years covered in grease. I had, throughout junior high, watched him rebuild a '57 Chevy truck for himself, and when it was done and I was on the verge of getting my driver's license, I convinced him to teach me to rebuild a car. It had resulted in Sally, the convertible Mustang I had once driven with great pride.

Which now lay unused under a plain gray dustcover.

I pushed off the bench and wandered to the far side of the garage to my car. I lifted the corner of the dustcover a few inches, just far enough to see a patch of bright red over a still shiny chrome bumper. I knew that if I lifted the cover higher, I'd find the black soft top stretched taut, in near-perfect condition. Just the way I'd left her. What a great car she'd once been. I'd been so proud.

Sighing, I let the cover drop into place again. Why I didn't just sell the dang thing, I couldn't say. It wasn't like I was using her . . . it. And certainly there were hundreds of other people out there who would love to get their hands on a classic car like Sally. I may not have appreciated the attention she got me, but that didn't mean she shouldn't be appreciated.

"Thinking of driving her again?" Dad asked, and I turned to find him watching me thoughtfully, the overhead fluorescent light glinting off the patch of bare skin on the top of his head.

"Oh. No," I said, crossing back over to him, to retrieve my purse before going in to see my mom. "What do I need with an impractical car like that?"

"Butch down at the parts store asked about Sally the other day. Remembered when you used to drive her around town. Might want to buy her, if you're interested."

Funny, I'd just had the same thought, but when Dad said it

out loud, it kind of made me want to cry. Like I'd be giving up part of my youth or . . . or a friend or something. "I think I'll wait on selling her for now, if you don't mind."

Again, he shrugged. "Not my car." He nodded toward the inner garage door. "Your mom'll be happy to see you. Don't keep her waiting."

I nodded and headed inside, feeling even more subdued than when I'd arrived and hoping I hadn't made a mistake in coming here. It was supposed to cheer me up, not drag me down even further.

"Absolutely, tell Matt that you need help, Connie," my mother was saying into the phone braced on her shoulder, as she used her free hands to dry the dinner dishes. Her eyes lit up as I stepped beside her and took the towel out of her hand so she could finish talking to my sister-in-law, with both hands . . . the way she preferred to talk.

"There's no reason he has to bowl *twice* a week when he can bowl once and help you with the twins the other night. Be firm."

It sounded like there was trouble in paradise.

"If he gives you any more crap, Connie, you just send him over and let *me* set him straight. Rachel's here. Gotta go. Love you, dear. Bye." My mother hung up the phone and tossed it on the counter. "Men!"

"Your precious firstborn giving Connie problems?" I asked with a chuckle.

"Of course. He's a man." Mom accepted the dish I'd just finished drying and put it away in the cupboard. "He'd rather bowl than change diapers. She's getting tired and wants a little more cooperation on the home front."

I frowned, imagining myself stuck at home, seven months pregnant and exhausted, with two needy toddlers clinging to my legs, knowing my husband was out drinking beer and throwing a ball, while I just wanted to take a nap and couldn't. My brother should be shot. Looking at it from Connie's point of view, it probably didn't matter that my brother couldn't be classified in the same category as *my* ex-boyfriends, the embezzler and the sex addict (and the other one I wasn't thinking about). If I was huge and pregnant and had an absent husband, I'd be just as pissed off as I had been at Mick, Aaron, and Eddie. Okay, maybe not *as* pissed off, but probably it felt like that to Connie.

Maybe all was not as peachy in Love Land as I imagined. Maybe coming here hadn't been such a bad idea after all. It just might end up making me feel better.

Setting down the towel, I handed Mom the last dish, then leaned back against the counter and chewed my thumb nail, watching her thoughtfully.

She was still an attractive woman, even in her late fifties. She was smart and had made good grades in school. She'd gotten her teaching degree and taught school off and on over the years, between babies. She and my dad had met and fallen in love in college and had been happily married for thirty-five years. Or had they? Maybe I had just projected my dream of happily wedded bliss onto them—and then onto Matt and Connie—because I expected them to be happy. Not because they really were.

"Do you ever regret marrying Dad?"

"What do you mean?" Mom started toweling off the damp counter.

"I mean, I remember you telling me once that you had always wanted to get married, but don't you ever kind of wish you hadn't?"

"Only when I land in the toilet water in the middle of the night because he forgot to put the lid down."

"Seriously, Mom." This might be my out. If she admitted that marriage wasn't all she'd hoped it would be, that she wished she'd pursued her career, or had traveled instead of settling down, then I'd be off the hook, right? I could attend family functions again, knowing that I wasn't *really* missing out on some blissful dream of True Love, but that I'd conjured it up in my imagination. If Connie wasn't really happy with my brother, and my mother wasn't really happy with my father . . .

Well, okay, that thought was actually depressing. It's not that I wanted the people I loved to be unhappy, but I was caught between fantasy and reality here. And maybe all I needed was a big dose of reality here to jerk my fantasies permanently out from under me.

"What are you driving at, Rachel?" Mom hung the towel up to dry and turned to study me. "Why would you want to know if I regretted marrying Dad?"

"Not Dad in particular," I corrected. "Just in general. Because, listening to you—and Connie—marriage obviously isn't all it's cracked up to be. You could have had a career. You could have moved to Europe. You said you always wanted to live in Europe. That's something you couldn't do while you were married with four kids."

"Marriage isn't perfect, but—"

"I'm not talking about perfection. I'm talking about whether or not it lived up to your expectations. I'm talking about whether you regret being tied to one man your whole life."

"Well. No."

"No?"

"You sound surprised," she commented dryly.

"Not . . . surprised." Disappointed, maybe. "I just . . ." I gathered my thoughts by retrieving a Diet Coke from the fridge. Gotta love a mom who stocks your favorite beverage just in case you show up once every two months. I handed her a Dr Pepper, her favorite. "I'm wondering if I have unreasonable expectations about marriage."

"Are we thinking about this because we have offers on the table?"

"God, no!"

She didn't appear to appreciate my indignation about the

idea, but kindly kept it to herself. "Well, what do *you* expect from marriage?"

Miracles? Perfection? Unerring blending of bodies, minds, and souls?

I shrugged. This wasn't working. I needed a new angle. "Aren't there things about Dad that piss you off so much you wish you'd never married him? Like . . ." I snapped my fingers, lighting up, "I know. You hate it when he sneaks cigars, right?"

"I hardly think that would be cause for regretting a thirty-five-year marriage. There're lots of other things that balance that out anyway. He's a good provider. A good father." Mom grinned and winked. "Not too shabby in the sack, either."

"Mom!" I made a gagging sound in the back of my throat that I hoped conveyed the extent of my disgust. "Too much information."

"What, you think we're celibate?"

"I think I'd rather spend the rest of my life believing you are, than ever again hear the words 'not too shabby in the sack' in reference to my father."

"Okay, but you asked the question."

"What about the bad stuff?" I said, guiding the conversation away from parental sex and back in the direction I wanted it to go. "What would you say are Dad's faults?"

"Well, we've already covered the cigar habit. He's also forgotten more birthdays and anniversaries than I can count. I started buying my own gifts before we'd been married a year. And, I once found fourteen dirty forks on his workbench after asking him a thousand times where all the forks in the house were disappearing to. And, I won't even mention how many times I've had to stick my hands inside smelly socks to turn them inside out before putting them in the wash."

See, I thought. All those things certainly didn't make marriage sound appealing. And we'd already established that my brother lacked in the "helping with the kids/house" department. Why would I want to be married anyway? I obviously wasn't missing anything except the headache of basically babysitting a member of the way-more-helpless-than-women-are opposite sex.

"So, really, I'm not missing anything at all," I muttered, as I took a swig of my Diet Coke, feeling better by the minute. Maybe I'd even show up at next Sunday's dinner. I'd be able to look at the two already established couples in my family and see that, behind the scenes, marriage was really more aggravation than it was worth. Plus, I could watch my sister Roxanne getting all lovey-dovey with Davis and know that all that blind bliss would soon be spoiled by the realities of "true love."

I glanced up to find my mother watching me carefully.

"What's going on? Why are you asking all these questions? Why are you here? In the middle of the week? Why aren't you out saving the world from apathy?"

"Gee, can't a girl visit her parents without getting the third degree?" Maybe I *wouldn't* be showing up for dinner, if I couldn't do it without interrogation.

"Not when the girl has missed Sunday dinner with her family for the past three months running." Mom raised one eyebrow in that way she had that reminded me of missing curfew in high school. "Grammy's worried about you."

I frowned. I didn't want to worry Grammy. She was one of my favorite people. She's who I aspired to be when I'm eighty. Ellen Greer was healthy and fit, played golf and bowled in a league, traveled, and every Friday toured the local casinos on the senior citizen bus with her cronies, just to keep busy.

"Wasting our inheritance," my father called it.

I called it good for her.

I wanted to be just like her. When my grandfather died fifteen years ago, Grammy didn't give up. She didn't sink into depression, like so many others did. She accepted the fact that she was now single and could either waste the rest of her life growing old, or she could live her life out as an active, productive person. Maybe, in light of what I'd learned tonight, my grandparents' marriage hadn't been all that noteworthy, either, and that was why it had been so easy for her to move on. She was finally free.

"Funny," I replied, keeping these thoughts to myself, so as not to start round two of Twenty Questions, "she seems to think you're the one worrying."

"We both are," my mother began. "We both think—"

"So is Connie really unhappy with Matt?" I needed again to steer the conversation back in a direction that might actually accomplish my newly discovered goal of finally realizing that my dream of Happily Ever After was a dream that no one *actually* had.

Mom frowned at me. "Not unhappy. Just a little frustrated. Why? Wondering if Connie regrets marrying Matt, too?"

"Does she?" I leaned forward. Too eagerly apparently.

"No! Rachel Ellen Greer, what's gotten into you?"

"Nothing!" She was looking a little possessed, so I wisely backed off. "I was just asking."

Apparently *she* wasn't backing off. "You've been acting very strange lately," Mom said in that Mom kind of knowing way. "Is there something you aren't telling me. Guy trouble?"

"No," I protested. "I'm not seeing anyone."

"Maybe *that's* the trouble."

I huffed out a breath. "How can you say that, when you just got through listing Dad's and Matt's bad habits?"

"Did you not hear me mention your father's good qualities also? And your brother, when he's not bowling, is a great husband and father, a thoughtful son, and makes people laugh . . . puts them at ease."

"But don't the bad qualities outweigh the good qualities? What's the use of being with someone when you have to spend so much time overlooking annoying things—or worse?"

"Well, let's see," my mother started in that stern voice she used when she lectured. Her hands were on her hips, too, which didn't bode well for me. "You, little miss, bite your nails . . . which, to those of us who have lived with the sound of your teeth making that little snapping sound for umpteen years, is enough to drive us off our rockers. You have never taken a shower without leaving the wet towel on the floor to be stepped on by the next unsuspecting—and inevitably barefoot—person to walk into the room."

I stared at my soda can wondering how long it was going to take her to run out of steam. And if I would survive the glaring recitation of my faults.

"You frequently get to talking, and don't let anyone else get a word in edgewise."

Wonder where I got that from, I thought wryly, as Mom continued without pausing for breath.

"You're often late for family functions. Your cousin Larry's wedding, for example."

I opened my mouth to protest that I did that on purpose, so as not to have to suffer through the agony of yet one more reminder that my own dreams of a wedding were permanently called off due to being unable to pick a groom who wasn't psychologically- or morally-challenged. I closed my mouth before actually vocalizing the words, which would have started another rant altogether.

"You have now taken to completely ignoring your family for the most part, leaving us all to wonder what we've done wrong."

I glanced up sharply at my mother, who, despite her angry tone of voice, looked on the verge of tears. "Aw, Mom."

"Don't 'Aw, Mom' me. I don't know what's going with you, Rachel. I know you had a hard time after Eddie—"

I reflexively groaned. I really, really didn't want to hear his name right now.

"I *know*," she repeated over my groan, "that you had a hard time after Eddie. And even though I don't know what happened between you two, because, lo and behold, there is another of your faults—refusing to share your problems with your own mother—but whatever it was, I really don't know why it caused you to turn your back on us."

Now she really *was* crying. Those silent painful tears that moms cry when their children hurt them . . . without meaning to.

"I'm sorry," I whispered, tears of my own stinging the back of my nose. "I just . . ."

"You just have your faults like all the rest of us," she said, the tears clearing now that she'd gotten what she'd wanted to say for the last year or so out of her system. "Just like all of us have, even us women. And we still love you, just like we love the men in our lives, faults and all, because *nobody* is perfect."

Yeah, but some of us were less perfect than others. Mick. Aaron. Eddie.

Me.

Mom didn't know the half of it.

I stood up. "I'm sorry, Mom. Really. You're right. I should be here more. It's just that—"

"The boys are growing up without you." Her voice softened when she spoke of my brother's twins, Nate and Brett, her only grandchildren until the new baby got here in a few weeks. "They ask where Auntie Rachel is every time they're here."

I feigned extreme interest in one of my mother's knick-knacks to keep from crying again. How could I explain how much it hurt to see them? How could I explain to my mother that seeing all of them, laughing and having fun and loving each other, seeing the boys, the babies, only reminded me that I had once dreamed of having a husband and babies of my own? And that, now that that dream had been squashed—not once, but *three* times—I just couldn't deal with it being shoved in my face anymore?

My mother's solution would be to get over it and go after that dream again . . . just like the heartbreak never happened.

Only, I didn't think my heart could take another fracture like that.

Unfortunately, my weak attempt at getting the dirt on marriage tonight had done nothing to change my mind at all. I still wanted it. And I still didn't have it.

And I still wasn't willing to risk it.

NINETEEN

Venus

The tips of my nails can't take much more drumming on the countertop.

And, my feet? Not much liking pacing in stilettos.

But, this godchild of mine is driving me to it! Can we say stubborn? Can we say unfocused? I've given her the golden opportunity for a little romance—not to mention red-hot monkey sex every day for the rest of her *friggin'* life—and she's not giving an inch. Can you believe how she tried to trick her mother into bashing marriage? Like that would let her off the hook? Not a chance.

I suppose I *could* let her take this at her own pace, but, she's just wasting time. Upon Zeus, do we have to drag this on forever?

Okay, it's been less than two weeks, but, that's *like* forever. I have places to go. Gods to seduce. Lounging to do! I'm not cut out for this fairy godmother shit.

I'm . . . I'm . . .

I am *not* a patient person.

I mean Goddess.

Goddess, I repeat quickly, starting to breathe faster.

Have I been here so long I'm forgetting who I am? Am I losing my identity?

No way. That's just not possible.

I am a Goddess.

God*ess*.

Like a god.

Only prettier.

Right?

Feeling a panic attack coming on—which in itself says I've been surrounded by weak humans far too long—I dash through the apartment and into the bathroom, where I stare at myself in the barely serviceable mirror. I look even more entrancingly gorgeous when gazed upon in the gold-and-jewel-framed looking glass I left behind when I was forcibly drafted into the Fairy Godmother Army of One.

My sigh is one of relief. Blond cascading locks like spun gold. Emerald eyes wide and wise. Slender, graceful neck. Perfect pert . . .

Well, you get the picture. I'm still me. I'm still Venus, Goddess of Love and Beauty.

And I have to get the hell off this planet before I've been here so long I *do* forget.

No more Ms. Patient.

TWENTY

Rachel

On Monday afternoon, I caught Venus sitting at Millicent's desk, using her phone.

"Would you excuse me a minute?" I asked the customer at my desk, and then vaulted out of my seat without waiting for an answer.

"What. Are. You. Doing?" I sputtered at Venus, when I arrived at my supervisor's desk.

She held up one finger to ask me to wait.

I'd have liked to hold up one finger at *her*, but it wouldn't be the "wait" finger.

"Of course," Venus was saying. She looked up at me, smiling and nodding, like I should be pleased with her.

I glanced around the room, trying to locate Millicent, so I could head her off if she caught Venus using her phone.

"Tomorrow afternoon at three will be fine. She'll be there. Thanks." Venus put down the phone and clapped her hands together like a fairy god-cheerleader. "I made your appointment for tomorrow at three. There was a cancellation or you'd have had to wait for another three weeks."

"What appointment? And get away from Millicent's desk

before she catches you." I grabbed her arm and dragged her out of the chair.

"No need to be so pushy," Venus said. "Millie gave me permission to use her phone while she was on break."

"*Millie?* Are you trying to get me fired?"

"Of course not." Venus headed back to her couch, where she had spent so much time the last week and a half that she had taken to storing packages of M&M's—which she ate in huge quantities, because apparently, they were lacking on Mount Olympus—in the seat cushions for snack attacks. She pulled one out now, opened it, and began retrieving the candies one at time with her outrageously long acrylic nails. "I needed to move you along—since you aren't moving along yourself," she added pointedly.

"Move me along?"

"I made you an appointment with Luke's next ex. The doctor."

"The *OB/GYN?*" I exclaimed. "Do you even know what that is?"

"Certainly. A woman doctor."

"A *woman's* doctor. Who deals with *womanly* things."

Venus's look was genuinely innocent. "Oh, you mean like periods and vaginal odor and stuff like that?"

"*Shh!* Yes," I whispered. "Stuff like that."

"I don't have that stuff, so . . ." She waved her hand like it was of no consequence to her.

Must be nice.

"Well, I didn't need an appointment with her. I just needed to talk to her."

"They wouldn't let you talk to her without an appointment. It's tomorrow at three."

"I don't get off until five."

"I told Millie you needed to leave early."

"And she was okay with that?" Millie . . . Millicent, never let anyone off early for anything short of death.

"I can be very persuasive."

"*I* told her you were filthy rich," I reminded her. "That's the only reason she listens to anything you say."

"It also got her to let me use the phone and give you three hours off with pay."

I sighed and chewed the end of my nail, still keeping a look out for Millicent from habit. "Just don't get me into trouble."

"I am the polar opposite of trouble. Get your finger out of your mouth," Venus demanded.

"Hi, I'm Rachel Greer. I'm here to speak with Dr. Steele."

The office was packed with women, most in various stages of pregnancy, or post-pregnancy, bearing infants in carriers, or attached to their exposed breasts. I tried not to look.

"What time is your appointment?" the stone-faced receptionist asked.

"Well, I didn't really need an appointment," I explained. "I just need to talk to her for a few minutes. Probably won't take very long at all—"

"What time *was* your appointment?" the receptionist repeated more firmly, as if she was speaking to a child.

"Three o'clock," I said. "But really—"

"Take this into the bathroom over there," she said, completely ignoring me, and slapping onto the counter a clear plastic cup with "Greer" written on it in Sharpie marker. "When you're done, put it inside the cupboard door. And then fill out this paperwork."

"But I don't need to give a uri—"

"Are you going to fight this *every* step of the way or are you going to cooperate and make this easier on all of us?"

Obviously *someone* was having a bad day.

"Fine. I'll pee in the cup."

And give Venus a piece of my mind when I got home. If she'd just let me do this myself, I would have explained to the receptionist on the phone that I didn't need an appointment, I just needed a brief consultation. A non-gynecologically–related consultation.

My mood wasn't any better when I came out of the bathroom. I hated peeing in a cup, far more often peeing all over my own hand than actually getting the body-hot fluid into the tiny plastic vessel. Then, I'd have to stand and wash my hands with my pants around my ankles, so that I didn't pull my pants up with pee-soaked hands.

Venus was climbing to higher and higher levels on my shit list.

I filled out the paperwork and turned it in to the barracuda behind the counter. "This isn't going to be sent to my insurance company, is it? Because I don't think they pay for peeing in a cup."

"No, honey. I'm going to pay for it out of my own pocket."

I rolled my eyes and took the only available seat. There were women on both sides of me with newborns. One was breastfeeding; the other trying unsuccessfully to quiet her squalling child by plugging its mouth with a pacifier.

"How far along are you?" asked the breast-feeding mom.

"Who? Me?" I pointed to my chest in confusion. "I'm not pregnant."

"Oh. Having trouble?" asked the woman on the other side of me, sympathetically, her baby now settling into silence.

"No. No. I'm not even married."

"Well, Dr. Steele is the best," said Woman Number One. "I don't think I could have had this little guy without her help. When it comes your time, you'll appreciate having her by your side."

Unconsciously my eyes were drawn to her contented-appearing baby. He was so beautiful, I almost couldn't breathe. It reminded me of my brother's twins when they were babies. When holding them, loving them, gave me hope—

I quickly looked away, focusing on a large poster on the

opposite wall of another cherubic-looking infant, whose big blue eyes bore into mine.

Reminding me.

God. How had I gone to the gynecologist every year for the past fourteen years without feeling like this? Oh, yeah. I went to a family doctor for all these things. A family doctor who didn't deliver babies. Strike *twelve* for Venus Cronus for putting me through this fresh hell.

"Want to hold her?" asked Woman Number Two, with a chuckle. "Now that she's quieted down."

Without waiting for an answer, she thrust the pink-clad bundle in my direction. I didn't have a choice but to take the baby to keep her from tumbling to the floor.

Oh.

Red-rimmed eyes looked back at me, blinking widely as she sucked the pacifier. It had been so long since I'd held a baby. Not since the twins were small. That had been three years ago.

When I still had hopes of having one of my own some day.

But no baby would come out of my body . . . no baby would nurture itself at my breast . . . no baby would bond me to a man I loved for the rest of my life.

Because I only chose men who qualified for the Loser List.

I felt like I was going to hyperventilate.

"I can't—" I shoved the baby back toward her mother. And, thankfully, simultaneously, my name was called. I leapt out of my seat and headed for the nurse at the other end of the room without so much as a backward glance.

"I'm Helen," said the pretty red-haired nurse, who wore a smock covered in colorful pictures of rattles and teething rings. "This is your first time here, Rachel?"

I nodded, still shook up enough that I couldn't speak.

"You look a little nervous," Helen observed. "You don't need to be. Dr. Steele is really very nice." She ushered me into an exam room and closed the door behind us. "I'll let you in on a secret. This is my first day. I was really nervous this morning, too. I was so afraid the doctor would be, like, really mean or something. But, she's great. She was even nice to me when I accidentally spilled someone's urine sample down the front of her outfit first thing this morning."

"Yikes," I said, finding my voice. "Bet that was embarrassing."

Helen nodded. "I was mortified. But she was really cool about it. She had a change of clothes in her office. Probably the only thing that saved me. So, let's get some information."

"Oh, we can skip that part," I said, with a reassuring smile. "I can make your job really easy. I just want to talk to Dr. Steele."

Helen blinked. "But I need to fill out the medical history. If I don't fill that out, Dr. Steele won't have the information she needs."

"But, like I said, I just need to talk to her. About a personal matter."

I swear Helen's lower lip quivered. "But, I don't want to get into trouble again. So, can't we please just fill this out?"

Far be it from me to make someone's first day of work harder than it had to be. So, I answered all of Helen's questions about my medical history (healthy), pregnancy history (nonexistent), sexual history (none of anyone's damn business, but I answered it anyway, grudgingly). By the time we were done, Helen was smiling brightly, far more cheerful now that she had accomplished something without smelly incident.

"So," she said, hopping up from her stool and rummaging through a drawer. She dropped a couple of items on the exam table and turned to me with a smile. "Get undressed and put these on, and the doctor will be with you in a minute."

"But, I said— You don't understand. I don't *want* an examination."

"Well, none of us do, silly." She bobbled her pert little head around and grimaced. "Do you think any woman *wants* to have a pelvic? Of course not. So, just get undressed—"

"I'm not getting undressed," I protested. "I just want to ask Dr. Steele about a guy."

"Sure, she'll answer all your questions about sexual partners, sexual positions, and/or sexual dysfunction after a thorough exam."

"I don't have a sexual dysfunction! And I don't want an exam, thorough or otherwise." I stood up, hoping that standing up would give me some advantage to sitting down. "I just want to talk."

Helen's face paled. "Are you going to make this difficult for me? If I screw up again today, I'm afraid I'm going to get fired."

"You're not screwing anything up. I'm just refusing to have a pelvic. It has nothing to do with you."

"It has everything to do with me!" she practically shouted at me. "If I mess up again today, Dr. Steele is going to fire me."

"Of course she won't. You said she was nice."

"That was to put you at ease," Helen whined. "I don't know what kind of person she is. For all I know she eats new nurses for lunch." Crocodile tears suddenly appeared on Helen's cheeks. "I can't lose this job. I have a little kid at home. My husband left me last month. I have to support my son. If you don't—"

I held up my hand to silence her. "Okay. Okay. I'll get my damn clothes off." There was no way I was going to cause another woman to cry this week. My mother had been enough.

"Oh, thank you, so much. It means the world to me to have you cooperate. I really don't want to get fired today. Not my first day—"

"Just go," I ordered. "Before I change my mind."

Helen high-tailed it out of the room without further comment, and I yanked the curtained partition closed so I could remove my clothes for a complete stranger, whom I needed to ask about a guy I didn't intend to date anyway, for a freakin' fairy godmother, who was probably a figment of my imagination, but who was, nevertheless, ruining my life. I debated just waiting it out fully dressed and explaining the situation to Dr. Steele when she got there, but I was afraid Helen would come back to check on me, and I didn't want any more hysterics.

After twenty minutes of sitting in the chilly room, in an open-backed gown with my bare butt hanging out, I wasn't feeling quite so generous toward whiny Helen, and was just about to get up and put my clothes back on, when there was a knock at the door. Dr. Steele entered on a current of perfume and fluttering lab coat.

"I'm Gwen Steele," she announced, without lifting her head from my newly published chart.

She was pretty. Not Miss Universe gorgeous like Raven Wolf, but attractive nonetheless. Her chestnut hair was cut in a chic, short style, perfect for the busy career woman, I'm sure. Under her lab coat, she wore no-nonsense navy slacks and paisley print blouse. Sensible shoes completed the doctorly ensemble. Gwen's more all-American-girl looks helped assuage my concern that Luke might figure out that, next to Raven, I was the plain girl next door and not worth his time.

Not that I *wanted* his time, but, still, no woman liked to be examined and found lacking.

"I'm Rachel Greer."

"I see that," she said, gesturing at me with the chart. "Let's get this examination over with, shall we? I hear you're a nervous one."

"I'm not nervous," I corrected, indignantly. I'd had pelvic exams before, and they didn't bother me any more than any other event where a virtual stranger gawked at my private parts like they were an exhibit at a museum. "I just couldn't get anyone to understand that I don't want an examination today."

"None of us do, dear. Now lay back."

"But, I just have questions," I said, even as Dr. Steele was easing my shoulders firmly back toward the table.

"I'll get to those as soon as we're done here."

"But—"

"Do I need to go get Brutus?" Dr. Steele asked, with a forced smile. "Just kidding," she added at my shocked look. "I just mention Brutus when my patients become difficult. Usually makes them laugh and puts them at ease."

Standing between my feet, she planted them in the stirrups.

I shoved the gown between my legs. "Really, Dr. Steele, I don't—"

"Do you need Valium? Would that help you relax?"

No, but it might make the whole farce of my life more bearable. I sank back onto the bed with a crinkle of paper, and read the poster on the ceiling.

God grant me the serenity . . .

Sheesh.

"Ask *her* how good he was in bed."

"What?" I asked the doctor, as she gathered supplies at the counter.

She turned to look at me questioningly. "I didn't say anything."

"Oh. Okay."

"Ask her how often he wanted sex."

"Excuse me?" I twisted around toward Dr. Steele.

"Ms. Greer, we're never going to get this done if you don't relax and lie still."

"You didn't say anything?" I asked, sure I'd heard a voice.

"No, I said nothing. Now lie back and *relax*."

I took a deep breath and tried to do as instructed.

Just as the doctor stepped up to begin the examination, I heard the voice again. "Ask her if he ever wanted a threesome."

Venus!

"Wait," I shouted, bolting upright and whipping my heels out of the stirrups. "I need a sec."

"Excuse me?"

I hopped off the table. "I need a minute to myself. Uh,

bathroom." I gestured vaguely toward the door. "Just . . . just a quick minute."

I tore out of the exam room, half expecting to find Venus standing in the hallway outside. She wasn't anywhere to be seen, but I spotted an open restroom a few doors down, so I headed for it, locking myself inside.

"Venus," I whispered. "Venus, where are you? I can hear you."

"Ms. Greer?" Dr. Steele's voice came from the other side of the door. "Ms. Greer, are you all right? Do you need something?"

I needed one very badly behaved fairy godmother out of my life. Or at least out of my exam room, during what amounted to a very private moment between me and my physician. Or rather between me and a potential future date's ex-girlfriend.

"I'm fine, Dr. Steele," I sang out with mock cheerfulness. "Just . . . I just need to use the restroom. I'll be back in a minute."

Dr. Steele answered affirmatively and after I was pretty sure she wasn't still listening at the door, I went back to my vicious whispering. "Venus, where are you?" I felt like Samantha Stevens in *Bewitched* when she used to excuse herself to the kitchen to hiss at her meddling mother to show herself.

"In your head," came the voice of the fairy godmother from hell.

"Well, get out!" I snapped. "You can't be in the exam room with me during something so private."

"I'm not," she said. "I'm on my bed."

"*My* bed."

"I know," she sighed. "We've gone over that. *Tirelessly*."

"*Venus*," I warned. "You are not to listen in on this interview. Or any other interview for that matter, if you can do things like that."

"Of course I can. And I might be helpful."

"No! You are not helpful." Hearing disembodied voices,

known or unknown, felt a little like losing my mind. "Did you listen in when I was talking to Raven, too?"

She hesitated. "Maybe."

"No 'maybe' about it. You are . . ." I grasped for the words that would tell her I was seriously pissed off at her for spying on me. "You are *banished* from listening in on any more interviews."

"Fine." I heard the pout in her voice. "I'm out of here. But I don't want to hear any whining when you need my help."

As if. "Not going to happen. Now go."

Turning my head from side to side, I listened for breathing or anything that might indicate Venus was still occupying my mind. Hearing nothing, I started to leave the bathroom, then stopped and decided to test the waters. To prove that she was gone, so to speak.

"Venus Cronus is an unattractive old hag, the mere sight of whom strikes limp, men and gods alike."

Lightning didn't strike, and there were no auditory hallucinogenic protestations, so I figured I was safe now.

I dashed back across the hall, gripping the gap in the back of my gown. The strange looks I received could have been because of my bare ass, or just the fact that most patients probably didn't try to physically escape from the doctor.

Dr. Steele was leaning her hip against the counter, arms crossed in front of her, one eyebrow raised. "Everything all right?"

I nodded. "Fine. Thanks."

She gestured toward the exam table. "Shall we try this again, or do you have any other errands to run?"

"Actually." I dropped the gown and straightened my back. "I don't want an exam. I have my own family doctor," I added, when she started again with the "Nobody *wants* an exam," line. "I have my own family doctor to do this. I only wanted to talk to you about someone."

"I'm not allowed to share privileged information," Dr. Steele said.

Were details about a past boyfriend considered privileged? "Um. I need to know about Luke Stanton."

Dr. Steele looked quite taken aback. "Luke? What about him?"

"Well." I looked around for a chair, and then, folding the gown behind me, I sat down. "This may sound weird, but—"

"Can't be any weirder than my patient rushing out of the room in the middle of an exam."

"*But,* Luke Stanton wants me to go out with him."

Dr. Steele raised an eyebrow again, and it suddenly occurred to me that she might be the jealous sort and not too happy that her ex-boyfriend was pursuing someone else.

However, she didn't comment, so I continued. "Luke wants me to go out with him, but I've made way too many mistakes in relationships. So my fair— my *cousin* suggested that maybe I should ask Luke's ex-girlfriends what kind of guy he is. That's not privileged information, is it?"

Dr. Steele looked a little shocked and then laughed. "You're checking out Luke's ex-girlfriends before dating him?"

"Yes. Basically." I squirmed uncomfortably under her scrutiny. "I really don't plan on going out with him, because there has to be something wrong with him, but, you know, I'm trying to get my cousin off my back."

Dr. Steele pulled up her stool and sat.

"It's like this," I continued, hoping it would appeal to Dr. Steele's intelligence to have me actually explain the reasoning behind what amounted to a very stupid idea. "I've had really bad luck with men. I have a Loser List a mile long. So, when Luke asked me out, I said no. But he's, well, persistent."

Dr. Steele's mouth twitched. "So, you're checking his references?" she asked, looking vaguely amused.

"Yes. Exactly like that. Except that I think it's just going to prove my point that Luke's a man, and men just aren't worth the trouble. It's completely silly—"

"No, actually it doesn't sound silly at all. You wouldn't enter into a long-term relationship with a car without test-driving it. So why should you enter a relationship without the same caution?"

"Oh-kay." Weren't intelligent women—like doctors—supposed to see through crap like this? I sighed, deciding I may as well get on with it. "So, can you tell me a little bit about him? His strengths and, more importantly, his weaknesses. That kind of stuff."

"Well. First of all, we broke up because he's not driven enough for me."

"*Driven* enough?"

"He's lazy."

"Lazy?" If Venus had been listening, she'd have lectured me for answering in questions, but sometimes things just needed questioning to be understood. "He seems very dedicated to the fire department. That doesn't seem like a lazy sort of job to me."

"Sure," she said with a shrug, "but a McDonald's fry cook can be dedicated. Luke doesn't have enough ambition. He's good at what he does. He could be chief by now."

"Isn't he only in his early thirties?"

"Doesn't matter. If he really *wanted* to be, he could be chief."

Okay. I didn't know all that much about fire department politics and protocol, but asking a firefighter to become chief in his late twenties (which would have been Luke's age when he was dating Dr. Steele) seemed to be pushing it.

"I could never get him to see the benefit in applying himself. In striving to be the best he could be, as soon as he could be it. He could even have had a political career, with his looks and trustworthy personality."

"I see." I didn't really, but it was obvious that Dr. Steele had strong feelings about dating men with type A leanings. "Anything else? Any other bad habits? Criminal tendencies? Disgusting fetishes?"

Dr. Steele laughed. "No. Besides the lack of drive, Luke was great in every other way." She pressed her lips together and with her heels pulled her stool closer to my chair. "Have you slept with him yet?"

"No!" I practically shouted, shocked by the question, and involuntarily blushing at the memory of Luke on the sidewalk last week, saying that he wasn't even *trying* to get me into bed. "I haven't even agreed to date him yet."

She reached into her pocket and withdrew a prescription pad and a pen. "Is your birth control prescription up to date? Because, as one woman to another, let me tell you . . . do *not* pass up the opportunity to let Luke Stanton make love to you."

"Excuse me?" So much for the jealous ex-girlfriend.

She wet her lips and looked a bit as if she might be damp in a few other places, too. "You will never regret the moment you let Luke Stanton touch you. Your wildest fantasies will be fulfilled. Your deepest places will be trembling."

"Really?" I leaned toward her. This was a decidedly different reaction to Luke's, uh, bedroom performance than Raven had given. However, we'd already determined that Raven's proclivity for women had probably rendered her incapable of sound judgment in this regard. "Dr. Steele, are you sure you should be sharing this with me?"

"Gwen," she said, with a sly grin and a pat on my arm. "Call me Gwen. After all, we are about to share a sensual experience."

"We are?"

She nodded. And giggled like a schoolgirl. "I mean, since you're about to embark on the Luke Experience."

I blinked. "The . . . Luke Experience?"

"The Luke Experience. The most sensuous experience of your life. Oh. My. God. It's unlike anything you could ever dream of." Gwen pressed a hand to the center of her chest as if to capture the breath that was beginning to come faster. Her gaze drifted absently into space as she continued. "He's attentive. He never lets you fake it . . . not that any woman being made love to by him would ever need to fake anything. He has just the right touch. Not too strong, but never wimpy. Oh, and the things he can do with his tongue."

"Ack!" I halted her. "Too much information." God. If I did ever sleep with Luke—which I wouldn't—but, if I did, I'd have to exorcise the vision I now had of Gwen and Luke's tongue.

Gwen leaned back in her seat, flushed and still breathing heavily, but starting to relax her suddenly memory-tense muscles.

"Why would you give all that up if it was so great?" I asked tentatively, praying she wouldn't start with the intimate personal disclosures again.

She sighed regretfully. "Sometimes even mind-blowing sex isn't the most important thing in the world."

"'Mind-blowing'?" I asked, in spite of myself. Wow. I wasn't sure I'd ever had mind-blowing sex. I thought back for a minute, to Mick. Nope. Aaron? Maybe a little closer to . . . well, no, still not mind-blowing by any stretch of the imagination.

And Eddie? Absolutely not. Truthfully, sex with Eddie had been mediocre at best. Functional but unimaginative. Faking orgasms became a fine art with me. And the last guy I had sex with . . .

Never mind.

"Yes," Dr. Steele—*Gwen*—continued, leaning forward, like she was a girlfriend sharing intimate gossip. "Mind. Blowing. As in toe-tingling ecstasy. As in the world tipping on its axis. As in multiple. Orgasms."

"Multiple orgasms?" I'd *definitely* never had that before. "Does that even really exist? I thought that was a myth."

"Not with Luke Stanton."

"Wow," I said, suitably impressed. But only for a moment. I didn't want to get sidetracked. I couldn't give in to the temptation of mind-blowing sex and forget about the very real problem that things in bed may be great, but that didn't mean that he was quality mate, er, date, material. "Seriously, though. Aside from all that, there has to be something wrong with Luke."

"There does?" Gwen stood up and wandered over to the counter, looking vaguely shaky. "Why?"

"He's a man," I said, is if that explained it all.

Turning, Gwen eyed me for a moment, before turning back to the counter and scribbling something on her pad. She tore off the top sheet and handed it to me. "Fill this. And get over it."

"Excuse me?"

"Get over whatever your hang-up is and do not pass up this opportunity." With a wistful sigh, Gwen leaned back against the counter. "I honestly don't think I've felt like a real woman since leaving Luke Stanton."

"Your plan *isn't* helping," I grumped, loading Diet Coke cans into my refrigerator. "My so-called *issues* aren't any closer to being resolved than before." I slammed the fridge door and turned to Venus, who was ignoring me and admiring my decor. "I told you this was a stupid idea."

"What *is* this thing?" Venus poked the hanging knickknack she'd been examining like it was a specimen from outer space.

"It's a kitchen witch. My mother gave it to me when I moved into my own apartment. It's good luck."

"Pish. There's no such thing as witches."

I blinked. "But, fairy godmothers are real?"

Venus grinned. "Of course."

"So, back to *my* problem," I prompted, reaching into the next grocery sack for the bread. "You told me that interviewing Luke's ex-girlfriends would solve whatever 'problem' I have that you insist I solve. But, it's not helping. Raven says he's a workaholic. Gwen says he's lazy. Raven says he didn't do it for her in bed. Gwen says I'll never get over the gloriousness of the experience. What the hell am I supposed to believe?"

"Zeus! My pores look like potholes!" Venus was examining herself in a compact mirror.

"*Ven*-us."

Venus slapped closed the compact and shrugged. "What do *you* want to believe?"

"Are you trying to be obtuse?"

"No. Subtle."

"You're about as subtle as a tsunami."

After folding the last of the paper bags, I retrieved a Diet Coke out of the fridge and popped it open. Drinking it luke-warm was in keeping with my lukewarm mood.

"Well," Venus continued, "telling you like it is doesn't seem to work."

"And if you *were* going to tell it like it is, what would you tell me?" I didn't stick around to hear her tell me like it was, because I knew she would follow me and tell me anyway, now that I'd given her an opening, and because I needed to get ready to go meet with my high school mentoring group.

She followed me into the bedroom. "I would tell you that you have the misbegotten idea that you committed some un-pardonable sin that is irredeemable."

"Ooh, big words," I snapped, now regretting I had asked for her opinion about the state of my life.

Venus continued as if I hadn't spoken. "You're punishing yourself for your 'sin' by eliminating all your own dreams, and filling up every spare moment of your time with activities dis-guised as helping others, but which really only amount to making sure you don't have one free second to think about what's missing in your life."

I turned to stare at her open-mouthed. "And you came to this conclusion how?"

"Aside from the fact that I'm the Goddess of *Love*—it's completely obvious to anyone who knows you well enough." Venus waved a hand in the air for emphasis. "You worked all day today, stopped by the grocery store on your way home, put away the groceries, and now where are you going?"

"I'm going to Sis-Men, my mentoring group."

"And then where?"

"I'm going to stop by the hospital and read to some of the sick children there. Nothing wrong with that."

"At eight o'clock at night?"

"I'm reading them bedtime stories. What time should I read to them? Eight in the *morning*?"

Venus again continued like I hadn't spoken. This was a recurrent move for her. "And then you will fall into bed tonight, exhausted, not having had a moment to yourself, and begin the whole process over again tomorrow. Work, walk pound pooches, rake leaves for elderly neighbors, serve soup in some kitchen, sleep. When do you have time to just think?"

"Think?" I asked, stomping into the bathroom with my change of clothes and closing the door most of the way behind me. I could hear Venus (which I wasn't so sure was in my best interest), but still had some privacy. "What's there to think about? I volunteer because I like helping out. Because it makes me feel good. Because I like to contribute to those less fortunate. Lots of people would be envious that I have time to do these things."

"And lots of people would think it was pathetically sad that those things are *all* you do."

Now dressed in something more appropriate for the evening's activities, I returned to the bedroom, where Venus was rearranging her cosmetics on the top of my dresser (now bereft of *my* cosmetics, which had been relegated to a bathroom drawer when she took over my life).

"That is not *all* I do."

At Venus's raised eyebrows, I forged on.

"I . . . I swim."

"And?"

"And, I . . . visit my grandmother." I squared my shoulders

and gave her an I-told-you-so look. "I am not pathetic. I play Monopoly with my grandmother every Saturday."

"For a half hour. *After* you do your volunteer work there, and only because you feel guilty for not spending any time with the rest of your family. Hell, your eighty-some-year-old grandmother has a better social life than you do. And, because I don't really care for your choice of best friends, I won't bother to expound upon the depth of her hurt feelings that you don't spend any quality time with *her* anymore."

I forced a quick recovery from the stab of guilt I felt and turned to face Venus with my hands on my hips. "You know, you sure are Miss High and Mighty. What do you know about self-sacrifice? What do you know about helping others? Somehow I don't think that getting Cinderella laid qualifies as bettering her life. I, at least, am trying to help out. Trying to give people who are less fortunate something to look forward to in their lives. What the hell's wrong with that?"

"Nothing is wrong with that," Venus agreed. "In moderation. What is wrong is that your life has become so consumed with making everyone else's life better, that you can't even see that your own life sucks."

"It does not." I turned away and went to retrieve my purse from the living room so I could get the hell away from her.

"Does, too," Venus said, keeping on my heels like a puppy.

"Does not," I insisted. "Come with me tonight and see what I do."

"Oh, no." Venus held up her hands in front of her and took a step back. "You're not sucking *me* into your ADD hell."

"Chicken?" I challenged, while at the same time silently beating myself up for impulsively asking her to go with me. Dealing with Venus the past few weeks at work and at home had been bad enough. At least when I was volunteering, I was free of her.

"No, I am not chicken."

"Then, come on." I headed for the door. "Unless you're

afraid I'll prove to you that volunteer work actually *is* a worthwhile activity."

"Fine. I'm coming." She snatched up her purse from the hall table. "But only because there's nothing good on TV tonight."

An hour later, watching Venus give makeup tips to the five teen girls in my mentor group, I vowed that my *new* mantra would be, "Keep your fucking mouth shut."

In the car on the way to the high school, I had explained to Venus what Sis-Men was, in the hopes that by the time we got there, she would understand the benefit of the program and why I felt so strongly about the time I spent with the girls. "Sis-Men stands for 'Sister-Mentor.' It's a Big Sister-like program run by the Cameron Creek School District. I mentor the girls. Give them someone to look up to, to talk to."

"Sounds like something I'd be perfect at," Venus said, brightening for the first time since she had reluctantly buckled her seat belt, obviously wanting to take back her agreement to come, as much as I wanted to take back my asking her. "Not that there's much—anything—I'm not good at, of course."

"Of course," I said wryly, before continuing my explanation. "I teach them a bit about finances and banking, while we're at it. Life skill stuff."

Venus shrugged. "But do they know how to have fun? Do they know how to find passion?"

"No! Geez, they're only fifteen or sixteen."

Venus sniffed. "Passion isn't only about sex. Although that *is* a wonderful by-product of passion. I was around that age—comparatively—when Zeus matched me with Hephaestus. Which was basically a ploy to control me, to keep the other gods from fighting over me." She flashed a movie star smile and shrugged. "Didn't work."

"Fifteen?" Geez, if I'd been forced to marry at that age, I'd have rebelled, too. "Must have been difficult."

"*Pfft*. The only thing difficult about it was being tied to a man who was so boring that watching grass grow was more entertaining. I found other outlets for my passion. I was born to make love . . . and to make sure everyone else got to make love, too. Quite a lot more work than it sounds," she finished off with a pointed look in my direction.

"Which is what got you into trouble with Zeus," I mentioned, getting my own jab in.

She simply glared. "Well, if some people would just take what they're offered, instead of fighting it—"

"Speaking of which." I pulled the car up to a stoplight and swiveled in my seat to pin Venus with a look. "Luke called me Cinderella the other day."

"So?"

"So . . . how do I know you haven't put some kind of spell on him? How do I know he really wants to go out with me of his own free will? Maybe you just waved your magic wand and forced him to fall in love with me . . . or *think* he's fallen in love with me."

Venus rolled her eyes. "You mortals are so stuck on that fairy-tale crap. Do you see me with a magic wand? Don't you think, if I could, that's exactly what I'd have done, instead of wasting my time arguing with you?"

"Maybe."

"Maybe nothing. I'm not a glutton for punishment. The easier the better, is my philosophy. So, believe me, if I could do it any other way, I would."

"Fine," I said, turning back to drive. "Just checking."

"Fine. Stop being so suspicious. So what are you going to do with those flowers?" she asked, changing the subject and pointing to the bouquet of fall blooms that were still in my backseat, where I had forgotten all about them. Mostly because they made me kind of uncomfortable. Luke had sent them to me this afternoon at work, with a note that said he had missed me the past few days while he'd been on his shift at the fire station. He'd included his cell phone number and said that he hoped the interviews were going well.

Well, if you called getting intimate sexual details from an ex-girlfriend, about a man you never intended to get that intimate with "going well," then I guess they were. I was trying to forget Gwen's confession that she hadn't felt like a real woman since breaking up with Luke. It tended to conjure up worries that I'd *never* feel like a real woman—because I wasn't going to sleep with Luke Stanton. I wondered if I didn't regret that just the tiniest bit. The "not being a real woman" part, not the "not sleeping with Luke Stanton" part.

But, really, I didn't know what to do with the flowers. They mocked me every time I looked at them. "Maybe I'll take them in for the girls to enjoy tonight," I suggested, as I turned down the street where the high school was located. "They don't get many flowers in their lives, I'm sure."

When we walked in with the flowers, by their reactions, I was sure that the girls *never* got flowers in their lives.

"Ooh, d'you get laid?"

I blinked at Mary Catherine Flaherty, the oldest and most streetwise of the group. "No, I did *not* get laid."

"Sadly," Venus murmured under her breath, from beside me.

"Give head?" Mary Catherine ventured.

"No!" I shot her a look. "How can a girl with such a sweet Catholic name have such a potty brain?"

"Guys don't give flowers for no reason," piped up Teeney Harvey from where her head was bent over her left knee to better concentrate on applying black nail polish to her big toe.

"Who says a *guy* gave them to me?" I tossed back with a warning glance at Venus, whose lips were taut from the effort not to laugh. "Women are completely capable of taking care of their own emotional needs—and physical ones, for that matter."

This prompted hoots and whistles from the gathering (including Venus), and a sudden embarrassed remembrance on my part that I wasn't in the company of peers, but of what basically amounted to little girls who probably shouldn't be encouraged to "take care of their own needs."

My gaze drifted to the eight-month swollen belly of seventeen-year-old Maria Munoz.

Or maybe they should.

"Okay. Okay." I held up a hand for silence. "They're from a guy. But not because I did anything to *earn* them." I shot a narrowed gaze at Mary Catherine, who snapped shut the mouth that had been open, undoubtedly poised to offer some other suggestion of what foul deed I'd performed to earn the bouquet.

"What does he want, though? That's the question," Teeney asked as she switched to her right foot.

A chorus of "yeahs" came from the gang.

He wants a date, I thought, wisely keeping this information to myself.

"He wants a date," Venus said, *un*wisely blurting this information out.

I shot her a murderous glare.

"Who're you?" asked Mary Catherine, thankfully distracted by Venus, which might mean that a discussion about my love life would not be forthcoming.

"Rachel's cousin, Venus," Venus said, smiling pleasantly.

"As in the planet?" Teeney asked with a snicker, looking up from her studious polishing.

"As in the goddess," Venus corrected, smugly.

I groaned and headed for the blackboard, where I started making notes on our evening's topic of how interest accrued on credit cards and why credit cards were a bad idea for young people. Usually we spent time chatting and catching up on our activities for the week, but I needed to steer the topic back to safe ground again. My plan was to teach the girls the value of saving money for what they wanted and how much trouble credit cards could cause in the long run, as the accrual of interest and making minimum payments to the cards every month could lead to them never paying off their debt over their lifetime. This was all information that would benefit the girls.

When the notes were complete, I turned around to find Venus standing over Teeney.

"Black?" she asked. "Any particular reason for making your toenails look like they have a nasty fungus?"

There were snorts from throughout the room and Teeney raised an eyebrow at Venus. "Got any better ideas?"

"Of course," Venus responded, then promptly dumped the contents of her purse onto an empty desk.

Upon seeing enough cosmetics to make up an entire theater troupe, the five girls—Mary Catherine, Teeney, and Maria, and even the quieter two of the group, Ariel and Naomi—pounced. Within minutes, I might as well have gone home, as compound interest was the last thing on their minds. They were more interested in the correct way to apply eyeshadow for daytime versus clubbing and which nail polish brand was less likely to chip yet didn't cost so much they had to take out loans to buy it.

So, they were getting *some* financial advice anyway.

I sighed and sank into the teacher's chair, watching Venus wow them with her girl talk, while I kicked myself for having asked her along. I should have made her stay home, boring TV or not. I was obviously no competition for the Goddess of Beauty.

Fifteen minutes later, the six of them were still eyebrow deep in mascara, blush, and foundation . . . and I had made a paperclip chain three feet long.

"Are you sure none of you want to hear about annual percentage rates and finance charges?" I asked lamely.

"Come here, Rachel," Maria called back, holding up a tube of lipstick. "I bet, with your coloring, this shade would be killer on you. Then that guy, Mr. March, won't give up on you because you keep dissing him."

I gaped at Venus, who just smiled sweetly and went back to instructing Naomi on the proper way to apply blusher to avoid looking like a circus clown.

"I'm going to the restroom," I said to no one in particular, since "no one" was the only one listening.

TWENTY-ONE

Venus

Something has to be done about Rachel. The girl has no sense of fun.

She wanted me to come to her Sis-Men thing on Wednesday night to show me the importance of the volunteer work she was doing. It worked. I saw how great it was to give those girls some *fun* in their lives, to show them how to be proud and strong women of the future . . . to tell them the difference between powder-based and liquid-based foundation and what skin types they work best on.

They loved it. You'd think no one ever talked to them about this stuff. *Sigh*. I guess I have to do more than just be a fairy godmother around here . . . I have to ensure that the young women of today have all of the essentials of life explained to them.

It was actually kinda fun. Even if it didn't have anything to do with capturing the men of their dreams. Really. I mean, I realized, once I saw how good they felt after a little primping that it was as much about how they felt about *themselves* as how they would look to the male population.

Seriously, I never thought about it that way before.

Turning this way and that, I examine myself in the bathroom mirror. Sans makeup. It's gruesome. On Mount Olympus, cosmetics aren't necessary. There's no Estée Lauder or Maybelline. There's no choice between lipstick and gloss. Goddesses are born beautiful . . . or at least *I* was.

The ravages of Earth, however, are a bit unkind, even to me. I'd been forced to become a cosmetics connoisseur.

But, why *do* I make myself up every morning? I wonder, beginning my routine. Do I do it just to attract men? After all, it got me what I wanted on more than one occasion. I bat my mascara-lengthened eyelashes and a new Fendi handbag appears on my arm. I pout my plumply painted mouth and earn myself a five-star dinner out. All right, they get a little more than that. They get a mental ego-plumping from me, too. But would they look at me twice in the first place if I wasn't made up properly?

It can't be all the cosmetics, can it? I mean, truthfully, there are beautiful women who never wear makeup. Men still flock to them because there is something about them . . . their carriage, their confidence. Something. Do they have that "something" because men think they are beautiful? Or are they beautiful because they feel beautiful, with or without the help of cosmetics?

I huff out a breath.

It makes my brain hurt to think about it all. Humans make things sooo difficult. I, however, know better than to waste time questioning things too deeply.

I finish applying my face and stand proudly at the thought that I made a difference in the lives of five teenage girls. I am more than a fairy godmother. Maybe I should branch out into *life* makeovers in general, instead of specializing in love lives. I'm apparently good at a variety of different things.

However, based on the exceedingly grumpy mood Godchild Greer has been in for the last two days, I don't think that fashion and hairstyles are what the Sis-Men group normally discuss when they meet. Like sixteen-year-olds give a fuck about financial analysis and the bottom line. Truthfully, I don't think Rachel does, either. It's just another subject that fills her time and keeps her from thinking about what she's given up. It's sad, really. I mean, I actually feel sorry for the girl. Deep down, I think she's lonely and won't admit it. The sad part is that she has so many people who love her . . . and I'm not just talking about Luke. I'm talking about her family. I'm talking about Hannah (with reluctance, mind you). She just can't see it. Or won't.

A few mistakes shouldn't keep a person from living their life.

Rachel needs a push. Just a nudge in the right direction. Of course, that direction would be *my* direction, not hers. Left to her own devices, she will be an old maid spinster crocheting doilies for the homeless just to fill her time. Unfortunately she doesn't seem predisposed to listen to anything I have to say about the state of her affairs . . . or rather lack of affairs. So, I am forced to admit that even fairy godmothers need help sometimes. And who better to get help from than Prince Charming himself?

Time to go light a fire.

I've never been to a fire station before; however, judging by the photos in the firefighter calendar hanging in Rachel's living room, some of these guys make even Hercules (voted Hottest God on Mount Olympus for thousands of years running) look a little "underdeveloped" by comparison.

One such fine firefighting specimen offers his services to me the moment I set foot on the premises.

"Noble Kipfer, at your service, ma'am."

A gloriously milk chocolate–colored hunk bends low over the hand I present him with. Ares used to kiss my hand whenever we meet. I feel faint with the memory of how it feels to be adored. Who cares if it's me or Estée Lauder evoking the adoration?

"How may I assist you?"

"I'm looking for Luke Stanton," I say, leaning closer, regretting that I can't linger longer with this one. "Although, maybe you would do just as well," I can't help but add, with a coy smile.

"I might do even *better* than Stanton," he replies with a wink. "There's been talk."

"That you might. However, I have business with Luke, not pleasure."

"His loss, I'm sure," Mr. Kipfer says, pressing wonderfully luscious lips to the back of my hand, of which he has yet to let go.

I may have to swoon. There has been a distinct lack of swooning in my life for the last two thousand plus years.

Out of the corner of my eye, I see Luke coming from the back of the station. Yum! So many gorgeous men crammed into such a relatively small building. Why don't single women just hang out at fire stations getting their blood pressure checked or volunteering to be CPR dummies? What better way could there be to find future husbands of the most sexy variety?

"Luke!" I call out, feeling immensely flattered at the territorial look that appears on Mr. Kipfer's face when the subject of my visit arrives. "How nice to see you again."

"You, too, Venus. Is Noble here bothering you?" He sends an amused look at my small white hand clutched in Mr. Kipfer's enormous brown one. Makes Luke's not-so-tiny hands seem pretty small in comparison . . . if you know what I mean.

"Not at all." I reluctantly extricate my hand from the warmth of its resting place before batting my naturally long eyelashes at him. "Thank you so much for your help, Noble."

"Any time." With another bow, seemingly tinged with regret, Noble leaves me with Luke, which isn't such a loss to me, seeing that Mr. March himself isn't exactly hard on the eyes.

"So, what can I do for you?" Luke asks, leading me into the station house. "Is Rachel all right?"

Depends on what you consider all right, I think somewhat wryly. However, instinct tells me that sharing Cinderella's issues with the chosen Prince Charming might just drive him away, rather than get him to agree to help me out a little.

"Rachel is fine. She enjoyed the flowers," I add, since I'm sure she stubbornly didn't call him and thank him, despite the not-so-subtle hint of including his cell phone number on the card. I don't understand her objection to him giving her his cell number. I thought it rather promising. Miss Pessimistic Pants, however, took it as a sign that he was hiding something, that he didn't want her to have his home phone number for some reason. Because that's what Eddie the rat bastard did to her, and he *did* have something to hide . . .

Luke's eyes light up, and for just a moment, it feels like they're lighting up for me instead of Rachel. It's been such a long time since a man's (or god's) eyes have sparkled for *me*. At least in that way. Love sparkles are different than "God, she's a babe" sparkles. Since I came to Earth—for*ever* ago—I've had to devote all my time to encouraging men to look at my fairy godchildren with love sparkles.

I try not to feel left out.

Sometimes it's not easy. Being a fairy godmother isn't all happiness and helping. It's kind of like falling in love over and over again. Only I don't get to participate in any of the actual loving.

Not that every match is about love, of course. Sometimes they're about duty, like with Princess Di and Prince Charles. Or about lust, like with Angelina and Billy Bob. I found that I prefer the love matches. Fine. So I'm a sucker for the fairy tale. Sue me! If I have to live this role, I get to have *some* enjoyment from it.

But, if I ever want to return to my home, if I ever want a prayer of a chance of being looked at with love sparkles again,

I have to shove these thoughts aside and selflessly concentrate on the task at hand.

"Yes," I repeat, prepared to lay it on thick. "Rachel is just fine. But, well, you know, she . . . she just needs some encouragement to leave her past behind. She's been hurt. Devastated really. Nearly damaged beyond repair." Okay, maybe that was a bit too thick, I think, as Luke's frown deepens. No need to scare the boy off. "I mean, nothing she can't eventually recover from, of course. You know she's had a hard time of it?"

Luke nodded, relaxing a little. "She told me she'd had some bad relationships in the past."

"Yes. She has. And, well, she's quite nervous about getting involved again. Which is understandable, of course."

Of course *not,* but I have to at least *sound* like I am somewhat sensitive to her feelings if I want to enlist his help in getting her to move the inevitability of this relationship forward a whole lot faster. I'm getting impatient. It's been almost a month since I took over as Rachel's fairy godmother, and it's taking far too long for my liking. Upon Zeus, it only took one night to get Cinderella hooked up . . . well, aside from waiting for the shoe-fitting thing. (That's the problem with the blind date setups. If names aren't given, there's got to be a foolproof way of making sure they find each other again. Hence the ingeniousness of the glass slipper. I try to avoid that scenario whenever possible.)

"I'm not out to hurt her," Luke assures me.

I lay a sympathetic hand on his muscular arm. "Deep down, I'm sure she knows that. She just needs a little encouragement, I think. A little time to get to know you."

"Can't very well get to know me if she won't go out with me."

Poor boy. He's as frustrated as I am. He's probably had a hard-on for the past six months. The Viagra ads say if it lasts more than four hours . . .

Well, anyway.

"So," I say, flashing him my brightest smile, "I think we should light a little fire under my dear . . . cousin. One that you, naturally, will be present to put out when the time comes."

Luke laughs. "And how do you propose we do that?"

"I have a plan."

And, leaning in close, letting my breast brush against his bicep (purely for my own benefit, of course; though, his being a man, there's probably something in it for him, too), I tell him the plan.

TWENTY-TWO

Rachel

ere. Put these on."

I swiveled in my desk chair to find Venus holding out a shopping bag. Clasping my hands to my bosom, I gasped dramatically. "You've brought me a ball gown, fairy godmother?"

Venus frowned. I know she told me not to call her that, but if I have to suffer with her constant butting into my life, then I get to have *some* fun.

"No. Jeans and a sweater. From your closet."

I took the bag from her, peering inside, at what was, indeed, my very own DKNY jeans and the sweater my mother had given me for Christmas last year. As well as a pair of tennis shoes in the bottom of the bag, by the feel of it. "What, I'm not allowed to go home and pick out my own clothes now?"

"You're not going home." Venus gestured toward the doors of the bank, which had been locked fifteen minutes ago, promptly at five. I'd been finishing up some paperwork.

"Is that my bike?" I asked squinting to see through the slightly tinted glass.

"Yes. We're going biking around Blue Lake. I borrowed Hannah's bike. She brought them over at lunchtime."

"We're biking around Blue Lake *now*?" I asked, catching Hannah's eye—and innocent wave—across the lobby. Something was fishy. Though the two of them hadn't come quite so near to blows in the last week or so, they certainly hadn't become exactly chummy. Even when they were ganging up on me.

"Yes," Venus answered firmly. "I'm feeling flabby."

"Wow, yeah," I said, turning back to her. "You might be up to a size two-and-a-quarter by now."

Venus fold her arms across her chest and ignored my teasing.

"I don't have time for that right now," I said. "I have plans. I told Twila I'd take a turn at walking the dogs tonight. Since you made me miss my last turn to go to the gynecologist. I was heading over there now. Well, after my swim and before going up to the hospital. It's in my planner."

Venus yanked my planner out from under my hand, flipped it open and frowned at it. Before I had time to react, she'd snatched a pencil off my desk and was furiously erasing the entries.

"Hey!" I made a grab for the planner, but she held the book over her head, threatening me with the pencil with her other hand.

"Stay back or you'll be sorry."

"What, you'll erase me to death?" I gestured at the eraser end of the pencil that was pointed menacingly in my direction.

Venus glared and lowered the pencil. "Look, I've wanted to bike around Blue Lake since I got here, and since you were going swimming tonight anyway, we're riding bikes instead. Otherwise, I'm going to throw a fit, right here in the lobby." She smiled sweetly, the Jekyll and Hyde of fairy godmothers, morphing from good to evil in the blink of a kohl-lined green eye.

I glanced at Millicent, who was watching us . . . probably, since she hated me, concerned that I might be threatening her best potential customer with bodily harm. She really was dense if she hadn't figured out after a month that Venus wasn't still sitting in the lobby all day, every day, deciding on her future fiscal relationship with Cascade National.

But, finally, not wanting to chance a scene, I stood, bag still in hand. "Whatever. You're changing clothes, too, right? Leather pants aren't quite appropriate for exercise. And spike heels and bike pedals don't mix well."

"I'm fine," Venus assured me, heading for the door.

Vanity apparently has no limits.

Venus

I'm being poked by the bike seat in places I don't normally like to be poked by things that aren't attached to a male body and don't rhyme with Venus.

I am vastly underpaid for this crappy-ass job.

This lake we're going to is on the edge of town, a couple miles from the bank. There's a path winding completely around the lake, flanked by trees that create the illusion of being at one with nature—even though the town was only a block away in some places. It is apparently a popular bike-riding, Rollerblading, running, walking spot.

As my stiletto heel scrapes on the asphalt path for the twentieth time in as many minutes, I'm thinking *man*-watching may be more my type of sport.

However, I don't think Rachel is much tempted to watch all the hunky men muscling their way around us on a variety of wheels or pounding past us on their own two powerful legs. With her prudish insistence on living like a nun, I'm not worried that she'll get too distracted. At least until we reach our destination and she sees the surprise I have for her.

"Are you going to be all right?" Rachel calls from behind me when I get a little wobbly. "You really should have changed shoes."

"Fine, fine," I call back. "You just worry about yourself."

Lance Armstrong's twin passes us on his bike, his butt tightly encased in black biking shorts molded to him like skin. I turn to watch him . . . watching me. Obviously my tight leather pants were the *perfect* outfit for this little jaunt. No matter what Miss Fuddy Duddy says about it.

"Just a little farther," I say over my shoulder. "You are trying not to sweat, aren't you? Sweating isn't very attractive."

"Oh, sure. No sweating going on here. I'm all about the attraction."

Pissiness will get her no brownie points.

When *I* feel a dripping sensation between my breasts, I glance down in horror. My cleavage is glistening. Ack! No sweating for me, either! It is not a good look for me. And, it probably means my makeup is running, too.

I try to slow down, to decrease the possibility of perspiration, but Rachel practically runs me over, so I have to speed up again. I try not to show concern on my face. Runny makeup on a pouty face is the worst. I pull my mouth into a casual smile, nodding at my admirers.

Apparently sweaty breasts and possibly imperfect cosmetics aren't any deterrent, as another guy almost kisses the dirt craning his neck around to check me out. Really there are some lousy bike riders out here. All men. They keep falling down. Maybe they're first-timers like me. Or maybe my theory about some women just "having it," even when they aren't made up to perfection, has merit. Just look at the continued attention I'm getting.

"Just a little farther," I say to Rachel, remembering what I'm out here for and remembering to play my part. "I'm feeling really, *really* good now. I think I'm developing calf muscles. Small ones, of course. Not those big manly ones like some women get. Just delicate ones. Toned. Sexy, of course. Men like toned and sexy calf muscles, right?"

"Oh, sure," Rachel replies sarcastically. "They don't seem to be having any trouble at all with your 'toned, sexy muscles.'"

"What's got your panties in a bunch?"

A teenaged boy on Rollerblades pulls up beside me, blatantly giving me the once-over. I bat my eyelashes a bit and try not to cringe when my heel grinds on the ground again. He's blushing, and practically drooling, as he darts sideways glances from my perfectly rounded ass to my high pert breasts. The sweating doesn't seem to bother *him*. He actually turns to skate backward to get a better look. Hmmm, even the youngsters can't resist me.

"Get a life!" Rachel scolds in a voice worthy of a drill sergeant, causing the poor kid to trip over his own feet and land in a heap beside the bike path.

"That wasn't very nice."

"What's not very nice is you dragging me out here just to watch men ogle you, while they completely ignore my existence."

"Jealous much?"

This is kind of shocking behavior on Rachel's part. Maybe this plan will work better than I thought. By the time we get to . . . who we're getting to . . . she'll be so starved for attention, she'll fall all over him.

"Seriously, are we done yet?" Rachel asks, adding a gasp when another half-inch of one of my heels grinds off on the bike path.

I try to readjust my foot on the pedal to raise my heel off the ground. Doesn't Manolo make strappy biking sandals?

"It's just up here a bit farther."

"*What* is?"

"Our meet— I mean, our finish line," I answer. "Where I can, I mean, *we* can turn around and go back. I'll have strong enough calf muscles by the time we get up to that willow tree, I think."

Rachel starts to reply, using words like "odd" and "psychotic," but I don't let her finish.

I wave and call out to the hottie by the willow tree. "Wow! Fancy meeting you here. Look, Rachel, it's *Luke Stanton*."

Just we reach him, my heel decides to imbed itself permanently in the pavement, sending me tumbling off the bicycle, landing in a pile beside the willow tree under which Luke and his bicycle are parked.

TWENTY-FOUR

Rachel

"Geez!"

Luke—quite suspiciously waiting for us under the tree—and I were off our bikes in a heartbeat, helping a slightly stunned and tousled Venus up off the ground.

"Are you all right?" Luke asked her, gripping her shoulders to steady her.

The little twinge I felt must have been adrenaline from watching Venus crash, not anything ridiculous like jealousy or wishing that I'd been the one to crash so that Luke's quite nice hands would have been on *my* shoulders instead of hers.

"Fine. Fine." Venus, looking slightly ruffled, but otherwise unhurt, brushed at her leather-clad thighs, and looked through her lashes at the other cyclists—all male—who had leapt to her rescue. "Thanks, boys."

As they nodded and tutted over her, I rolled my eyes. This entire bike ride had been Venus on parade for the local boys. By the time the ninth or tenth guy had nearly taken a nosedive checking Venus out—while completely ignoring the fact that I

was even in the same vicinity—I got cranky. And the fact that
I got cranky about being the Invisible Woman, made me even
crankier. I'd ridden this bike path a hundred times in my thirty
years, with nary a thought to whether or not men were noticing
me. But riding with a former goddess who got more attention
than Paris Hilton on the red carpet, made it very noticeable
that I was being ignored. Passed off as the ugly cousin.

Or Cinderella . . . pre-makeover.

Luke let go of her, stepping back to let her admirers take
over. The relaxing of my clenched stomach muscles, of course,
had nothing to do with relief that Luke wasn't as gaga over
Venus as her other rescuers were. He didn't seem to notice
her for more than a second or two before turning to smile at
me. I gave him a slight smile back.

Venus lifted her bike—with the help of at least three pairs
of male hands—and turned to Luke and me. "Well, I'm tuck-
ered now. Why don't you two continue on? I'll see you back at
the apartment later, Rachel. Maybe after one of these hunks
buys me dinner."

Without waiting for an answer, Venus got on Hannah's
bike and headed back the way we'd just come, flanked by her
newly self-appointed bodyguards.

"I smell a setup," I commented, with a pointed look at
Luke.

His mouth quirked at one corner. "Don't know where you
got that idea."

I swung a leg over my bike, apparently deciding that I was
allowing myself to be set up. "Because Venus is a lousy actress."

Luke laughed. "Have to agree with you there."

A minute later, we were back on the path around the lake,
riding smoothly side-by-side, and I relaxed—probably because
I didn't have to watch Venus's expensive shoes being destroyed
anymore. Or the fact that, with Luke by my side, I no longer

noticed that men weren't ogling me. Because Luke was ogling me instead.

There was nothing else special about this ride. Luke and I were simply getting a little exercise—together. It had nothing to do with anything.

And it certainly didn't constitute a date.

"So, how'd you get suckered into this?" I questioned. "Did she bribe you?"

Luke laughed. "Haven't you figured out yet that I don't need to be bribed to spend time with you?"

"Well, it's obvious that this was planned."

"Sure." Luke shrugged and swerved deftly around a Rollerblader before joining me again. "Would you have agreed to spend time with me without being set up?"

I blushed. "Got me there."

Luke gave me a minute to recover from my embarrassment and then continued. "So, been interrogating any more of my ex-girlfriends lately?"

My face had barely drained off the blood from the first blush, when the second one came rushing back. "Um, yeah. Gwen."

Gwen, who "no longer felt like a woman" after dumping him.

Gwen, who thought Luke's tongue deserved some kind of performance trophy.

Gwen of the multiple Luke-induced orgasms.

"How'd you like her?" Luke asked, with complete innocence.

Or *was* he completely innocent? Being a man, he was probably fully aware of how women reacted to him sexually. Maybe he knew exactly how Gwen would describe him. Probably bragged about it down at the station house.

After all, he'd been there . . . done her.

But, no, his blue—really blue, now that I looked closely—eyes didn't seem to be hiding anything, so I beat down my doubts as to his sincerity and continued. "She was very nice," I said, because she had been, once she got over my irrational, Venus-induced behavior and had warmed up to the subject at hand. "Don't ask me to share details, though. I don't interview-and-tell."

"Are you sure? You've turned me down so often lately, I could really use an ego stroking."

I nearly choked at the thought of stroking anything of Luke's. Instead, I forced a laugh. "Of course, I'm sure." God, yes, I was sure. There was no way I was sharing with him any of what Gwen had told me. Odd, though, that he seemed to know that whatever I shared would be "ego stroking."

"So, while we're here, together, with another fifteen minutes before we get around the lake, why don't you ask *me* some questions."

I glanced at him. "What kinds of questions?"

"Name. Rank. Serial number. The basics. Since you haven't allowed me to actually fill out an application, as is typical when interviewing for a job—"

"You're *not* interviewing for a job," I interrupted, wanting to make it very clear that despite being coerced into this little game, I still had no intention of dating him.

"Anyway," he continued, ignoring me. "I think you should know more about me. And I should know more about you." He turned and smiled, and the heated look he sent me almost had *me* falling off my bicycle. It definitely gave me the wobbles. "But I'll go first as a warm-up."

"O-okay," I stuttered, then took a deep breath to compose myself. Knowing the basics about someone didn't constitute starting a relationship with them. And, I couldn't very well be rude and tell him I didn't care. Maybe because I did care . . . a little. Statistically speaking. For curiosity's sake. Not for any personal reason, of course.

"So, name, rank, and serial number," I said lightly.

"Name: Lucas Robert Stanton," he started.

"I knew that from your bank account."

He grinned. "But, I bet you didn't know that I was named after my mother's uncle Lucas and my father, Robert."

"No, I didn't know that."

"I'm thirty-one, and my birthday is March thirty-first, making me an Aries with Scorpio rising."

I looked at him, surprised. "Guys don't usually know those kinds of things, do they?"

"They do when they date Raven Wolf. I can also give you a rudimentary palm reading if you'd like."

I laughed. "I'll pass, thanks. Raven read my cards."

Luke raised his eyebrows. "And? What did they say?"

That my true love was near. "Nothing," I replied, looking away. "Nothing important at all."

He probably didn't believe me, but he left it. "So, to continue. I've been with the Cameron Creek Fire Department for the past eight years. Always wanted to be a firefighter, from the time I was small."

"What makes a person decide that's the job for them?" I asked, truly interested, remembering how, for a brief time when I was in high school, I'd wanted to be a mechanic. Or better, an auto refurbisher. Something about the thrill of building a car, making it come to life, like I had with Sally. I pushed that vaguely depressing thought aside, remembering my once beloved car wasting away in my father's garage.

After that phase, I'd wanted to be a wife and mother. I'd worked as hard at that as I had at building Sally . . . reading books on how to attract the right kind of man, actually using the tips on fashion and makeup that Hannah gave me instead of laughing at her, and . . . and I'd decided against the University of Washington and attended business college instead. Because who needed a four-year degree to be a wife and mother?

The only difference between the two dreams was that I had been good a rebuilding cars. Horrible at building relationships with men.

"My dad was a fire chief before he died. I wanted to be just like him."

"I'm sorry to hear that," I said, turning my attention back

to Luke, out of common courtesy if nothing else. "That your father . . . you know."

"Died?" Luke smiled wistfully. "It was a long time ago. I was ten. My mom remarried my stepdad, Walter, when I was twelve. I now have two ugly stepsisters, who—"

"Stepsisters?" I stared at Luke, eyes wide. "*Ugly* stepsisters?"

"Sorry," Luke cringed. "Old joke between us kids. I don't really mean that they're ugly. Emma and Regina are actually quite nice-looking. For sisters. It was just a kid thing."

"Oh." I looked away and took a deep breath, getting a grip on myself. It wasn't that I worried about any lack of respect on Luke's part for calling his stepsisters ugly. I'd called my siblings my fair share of derogatory names over the years. But, for some reason, "ugly stepsisters" made me think of Cinderella, and Cinderella made me think of fairy godmothers, and fairy godmothers made me think of Venus, and once again, I worried that this whole thing with Luke was one big . . . spell or something. But, there was no spell. There couldn't be, because spells didn't exist.

But then, up until a month ago, I didn't think fairy godmothers did, either.

So, how was I to know that Luke's feelings for me were real? How was I to know that Venus just didn't go around casting love spells on people—despite her reassurance that spells were mortal make-believe—getting them together in an effort to rack up brownie points with Zeus, so he'd take her back? How did I know that Luke wasn't just acting under some kind of duress?

And, why did I care? I *wasn't* going out with him anyway.

"Rachel, I'm sorry if that offends you."

"What?" I came out of my thoughts with a start.

"The 'ugly stepsisters' comment. It really doesn't mean anything. If you met my sisters you'd understand that we call each other stuff like that all the time. I was Rat Boy for years."

"Rat Boy?" I cracked up. "Were you homely?" Unlikely as

that might be, I added to myself, gazing sideways at the body that had won the honorable—and well-deserved—spot as Mr. March.

"No," Luke said, matter-of-factly. "They called me that because I ratted them out a lot when we all moved in together. It was my pleasure to tell on the new big sisters I didn't want in the first place. You know, when they broke curfew or snuck cigarettes out behind the garden shed."

"Oooh, that was always fun, catching your siblings in compromising positions." I laughed. "I once caught my older brother in the backseat of his car, with his girlfriend's shirt off. I made him pay me twenty bucks to keep quiet about it."

"Ah, so you have a devious streak, do you?"

"Maybe," I said, surprised at how much the memory made me miss my brother and Connie, the shirtless girlfriend in question.

Which then reminded me how I'd watched them get married a few years later, knowing they were perfectly right for each other and would be together forever. And deciding right then that that's what I wanted for myself. One love I could count on forever. A love that lasted for thirty-five years—like my parents—and beyond. A love that meant never having to be alone.

It had taken years—and the realization that I had enough failed attempts at love to create a Loser List—to come to the conclusion that this dream wasn't like the dream of owning a red convertible Mustang. Or of rebuilding cars for a living. This dream obviously required skills I didn't have and never would.

The end of the trail came in sight just then and I was almost disappointed. Almost. Of course, I wasn't disappointed to be leaving Luke's company. He was just forcing thoughts into my head about things I tried not to think of whenever possible. It was just . . . probably that the bike ride had been pleasant, the air fresh and cool, the lake relaxing. It didn't have anything to do with Luke Stanton.

"So, I'll give you a lift home," Luke said, slowing to a stop and getting off his bike near the parking lot that flanked one end of the lake.

"What?"

"You. Your bike." Luke gestured in our direction. "You don't live close enough to the lake to ride home, do you?"

"Well . . ." I lived about five miles away. And, while I wasn't an exercise wimp, it would be dark within . . . well, a lot less time than it would take me to get home. My decision was made for me. "No. I don't live close enough to ride home. I'd . . . be grateful for a ride."

Luke's mouth twitched. "Try not to sound so enthusiastic. I don't think my ego can take it."

"I'm sorry. It's just that—"

"You can't very well keep your resolve not to date me when you're forced to spend time with me?" Luke didn't wait for an answer, but headed for his big red truck, pushing his bicycle.

"It's not that," I protested, following behind him.

"Oh, so you *want* to spend time with me?" he asked, with a flash of a smile over his shoulder.

"No! I . . . I . . ."

We arrived at the truck and Luke lifted his bike into the back—all flexing biceps and triceps—and then reached for mine. When it was secured in the truck bed, and I had sufficiently recovered from admiring his, uh, strengths, Luke turned toward me again. So close that his breath warmed my face.

"I like knowing that I leave you speechless."

For a second I was *more* speechless, but I recovered quickly. "I'm not speechless," I assured him, moving past him to climb into the passenger seat before I lost my nerve and *ran* home instead of accepting his offer of a ride. "I just don't know how to convince you that this whole thing is a bad idea," I continued once he joined me in the truck.

He turned the key and the diesel engine roared to life, vibrating the seat beneath me. After checking gauges, he turned to face me resting an arm casually across the top of the steering wheel. "What if I think it's the best idea ever?"

For a moment I just looked at him. He seemed so sincere, so serious, like he really believed what he was saying. But how could he? He didn't know me. If *he* had been the one interviewing *my* exes . . .

I looked away, out the window of the truck. Bad memories threatened to ruin the whole afternoon, which I had to admit had been pretty nice. I'd spent much of the last two years trying to crowd those memories out of my head . . . just like Venus said. If I was busy, I didn't think. If I didn't think, I didn't remember. Which was fine with me.

Because remembering hurt too much.

If only Luke could see how ridiculous it was to pursue this plan, I could go back to my nice safe little world, where I didn't have to think about my mistakes, my failures. Eddie had broken my heart and I wasn't at all eager to be in that position again.

"How can you not think it's a bad idea?" I finally asked, keeping my expression serious. "How do you know what kind of person I am, when we haven't spent more than a few minutes together at any given time?"

"Not by my choice," he started to joke, but noticing my frown, he stopped and took on a serious look himself. He reached across the seat back, and pushed a strand of errant hair out of my eyes. "It's a hunch," he said. "Intuition. Whatever you want to call it. I just have this feeling we're meant to be together. That feeling has been there from the minute I met you."

I stared at him suspiciously. That was one of the things that bothered me. True, he came into the bank months before

Venus arrived on the scene . . . before *I* knew she'd arrived on the scene anyway. But, what if she'd been watching from afar long before we bumped into each other in front of Starbucks? What if she'd gone to work on Luke before she'd ever announced herself as my fairy godmother? What if the "hunch" he had wasn't really a hunch at all?

I couldn't say that to him, though. Not without sounding like a crazed loon if I was wrong. So, I tried to brush him off the only way I could think of. "You spent too much time with Raven," I said. "Hunches and intuition aren't real."

You didn't believe fairy godmothers were real, either, until a certain lightning display, reminded a voice in my head that sounded suspiciously like Venus. I was spending far too much time with her.

"I'm not so sure," Luke continued, then turned away to drive. "My dad once told me he knew the minute he saw my mom that she was the one he'd marry. I've always believed, since I was a kid, that I'd recognize the right woman when I met her, too."

"A father's fairy tale," I said, as we pulled out onto the road.

Then my brain processed what he'd said.

He'd implied that *I* was the right woman. For him.

Like *Mrs.* Right.

Oh, God.

I felt like I was having a panic attack. I darted what I'm sure was a clearly terrified look in his direction before turning back to the window, trying to get some control back. My breathing alternately felt like it was coming too fast and then getting choked off. I had to figure a way out of this mess, before it was too late and I did something stupid.

Like starting to believe Luke the way I'd obviously been coerced into believing Venus.

I turned down Luke's offer to go to dinner by telling him I had other plans for the night. I didn't tell him that the plans were walking dogs at the pound, which it would probably be too dark to do anyway by the time I got there. I just knew I needed to get away from him as quickly as possible tonight. His words were echoing in my head . . . and I wanted to forget them.

I directed him through the streets toward my apartment. It appeared that my car had found its way home . . . probably courtesy of Hannah, Venus's apparent new partner in crime. It was in its usual parking spot out front.

Luke insisted on carrying my bike upstairs for me, and I let him, as it was always a struggle for me to get the awkward piece of equipment up two flights of stairs.

"So," Luke finally ventured again, as he carried the bike through the apartment, where I directed him to the storage locker I had on my lanai, while trying to keep my attention anywhere but on him and the again flexing muscles of his very nicely toned arms. "If you're so sure my hunch about us is wrong, why are you going to so much trouble? With all the interviews and everything?"

Because I have a very pushy, demoted-goddess-turned-fairy-godmother who refuses to take no for an answer, I thought.

"It hasn't been that much trouble," I lied instead, pushing aside the humiliating experience of hearing a rundown on his outstanding sexual prowess while sitting nearly naked with his ex-girlfriend and narrowly avoiding a completely unnecessary pelvic exam. "And, I'm only doing it at all to prove you— and Venus—wrong. I think I mentioned that once before." Luke set the mountain bike down, and I maneuvered it into its place alongside two folding lawn chairs and several empty planters I'd put away after the summer blooms had died, and locked the storage room door. "Venus is very persistent. So are you, in case you didn't know that already."

I pushed past him into the apartment to see him to the door. He stopped me with a hand on my arm. I tried not to re-act to his touch, but a shiver ran through me nonetheless. A shiver he noticed, based on the heating up of his expression.

"Persistence is one of my best qualities," he said, stepping closer, anchoring me in place with a firm hand. "It's gotten me a lot of things I really wanted in my life."

I cocked my chin up, in an effort to look a whole lot stronger than I felt. My knees were liquefied rubber. My lungs only seemed to hold half the amount of air I needed to breathe. If he didn't leave soon, I was going to need a defibrillator to get my heart going again.

"Persistence is overrated," I said, in a strained voice, barely over a whisper. "I know that better than anyone. No matter how persistent you are about something, if it's not meant to be, it's not meant to be. You aren't going to 'get me.' It won't happen. It can't."

"We'll see about that." Luke moved even closer, until our foreheads touched. All my concentration was spent trying to keep from vibrating with the tension flowing through me. "By the way," he said, his voice husky and deep as he matched my whisper, "I'm officially applying for the job of your boyfriend, whether you like it or not. Consider this my application."

Luke lowered his head to mine and kissed me.

My heart suddenly slammed into overdrive without the help of a defibrillator, as his warm lips moved against mine in the first kiss I'd had in a very, very . . . Very. Long. Time.

As if propelled by some magical force, I accepted his "application," melting into him, leaning forward, taking his kiss . . . as well as giving back. It only lasted a moment, and then he was gone.

I gasped as he stepped back, then met his steamy—and amused—gaze.

"That was just one of the things I've wanted," he said, with a grin and an arch of his eyebrows. "Guess my persistence paid off."

I swallowed the lump in my throat, before tossing my hair back out of my face. "It didn't mean anything. You can't just apply for a job that doesn't have any openings."

Luke just smiled. "Oh, I think there's an opening all right." His eyes flicked over my shoulder as he let go of me. He gestured in the direction of his gaze. "Nice calendar," he commented.

I turned to see what he was referring to, eyes widening as they lit on the likeness of the man who had just kicked up embers I'd thought were long cold.

"You do realize," he commented, "that it's September . . . not March?"

TWENTY-FIVE

Venus

It took four nails—and superglue—to ensure that the calendar stayed on the wall.

Rachel is furious at me and I have no clue why. Upon Zeus, that kiss looked so hot, I'd have thought she'd be ready to kiss *me* in thanks for stoking her fire again. I saw it. I saw how she reacted. That long lost libido of hers came back in a *big* way.

Sigh. Wish I could have actually felt what Rachel was feeling when Luke kissed her. I tried to remember what being kissed like that was like, but it's been so long . . .

But, damn, it *looked* good from my vantage point behind Rachel's eyes. Yes, I know I promised . . . but, she banished me from listening to any more *interviews,* not from listening in on her and anyone else. A technicality is a technicality after all. Must use them to my advantage.

So, anyway, the increased pressure is obviously working. During the bike ride, they got to know each other and I think Rachel actually relaxed a little, let her guard down a bit. Hell, a week ago, she'd have karate kicked him if he'd tried to kiss her, so we are definitely making progress.

With a sigh, I tuck the narrow box containing my Golden

Girdle back into its resting place in Rachel's dresser drawer. I know I shouldn't even be looking at it. It's far too tempting. But really, I was only thinking of Rachel. If the girdle worked for mortals, I'd have put it on Rachel weeks ago and been so out of here by now. Okay, so it wasn't only for Rachel's sake. It's just that I want to go home so much that I'd be willing to do just about anything to hurry it up. Even use my most precious possession . . .

Instead I have only my memories of the Golden Girdle's effect on me . . . or rather on the male of the species. The feeling of being irresistible is like a drug, feeding the ego, the heart, and the libido all at the same time. I miss that.

Shaking my head, I push away from the dresser. There's no sense feeling sorry for myself. Time marches on and I need to press forward.

But, I would so love to spend the winter on Mount Olympus.

TWENTY-SIX

Rachel

"Hello?" I said, answering the phone Saturday morning. I had no clue who'd be calling me this early, before I'd even had my morning Diet Coke.

Glaring at the calendar from hell—nailed at all four corners with three-inch-long spikes supplemented with superglue and Scotch tape repairing the tears created when I'd ripped it off the wall—I turned my back on it and plugged one ear, trying better to hear the person on the phone. There was a man's voice hollering in the background, as well as what sounded like several shrieking children, which made it very difficult to understand the caller.

"Say again?" I practically shouted.

Venus came out of the bedroom right then, looking awfully bright-eyed and put together for the early hour. I raised an eyebrow at her curiously, until I remembered I wasn't speaking to her. I turned my back on her, too.

Which unfortunately put me facing the calendar again.

"Is this Rachel?" the caller finally asked, clear enough that I could understand her.

"Yes, this is Rachel Greer."

"This is Harry Rogers. Shut the hell up!"

"Excuse me?" I answered, preparing to hang up. I don't do rude phone calls. At the same time, I registered that this was a woman's voice, but I swore she'd said her name was Harry.

"Oh, not you. My husband. I'm Harry. You called."

"I did? I think you have the wrong number. Sorry." I started to hang up but heard her shout again.

"You called about Luke Stanton."

I frowned into the phone. "*I* called *you* about Luke Stanton? I don't think so."

Venus chose that moment to tiptoe past me into the kitchen, avoiding eye contact.

"When exactly did I call you?" I asked this Harry person, narrowing my eyes at Venus's retreating back.

"Last night. I have that information you want. About when I used to date Luke."

Suddenly that corner of my brain that was trying hard to forget all about Luke Stanton kicked into gear and I remembered that one of his exes was named Harry.

"Did you say your last name was Rogers?" I asked. "I thought Luke's ex-girlfriend's last name was Middle-something."

"Middleton. My maiden name. Goddamn it, I'm on the phone, I said!"

I held the phone away from my ear as Harry began a lengthy ass-chewing that was so loud, Venus stuck her head around the corner.

"She's even louder today than she was yesterday," Venus said, before ducking back into the kitchen.

Harry didn't seem to be done yet, so I covered the mouthpiece of the phone and followed Venus. "What did you do?" I whispered furiously. "Did you call her?"

Venus nodded and went back to slathering cream cheese on a sesame bagel. "You certainly weren't going to be doing it anytime soon, and I don't have all fucking century to wait around for you to take action yourself."

"You don't—" I stopped when I heard my name being called, and held the phone back up to my ear while shooting eye-flames at Venus.

"Rachel?"

"Yes," I said as patiently as possible.

"Anyway, I have that information for you."

"Information about Luke?"

"Yeah. Are you with the FBI or something?"

"FBI?"

I stared at Venus, wide-eyed. Oh, my God. Maybe Luke had some sort of shady, secretive past. After all, one of my ex-boyfriends was an embezzler. Maybe Luke was an arsonist or something and Harry had information about his clandestine activities. Maybe I was right to be suspicious that he seemed too good to be true. Not that I wanted to be right about something as serious as arson or anything, but I most definitely wanted to know why one of his ex-girlfriends would even *suspect* that the FBI might be investigating him.

"Oh," Venus said, "I told her you needed information about possible criminal activities he might be involved in."

My jaw dropped.

Harry continued, "Yeah. Has he done something wrong? I always knew something was fishy about him."

She did? "You did?"

"Sure. I mean, he was so serious about that job of his. And what's the big deal about putting out fires? There had to be something wrong with him."

Of course there did, I thought, getting more confused by the minute. Because letting people's houses burn made so much more sense.

"So," I asked. "What did I say to you when I called you yesterday?"

"You agreed to take me out to dinner tonight," Harry replied, seeming not to think it at all odd that I didn't remember our previous conversation. "My choice of restaurants, seven P.M. tonight. I made reservations."

Still a little stunned, I took down Harry's address and directions to her home and hung up the phone, before turning to Venus.

"Why'd you lie to her?"

She paused with the bagel—now also dotted with the M&M's she seemed addicted to—halfway to her mouth. "Did you hear her? She spent more time yelling at her kids and her drunk of a husband during our ten-minute conversation than she did talking to me. I had to say something to get her attention."

I shuddered as she bit into the sesame, cream cheese, and M&M bagel, then turned my attention back to the subject at hand, rather than her nutritional fetishes. "How do you know her husband is a drunk?"

"She told me," Venus said, with a roll of her eyes. "In the first three minutes of our conversation. She didn't even know who I was."

"Who did you *tell* her you were?"

"You." Venus smiled sweetly and popped the rest of her freaky bagel in her mouth.

"I don't know what you're so flipped out about," Venus said, glaring up at the slight Pacific Northwest drizzle that had been coming down for the last hour. Those of us from western Washington didn't even consider it rain. Unless it was causing flash floods, it wasn't even considered bad enough to bother with an umbrella.

We—or rather I—was working on the Habitat house, planting shrubbery donated by one of the local garden centers, while Venus hid under the eaves, attempting to keep her hair from frizzing. She'd tried to talk me out of coming today, but

I'd been unfocused enough lately. I refused to be further distracted from making people's lives better. *Somebody's* life had to be better.

"I'm not flipped out," I said, stabbing the dirt with my trowel. "It's just . . . he shouldn't have kissed me like that. I didn't want to be kissed."

"Sure you did. You were sending out vibes."

I pushed myself half up off the ground with the trowel. "How do you know I was sending out vibes?"

For a minute, I could have sworn Venus looked guilty. But she just blew a puff of air out between her lips. "I've seen you with Luke. You give off vibes every time he's anywhere near you. I just . . . assumed you must have been giving off vibes when he was in the apartment. I still can't believe you blew him off like that."

"I didn't blow him off. He left."

Thank God. One more minute alone with him, and I might have been tempted to do just what Venus was suggesting I should have done to him. With him.

"Look, as your fairy godmother, I feel it necessary to point out—again—that he's the perfect guy for you, and if you'd just give him a chance—"

I stood up abruptly, stopping Venus from going any further. A quick glance around showed we were alone, but I kept my voice low anyway. "You just don't get it, do you? That Loser List isn't just about the guys. It's about me. *My* mistakes."

Venus shrugged, curling her lip in distaste at the bit of mud clinging to the edges of her Anne Klein heels because she insisted on standing in the flower bed to avoid the rain. "So you made a mistake—"

"Two mistakes," I corrected, holding up two fingers in case she didn't understand that two was twice as many as one. "Two *big* mistakes that could have hurt a lot of people."

"They weren't your fault." Venus looked me straight in the eye when she said it, and for just a flicker of a second, I wanted to believe her. After all, she didn't often take anything so seriously.

But I knew better.

The Eddie Incident was my fault because I wasn't observant enough. I hadn't paid attention to the signs. Maybe because I was getting so desperate by then. I'd been working toward finding the right guy to settle down with for years. I'd watched my brother and Connie have their first baby (babies, in their case). I'd celebrated my parents' more than three decades of marriage and had witnessed how in love they still were. I even watched my little sister, Roxanne, find the perfect guy for her.

All of that made me completely blind to Eddie's faults.

It made me believe him when he called me Mrs. Right.

Maybe because I knew it would be my last chance, that I wasn't capable of following this dream any longer. If I failed once more, I'd be forced to admit that choosing a man to spend my life with was something I simply wasn't capable of doing.

Sure, logically, maybe Eddie should shoulder some of the blame, but it was my mistake to not have noticed something was wrong with our relationship.

And totally aside from that, what happened *after* the Eddie Incident was most definitely, 100 percent, my fault.

"You don't understand," I said, shaking my head and dropping back down to my knees to shove the azalea I was planting into the dirt. "How can you? Aren't gods and goddesses all about free love? Like stuck in the sixties or something?"

"That has nothing to do with you martyring yourself for the rest of your life. Like you had any control over what happened with Eddie and . . . what was the other guy's name?"

I had no clue. And *my* inability to conjure up the name of my second mistake was only emphasized by the fact that *she* didn't know, either, since she knew everything about me that I knew.

Feeling vaguely sick to my stomach, I just shrugged.

"Be that as it may," Venus continued, "what's going on between you and Luke—"

"Which is nothing," I interrupted.

"—has nothing to do with Eddie or that other guy."

"Can we drop this conversation?" I said, scooting over a few feet to dig the next hole. "Because if you're trying to make me feel better, you need to work on your technique."

"I'm not trying to make you feel better," Venus replied honestly, as she delicately stepped around the freshly turned dirt and found a new, mildly dry spot up against the house. "I'm trying to make you see that humans are the only animals that even have the concept of mistakes. You don't see female baboons cutting themselves off from society because they fucked the wrong male baboon, do you?"

I glared at Venus in disgust.

"Well? I'm right, aren't I?"

"Maybe I should just tell him," I sighed, suddenly really tired of arguing with Venus about it. Of thinking about it. Of hiding my secrets. "I should just get it over with. Tell Luke and let him leave. Let him give up on me."

"What if you tell him and he doesn't give up on you?"

"He would," I insisted. "What guy wouldn't?"

"One who really cares about you." Venus's voice was so soft, I was startled. Once again, she was being serious.

"You can't know that," I said.

She shrugged and brought her hand up to her face to examine her nails. She seemed almost as uncomfortable as I was. "Think what you like. I've only been a fairy godmother for two thousand years. What the fuck do I know?"

Harry Rogers, née Middleton, was a chain-smoking, foul-mouthed, shrieking shrew.

This I determined before she even got into my car, as she stood on the cluttered front porch of a ranch house in a nice middle-class, suburban West Seattle neighborhood—similar to the neighborhood I'd grown up in. She seemed to be reading the riot act to some unseen figure inside the house. As soon as she was done, she tossed down a cigarette butt, ground it out with her heel, and pulled another from a pack. Thankfully, she seemed to think better of lighting it and stuffed it back in her purse before getting in the car.

The instant personality assessment was confirmed the moment she slid into the front seat beside me in a choke of clinging smoke and slammed the door behind her.

"Damn asshole. I told him I was going on a job interview, and he wanted to know if I was interviewing with a pimp, cause what fucking business was open at this hour? Son of a bitch just didn't want to watch his own damn kids for more than five minutes. Might be forced to get off his ass to pour a glass of milk or wipe a snotty nose or something."

As Harry buckled her seat belt, Venus and I exchanged shocked glances over the seat. Even my not-so-clean-mouthed fairy godmother appeared startled at the verbal "runs" that had accompanied Luke's ex-girlfriend into the car.

"See, even Luke makes mistakes," Venus muttered.

Without knowing how to comment, but fearing this evening's meal was going to be the longest of my life, I put the car, which apparently wasn't up to Harry's high standards, into reverse.

"This the only car you have?" she asked, with a sneering perusal of my two-year-old Subaru. "You'd think the FBI paid better than this."

"You'd think," Venus agreed, due to her own hatred of my supposedly "uncool" ride. I glared at her.

"We need to correct a misunderstanding here, Harry," I said, feeling odd calling her that, but remembering Luke's warning that calling her Harriet would be a mistake. Seeing as how she looked like she might pack heat, I was inclined to take his advice. "I'm not with the FBI."

Harry stared at me for a moment, then looked back up toward the house, where three small round faces were pressed against a window, staring out at us. Two of them appeared to be contorted into some sort of scream.

"I don't care what the fuck company you work for," she said. "If you can get me away from this hellhole for a few hours, you have my undying attention."

With a sigh, I took the directions to the restaurant that Harry handed me and pulled out onto the street.

Twenty minutes later—which were filled entirely with a bitter diatribe on the hell that was Harry's life—we pulled up in front of Pacifique. Seattle's most expensive restaurant.

"God, I've always wanted to eat here," Harry said, stepping out onto the sidewalk.

Rather stunned, and not sure how to get out of having to pay for dinner for three at a place I could ill afford, I nevertheless handed my keys over to the valet. The tips I was going to have to fork out tonight alone were going to take a bank loan.

"You, uh, eat in places like this often?" I asked, as a doorman held the door open for us, and I followed Harry in.

"Not since marrying Asshole," she replied. Asshole was apparently her husband's name, as she hadn't referred to him by any other moniker since getting in my car. And she had referred to him several times.

I groaned as the maître d' who'd stepped up to greet us blinked at her language. Harry gave her name, confirmed her reservation, and was shown to the table.

"I can't afford this place," I whispered frantically to Venus as we trailed along.

"Don't look at me," she whispered back. "Zeus didn't give me an entertainment allowance."

"How am I supposed to pay for it?"

"Use your credit card."

Easy for her to say, I thought, as we arrived at the table and my chair was held out for me, giving me little choice but to sit down or make a scene. Venus wouldn't have to pay for the dinner plus 13 percent interest, since I highly doubted, based on the shocking prices listed in the menu, that I'd be paying the card off anytime soon.

"We'll start off with a bottle of Dalla Valle Cabernet Sauvignon 1999," Harry was saying.

I didn't know anything about wine, but anything that had four words and a date in the title had to be expensive. A check of the menu revealed it to be pushing two hundred dollars per bottle. I started to protest that we would just drink water, when Harry continued.

"I need to relax," she said, shoving her hands through her spiky-cut black hair. "If I don't relax, I won't be able to answer your questions about Luke. I hate to say bad things about people, so I need to loosen up, if you know what I mean."

No, I didn't know what she meant, considering she'd just spent the last nearly half hour quite "loosely" telling us lots of bad things about the Asshole she was married to. What, she suddenly developed tactfulness when it came to Luke?

And what did she have to say about him that was bad? I wondered, suddenly realizing exactly what she'd implied.

"So who are you guys, really?" Harry asked, as the waiter brought the wine. When he tried to have her taste it to see if it was to her liking, she waved him off. I had a feeling that it could have tasted like toilet water and she would have thought it was fine, as long as it was alcoholic. "If you're not FBI, then who are you? CIA? Secret Service?"

"Why would any of those agencies need to ask questions about Luke?" I asked, taking a huge gulp of the wine that had just been set in front of me. If I had to fork out a day's salary to pay for it, then I may as well get the medicinal benefit from it, I thought, even though I hadn't been much of a drinker in the past few years. Tonight I needed a bit of relaxation myself.

"He was just always one of those too good to be true kinda guys," she said. "There had to be some deviant behavior in there somewhere. All men are pigs deep down."

"That's what Rachel thinks, too," Venus offered, all smiles and innocence.

"Oh, then you know what I'm talking about," Harry said, putting a blue fingernailed hand on my arm, like we were best buddies. "I mean, my God, that Asshole I'm married to will fuck anything in a skirt." She paused briefly, then gave the hovering waiter her order, which, I noticed, was the most expensive item on the menu.

Venus ordered some smoked salmon thing that came in a close second, price-wise. It earned her a glare from me.

I ordered a side salad. At Harry's raised eyebrow, I explained, "I'm watching my cred— er, waistline."

"Yeah, I can see where you might need to."

Venus snickered and I kicked her under the table.

"So, back to Luke," I suggested.

"Yeah, so what did he—" Harry paused and downed her entire glass of wine, poured herself another, and then continued, "what did he do?"

"He didn't do anything," I assured her. "I just want to find out what kind of guy he is."

Harry looked from me to Venus and back again. "Really? Just what kind of guy he is? You're paying for all this just to find out whether he lies when he goes out with the guys? Or chases skirts?"

"Does he?" I asked, leaning forward with interest. I mean, an affirmative would solve all my problems and put a halt to this entire farce right here and now.

She shrugged. "Don't remember." She tipped her head back and poured another whole glass of wine into her mouth, her throat working to take it all in. "Another, please." She signaled the waiter for another bottle of wine and I blanched.

All for a good cause, I told myself. My nightmare could be over tonight . . . if only I got the info I needed to convince Venus that Luke and I were never going to happen.

"So, how long did you date Luke?" I asked, trying to keep on topic.

"A year."

That long? I thought. Luke had to be a saint.

"Why'd you break up?" Venus asked, and instead of being mad that she was butting in, I was grateful, since I was having trouble breathing watching Harry chug down another roughly fifty-dollar glass of wine like it was tap water.

"'Cause he didn't provide me with what I needed from life."

"Oh, he was a loser in the sack?"

"Venus!" I gave her another swift kick under the table, causing her to yelp in pain.

"Nah, he was okay in bed," Harry began.

I interrupted quickly, so as not to have a repeat of the conversation I'd had with Gwen last week. "What did you need that Luke couldn't provide?"

"This." Harry pointed at the plate of beef medallion tenderloin things that had just been set in front of her. "I grew up dining in five stars. But do you think I could get tightfisted Stanton to take me places like this? Fuck no. He kept his wallet tucked in his tight ass, so he didn't have to fork out."

Smart man, I thought, seriously fearing my credit record would never recover from this meal.

"Weren't you, like, college students when you met? Surely, most college kids can't afford to eat in places like this?"

"Lots of them can," Harry scoffed, washing down some sautéed mushrooms with another swig of cabernet sauvignon. I was beginning to think we might need to accelerate this conversation before she was too blitzed to think. "Even Asshole could afford to bring me here, and *he* was in college."

"So you come here often now?" Venus asked, closing her

eyes in ecstasy over a piece of salmon that looked so much more appetizing than my plate of lettuce that I got even crankier. I didn't get to come to places like this very often—okay, ever— and I wasn't even getting to enjoy it.

With a brief mental prayer to win the lottery I never bought tickets for, I hailed the waiter and told him I wanted the same thing Venus had. If I was going to pay for this meal—in more ways than one, I thought, grimacing at Harry—I dang well should get some compensation for it.

"Hell, no," Harry continued. "Never. Asshole may have had dough in college—inherited, by the way, not through any sort of accomplishment on his part—but he gambled it all away just about the time I got pregnant with baby number two of four. God, I was stupid. If I'd had a fucking bit of sense I'd have let Luke knock me up instead of Asshole. Luke didn't turn out to be an asshole, did he?" she asked.

"Uh, no," I said, though my brain was still processing the "let Luke knock me up" comment. Like Luke would have felt honored to have been granted that privilege. "He's very nice."

"Which is why she won't go out with him," Venus inserted pointedly.

"Venus!"

"Well, it's true," she muttered.

"Well, don't be counting on any special treatment from him," Harry continued, as if we hadn't even spoken. "Like I said, 'Tight' is Luke's middle name. We spent so much time at Denny's, I thought my taste buds were going to rot out of my head."

"I don't need restaurants like this," I answered. "I'm really more of a Denny's type of girl."

"Whatever." Harry dismissed me with a wave of her hand. "Luke's too much of a goody-goody, anyway. I once tried to get him to sneak out of history for a quickie and he wouldn't do it. Something about wanting to actually *learn* in college."

Imagine that.

"He was so boring. He was always trying to get me to do thing besides clubbing or going to frat parties. Like anything else was important. That was the only way to see and be seen. He always wanted to do stupid stuff, like hiking or bike riding. What girl thinks that kind of stuff is fun?"

Out of the corner of my eye, I saw Venus cast me an amused glance, as involuntary visions of a certain bike ride around Blue Lake popped into my head.

I needn't have bothered formulating an answer to the completely hypothetical question, though, as Harry was having too much fun listening to herself talk. "Luke doesn't understand the upper class at all. Like what's important to us. He's critical, demanding, fucking inattentive—"

"Wait a minute." I held up a hand to halt the tirade. "Are we talking about *the* Luke Stanton? The same Luke Stanton who risks his life to help others on a daily basis? Who had a picnic for me in the back of his truck just to be nice, even though I was asking him to let me completely invade his privacy? Who carried my bike up two flights of stairs so I wouldn't have to?" The volume of my voice increased with each sentence, until half the patrons of Pacifique were staring in my direction. I lowered my voice . . . fractionally. "How can you accuse him of being inattentive? And what did he demand of you? A bit of politeness? A modicum of tolerance for someone who didn't come from the same class that you did? A tiny amount of—"

"Whoa. Rachel." Venus stuck out a hand and dug her fingernails into my forearm.

I jerked my head in her direction. "What?" I snapped.

"Chill."

"I shouldn't have to chill. Tell her to chill." I waved a hand at Harry, who was blinking at me in surprise . . . or intoxication. "She's acting like a spoiled brat because there are people in this world who won't bow and scrape to her every whim."

"Said like someone who doesn't get what it means to *be* upper class," Harry commented snidely.

"Just because I didn't grow up in a mansion on the hill, doesn't mean I don't know what it's like. My best friend probably lived in the same neighborhood you did, and she isn't shallow *or* mean-spirited."

Okay, Hannah *could* be a tad shallow at times, but she sure as hell didn't expect her dates to treat her like some kind of pampered princess just because her parents filed in a higher income tax bracket than they did.

"Whatever," Harry said, completely unconcerned that I'd insulted her. "Don't say I didn't warn you. And another thing . . . Luke Stanton is completely old-fashioned. I guess that's something to be said about Asshole. He, at least, knows that nobody lives by those old rules anymore."

Before I had a moment to interpret what she'd just said, the wine got to her and Harry Rogers took a nosedive into her garlic mashed potatoes. A half hour later, Venus and I dragged her to her front door, deposited her on the doormat, rang the bell, and ran. We had no desire to see if Asshole really was one.

"So you were defending him," Hannah said around her pastrami on rye. We were eating our lunch at Goodman's Deli, around the corner from the bank. Venus was stalking men on the waterfront, trying to find a buyer for the new purple leather mini she had her eye on in one of the boutiques.

"I wouldn't call it defending *him,*" I replied, waving my dill pickle at her. "Just the middle class in general. She was such a snob."

"Wonder why he dated her? She was probably good in bed."

"She couldn't have been anything but selfish in bed," I replied, snidely. "Probably directed the whole show and then complained anyway."

Hannah smiled slyly. "You *were* defending him! You like him."

"Of course I like him," I said, avoiding Hannah's eyes, and pretending to be fascinated with my tuna sandwich and trying not to think about the picnic in the back of Luke's truck—when I had last eaten one of Mr. Goodman's tuna sandwiches. "Luke's a nice guy. Anyone can see that. That's not the issue."

"Ah, yes. The issue. That would be your phobia about being human."

I just glared.

"The idea that you're the only one in the world who could make a mistake."

"I never said I was the only one who made a mistake. Obviously, Luke might consider dating Harry a mistake, although I'm certainly not speaking for him." I frowned and poked at my pickle with my knife, the pungent odor of dill prickling my nostrils. "There are just those of us who make mistakes and don't learn from them," I muttered under my breath.

"How can you know whether you learned from your mistakes if you never ever try again?" Hannah demanded. "It's not like you've even given it a chance. How do you know you can't do it right this time?"

Because I did take another chance, I thought. Just not one that Hannah knew about.

I shrugged. "It's not worth the risk."

"Luke's not worth the risk?" Hannah said, her tone soft. Highly un-Hannah–like. A lot like the un-Venus–like tone my fairy godmother had been using on me the other day. What was it with these two? "You—nice, polite, don't make waves Rachel—chewed a *stranger* out in a fancy restaurant. You defended a guy that you profess not to care about, and won't go out with, even though he obviously adores you—"

"He wants something," I protested. "Not the same thing as adoring."

"So he wants you," Hannah conceded. "What guy wouldn't

have given up long ago? Being repeatedly turned down isn't generally high on a guy's list of things to do for fun."

"What if he likes the pursuit, and then as soon as he's made the conquest, he's done? What if he just likes the thrill of the chase?"

Hannah snorted. "Does he look like the kind of guy who needs to do much chasing?"

She had a point there.

But still. She really didn't have a clue what was holding me back. And, even though Hannah had been my best friend for fifteen years . . . the disappointment I knew I'd see in her eyes held me back from being completely truthful. It kept me from being completely honest with Luke, too, despite my threat to just tell him and get it over with. I should just spill the beans and let him know that the girl he was pursuing, wasn't the type of girl he really wanted. But the fear of seeing that light go out of his eyes . . . I just couldn't bring myself to make good on my threat.

And, really, by this time, it wasn't so much that I worried Luke would end up just another name on my Loser List . . . because truthfully, I sensed that he wasn't like the other guys on that list. He probably was honest and kind . . . and law-abiding.

What scared me more than anything, even more than seeing his disappointment when he found out what kind of person I was, was finding out that I had made yet another mistake and having to finally admit that *I* should be the one to head up that Loser List.

"Got time for coffee?"

Luke stood at my desk, looking completely hot in jeans and a fleece jacket. I felt my heartbeat kick up a notch.

"I really can't," I said, unable to completely keep the tinge of regret out of my voice. Where had that come from? "I promised I'd go after work and help out at the soup kitchen. I'm due there in a little while."

Luke smiled. "Can anyone help or do I need an invitation?"

Surprised, I blinked. "You'd be willing to help with something like that? Most people are kind of turned off at the idea of serving meals to the homeless." Like Venus, who had blanched at the idea when I'd asked her. Of course, I'm not sure which part of the idea bothered her the most . . . the idea of being around people who weren't current on their fashion trends or being asked to do anything involving food preparation. If it didn't come from an invisible kitchen at a restaurant, Venus seemed to feel the "magic" was gone from the meal.

"Sure, why not? I do my share of volunteering," Luke said. He nodded and smiled at Hannah, who passed my desk on her way through the lobby. Behind his back she turned to make kissy faces at me, which I pointedly ignored.

"Do you?" I asked, removing my purse from the drawer and coming around my desk, apparently unconsciously deciding to take him up on his offer to go with me. "What kind of volunteering?"

An hour later, we stood side-by-side, cloaked in matching aprons, spooning up mashed potatoes and green beans to those who gratefully accepted the warm food. I'd discovered that Luke really did enjoy volunteer work as much as I did. He co-coached a high school softball team in the spring with one of his fellow firefighters. He had had a Little Brother for a while, until the boy had moved away with his family during the summer. He also frequently visited the pediatric ward when there were sick kids who dreamed of meeting a real fireman. I was surprised we'd never run into each other there.

With every new revelation, I grew a little fonder of Luke Stanton. And a little sadder that I couldn't let myself fall for him.

We finished up about eight o'clock and I set aside my worries—and my exhaustion—long enough to take Luke up on a cup of coffee, following along behind his truck back to the Cameron Creek Denny's. We continued our discussion about volunteer work over coffee and the piece of chocolate cream pie Luke insisted on. He handed me my own fork, and I couldn't help wonder why Harry Rogers was so much happier eating in Pacifique's stuffy atmosphere than in a nice cozy booth at Denny's twenty-four-hour diner.

"Volunteering saved me, I think," I admitted, poking my fork at the frothy white cream on top of the pie.

"In what way?" Luke asked.

"Two years ago, when my last relationship ended so badly, I needed something to do, anything to keep my mind off of . . . everything." I paused and frowned. I really didn't know why I'd let the conversation drift from casual to personal. I also didn't know why it felt so good to get this off my chest. "I volunteered for Habitat for Humanity to keep busy, and found that suddenly my problems didn't seem so huge anymore."

"That you could do something good, even when things seemed bad," Luke said.

I nodded. "Yeah. And since that felt so good, I started looking for other opportunities. Mentoring the girls at the high school, reading to the kids at the hospital . . . there are so many ways to give back, to make other people's lives better. I've even toyed with the idea of going back to school to become a high school counselor. Banking was never my first choice." It was a job until I got married and had kids. Which, of course, I'd never done and never would. Still, I was stuck with the job.

"Why don't you? Go back to school. My stepsister's going back this year to get her teaching degree, and she's married with two kids."

"Not enough time." I shrugged. "Too many other things going on."

"You don't have to volunteer for everything yourself, you know."

"I don't," I protested. Not someone *else* telling me I did too much.

Good thing for him, Luke decided to change the subject. "So, how's the interviewing process going?"

I opened my mouth to answer, then clamped it shut again. I wasn't sure how to answer Luke's question without either giving away too much, or completely insulting his taste in women. "It's going," I said blandly, settling for the vague approach.

I should have known that Luke would accept anything but vague. "So, you've interviewed Harry?"

I reluctantly nodded. "She's married now. Did you know that?"

He shook his head as he slid a bit of the chocolate pie between his lips.

I swallowed and averted my eyes. "Yeah. She has a couple of kids, too. Four actually."

He looked at me in disbelief. "Four kids. Harry *Middleton*?"

"Actually Harry Rogers, now. Apparently she married some guy named Asshole." In horror, I clamped my hand over my mouth. "I didn't say that."

Luke cracked up. "That bad, huh? Wow. Married with four kids. She certainly never expressed any interest in kids when we were dating. In fact, she was extremely careful to make sure that *didn't* happen."

"I don't think it had anything to do with a desire for children and motherhood," I said, forking off a bite of pie. Our forks clashed when we reached at the same time. Our eyes met as we shared a smile. "I think it had to do with snagging just the right guy. At least *her* estimation of the right guy."

"And who would be *your* estimation of the right guy?" Luke asked, softly.

My breath jammed in my throat. I could see from his look he was seriously asking me to answer the question. But I couldn't. Because, more and more, I was thinking that the answer might be, "A guy like you."

"Well," I started, then had to clear my throat to achieve a lighter tone. "Since I'm not looking for a guy, it doesn't matter, does it?" I tried for a bright smile, failed miserably, I'm sure, but Luke let me off with just a knowing nod.

"So, what did Harry have to say about me?" he continued, setting down his fork and pushing the plate with the last bit of pie on it in my direction. I was more than happy to finish it off, because it gave me something to concentrate on besides him.

"I'd rather not say," I said, thinking how mortifying it would be to repeat the awful things she'd said about him.

"Pretty bad, huh? Let me guess . . . I'm tightfisted, didn't party enough, studied too hard."

I laughed in surprise. "You knew what she was going to say about you?"

"Wasn't the first time she ever said all that."

"Seriously. Why'd you go out with her? And for so long?" I asked, sipping the hot coffee the waitress had just refreshed. "She didn't seem your type at all. Surely you weren't that different back in college."

"No, I don't think I was. But guys do tend to have their relationships driven by hormones. At least at some point in their lives."

"Is that why you're pursuing me? Hormones?" As soon as the words slipped out of my mouth, I groaned. "Forget that. You already told me you weren't trying to . . . you know."

"Get you into bed?" The amusement was evident in Luke's voice, and I cringed before nodding. "No. I said '*What if* I wasn't trying to get you into bed?' I never said I *wasn't*."

Luke reached out and slipped his hand over mine. I just stared at our hands—mine small, and his so . . . big, as Venus had pointed out once—and tried to keep my breathing under control. It wasn't easy. Especially when I was remembering that kiss in my apartment, and all the feelings it had made me feel. The ones I'd thought were buried for good.

"So, back to Harry," he continued, his thumb moving in little feather-light circles on the back of my hand. "I dated her because I was attracted to her. When she didn't turn out to be the kind of person I wanted, I didn't want to just dump her. I figured I should give her a chance. I gave her a year before . . . well, let's just say our differences became insurmountable."

I forced my eyes away from our intertwined fingers and met his gaze. "She said some pretty mean things about you. I couldn't believe she'd say that about someone who is so obviously *not* selfish, boring, or inattentive."

He grinned, obviously unoffended by my unthinking recitation of Harry's description of him. "Did you defend me?"

I blushed.

"You *did*." Luke tugged my hand closer to him across the table. "There's hope yet, isn't there?"

I shook my head, but it wasn't convincing . . . even to me.

I was saved from having to further convince him of the lack of hope for a relationship between us by the appearance of the waitress with our check, which Luke insisted on paying—probably so I wouldn't accuse him of mooching money off me again. Leaving cash on the table, he pulled me up by the hand and led me outside.

I should have protested. I should have walked on my own, but my hand felt so comfortable in his that I just couldn't bring myself to take it back. What harm was it doing, after all? It was only holding hands. It wasn't like I was agreeing to date him under false pretenses or anything. I wasn't leading him on or making him believe that I might be willing to go out with him. I'd shaken my head no when he asked if there was hope. He knew where I stood. Very firmly.

When we got out to our cars, I suddenly felt awkward. Well, it really wasn't so suddenly, it just seemed to be more exaggerated than before. Luke pulled me until we were standing with our chests practically touching. I stared at the zipper on his jacket and fought the desire to gnaw on a fingernail the way a smoker trying to quit fights to keep from reaching for a cigarette.

Luke reached up and cupped his warm hand around my

cheek. It felt even better than his other hand holding mine did. "You know, Rachel, you don't have to worry about what Harry said about me."

"I didn't *believe* her," I reiterated, a bit breathlessly inhaling his warm coffee-and-chocolate-scented breath.

"I know. But there's probably still that doubt. You have to trust your instincts, though. I know you said you thought you had poor judgment when it came to men—"

"I once dated thirty men in thirty days in an effort to find the right man," I interrupted. "Not one of them was worth a second date."

"*Who's* persistent?" Luke smiled, then got serious again. "I bet if you really examined your thoughts when you were dating the guys you dated longer than three hours, maybe you really *did* have a feeling something wasn't quite right way back in the beginning of the relationship. Maybe you just ignored it."

I definitely couldn't ignore the stroke of his thumb on my cheekbone. Or the deep, deep blue of his eyes, which held mine as captive as my fingers in the gentle grip of his hand.

"Give your judgment another chance," he said.

The judgment comment was just a cover, I protested silently.

"I may have made a mistake dating Harry all those years ago. But I'm not making a mistake with you."

Luke slanted his head over mine and captured my lips with his. Our last kiss paled in comparison.

As Luke leaned his body into mine, pressing me back against the cold metal of my car, I came alive. I couldn't help it. Everything about him was so right. The way his rough cheeks felt beneath my fingers. The way his muscled chest and thighs heated my body everywhere they touched. The way he smelled all male and sexy at the same time. The way he held my lips like he couldn't get enough of the taste of me.

The way *he* tasted better than anything *I'd* ever tasted before.

When he stopped, I had to catch myself, my knees buckling.

He smiled knowingly, tucking me in close to him while I regained my balance.

I wanted to tell him he shouldn't have done that. But no matter how many ways I said it inside my head, I couldn't even make *myself* believe it. So obviously I wouldn't be able to convince Luke.

When I'd finally relaxed a bit, I forced myself shakily out of his arms. Without trying anything else, Luke settled me into the driver's seat of my car, rolled down my window, closed the door, and leaned his elbows on the window ledge.

"No more worrying about Harry," he said, one finger gently teasing the back of my hand where it gripped the steering wheel to keep from grabbing him again. When his eyes met mine, his look was serious . . . and maybe a bit sad. "It doesn't bother me at all what she said about me. I know the truth. I think you do, too. She's bitter because I wouldn't tolerate it when she cheated on me. That's the one thing I will never accept in a relationship."

TWENTY-SEVEN

Rachel

I had to call you over," Venus said, as she came back into the room. "I don't know what to do with her. Mortals drinking themselves into cosmo comas aren't my area of expertise."

Hannah, who had just stormed past Venus into my living room, was apparently too intent on looming over me to notice that Venus had called us "mortals." As differentiated from *im*mortals. That would be *her*.

"What's the matter?" Hannah demanded to know.

I opened my left eye to join the right eye I'd been staring at her with. She looked like she'd just gotten out of bed, and I'm pretty sure it was only around midnight, so she'd probably been in the middle of sex with Griffin when Venus called her.

"I'm yust fine," I slurred, er, said. "Venus did'n' need to call you." I tipped the giant mug of vodka and cranberry juice mixture into my mouth only to have Hannah yank it from my hand, spilling it all over the front of my blouse. "Hey!" I protested, starting to sit up on the couch. It was way too much effort, though, so I dropped back down onto the pillows to finish the protest. "This is one of my favor' blouses."

"Favorite," Venus corrected.

"Shaddup," I said. "This is all your damn fault anyway."

"What did you do to her?" Hannah asked Venus.

I waved a hand wildly in Venus's direction. "She popped in here being all fairy godmothery—"

"Rachel," Venus warned.

"No," I snapped back, only I don't think snapping is as effective when the snapper's eyes are closed. "I don' care if she knows. Maybe I am crazy. Crazy to let you talk me into doing this at all."

"What are you talking about?" Hannah demanded. "Go make some coffee, Venus."

"Me?" Venus squeaked. Like *she* knew how to make coffee.

"There's probably instant in the cupboard. Even you can't screw that up."

Yes, she can, I thought, having experienced her screwing up boiling water once and almost catching the stove on fire.

Hannah waited. About the time I heard a cupboard door squeak open in the kitchen, Hannah sat down on the edge of the couch beside me. "Scooch over."

I scooched.

"Now what's going on?"

"Give me my cosmo back."

"I'm not giving you your cosmo back. You don't drink."

"I used to. I do *now*." I frowned.

"The last time you drank was when you found out about Eddie."

I sneered. Drinking after finding out about Eddie (mistake number one) had led to mistake number two, which was the real reason I tried not to drink anymore. Only Hannah didn't know about mistake number two, and I wasn't quite drunk enough to reveal it to her.

"What did Venus do? I'll kill her if you want me to."

I opened one eye and stared at my best friend, whose dark face, like a smoothly frosted chocolate cake, was pretty indistinguishable in the dim light I'd insisted upon when the alcohol had begun affecting my eyeballs. "Yer so sweet," I gushed. "I love you."

"Yes, I know you love me," Hannah said. "You've told me before. Now tell me what Venus did, so I can go pick her eyeballs out with tweezers."

"Tha's so nice. I'll drink to that." I lunged for the mug on the floor, and actually managed to get another mouthful before Hannah snatched it away again. "Venus made me like Luke. Damn her. Is all her fault."

"Oh, like you wouldn't have liked him anyway?" Hannah said, wryly. At least I think it was wryly. It was hard to tell with all the sloshing going on in my skull. "Hell, I've been trying to get you to like him for months."

"But she's my fairy godmother."

"Right."

"She is!" I protested, even opening my eyes to prove it.

"How many of these did you have before I got here?"

"Two. Three. I don't remember. Less than ten. But tha's *not* why Venus is my fairy godmother. She's Aphrodite, only she got in trouble, and Zeus made her come here to be a fairy godmother. She's been here two thousand years," I told her. "Can you imagine havin' a job you hate for two *thousand* years? I wanna be just like her." I waved a hand wildly again, and Hannah ducked out of the way. "She gets to love anybody she wants . . . even *gods*," I whispered conspiratorially. "And she doesn't have to worry about disappointing anyone or . . . or getting her heart broken. She's so lucky. I envy her. Hey!" I popped up in my seat. "I have Venus envy!"

As I dissolved back onto the couch in drunken giggles mixed with tears, Venus came back into the room with a steaming cup in her hand.

"What was she smoking before she started in on the cosmos?" Hannah asked her, peering into the cup that Venus handed over. She sipped it, grimaced, and then pushed it toward me. "You drink this. You obviously need it. I don't think it'll kill you."

"Tell 'er, Venus," I said, tossing my head and then leaning it awkwardly back on the couch, exhausted from laughing. "Tell 'er who you are. Tell 'er you're immortal and how Zeus is your dad."

"She obviously stopped by a crack house on her way home," Venus told Hannah with a roll of her eyes.

"Hey!"

"Look, Rachel—" Hannah grabbed the cup of the alleged "coffee," which tasted more like sewage, when I tried to set it on the coffee table and nearly missed. She turned and pushed me back on the cushions. "Are you sure you don't think Venus is your fairy godmother because deep down you really *want* to have a fairy godmother force you into opening your eyes and seeing that Luke's the right guy for you?"

"No! He's not. He's really, really not."

God. Hannah had just reminded me why I started drinking in the first place tonight. The minute I'd arrived home from Denny's.

"I can't ever, ever be what Luke wants. Never. He told me."

"He broke up with you?"

"How could he break up with her when she wouldn't go out with him in the first place?" Venus asked.

"You know what I mean," Hannah snapped, then turned back to me. "Rachel, honey, did he tell you he didn't want to date you after all?"

I shook my head. "He *kissed* me."

Hannah raised her eyebrows.

"That's been happening a lot lately," Venus said.

"How come she knows about that, but I don't?" Hannah whined. "I'm your best friend."

"But she's my fairy godmom."

I saw Venus shrug and roll her eyes, before I closed mine

again. "It's the second time he did it. I can' take it. I'm all wrong for him. If he finds out—"

"He's not going to find out, if you don't tell him," Hannah said.

"But I'd feel guilty forever."

"That's just because you're stupid," Hannah said, standing up and walking away. The next time she said anything it came from the kitchen. "You have no reason to feel guilty. Eddie was the guilty party, not you."

"I shoulda known."

"And we should have known tech stocks were going to tank when they did, but we didn't and we all lost money. Boo. Hoo."

"Snot the same thing." I pouted, feeling a bit more sober than I had five minutes ago. Sober enough to remember that Hannah was still working on the assumption that I'd only made a mistake with Eddie. The mistake I made with what's-his-name didn't even exist in her mind. If she knew how much I'd really done . . . she'd react the same way I knew Luke would react if he knew what I'd done. With either of them.

The reason for the demise of Luke and Harry's relationship was enough evidence for me.

Hannah came back in the room with a Diet Coke and a glass of water, which she handed to me, gesturing that I had to drink it before she passed over the Diet Coke. "This has caffeine. See if that helps more than Venus's poisonous coffee."

Venus stuck her tongue out at Hannah's back.

"Maybe you need to confront Eddie," Hannah suggested.

"What?" I sputtered on a mouthful of pop. My stomach heaved, and I didn't know whether it was from the vodka or the thought of confronting Eddie Glassner in this lifetime. "Why would I do that?"

"Because you've decided that you're the bad guy in this situation. Maybe if you talked to Eddie, you'd remember that he's the bastard, not you."

Venus was watching my reaction, the only other one in the room who knew that it had to do with more than just the Eddie Incident.

I shook my head, then moaned and clutched it between my hands, as the after-alcohol headache commenced. "It wouldn't help. I should have *known*."

"Sing a different tune, for God's sake," Hannah groaned. "You're not fucking psychic. I'm so tired of hearing how it's all your fault." She picked up her coat before turning to Venus. "You can handle her now. Don't let her have any more cosmos, make her drink a couple more glasses of water, and call her in sick tomorrow, because she's not going to be able to stand up. I can't watch this pity party anymore."

"Be that way!" I shouted at the retreating back of my best friend. My *unsympathetic* best friend.

The best friend who didn't even know what a truly miserable human being *her* best friend really was.

TWENTY-EIGHT

Venus

Rachel finally slept. She'd lain awake for a long time after Hannah left, bitching about how no one understood her. I just sat up in my chair, listening to her with one ear and dozing, until I was sure she was asleep and wouldn't get up and mix any more of those apparently lethal-to-mortals cocktails.

I'm *supposed* to understand her. And I guess I do. A little. She did things she's not proud of . . . even if *I* don't agree that they were bad things, she thinks they are, so that's all that matters.

Apparently, Luke unwittingly fed her even more guilt by telling her the reason he and Harry had broken up.

So, who's left to pick up the mortal messes? Me, of course. Me, the fairy godmother. Me, the *goddess,* who should be enjoying a life of leisure and pleasure—which might have included some of the same so-called mistakes Rachel claims to have made. Instead, I'm left trying to figure out how to fix this mess, so that Cinderella and Prince Charming can live happily ever after.

So, I think, finally crawling into my own bed (okay, Rachel's bed, but I've become so fond of it, I think of it as mine—and she really does look completely comfortable passed out on the couch), Hannah wasn't so far off. If Rachel could remember what a creep Eddie was (we'll have to work with him, since we can't remember the other guy's name, although he was equally creepy), she'd realize that she couldn't have done anything differently to change the outcome of the situation. She was completely at his mercy, short of hiring a private dick or something, to have had him followed, and that would only have worked if he weren't such a great con artist. Rachel would have had to suspect something before it would have occurred to her to have him checked out. Not noticing someone's deviant behavior isn't the same thing as knowingly doing something wrong.

So, it may just be necessary to be a little devious in my fairy godmothering.

She'll get over it.

TWENTY-NINE

Rachel

Through the hangover haze I'd been in the day before, lying on my couch/bed, I'd made my decision. I was going to put an end to Luke's pursuit of me once and for all. I had no idea how, but I was going to do it.

However, I was too chicken to face him before I'd finalized my plan of action, and knowing he'd probably come in on my lunch break, I'd taken my lunch early and had hung out in the lunchroom with Venus, making Hannah tell Luke that I'd gone to run errands. I felt awful lying to him and disappointing him, but the real disappointment was still to come, and I couldn't face it yet. If I could just avoid him for the rest of today, he'd be back to work for the weekend, and I could avoid a confrontation until Monday at least.

I noted that Venus was busily chatting with Millicent, probably pretending to be on the verge of opening that multimillion-dollar account Millicent had been drooling over for the past five weeks.

Venus was going to be upset, too, I knew, but I really didn't have a choice. My sanity dictated that I put a halt to what never should have been started in the first place. I had to take my life back. I wanted to be happy again. Surely, Venus would understand that. I mean, after all, that was her goal, too. To have her old life back. To be happy. She had to see that our goals for ourselves were one and the same. Only, if I didn't reach my goal, if I didn't take whatever steps were necessary to get my old life back, and to get Luke Stanton firmly behind me, I stood to have my heart broken. Venus didn't risk that.

I realized that I had been telling the truth when I said I envied Venus, because I really, really did. Even now, my heart aching, if not yet broken, I wanted nothing more than to be just like Venus. Immortal, immovable, invulnerable. She didn't have to worry about love or feelings. As a goddess, she could just take her pleasure and move on, without worrying about being hurt. She didn't worry about making mistakes or what people thought of her. If only I had the same ability. I'd take what Luke offered, without a second thought to getting hurt . . . or hurting him.

But, I was mortal, and I did have feelings. So, I was stuck making the hard decision to quit while I still had some dignity left.

I checked my watch and realized that it was finally four thirty. Almost time to go home. With any luck, Luke wouldn't show up after work today. Maybe he'd be busy. Maybe he'd changed his mind about me. Maybe—

A pretty blond woman stepped up to my desk. "I'd like to open a checking account," she said. "My husband will be here in a few minutes, but I'd like to get started now, if I can."

"I can help you," I replied with a smile, standing and shaking her hand, grateful for the distraction that would last almost until it was time to leave. "Please have a seat."

I dug out the necessary forms and passed her the papers and a pen, asking the preliminary questions about what type of checking account she wanted, et cetera.

When she finally handed the papers back to me, I had her

account information ready to fill in, beginning with their names—

    Tami and Edward Glassner, I read.

    Glassner, I typed. Tami and Edward.

    Eddie. Eddie Glassner.

    Shit.

THIRTY

Venus

Turning away from Millie's monologue about the benefits and risks (or lack thereof, according to her) of opening a jumbo CD with Cascade National Bank, I watch Rachel out of the corner of my eye. I can only see the back of her head, but the stiffness of her shoulders is apparent even from a distance.

She needs to trust me on this. She will thank me in the end. Confronting her past is exactly what she needs. She'll see that none of her "sins" were really her fault at all, and then she can get on with her life.

I take a deep breath and turn my attention back to Millie. As much as I want to help, I have to let Rachel deal with this on her own.

THIRTY-ONE

Rachel

Oh, my God.

If I had been Catholic (unlike Hannah, who takes her Catholicism so lightly as for it to be nonexistent), I'd have been Hail Marying my heart out. Speed genuflecting. *Drinking* holy water.

I wasn't Catholic, though, so I was stuck waiting for lightning to strike. Cursing my parents for not taking us to church, for not giving us an out for when we screw up so badly only God can make things right.

I resisted the urge to turn around and get Venus's attention. Surely if Zeus (a "god" in some sense of the word, I guess) put her in charge of me, then he should feel some responsibility for keeping me out of trouble like this. Shouldn't he? I mean, what was the point of sending a goddess my way if she was helpless to get me out of jams?

However, it would look more than a little odd to my customer to call Venus over to sit with me for protection while doing something as simple as opening a checking account.

"Oh, and this is just my fairy godmother. She'll be holding

my hand while I open your account, so that I can avoid being struck by lightning."

I stole a look at Tami Glassner under my eyelashes. She sat patiently, hands relaxed—surprisingly *not* poised to wrap around my neck—staring unseeing at my nameplate, waiting for me to finish inputting her information into my computer. I had no reason to believe that she would connect—or even remember—my name. Lots of people were named Rachel, and she'd mistaken me for someone else anyway the one time I'd spoken to her.

She glanced at her watch and I reflexively swallowed, darting a glance at the door. This woman really had no reason to know who I was, but Eddie, due here any moment . . . was a whole different story.

Oh, dear God, I prayed silently, I will do anything . . . *anything* . . . if you get me out of this without a scene. Really. I'll become Catholic, join a convent, give up sex for the rest of my life. (I'd given it up for the past two years, so how hard could it be to go the rest of my life?) I'd take a vow of poverty and live in a box under a bridge, so nothing would distract me from my devotion to the needs of the less fortunate (or less sinful, as the case may be).

I'd devote myself to helping others. I'd also done *that* for the last two years and had planned on continuing to do it the rest of my life. Until I'd been distracted. Obviously Eddie showing up (or about to show up) was punishment for straying from the life of servitude that I'd chosen to make up for my shortcomings. My mistakes.

My *sins,* I thought, glancing at Eddie's wife and stifling a groan from the rising hysteria I felt.

If only Eddie wouldn't make a scene when he got here.

Maybe I looked different. It had been two years, after all. Maybe he wouldn't recognize me.

I darted a glance at my nameplate. Shit. Even if I looked

completely different than I did when Eddie and I were together (which I didn't, unfortunately), names didn't lie. His wife may not recognize my name, but Eddie certainly would.

Thinking fast—or not at all, possibly—I faked an explosive sneeze, flinging my hand out and knocking my nameplate off the desk, narrowly missing my customer as it flew through the air and landed on the floor beside her.

"Oh," exclaimed a startled *Mrs. Eddie Glassner,* who picked the metal nameplate up off the floor and handed it to me. "Here you go." She looked at me a little oddly as I took the nameplate and pretended to examine it closely.

"Oh," I said with mock concern. "It's damaged. I'll have to send it in for repairs." I quickly shoved it in my desk drawer, slamming it shut, and went back to my computer as if what I'd just said wasn't obviously a complete and utter lie. And downright stupid to boot.

Maybe it would save me. Maybe I wouldn't look like myself for five minutes. Maybe when Eddie arrived, he'd have developed a case of amnesia and—

A slight change in air temperature alerted me to the front door opening, and I automatically looked up . . . and met the hard brown eyes of Eddie Glassner.

Who instantly saw through all of my attempts at mentally disguising myself. As the dawning of recognition showed in his expression, and his widening eyes darted to the back of his wife's head and then to me again, I felt all the color drain from my face.

I was completely dead.

"Honey." Eddie stepped hesitantly up to the desk and kissed the top of his wife's head as he joined us. I could have sworn he said "Honey" with extra emphasis for my benefit. As if I needed any reminders that he was married.

"Oh, good. You're here," Tami smiled up at her husband as he took a seat beside her. "I have to leave to go pick up the

kids in a minute. I've signed the signature card, so you can fill
out the rest and finish up here." She turned to me with an
easy—uncomprehending—smile. "This is Rachel. Right?"

I nodded, completely mute. Then I remembered I wasn't
supposed to know him and it would have been impolite not to
greet a new customer. "Nice to m-meet you . . . Mr. Glassner."

Eddie nodded briefly in my direction, his jaw tight. A
muscle in front of his ear jerked as he gritted his teeth.

I closed my eyes, blew out a breath, and turned back to my
computer screen, typing as fast as I could go. Maybe if I could
finish up before Mrs. Glassner left, I wouldn't be left alone
with Eddie.

"Stupid," I chastised myself under my breath. I wasn't really alone with him anyway. We were in the middle of a bank.
My coworkers were all around us. Customers drifted in and
out, bringing in paychecks for deposit, taking out car loans.
Eddie wouldn't kick up a stink in public.

Would he?

The last time I'd seen him, he'd been ranting at me like a
lunatic . . . in the middle of Roxio's dance club.

I shoved the memory aside and concentrated on entering
their information. I was all thumbs, unfortunately, and spent
more time typing backward than forward.

My luck ran out when Tami Glassner stood to leave. "If you
can do the rest of it without me, I really need to be going."

I nodded mutely, then found my manners. "Thank you for
opening an account with Cascade National," I murmured by
rote. "We're happy to have you as a customer."

Tami said good-bye, bent to kiss her husband on the
cheek . . . something I couldn't help but remember doing myself once upon a time. When I thought he might become *my*
husband. Before I knew he already *was* a husband.

I barely stifled another groan as I buried my head in my file
cabinet, searching for the appropriate deposit slips needed to
get their account opened. The faster I got Eddie out of here

the better. Even though his wife was gone, it didn't mean I was off the hook by any means.

Then another horrible thought occurred to me: if the Glassners opened an account at this branch . . .

God, I'd have to see Eddie on a regular basis. To be reminded of my mistakes.

I was going to have to change jobs.

Okay, if I joined the convent because God got me out of this situation unscathed, the new job thing would be moot. So the only reason I'd need to worry about changing jobs was if I didn't get out of this—

"Stop."

My head shot up as Eddie spoke, and again I felt the blood drain out of my face as he stared at me with eyes filled with complete and utter disgust.

"S-stop what?"

"Stop opening the account," he hissed, through gritted teeth. "For God's sake, do you think my *wife* and I can really have an account here, while you're working here? I'll just tell her I didn't like the way the bank worked. That the customer service sucked."

For a brief moment, my temper flared. But then I remembered who I was talking to and what I was guilty of. "N-no," I stammered. "I suppose not."

I quickly shoved their paperwork into a pile, preparing to delete everything I'd done. If I avoided eye contact, maybe I could avoid any further conversation with him. I'd cancel the account, Eddie would leave, and I could make my escape.

No such luck.

"What are you doing here anyway?" he whispered, leaning forward over the edge of my desk. "I thought you worked at the Seattle branch."

"I did," I whispered back. "I transferred here . . . two years ago." *To get far away from you.*

Eddie continued to glare at me, and I found myself unable

to look away. It amazed me that he could hate me so much. We'd once loved each other. Well, I'd loved *him* anyway. I don't know what he really felt for me. I'd once thought it was love, but after I found out about his wife, I wasn't sure.

"Here you go." I passed back to Eddie the cash his wife had given me to open their account.

He grabbed the money from my hand, his fingers brushing mine and sending a shock through my fingers. And not a good shock.

He rose quickly and loomed over me. "I just want to know one thing," he barked.

I stared at him, unable to speak, my heart pounding in my throat. The fact that there were people around us registered at the edges of my consciousness.

"I want to know why you cheated on me."

"I did'n—" I reflexively flew out of my chair, aware that another customer had entered the bank and stood a few feet behind Eddie. "I didn't."

Eddie fairly growled at me, leaning in so close to my face, I could smell stale coffee on his breath. "Don't lie!" he snapped, his voice getting louder. "I saw you leave with him. You *told* me you were going to fuck him. You were *my* girlfriend."

The protest on the tip of my tongue . . . stuck like glue. I couldn't spit it out. I couldn't defend myself. I swayed above my chair, and just as I felt like I might collapse, the new customer stepped up beside me grasping my arm. I barely had time to register who it was before he spoke to Eddie in a hushed voice that carried such authority Eddie backed up a few steps.

"Don't *ever* speak to Rachel like that again."

Eddie regained his bravado and leaned forward, looking like he was ready to go to blows if Luke insisted on standing up for me. "Who the hell are you? Her latest fuck buddy?"

I gasped simultaneously with a sudden flurry of activity all around. Venus shoved her way in, retrieved my purse from my desk drawer, and stuck it into my free hand.

"Go," she ordered. "Go now."

I glanced wildly around the bank, automatically searching for Millicent, my employee sense kicking in and knowing I couldn't just leave.

"I'll clear it with Millie," Venus said, interpreting my panic. "Just go. *Now*."

I went.

THIRTY-TWO

Venus

"You may leave now," I say in my most haughty, goddesslike voice, to the object of two years of misery for my godchild. "There's no reason for you to be here."

"Who the hell are you?" Eddie snarls, glancing at the door, then at Luke, torn between going after Rachel and taking his pent-up anger out on us.

Luke doesn't give him a chance to take anything out on him. He's out the door after Rachel. He's *definitely* the prince I thought he was. If only he can convince *her*.

I try to keep from shaking, but don't succeed. I lean toward Eddie, turning on every ounce of goddess charm I have in me. Usually I use it to get men to buy me things, but it should work to get them to do anything I wish them to do.

Even go fuck themselves.

I give my eyelashes a flick. "I'm your worst nightmare. Leave. Now."

Eddie blinks before backing off. "Fine, I'm going."

"Good. Go."

Upon Zeus, I hope I've given Rachel and Luke enough time to escape, because I'm sure Eddie would have no qualms about continuing this little scene out in the middle of Main Street.

He finally goes and I sag into Rachel's deserted chair and struggle to keep from lowering my head to the desk.

What went wrong? It was going so well. Eddie was going to come into the bank, be the jerk that Rachel had forgotten he was, and she was going to realize that anything she did two years ago was only a result of his lies.

Eddie wasn't supposed to cause a scene.

Luke wasn't supposed to show up and witness it.

Rachel wasn't supposed to be in so much pain.

Hannah arrives at Rachel's desk, her expression at once confused and murderous. "Was that Eddie?"

Mute, I just nod.

"Did he say . . . ?" Hannah looks askance at me, like I have all the answers. Only I don't.

Unable to stop myself, I do lower my head to the desktop. Since when did fairy godmothering become so difficult?

THIRTY-THREE

Rachel

The heel broke off my shoe three blocks from the bank. I kept going.

I didn't even know what I was running to. Only from.

The person calling my name from a few blocks back.

I ignored him and turned down a side street, almost bumping into a woman holding a fluff ball of a dog. It reminded me of the dogs at the shelter. Which reminded me that the shelter was only a few more blocks away.

That's what I'd do. I'd get the dogs and take them down to the beach. We'd walk. They'd poop. I'd forget.

That was the plan anyway. Hasty, but foolproof, I thought. After all, volunteering—helping out—had been what saved me from mortification two years ago, so why not now?

Twila, the caretaker at the shelter, looked up when I burst in through the office door a few minutes later, out of breath.

"I need some dogs," I panted. "Now."

Twila smirked. "Is this like a doggy stickup? 'Cause all I have to give you is some pooper-scoopers."

"Ha," I replied. "Very funny. Just give me some dogs to walk and no one gets hurt." She didn't even realize, in my current state, I wasn't much kidding about that.

With a shrug, Twila led the way to the back of the kennel, where the dogs set up a resounding welcome. I tried not to limp on my broken shoe so she wouldn't feel the need to ask me any questions I didn't want to answer. "Jeremy already walked most of them today," she said, nevertheless lifting some leads off their hooks. "It's not your day."

"You can say that again," I muttered, taking the first dog from her, a little beagle, who alternately stared at me with sad eyes and bayed in response to the other dogs barking. "I just need . . . I just thought the dogs could use an extra walk maybe."

Twila shrugged. "Can't hurt." She handed me the other leads and then looked at me closely. "You okay?"

"Sure," I replied nonchalantly, then tried to appear engrossed in the dogs, so she wouldn't see how close I was to a breakdown. "We'll be back in an hour or so."

As if an hour was going to fix my life.

The beach was fairly deserted. September wasn't a big beachcombing month. Especially not at 5:00 P.M., when it was starting to get dusky . . . and chilly.

I wrapped my arms tightly around myself, keeping the leads tucked close in. Luckily, the four dogs Twila had given me were pretty quiet, more intent on finding the perfect potty spot than on causing mischief. This left me free to think.

Maybe that was *un*lucky. Because thinking left me open to remembering. And remembering left me seeing pictures in my mind that I didn't want to see again. Like the look on Luke's face when Eddie had blurted out all my sins for the world to hear . . . or at least everyone in the bank lobby.

"You *told* me you were going to fuck him. You were *my* girlfriend."

I groaned aloud. How could I have been so stupid? I'd

talked about telling Luke the truth, about confessing what had happened with Eddie, but I'd always imagined that I'd have had control. I'd have been able to break it to him gently.

But, I hadn't. And before I ran, I'd seen the look on his face. Anger. Disappointment.

Unable to hold it in any longer, I threw back my head and let out a half-cry/half-growl of frustration. The beagle howled along with me. The mournfulness of his baying made me tear up. Which only made me madder. Which only made me cry harder.

Which only made me more thankful that Venus wasn't here witnessing this. She'd never let me hear the end of it. She'd tell me to buck up, to snap out of it.

Being a goddess was obviously so much different—better—than being human. Venus probably never shed a tear over *any* of her lovers. She'd loved them and left them without regrets. If they turned out to be different from her expectations, she moved on to the next man (or god) who caught her fancy. Being a goddess, things were just easier. They had to be.

I kicked off my broken heels and sank down onto the damp sand, heedless of what it would probably do to the suede skirt I had on. Even when things were hard, Venus was a better person than I was, I thought. She'd been cast out, shunned by her peers, banished to a place completely foreign to the home she loved. All she wanted to do was to get back there. And Venus had focused on her dream of getting home again . . . for two thousand years. My dream had once been to have a husband and a family. To love and be loved exclusively . . . madly.

My dream had barely lasted thirty years. It was just too fucking difficult.

The dogs all set to barking and made a mad dash toward the street behind me, pulling me onto my back. I held fast and just stared at the gray sky above, really not caring what damage the sand was now doing to my blouse . . . or to my hair. It served me right. The cold dampness on my back and scalp was further punishment for my transgressions.

"Cinderella, I believe?"

I rolled my eyes back at the sound of Luke's voice. He was upside down, holding out the heel of my shoe. I quickly sat upright and wiped at my runny nose with the sleeve of my blouse.

"It's not exactly a glass slipper," he commented, coming around to the front of me, ignoring the dogs jumping all over him, his expression far more serious than his light words. "But, I do believe it fits." He gestured to my obviously broken shoe being stepped on by a schnauzer.

Swiping at my damp eyes with the back of my hand, I took the heel and stuck it in my purse, without meeting Luke's eyes. I didn't think I could stand to see the look there.

Dropping to the sand beside me, he absently petted the whitish-gray mutt climbing on his lap and stared out at the water. He didn't seem inclined to say much. I didn't know why he was even inclined to be here . . . with me. Not after what he'd heard.

I made myself look at him. Time to get the inevitable over with. "Why are you being nice to me?"

He shrugged. "I'm a nice guy."

I couldn't say anything to that. I couldn't form a coherent thought, let alone words.

"I need to go." I stood. "I need to get the dogs back."

"I'll help." Luke took my arm and helped me up, eyeing my mismatched shoes with doubt, as I slipped my feet into them. He took two of the leads from me, and we walked back toward the street.

When he turned with me toward the shelter, I looked at him questioningly. "What about your truck?" It was parked on the street next to the boardwalk. Hard to believe I hadn't heard it coming. Pain is apparently deafening.

"It's not important."

I still ranked somewhere higher than Luke's truck. That was hard to believe.

The six of us walked—or limped, in my case—silently back toward the shelter, the dogs dancing around us, oblivious to Luke's anger and my shame.

When Luke finally spoke, I just wanted to sink into the ground and disappear. "Is he why you wouldn't go out with me?"

Not *won't* go out with me. *Wouldn't*. Past tense. In other words the offer didn't stand anymore.

Like there was ever a chance anyway.

I nodded, stepping around the beagle, who had stopped to scratch. "One of them."

"Tell me what happened."

I shot him a startled glance and felt like I'd been struck when I saw the disappointment again in his eyes. There was no sense in prolonging the agony. "There's no reason to tell you. You heard him. I slept with someone else."

"I don't believe it," Luke said, his disbelief not very evident in the coldness of his eyes or the hard set of his jaw. Gone was the guy joking about Cinderella on the beach. In his place was the guy who probably couldn't believe how stupid he had been to fall for a girl like me.

"It's true," I assured him, staring unseeingly ahead of us. I couldn't bring myself to look at him anymore. Just this morning, I'd been ready to tell him the truth about my past, to tell him that I'd done to Eddie what Harry had done to Luke. But now that the time had come, I wasn't as keen on the idea as I thought I would be. "I cheated."

"Why?"

"What do you mean 'why?'" I asked. "Because I'm a screwup."

"You're not a screwup or you wouldn't care that you cheated."

I shrugged.

"Why, Rachel? Tell me why you would cheat."

"Revenge, all right?" I shouted, then repeated in a whisper. "Revenge."

"What did he do to *you*?"

My laugh came out in a huff. God, which was worse? Having to admit your own mistakes? Or having to admit that you'd been completely made a fool of by someone you loved? Either way, it was humiliating.

Luke watched me intently, eyes slightly softening, for some inexplicable reason still wanting to think the best of me. If I was going to humiliate myself, I decided, I'd better do it all at once. Get it over with, so I could crawl back into my hole and be left alone with my miserable memories. They were, after all, all that was going to keep me company the rest of my life.

I took a deep breath and just blurted it out. "If you'd come into the bank five minutes earlier, you'd have met Eddie's wife."

Luke's face relaxed fractionally. "He's married now?"

"He was married *then*."

The play of emotions on Luke's face might have been humorous in different circumstances. "You were . . . dating a married man?"

"Apparently," I said, instantly flooded with all the feelings I'd had two years ago, when I'd discovered that little fact myself. The horror. The shock. The feeling of dirtiness that a week's worth of showers didn't wash away. "In my defense," I continued quietly, not particularly wanting to hear my own voice out loud, "as little as it's going to help, I didn't know he was married at the time."

He accepted my explanation all to easily. "All right. So tell me about it."

I stared at him, stunned that he hadn't just dropped the leads he was holding and turned back toward his truck. "Luke, it's not going to matter."

"It might," he insisted.

"It *won't*," I protested. "Harry cheated on you. You told me that was the one thing you couldn't forgive. I cheated on Eddie. You'd always look at me and remember that."

Luke regarded me closely. As hard as it was, I didn't break eye contact, deserving whatever discomfort I got simply because I hadn't been honest with him in the first place.

"Tell me what happened," Luke finally said again. I opened my mouth to repeat my protest, but he interrupted. "I'm *not* wrong about us, and I'm not giving up."

I swallowed and turned away, closing my eyes against the tears that were forming again. He *was* wrong about us. And I owed it to him to prove it. It would save us both a lot of agony. I'd spill the whole sordid tale, accept his rejection, and then life could go back to normal.

Because Luke wouldn't want me anymore.

So I told him what happened two years ago . . .

Hannah and I had been dancing at Roxio's, our favorite club. Hannah's boyfriend was working late, so wouldn't arrive for a few hours. Eddie, my fiancé, should have been there already, but wasn't. I finally decided to call his cell phone—the only number I had—and check on him.

A woman's voice answered. Confused, I asked for Eddie.

"He's not here right now," the woman said brightly. "Left his cell at home by accident. Can I take a message? This is his wife."

In a supreme act of self-control, I did not collapse to the floor in a heap.

When I didn't answer right away, she repeated her request that I leave a message.

I was so stunned, I didn't even think to just hang up. "Tell him . . . Rachel called." Then I hung up.

One hour—and many drinks—later (on top of the one I'd already had), Eddie showed up at Roxio's to find me in the arms of a nameless guy. I'll call him Jerry. "Jerry" and Hannah had spent the last hour watching me pour drink after drink down my throat, listening to me complain about what a bastard

Eddie was, and how I should have known he was married because he didn't give me his home phone number, and how all I wanted out of life was a nice guy, but just continued to pick losers. Jerry told me *he* was a nice guy, and since he was nice enough to keep me supplied with alcohol, I believed him.

When Eddie showed up, I told him he could go fuck himself.

Because *I* was going to go fuck Jerry.

I don't think, when I left, I really intended to follow through with that. I didn't pick up strangers and take them home. But I was furious . . . and indignant . . . and mortified. All at the same time. Eddie had knowingly put me in the position of being a cheater, of helping him—a married man—cheat on his wife. The rage I felt, on top of being completely blitzed by that time, clouded whatever little bit of shitty judgment I had. Which wasn't much, as evidenced by the kind of men I hooked up with.

So, leaving Eddie at the club with his wild-eyed, tongue-lashing protests—none of which included an apology for being a liar and a cheat—I left with Jerry. My one and only thought was payback, revenge. I wanted to show Eddie how it felt. My inner moral compass was obviously affected by alcohol, because I was soon to discover I'd made mistake number two.

"A few hours later," I told Luke, now nearly completely numb from the telling of my story, "Jerry left me to go home. To *his* wife. Who he forgot to tell me about until we were through."

Luke raised his eyebrows and blew out a breath. "Wow."

"Yeah."

We stopped in front of the shelter and I reached for the leads Luke was holding. Looking a little stunned, he handed them to me. I tried not to notice how good it felt to touch his hand, because it wouldn't be happening again. I'd done it. I'd given Luke all the gory details . . . all the ammunition he needed to run the other way as fast as he could. I'd given him permission to leave. "Now you see why I can't go out with you."

Without waiting for his answer, I turned and pulled the dogs into the shelter.

Ten minutes later, I came back out.

Luke was still standing there waiting for me. "No," he said.

I stared at him in shock. "No, what?

"No, I *don't* see why you can't go out with me." He was back to looking mad again, which I guessed was better than disappointed, but was confusing the hell out of me.

"How can you not see how totally wrong I am for you?" I asked, starting off down the street toward the bank, so I could pick up my car and go home. I probably still had enough vodka for a few cosmos. "I cheated, not once, but *twice*."

"No, you didn't," Luke said, taking long strides to keep up with me. "*They* did. How can you be guilty of something you weren't even aware of?"

"I should have *known*. How can you date someone for two years and not know they're married?" I threw up my hands in complete frustration. Frustration I'd been holding inside for the past two years. "How could I have been so completely blinded by his . . . his charm, or whatever it was that made me believe all his lies? I should have *seen* it."

"Rachel—"

"And, going home with '*Jerry*,'" I interrupted, "was just plain stupid. I don't have one-night stands. I don't do casual sex, safe or otherwise. Sex isn't about bodies. It's about feelings. Sex definitely is *not* about revenge, and that's what it was when I took Jerry home with me. Getting revenge. I'd never done *anything* like that before in my life, and what do I do?" The laugh that burst from my chest was verging on hysterical. "I find out I've helped a guy commit adultery, so I take a total stranger home with me for revenge sex and he turns out to be married, too!"

"Rachel." Luke grabbed for the hand that I'd been waving in the air to emphasize my faults. "Stop. You didn't know. You made a mistake. Everyone makes mistakes."

I deflated right there on the sidewalk. I couldn't move another step. I didn't know whether his confidence in me was flattering or stupid.

"Everyone makes mistakes," Luke repeated, his voice gentle. "You can't let it ruin the rest of your life."

Oh, but I could. And I had.

"Do you have a pen and a piece of paper?"

I blinked and stared at him like he was nuts.

"Do you?" He gestured at my purse.

Sighing, I rummaged around my bag until I came up with a pen and a clean napkin. Luke took them and scribbled something on the napkin and handed it to me.

"Just so we don't proceed under any false assumptions."

On the napkin was written his cell phone number, his work number, his home number . . . *and* his address.

"Don't want you thinking that because I only gave you my cell number with the flowers, that I'm hiding a wife and three kids back at home."

I blushed, remembering that that's exactly what I thought. "I . . . but—"

Luke silenced me with a finger. "The only reason I gave you my cell instead of my home number is that I wanted you to be able to call me anytime, not just when I was at home."

"Really," I started, searching for the words to finally make him see. "I just don't think—"

"Stop thinking," he said, with a smile that made my throat tighten. "It's only gotten you two years of self-inflicted misery."

I could only stare at him. Really, I wanted to believe him. I wanted to just take his words and wrap up in them and finally be warm again after two long years. But, I couldn't.

It would require forgiving myself.

It would require being vulnerable again.

It would require some sort of magic that I didn't have in me.

Luke raised his eyebrows in a silent question. Could I take a chance?

Inside my head, I groaned, and closed my eyes.

No.

I couldn't.

When Luke tugged at my hand, I held firm. "No."

"No?"

"No," I repeated, pulling my hand out of his. "I can't do it."

I opened my eyes and finally looked back at Luke. The hurt in his eyes was like a slap in the face, but, I couldn't give in. I had too much to lose.

"There's nothing between us, Luke."

For a minute he just stared at me, his jaw clenching and unclenching. Finally something changed in his eyes. "I guess if you can't see it, I can't *make* you see it," he said.

Then, he turned around and walked out of my life.

THIRTY-FOUR

Venus

What do you mean?" Rachel stares at me with her mouth hanging open. "*You* sicced Eddie on me?"

"Not 'sicced,'" I insist, from my place on the bed, regretting instantly that I'd admitted my part in today's little drama. "Just gently suggested. I didn't mean for all *that* to happen. I just wanted you to get a little reminder what a shit he was. And, Zeus knows, that's exactly what happened."

"That's not what happened!" Rachel says, throwing her hands up. "I . . . I looked like a fool. I . . . you ruined it with Luke."

I blink and sit up. "What do you mean? I didn't ruin anything. You guys talked—"

"And Luke left."

"He . . . what?"

I don't get it. I swear when he went after her, he was planning on telling her all was fine. That he loved her. I swear he was. I'd even started packing—either for home or for my next assignment, depending on how much of a prick Zeus decided to be about this punishment crap.

Because, seriously, if I thought all was lost, I'd be drowning myself in the Sound by now.

"He left," Rachel repeats, her voice breaking. "He said, if I couldn't see . . . *it*—whatever the hell 'it' is—then he couldn't *make* me see it."

"What's 'it'?" My voice rises in panic. Things weren't supposed to happen like this. I'm supposed to be on my way home.

All pride forgotten, I flash a look heavenward. Give me a break here, Zeus . . . *Dad*, I plead. I never screwed things up like this. Never. As crazy and warped as humans are, my instincts are never off about who is meant to love whom. I was born to get it right.

Now is not the time to start being wrong.

"What is 'it'?" I repeat more firmly, needing to get to the bottom of this before I completely lose it.

"You tell me."

The pain in Rachel's eyes is almost unbearable. And I don't get why it's getting to me so much. I'm a make-'em-fall-in-love-and-leave-'em kind of fairy godmother. No attachments, no regrets. Just put another gold star on my chart and move me along to the next godchild. So why is the look on Rachel's face making me so itchy? Like . . . like little spiders of guilt are crawling all over me.

This just isn't right. I'm letting emotions—upon *Zeus*, where did those come from?—get in the way.

No time for this. It has to be fixed. I have to take control again. And, I can't let Rachel know that I don't know what the hell is going on.

I have to be the fairy godmother again.

Jumping off the bed, I plant my hands on my hips and frown at Rachel. "A fine mess you've made of things."

"Me? Are you kidding?" The pain in her eyes is replaced by anger.

Anger, I can deal with. "Yes. You. I gave you every chance to redeem yourself, to . . . to have the love of your life. And you . . . messed it all up with your issues and your pride."

"I *have* no pride left after today." Rachel turns away from me and leans heavily against her dresser. A moment later her shoulders sag. Oh, no. Not back to the pain again. "How could you send Eddie to the bank?" she asks. "How could you think so little of me that you'd flaunt my biggest mistake in my face? I *loved* him, Venus. He broke my heart."

She loved him? Was she kidding me? Was she kidding herself?

Hey! That was it.

"You didn't love him," I say, crossing my arms, trying to look stern and gain control of the situation again. I feel a bit like a relationship detective who has finally broken a case.

She whirls around, eyes flashing again. "I wanted to marry him. I did *too* love him."

"No, you didn't. Because if you did, you couldn't have replaced him so easily."

Rachel stares at me, chest heaving, looking completely confused. "Excuse me?"

I'm onto something. I can feel it. I decide to just go with my goddess intuition on this. "If you'd loved Eddie so much, you would've been heartbroken. Sad. Not mad. And you wouldn't have slept with Jerry—which, by the way, wasn't his name."

"I *know* that wasn't his name! And, I *did* love Eddie. I did. Jerry was just—"

"Revenge," I say, knowing I've finally gotten it right. Now I just have to make her see it. "When you truly love someone, no matter how they fail you, you don't seek revenge."

"Why not?" Rachel demands. "He hurt me. He used me. He deserved it."

"I don't deny that. But, if you really loved him, you wouldn't have thought that. You'd have been devastated, hurt, sad. Not ready to slash his throat. *True* love isn't like that."

Rachel scrubs at her eyes and drops into the chair by the

window. "I don't get it. I just . . . you *can't* be right. I spent two years of my life on Eddie. You don't do that when you don't care . . . don't *love* a guy."

"Humans do all kinds of stupid things." I shrug. "Never said you all were very bright."

Rachel glares at me. "Very funny."

"Not meant to be."

Needing distance, I go out to the kitchen and retrieve two Diet Cokes. While I'm there, I let out the sigh that's been holed up inside me for the past hour. Sagging against the refrigerator, I try to chill out again. And I completely don't get why I even *need* to chill out. What the hell is happening to me that all this inconsequential, little shit—like *human* emotions—is getting to me all of a sudden? Something's wrong. Terribly wrong.

Something that might require, like, I don't know, Xanax or something. Yes. Xanax. I heard some women talking in the boutique the other day about Xanax. "Miracle drug," one of them had called it. Completely made her forget all her troubles.

That's what I need.

However, unless Rachel has a prescription for it kicking around somewhere, I'm shit out of luck.

I need to go fix things and get rid of the sinkholes that have developed on Rachel's road to True Love. That's the only way I'm getting out of here.

"Here." I hand her an icy can upon returning to her bedroom. At her quizzical look (probably because I'd never been the one to bring *her* a Diet Coke before; it's always the other way around), I just shrug. "Drink it, roll it around on your forehead to get rid of your headache, put it on your heart to ease the hurt. Whatever."

"You're wrong," she says again, like we're still having this conversation. She stares at the lid of the can, tracing the tab with a newly-mangled fingernail. "I loved Eddie."

I sit on the bed opposite her, getting impatient. "You *thought* you loved Eddie. I'll give you that. Humans *think* they're in love all the time."

She arches an eyebrow. "Goddesses don't?"

I sigh. How much to reveal? How much should remain a mystery? Chewing my lip, I give her what I can. "Goddesses—being far more enlightened than humans—don't *think* they are in love when they're not. We know that we either are . . . or we aren't."

"But, you're the Goddess of Love. Doesn't that mean you love everybody? Doesn't that mean that every time you date, or whatever it is you do, that you love who you're with?"

"No. My job is to bring love to others. Not that I don't get it for myself, too, but when it's just not there . . . a little pretending never hurt anyone."

Like with my husband. For a while, pissed as I was at Zeus for forcing my hand, I tried to be happy . . . to be in love. I pretended we were blissfully over-the-top about each other, Hephaestus and I. I needed that. I needed to have hope that one day it might turn into the real thing. Only it didn't work for very long and I soon gave up. But I didn't try to fool myself that it really *was* True Love. I was fully aware I was faking it with everything I had.

Rachel looks more confused than ever.

Suddenly antsy, I get up to pace the room while I talk and reveal secrets I've never told any human before. But, desperate times lead to desperate measures, right? I have to get off this godforsaken plane of existence and back to my home. I have to spill it.

"We fake it," I finally blurt.

"Fake it," Rachel states. "Like orgasms?"

"Right . . . only we *never* fake orgasms. A goddess would never fake that," I say sternly. "We are very good at orgasms."

Rachel snorts, a tiny smirk on her face. "Of course."

"But," I begin again, before I lose my nerve, "we do fake love. Sometimes. When absolutely necessary."

"Why would you fake love?"

"Because," I whisper, avoiding Rachel's eyes, "sometimes the feeling's just not there. And sometimes, you need that feeling more than anything in the universe . . . right at that particular moment." I pause and rub my hand against my belly. Right where the Golden Girdle lays when I wear it. "Sometimes, feeling love is more important than breathing."

Rachel's silence blends with mine, until I can't stand it anymore.

Shaking it off, I whirl around, a tight smile plastered on my perfect lips. "But, we goddesses are smart enough to *know* when we're faking it. We fake on purpose. You humans fake it without realizing it . . . sometimes to the point where you actually so *convince* yourselves you're in love that you keep it up for years on end. When really, all you are is a damned good actress. Then, when you get called on it, or your partner decides they don't want to play anymore, you get pissed. Not hurt. Not sad, like you would with a *real* broken heart. Just ticked off. *Revengeful.*"

Rachel continues to stare, only I can feel the change in her. She's starting to get it. Hope slowly seeps back into my soul. Maybe all is not lost.

Slowly, she rises from her seat.

"I think you're full of crap," she says.

I just blink at her as she pushes past me and slams the bedroom door behind her.

THIRTY-FIVE

Rachel

It was a fine time to become an insomniac.

I lay on that couch staring at the ceiling for hours. And hours. The pendulum of the antique clock that had belonged to my great-grandmother announced with its incessant ticking every single second that passed over those hours, until I was ready to rip it off the wall.

Because lying awake meant thinking.

And thinking was nothing but trouble.

It started out easy enough. I was so mad at Venus . . . so completely irate about her manipulating my life, that I had something to think about that wasn't too difficult. Like ways to burn all her shoes. Or cause her perfectly highlighted hair to fall out in clumps overnight.

But as the anger wore down and gave way to a repetitive replaying of our conversation, I found myself more and more agitated.

She was wrong. She had to be wrong.

I *had* loved Eddie. I *hadn't* wasted two years of my life. Okay, I had, but not because I was faking love or anything. It was a waste because it had turned out I was wrong about him.

It was a waste because I'd given him my heart, my time, my . . . my . . .

I started to tell myself that I'd given him my soul. Only I realized that I hadn't. My soul was intact, because surely if my soul hadn't still been intact, I'd never have felt the guilt I did for sleeping with Jerry. I'd never have thrown myself into volunteer work to fill up time and to avoid having to listen to my soul's urgings that something was still missing from my life.

Because, I realized, as I stared into the blackened living room surrounding me, that's what I'd been avoiding this whole time. I honestly think the guilt had only lasted a little while. It was the emptiness left behind by Eddie being out of my life . . . no, not by *Eddie* being out of my life, but by *love* being out of my life. That's what I missed. That's what I was trying to replace.

In the years leading up to Eddie, I'd seen so much evidence of love . . . the love of my parents, of my brother and his wife, even of my younger sister, Roxanne, and her soon-to-be husband. I'd seen them and I'd been jealous. And when Eddie was with me, spending time with my family, charming them with his wit and good humor, making them—and me—laugh, I'd had everything they had.

It took hours, but I finally realized Venus was right. When Eddie came along, I'd somehow started pretending that I was in love, too. Eddie made it easy. He was a nice guy (before I knew what I now knew). And, I'd pretended to be in love so well, and for so long, that I'd come to believe it. I had completely accepted our "love," our relationship, as being the real thing.

Flopping over on my side on the couch, I poked at a throw pillow lumping up underneath me.

So was Venus right about the reason I was mad after finding out Eddie was married? Was it not because I was heartbroken, as I'd thought for the last two years, but because I'd been pissed at him for blowing the little act I'd been putting on? For wrecking the "love" that had been the focus of my life for two years?

As soon as I'd hung up the phone that night, after talking to Eddie's wife, it was like my life flashed before my eyes . . . not the life I'd led, like happens when you face death, but the life I was *going* to have to lead. The one where I had to confess to my family that, once again, I'd failed at a relationship by picking the wrong guy. The one where humiliation was my middle name. The one where I had to admit that things hadn't been perfect between Eddie and me.

The one where I was once again alone.

Now, with my eyes open and my heart laid as bare as it could be, I could completely see all the little imperfections in my relationship with Eddie. It wasn't just the thing about his cell phone being the only number he ever gave me. It was all the *other* things I'd ignored in an effort to sustain the illusion I'd created that we were in love and would be together forever. Like the fact that I'd never met his family, though he talked about his parents and siblings who supposedly lived just an hour away. I accepted—because ours was "True Love"—when he told me that they were shy and unsocial, but that he had "almost warned them up" enough to meet me.

I'd ignored the fact that I'd never met his friends. He said—while kissing my neck in that one particular spot that drove me wild—that he had no time for friends anymore, because our love was so big that it encompassed his whole life. He didn't need friends anymore.

I'd ignored the fact that he never spent the night at my apartment and he never invited me to his. I accepted his explanation that he had to feed his cat (so he couldn't stay at my place) and that he was such a slob (said with appropriate humbleness and shame) that he would be mortally embarrassed for me to see his apartment, without a second thought.

I had so convinced myself that I loved him, that any little inkling that something was wrong was pushed aside, because,

as Venus so rightly said . . . the feeling of love had become
more important to me than breathing. And accepting that
that love was flawed would have been like taking myself off
oxygen . . . removing my life support.

Pulling my knees up to my chest and holding them as
tightly as I could, I squeezed my eyes shut, willing sleep. I
couldn't think anymore. I couldn't face me anymore.

Because two people had been right about me tonight.

Venus.

And Luke.

And tomorrow I was going to have to do something about
"it."

I was up before Venus the next morning. I hurriedly dressed
in a pair of casual low-riding khakis and a blouse, tugged a
brush through my hair, and decided to skip the makeup. Humility has no fashion sense.

Not knowing what Luke preferred, I picked up bagels *and*
doughnuts to go with the Starbucks coffee. Before I'd left the
house, I'd found his address on the crumbled napkin in my
purse and mapped it out on the Internet. As I drove, I played
the radio as loud as possible to avoid listening to anything going on inside my head that might try to talk some sense into
me. I was practically sick with nerves and wouldn't have
needed much encouragement to turn around and go home.

Luke's house was in the hills above Cameron Creek. Not in
the ritzy-glitzy mansion-packed neighborhood where Hannah's parents lived, but in the still-wooded area to the north.
The house was older and appeared to be "a work in progress"
as evidenced by the various stages of construction visible. A
small opening in the trees framed the water of the Puget
Sound through a hazy layer of clouds.

Smoke curled from the chimney, indicating that Luke was
probably home. I knew from memorizing his on-four-days,
off-two-days rotating schedule—which I did so he wouldn't

catch me by surprise when he showed up at the bank—that he wasn't working today. He didn't answer my knock, though, and as the moments passed and I tried again, I glanced back at my car, wanting more than anything to flee. But, I couldn't. I'd decided during my long hours of soul-searching last night, that I would no longer run scared. I would face up to my feelings and do something about them instead of running from them.

A small gray cat appeared, meowing for some attention. I bent to pet it, welcoming the distraction.

"You looking for Luke, too?" I asked. "Maybe he's around back."

Juggling the coffee and pastries, I headed around the side of the house, along a gravel path. The view out over the water would have been spectacular if it hadn't been so cloudy and overcast in the typical western Washington autumn way.

I smiled down at the cat. "You have a great view here. Wish me luck that I'll be allowed to come back and see it when the weather clears up." My attempt at light humor did nothing to relax me.

As we rounded the corner, I heard the sharp crack of ax against wood. I took the few steps up onto the deck that stretched across the back of the house and reached into the trees overlooking the Sound, and finally spotted him on the other side of the deck. His back was to me and he was fully involved in splitting a huge stack of firewood. He was shirtless, but I was too nervous to give more than a cursory notice to the nicely defined muscles spanning his back and shoulders with each ax swing.

I winced as the blade bit into the hunk of wood again. Hopefully, he wasn't imagining my head on that block as he brought the ax down on it. Only God knew I deserved it after the way I'd treated him.

Sucking in air and courage, I stepped forward and called out to him between swings. "Luke?"

He turned and wiped his brow with the back of his hand. His look was inscrutable.

"I brought breakfast. If you want." I shrugged, not knowing what else to say yet. So much depended on him.

He retrieved a flannel shirt from the deck rail and slipped his arms into it as he mounted the steps. He didn't say anything. And he didn't look at me. Emotions I couldn't put a name to rolled off him in waves.

"Here." I thrust the Starbucks cup at him. "Black. I think that's how you take it."

He accepted the coffee, but he didn't look happy about it. "This doesn't make things right."

"I know." I rolled and unrolled the top of the bag in my fists, mashing it until it threatened to fray in my fingers. "I'm sorry. About yesterday. About everything."

"What's there to be sorry about?" he asked, setting the coffee on the rail beside him, untouched. "If there's nothing between us, there's no reason to be sorry."

"I may . . . I may have been wrong about that." I felt so sick to my stomach, I didn't think I could go on. I wasn't ready yet. I needed time. I needed him to throw me a bone. To let me know that I wasn't here for nothing. "I brought bagels. And doughnuts, too." I thrust the bag into his hand. "Because, you know, I don't know what you like in the morning, plain or sweet. Some people hate sweet stuff in the morning, but I didn't know."

The corner of Luke's mouth looked like it may have quirked up, but I couldn't be sure. "I like sweet in the morning. In more ways than one."

A little choking sound escaped my throat, and my shock must have shown on my face, because he reached out his free hand and wrapped it around my neck, pulling me close. He planted a rough kiss on my forehead before releasing me and retreating with the bag and the coffee.

"I'm here to explain," I said hastily, a bit breathless. His kiss-and-retreat was confusing. It was like he forgave me . . .

but not. Maybe he was at least thinking about it. "If I *can* explain."

"Should I get comfortable?" He sank into a nearby lounge chair, setting the coffee on the deck beside him before digging into the bag. "There better be maple bars in here. My mood might improve fractionally if I have a maple bar."

I breathed a tiny bit easier knowing that I'd at least done *that* right this morning. I may not be able to *say* anything right, but at least his pastry of choice was available.

The cat nosed around under my feet. Feeling like something to anchor me, I picked it up. "Your cat?"

Luke nodded, eyes hooded, though obviously enjoying the pastry. "Her name is Cat."

"Creative."

"She just showed up one day, decided she lived here. I wasn't sure she'd stick around, so it didn't seem worth the effort to pick out a name." Luke opened his eyes and looked at me.

That was as good an opening as any. "I guess that's kind of why I've been reluctant to, uh, name *it*." I gestured back and forth from Luke to myself. "What's going on between us." I'd finally figured out what the "it" was Luke had been talking about yesterday afternoon.

"You think I'm going to leave you."

"I think it's always a possibility." I gave the now-purring cat a stroke behind the ears. "You have a cat you didn't take the time to name, because you don't know where she's come from or where she's headed. I guess it's the same with me. And you."

Luke continued to silently eat his breakfast, letting me go on uninterrupted. His look was still unreadable. Was he prepared to forgive me? Or was he just letting me talk to get a free breakfast before he tossed me out on my ass? I probably deserved the latter.

Maybe he just sensed that if I stopped, I might not very easily be coaxed into finishing.

"I'm not sure where you're coming from," I continued, "or

if you're going to stay. So, I'm not at all sure I want to name what we have."

Luke dropped his feet over the side of the lounge chair and leaned forward, resting his elbows on his knees, his shirttails flapping a little in the breeze. "So, tell me what you do know," he said. "About us. About you. Whatever."

A bit of hope blossomed within me. He wasn't kicking me out. He wanted to hear what I had to say. Maybe there was hope.

I put Cat down and wrapped my arms around myself before taking a deep breath. "Okay. Venus and I talked last night." I started pacing back and forth across the deck planking, mostly so I wouldn't have to look at Luke, or see Luke looking at me. "Venus thinks I was never in love with Eddie. That I was . . . faking it."

A sideways glance at Luke showed his brows raised. "Like faking orgasms?"

I nodded. "Kind of. It's a fact of life," I said. "No matter how much guys hate it, women fake orgasms."

"Not in my bed," Luke muttered, leaning back again, digging in the bag with a frown.

"So I've heard," I muttered back.

He shot me a questioning look.

"Never mind." I went back to pacing. "So, Venus thinks that I was faking love. With Eddie."

"Why would you do that?"

"You've never been a little girl," I said. "You probably wouldn't understand. But, ever since I was small I've watched the people I love *be* in love. My grandparents were in love until the day my grandpa died, and even now, my grandmother still loves him with every fiber of her being. My parents celebrated their thirty-first wedding anniversary just before Eddie and I got together. That's a miracle these days."

Luke nodded, eating a chocolate-covered doughnut at the same time. But I could tell he was listening.

"And, I've watched my brother and his wife, raising a family, doing exactly what I've always wanted to do. And, even my sister," I said, throwing my arms up for emphasis. "Even my *little* sister found the love of her life and is getting married next year." I stopped and faced Luke again. "I looked at all that, and I wanted it, too."

"So far, I'm following you," Luke replied, resting his coffee cup on his thigh. I couldn't help but notice the way he reclined in the lawn chaise was much like his calendar pose. Even down to the bare chest, since he hadn't rebuttoned his shirt. Under other circumstances I might have taken the time to enjoy the view. "But, I don't get the faking part. And faking is kind of serious to a guy."

I smiled and we shared a moment. It made me relax a bit before I continued. "Venus thinks that, um . . . that women who want to have love in their lives will sometimes take the wrong guy and convince themselves they're in love with him. Like, *fake* love until it seems so real they don't know the difference."

"So, she thinks because you saw everyone else in your life as happy and successful at relationships, that you playacted your way into believing you and Eddie were for real?"

"Basically."

"Do you agree?"

Again I threw my hands up in frustration. "I don't know! I didn't think so. I totally blew her off last night. But then, during the night . . . I thought a lot about it." He couldn't know how huge that was to me, that I'd spent the last two years doing everything in my power *not* to think at all.

"And what did you conclude?"

"That maybe she's right. If I was really in love with Eddie, my heart would have been broken when I found out he was married. But, I don't think broken hearts go out and grab the first willing guy and jump into bed with him." My face grew hot at bringing up that sore subject again, but I plunged on anyway. "Venus thinks I was mad at Eddie, not because he broke my heart, but because I was embarrassed and upset that the little dream world I'd built was destroyed. That I was going to have to tell my family and friends that I'd failed again." I looked back at Luke. "I don't really like failure."

"No kidding." His sarcasm was tempered with a bit of a smile. One that I was so grateful for I could have kissed him.

But not yet. I wasn't finished baring my soul yet.

"I do think she was right about that. There were little things I noticed along the way. Red flags, I guess, that should have told me things with Eddie weren't as perfect as they seemed. But, I never talked about them to anyone . . . not my mom, or my sister, or even Hannah. I felt like, if I shared that there might be problems, Eddie would look bad in their eyes, and they might try to talk me out of being with him. Or worse, they'd think badly of me because I chose to be with someone who wasn't perfect . . . or who potentially had something to hide."

"You'd made mistakes before."

"And every time I did, I felt worse and worse. This was like the final straw. If I screwed up another relationship—"

"But you didn't screw up the relationship," Luke corrected. "Eddie did."

"But, I *chose* Eddie. Don't you see? It's like . . . I don't know . . . like buying spoiled milk from the grocery store over and over again, because you never bother to look at the expiration date. After a while, your friends and family just start expecting spoiled milk, and you try really hard not to let it happen again, just so you can prove them wrong."

"So you faked like you were in love with him, so you didn't have to face telling your family that you'd made another mistake."

"Yeah. I think I did." I stared down at the decking, not knowing what else to say.

"So what worries you about us?" Luke casually licked his sticky fingers.

Except that it didn't seem casual at all from my point of view. Sometime during the night, my newfound revelations had given way to something else . . . tentative fantasies of what life could be like with Luke if I just took a chance.

And the licking of sticky fingers was bringing some of those fantasies right back to the forefront of my mind.

I shook my head. I wasn't ready yet. I wasn't sure. "I don't know," I admitted. "One part of me can think of a thousand reasons—worries—about why it wouldn't work with us."

Luke stood and stepped toward me, not quite frowning anymore, but not smiling, either. "And the other part of you?"

I lifted my shoulders so fractionally that I'm sure he didn't even see.

He stopped bare inches away and looked so deeply into my eyes, I started to burn inside. "I think the other part of you knows that what we have between us could be real . . . and that scares you just as much."

I blinked and backed up a step. "Why would that scare me? Wouldn't that be perfect . . . great even?"

"Would it?"

"Why . . . why wouldn't it?" I whispered, confused and feeling like my chest was caving in with the weight of the tension between us.

Luke reached for my hand, and brought it to his chest, laying it flat on the warm, bare skin overlying his heart. "Because if it's real and I let you down, your heart might *really* be broken this time."

Even as my head jerked side to side, tears overflowed and a sob escaped.

Luke leaned forward, pressing his forehead to mine. "Not. Going. To happen."

"How do you *know*?" I practically begged him to reassure me.

"I just do." He tugged me into his arms and I took what he gave, nestling my cheek against his warm skin, wrapping my arms around him under the loose shirt he wore. He was so solid and felt so good, I never wanted to move. "I've never felt this way with anyone, Rachel. This is not a trial run for me."

Mute with emotion, I simply nodded.

After a few minutes, I looked up at Luke's chin. "Have you ever done anything you really, really regretted?"

His eyes were warm as he tipped his head and met my gaze. "Regretted?" He shrugged. "Sure. But, not lately."

As I searched his eyes, maybe for the forgiveness I couldn't yet give myself, the air charged with electricity. By the time Luke lowered his head the last few inches to mine, my breath was ragged and shallow, my heartbeat irregularly loud.

The kiss was soft and sweet. Filled with all the forgiveness I still wasn't sure I deserved, but needed so desperately. He obviously had no clue what he was doing.

The kiss lasted only a moment.

"What about now?" I whispered, terrified of his answer.

Instead, he grinned broadly. "Nope. Still no regrets."

After a few minutes of soothing me and allowing me to get used to the idea of being in his arms, Luke set me away from him. "Don't move."

I nodded and watched him go retrieve my coffee cup from where I'd left it on the deck table. He brought it back to me.

"Drink."

I took the cup from him, but raised a questioning eyebrow at him before drinking.

"I have a feeling you didn't drink or eat anything before coming up here to spill your guts."

I flushed. "No."

He grinned. "Bet you didn't sleep last night, either."

"Guilty."

"Good. I didn't, either," he admitted. He took my hand and started toward the open French doors leading into his home. "I decided I'm not willing to wait for months until you figure out that I am who I say who I am. So we're going to do something about it."

Just before we reached the house, I paused. "Can I just have a minute?" I asked. "I left the apartment this morning without telling Venus. I should let her know I'm okay."

He nodded. "I'll go start a pot of coffee."

Hannah picked up the phone when it rang. "Where *are* you?"

Venus must have been *really* worried, or have been very convincingly worried when she called Hannah anyway, because my best friend never got out of bed before noon on Saturdays—except for the occasional Saturday-Only Sale. I reassured her—and Venus, who apparently, for my sake, had set aside any remaining animosity she had toward Hannah—that I was fine.

"We're just going to talk," I said, after briefly explaining to her what had transpired since I left the bank yesterday afternoon.

"Talk, my ass!" Hannah exclaimed. "You've finally given in."

"No, I haven't," I protested. "It's only nine A.M."

"Sex doesn't have a happy hour, Rachel. You don't have to wait until after noon like drinking. You can have sex anytime you want. In fact, the more the better—"

"Hannah!" I shouted to get her attention. She quieted down. "I just . . . Luke seems okay with things. Now. I told him what happened."

"Good. I knew he wasn't as shallow as you thought he was."

Hannah had no clue how really wrong I'd been about Luke's shallowness.

"Rachel? Don't let him get away." Hannah's voice was serious. An unusual tone for her. "He's a good guy."

"I know," I said. "But I don't know if I'm ready for . . . whatever."

"Just give it a chance."

I didn't promise, because I wasn't sure I could keep that promise. Luke was obviously a great guy . . .

I just couldn't get over that feeling that the other shoe had to drop sometime.

"You need a crash course in the life of Luke Stanton."

I laughed. "A crash course?"

"Yep. I'm going to come completely clean. Even if it takes all damn day."

I shot him a worried glance. "Do you have so much to come clean about that it could take all damn day?"

"Let's hope not," Luke said, sidling closer and planting a hand firmly against the small of my back. "'Cause we have better things to do."

I let him kiss me again, trying to remember when I used to be daring. Believe it or not, there was a time when I would have been the one tugging the guy to *me* to plant a big one on *his* mouth. When I was the one to initiate sex. When I used to be brazenly confident in my ability to turn on a man.

Just as I felt my bravery return, Luke broke the kiss off, leaving me hanging.

"Not yet, though," he said, stepping away. "We have a job to do."

I turned away so that he wouldn't notice how much he affected me. "A job?"

Luke swept a hand around the room we were standing in. "To reveal my house . . . and my life."

I blinked. "Your life?"

"Yep." Luke took my hand. "I can see those wheels turning in your head, wondering what my deep dark secret is. So, we're going to unearth any secrets I may have hidden."

"Luke, you don't have to—"

"No arguing. My soul will be laid bare for you."

I couldn't keep from snorting as he dragged me over to the entertainment center against one of the living room walls. Videos and DVDs cluttered the shelves.

"Obviously, I'm not a perfect housekeeper," he said, taking

a swipe at the top shelf and showing me the gray dust frosting his finger. "My mother gives me a cleaning lady for my birthday and Christmas, and anytime she starts to feel the need for snowshoes due to the depth of the dust. I'm also not Mr. Organized. I don't alphabetize my movies or care if they're sorted by genre."

"That would be excessive," I agreed.

"I also don't own any porn," Luke continued in mock—or not so mock, I couldn't tell—seriousness. "My favorite movies include *Die Hard*—one, two, and three—*Lord of the Rings*, and *The Matrix*."

"Typical guy."

"There *are* a few surprises, however," he continued. "Some Disney classics. *Shrek* and *Ice Age*. For when the nieces and nephew come over, of course."

"Of course."

He opened all the cabinet doors, to let me view the contents, which I did, out of curiosity, but also because Luke's playful mood was finally relaxing me.

"No porn."

"No porn," I agreed.

"Unless you *want* me to get porn," he added.

I nodded. "Unless I— *What?*"

He flashed me a grin. "Gotcha." He pressed a quick kiss to my lips, then stepped back and winked. "Onward to the next stop on the Honesty Express."

I laughed, mostly to get my heart started again, and allowed myself to be pulled along. It had been a long time since I'd felt such easy intimacy. It felt good.

On the way down the hall, Luke opened his coat closet, to demonstrate that there were no "skeletons." We checked out a spare bedroom, neatly furnished, but sparse. And then we peered into an office, which kind of looked like an exploded office supply store.

"Again, neatness is not my forte, as you can see."

"If it makes you feel better," I said, "I leave wet towels on the bathroom floor sometimes."

"Oh, man." Luke cringed. "Not sure that'll work for me."

My surprised look earned me another kiss and a "Just kidding."

As we continued, I fought the voice in my head that emphasized all the reasons I should just give up and fall for Luke. The fact that he wasn't a perfectionist. The fact that he wasn't a neat freak—which worked for me, since, besides the wet towel thing, I'd been known to heap my clean laundry in the armchair in my bedroom, pulling out clothes as the need arose until there was no actual need to put any clothes away at all. Luke didn't seem like the kind of guy who'd come unglued if I didn't keep an immaculate house.

Not that I was thinking of keeping house with him, I told the overeager voice in my head, who was getting way ahead of herself.

"And finally, the Chamber of Secrets," Luke announced in an ominous voice.

The final room at the end of the hall was Luke's bedroom.

I covered my sudden hum of nerves with humor. "Oh," I said lightly, stepping into the room and trying to appear nonchalant. "Harry Potter lives here?"

"No, but I have been known to work magic in this room," Luke said with a grin and a wink.

"I've heard," I blurted out, then clamped my mouth shut in horror. "Oh, God. Forget that."

It was Luke's turn to look surprised. "Is that so?"

"Never mind," I said, pulling my hand out of his and getting as far away from him as I could. "So, what's in this closet?" I asked, changing the subject.

Leaning around me—and purposely leaning *into* me—Luke opened the closet. He was hard and muscular in all the right places. And warm. It had been far too long since I'd felt warm like that. And that little taste of warm out on the deck a little bit ago? I was thinking that probably wasn't enough to satisfy me.

For the next ten minutes, Luke pulled every item out of his closet. He didn't have anything incriminating . . . no priceless artwork to indicate thieving tendencies, no bronzed baby shoes to indicate parenthood, no lace-covered photo album of OUR FIRST YEAR OF MARRIAGE.

"Luke, really," I said, when he began taking boxes off the top shelf. "I'm really okay. Honest."

He raised a doubtful eyebrow.

"I swear. I believe that you aren't a cross-dresser and you don't appear to have a wife, a secret love child or a live-in girlfriend."

"Yet."

Before I could stop him, he had a hand on my cheek and warm lips on mine.

God, he was a good kisser.

The best ever.

Made me wonder what else Luke might be the best at. Which again, brought back Gwen's voice in my head, raving about the skill of Luke's tongue—which I could now vouch for—and multiple orgasms.

Too soon! I thought, pulling away quite suddenly. Although my lips were more reluctant than my brain and tried to stay behind.

Forcing myself to turn around, I focused on the rest of the room. An involuntary glance at Luke told me the kiss had definitely affected him as much as it had me. I just needed to breathe a minute. Focus on something nonthreatening to my sanity.

Beside the bed sat a pair of heavy black boots, nesting in yellow fireproof pants with suspenders draped over the sides, ready to jump into at a moment's notice. The matching coat hung on a peg on the wall.

"You're prepared," I said, gesturing to the gear standing by.

The minute Luke was called to save someone's home . . . or their life . . . he could be dressed instantly, night or day.

"When I'm not on duty, I don't get called out often," he said. "But when I do . . ."

There was something touching about that. Definitely not the selfish guy Harry had ranted about.

"You chose an admirable career."

He just shrugged, humble.

Behind me was a dresser covered with framed photographs. Leaning down, I examined them. An older couple was featured in one of them, the woman obviously Luke's mother, with matching blond hair and ocean blue eyes. She smiled out of the photo with Luke's smile. The man was Luke's stepfather, I guessed, surmising that the photo was fairly recent, and Luke's father had been dead for a long time. There were pictures taken at the beach and in the mountains, of a little blond boy and two older, dark-haired girls . . . probably Luke and his "ugly stepsisters." They weren't, of course, ugly, and I smiled, remembering how my siblings and I traded insults as a form of affection.

The last photo was of Luke in his fire gear, a small boy in his arms . . . a beautiful brunette by his side, practically glowing.

My heart stopped, my shoulders sagging under the weight of the discovery. I knew it! Or, I should have known, with *my* history. He was married. That woman was looking at him like the sun rose and set at his command. And the little boy was blond. Just like Luke, who could only be . . . his father.

I whirled around, shoving the picture in his direction. "Who is that? And don't tell me it's not your wife, because I won't believe you."

Luke's mouth twitched. "That's not my wife . . . that would be me." He pointed to himself.

"No kidding." Covering up my devastation with sarcasm seemed my only defense. "I don't mean you."

"Oh, then you must mean Austin." He pointed to the little boy in his arms. "My nephew."

I knew it! He had a— "*Nephew?*"

He nodded. "This was his preschool graduation day. His dad was out of town, and Austin is completely hooked on firefighters, so I agreed to come in full gear to take his mind off his dad not being there. I was his cool uncle."

"Oh." I frowned. Reaching out a hand, I tapped the woman in the picture. "And I suppose you're going to tell me this is—"

"Gina," Luke said, "my stepsister."

"Ah-ha! Your . . . stepsister?"

Luke nodded, his lips pressed together to keep from laughing. "Regina. My stepsister. Austin's mom." He pulled his cell phone from his pocket and flipped it open. "I have her on speed dial. Should I call her to vouch for me?"

"Uh. No." I tugged the picture out of his hand and turned to replace it on the dresser, cursing myself under my breath. I was so lame. "I'm fine now."

Luke laughed, which only made me feel lamer. "Obviously you aren't fine yet," he said, pulling me back up against him.

"About three weeks ago, I tried to get my mother to tell me she was sorry she married my dad. Because it would have given me an excuse to stop wanting a relationship."

"Bet that went over well," Luke replied, stroking his thumb along my forearm.

"Not really."

"I'll get you there, I promise. *Wanting* a relationship, not trying to make excuses why not to have one." Luke let go and turned me around. "Maybe going through the dresser will help. Because otherwise you'll keep worrying that I wear women's underwear."

"I never worried about that." I worried he had someone *else* living here who wore women's underwear . . . like a woman.

He ignored me and opened the top drawer.

Nibbling at my thumbnail, I tried not to be completely mortified as Luke showed me that the only things in his drawers were boxer shorts and T-shirts, socks and long johns.

"Better?" Luke asked, finally turning around, struggling not to laugh, probably at the stricken look on my face.

"No. Now I'm embarrassed."

"Don't be," Luke said. "I'm glad you came."

I sighed. "It wasn't easy."

"You know why?" Luke put his arms around me. I shook my head. "Because you really are worried this might be real. I get that."

"Do you? Because I don't. A sane person would *want* it to be real." I sighed and looked up at him, our faces so close we shared our breath. "I don't want you to be the wrong guy," I admitted.

"That's good. Means you *do* want me to be the right guy."

I nodded, the truth of his words choking off my voice.

"Give me a chance," Luke said, pressing a kiss to my forehead.

Forehead kissing wasn't enough. I was tired of . . . of running scared. Of pretending I wasn't attracted to Luke so that I wouldn't feel bad telling him no over and over.

Well, I *was* attracted to Luke. He was hot. He was nice. He was fun to be around. A very wise ex-girlfriend of Luke's had told me that if I looked for things to go wrong, the Universe would accommodate me. But if I looked for things to go right . . .

So I took the plunge, turning my face up to his and taking from him the kiss that I wanted more than anything right now. I felt his lips curve into a smile when his mouth met mine, and it made me smile, too.

It didn't take long for the kiss to escalate to the point where I was ready to push him back on the bed and take more than just his mouth. Apparently aware of the change, Luke broke it up with a groan and backed off, breathing just as heavily as I was.

"As much as I'd love to take this further . . ." he said, hands held up in surrender.

"Oh. I thought . . ." My face flushed at how close I'd just come to attacking him. I was an idiot.

"No *sorry* necessary," Luke laughed. "We'd just better stop . . . for now. I have a feeling we need more to sustain us than doughnuts and coffee to see us through this day."

Luke headed out the door leaving me alone in his bedroom.

Hot. Bothered.

And thinking maybe he was right about the sustenance thing. I suddenly felt like I had two years worth of suppressed hormones just itching to bust out of the prison I'd held them in.

Two hours later, we'd eaten an early lunch of nuked leftover pizza, drunk most of a bottle of wine (even though it wasn't yet noon), and sat on the living room floor against the couch, with our legs stretched out under the coffee table. We'd talked about our jobs, our hobbies (well, he talked about his hobbies and I talked about the stuff that filled my time), and our families. Finally, there was a lull in the conversation. Even that was comfortable.

"To us," Luke toasted, tipping his wineglass in my direction.

I met his eyes, floated on the sheer blue of them for a moment, and then sighed. Now that my libido had died down a bit, I was suddenly unsure again. I'd told him yesterday I didn't do casual sex, and I meant it. So the only way I could sleep with him would be to have a relationship with him. And, I just wasn't sure I could do that. "Luke—"

"Nope," he said, never taking his eyes off me. "I'm not taking no for an answer. Yeah, your past sucked. Everyone's does."

"Yours doesn't," I reminded him. "You have two ex-girlfriends who basically say I'd be a fool to let you go."

"Brilliant women I've dated," he said, with half a grin. "But, that's only two out of four. You haven't talked to Sarah. And Harry didn't recommend me."

"Harry wouldn't reco.nmend anyone but herself."

Luke laughed. "Probably not. But, there you go . . . I made a shitty choice dating her, didn't I? I fully admit I dated her for sex."

I raised an eyebrow. "I thought you said you dated her to give her a chance."

"No, I said I *kept* dating her because I felt I should give her a chance. I believe I mentioned attraction as the reason I dated her in the first place. That would be the sex part."

"Well," I said, touching my wineglass to his, with a soft clink. "Here's to *honesty*."

Luke narrowed his eyes in amusement, fully aware that I'd not-so-sneakily averted the toast he'd proposed . . . to "us."

"So, I've been recommended by two out of three exes surveyed. Not bad odds. But, I bet they didn't have *only* good things to say about me, right?"

I shrugged, my mind flashing back to my conversations with Raven and Gwen.

"The point is," Luke continued, "I'm not perfect. I can be a slob. I don't always finish projects in a timely manner." He stabbed a thumb toward some stacks of tile on the counter in the kitchen he'd been working on for several months. "Especially if there's any mediocre reality TV on to distract me."

I grinned. "Well, heck, no wonder you like me. My life *is* mediocre reality TV."

Luke grew serious and leaned closer. "This is more than 'like,' Rachel."

I bit my lip and didn't say anything. What could I say? I had no clue how to put into words what I was starting to feel for him. It was sexual, yeah. His smile, his hard firmness, the smell of him. That was all just calling to me. But there was more. I think.

"Tell him you like him, too."

I blinked and narrowed my eyes at Luke. His lips hadn't moved, but—

"Did you say something?" I asked.

"I said, this is more than *like,* and I think it's more than that for you, too."

"Luke, I—"

"Tell him it *is* like that for you. Tell him you can't stop thinking about him. Get on with it already. We're almost there."

I sat bolt upright and stared around the living room, dropping the wineglass onto the coffee table. I'd apparently had more than enough. "Did you hear that?" I asked Luke. "A voice?"

He shook his head. "Are you all right?"

"I'm—"

"Get a grip on yourself before you scare him off," the same voice hissed in my head.

Venus!

I shot up off the floor. "Uh, my cell phone." I gestured toward my purse on the counter. "I think it's, uh, ringing."

"I didn't hear anything."

"No, it's a . . . really quiet ring." I dashed for my purse and dug out my phone. "I'll just . . . I'll take it outside."

I couldn't get out the door fast enough. My hands were shaking as I dialed my apartment. I couldn't risk talking to her out loud, in case Luke decided to watch me from the window. Besides that was just too weird.

Venus waited three rings before picking it up—like she hadn't been sitting right there.

"What are you doing?" I snarled at her. "Who do you think you are, Cyrano de bloody Bergerac?"

"Who's that?"

"A guy who— It doesn't matter who he is." I growled into the phone. "What were you doing in my head?"

"Trying to make sure you don't blow it," Venus replied.

"You only get so many chances. You already almost blew it with that picture thing."

"You were spying!"

Venus's shrug was obvious even through the phone lines. "Well, duh. It's my job. I'm the fairy godmother. You're the client."

"No. *Clients* have choices," I snapped. "I am an unwitting victim of a naughty goddess and her pigheaded ass of a father."

I squealed when a warning bolt of lightning struck the ground fifty feet away. The simultaneous thunder rumble and subsequent torrential downpour had me pressing myself against the side of the house. "Shit!"

The French doors opened and Luke stuck his head out, staring in surprise at the sudden rainstorm. "Rachel? Are you okay? What was—"

"Nothing," I called back, squinting at him through the rain. "I'm fine. Venus just found some cellulite on her thighs and she's a bit freaked out."

"Rachel!" Venus screamed into the phone. "You take that back right this minute."

"Too bad," I said sweetly, turning back to the phone. "Luke's already back in the house. He'll forever think you have cottage-cheese thighs."

"That was just cruel," she pouted.

"No more cruel than *spying* on me." I leaned farther into the outer wall of the house, as the gutters started overflowing, pouring over onto me. I was too pissed off to be making any apologies to the Big Guy, though. He could just let loose his worst for all I cared.

"I have to keep track of my investment," Venus argued.

"Don't you mean *my* investment? You live rent-free, eat my food, use my gas."

"Twin bed, boring food, and completely uncool car. Oh, by the way, Luke would *love* the car in your parents' garage. You really need to retrieve it and ditch the Subaru. Insurance in case you start to bore him."

"Venus."

"What?"

"Stay out of my head," I warned. "Stop telling me what to say to Luke."

"Fine. I'll stop telling you what to say. I just want to remind you that the sooner you get this little love match solidified, the sooner I'll be out of your hair."

As heavenly as that thought was— "You are to stay out of my head. No more spying."

"But, Rachel," Venus whined, "that's the only fun I have. There's nothing on TV today and the fireworks are just starting between you two."

"They are *not*."

"I saw you earlier. You were ready to rip his clothes right off. There'll be fireworks."

"No, there won't."

"Yes, there will. Want to bet?"

"*No*, I don't want to bet."

"Chicken?"

"No!"

"Fine, I bet you that new pair of Kenneth Cole pumps I've been eyeing."

"Fine," I said. "There won't be anything happening between Luke and me and if it takes a pair of shoes to prove it to you—"

"Of course, that means I get to stick around to be sure you don't lie about stripping down—"

"Stop it!" I closed my eyes and counted to ten . . . okay, only five. I *needed* my anger to get it through her thick, blond skull. "I banish you from my head, Venus. I mean it. No more listening in to our conversations."

"But—"

"*Banished*, Venus. Do you understand me? Stay. Out. Of my. Head."

"Fine," she snapped. "But when you say something stupid—"

"I'll deal with it."

"When the *fireworks* start and you can't remember how to do it because it's been so long since you got it on—"

"Venus. There will be no fireworks."

"Good luck with that. I'll go pick out a dress to wear with my new shoes." She slammed the phone down, nearly taking out my eardrum.

Ohhhh! She thought she was so damn smart. Just because I might admit that Luke could possibly be the guy for me, didn't mean I was going to jump right into bed with him. I wouldn't be pushed. Venus could pick out all the dresses she wanted, but she'd be going barefoot. And Zeus had another thing coming if he thought I was going to do whatever his spoiled brat of a daughter wanted me to, just so he got the satisfaction of watching her squirm.

"What the hell did I ever do to you?" I shouted at the sky—having no clue where Mount Olympus might be located. This wasn't only Venus's fault. Zeus's daughter might be the psychotic one, but it was his fault she was here in the first place. "You're an even bigger control freak than she is, you know that?"

If it was actually possible, it rained *harder* as I made a mad dash back up onto the deck. Just as I got the door open and started to duck through, the gutter above me cut loose, dumping a gallon—or twelve—of water on my head.

"Venus okay?" Luke started, gaping when he turned to see me standing in the doorway looking, I'm sure, like a drowned puppy. He set down the wineglass he was refilling, his eyes darting to the front of my blouse, then quickly back to my face.

I looked down and groaned. My white blouse and bra were

now a rather see-through gray, plastered to my chest with rainwater. There was nothing much left to the imagination.

On top of that, I was now cold. And when women get cold . . .

I quickly crossed my arms and nodded, trying to smile. "She's fine. You know how those high-maintenance women worry so much about their appearances. Uh, so, I don't suppose you have any spare shirts around?"

Mutely, Luke nodded, his eyes going dark as he watched me dripping on his carpet. Finally, he backed away a few steps, then turned and headed toward his room.

By the time he took his eyes off me, my heart was doing a little jumpy thing in my chest. Hormones again. I rubbed my arms to try to warm up and did a quick nipple check again to find that they were still broadly at attention. No problem, I thought. I'll just get into a dry shirt, and then I'll go home. Luke and I can get together later. When I'm dry. Not so . . . exposed. And that would solve the problem of whether I was going to sleep with him or not. Since I wouldn't be here, the answer would be not.

However, when Luke came back into the room, carrying a white dress shirt, he didn't look like he had any intention of letting me go home.

No fireworks! I told myself. Venus is *not* going to win this round.

Only my body didn't seem to be listening, because as Luke crossed over to me, I got warm—hot, even—in places that weren't previously warm at all. In fact, I had started shivering, and I wasn't at all sure it was from being wet.

It was like little sparklers going off . . . the prelude to the *big* fireworks display.

I was just . . . *wet*, I told myself. From the rain.

Because it couldn't have been the bold way that Luke was staring at me. It couldn't be because my feelings for him had kind of outted themselves in the last hour.

It had to be the rain . . . and all that talk of fireworks.

That was it. Really.

Not the look of heat in Luke's eyes as he padded barefoot across the carpet.

Not the way he leaned into me when he reached me, pressing me into the cool glass at my back, or the way he palmed the dripping hair off my forehead, tipping my head back for easier access.

It wasn't how he kissed the rainwater off my cheeks . . . my eyelids . . . my nose . . . that ridge along my collarbone . . .

By the time he finally—*thirstily*—captured my mouth, tasting like wine and warmth, I was willing to admit I was wrong.

There *were* fireworks.

And the fireworks were so good, I knew I wouldn't even cry over the two-hundred-dollar check I'd be writing for Venus's new shoes.

Because I was suddenly getting my brazenness back, and now that we were completely alone, without any meddling fairy godmothers, maybe waiting wasn't *really* what I wanted to do.

Wait—

I pulled back and scrutinized Luke for signs of tampering. Not that I'd know what someone might look like who had been tampered with by fairy godmother magic. But, I knew Venus's desire for shoes, and anything was possible.

"Do you feel all right?" I questioned. "Not light-headed or anything?"

"Any light-headedness," he murmured, as he dove back down in the direction of my neck, "is a result of kissing you."

"Mmmm." I closed my eyes and tipped my head back, completely forgetting about Venus.

Finally, with a groan, Luke fisted his hands in my shirt front, the backs of his finger brushing against my now no longer cold, but still fully aroused nipples. "We need to get away from the window."

"Oh." I let him guide me toward the fireplace sneaking a few kisses along the way.

We stopped and Luke dropped my replacement shirt to the floor. "You don't need that."

"I don't?"

He shook his head and began unbuttoning my blouse. One button . . .

At . . .

A . . .

Time.

"Wait." I glanced down at his hands, where his knuckles brushed my belly, raising goose bumps. "I'm not . . . sure."

Luke dipped his head until he caught my eye. "I'm sure enough for both of us," he whispered. "Rachel."

I looked up.

"I love you."

And as my heart clutched in my chest, suddenly . . . I *was* sure.

And when he kissed me again, I forgot all about exes and liars and cheaters, and just remembered—whether because it was real, or because I wanted it so badly—what it felt like to be cared for, to be . . .

Loved.

Tossing my wet shirt to the floor, Luke reached around me to unhook my bra. I was too busy unbuttoning his jeans to notice that I was now nearly naked in front of him. The first man I'd been naked with in a very, very long time. I was glad I'd waited for him.

We made quick work of the rest of our clothes, Luke remembering to snag a condom from his jeans pocket before I flung them onto the couch.

He held it up with a wink and a sly smile.

"Feeling lucky when you got up this morning?" I asked.

"Not until I saw you standing there all wet and beautiful."

He stepped up to me, put a hand on my butt, and pulled me flush against him. He was hot and hard and ready.

So was I.

Wrapping my arms around his neck, I gave a little leap and wrapped my legs around his waist. Luke let out a laugh and resettled me more comfortably pressed up against the hard length of his erection.

"A little more eager now, are you?"

"Maybe," I replied, leaning over to lick his earlobe.

"I'm going to have to make sure you get caught in the rain more often."

He took a few steps forward and boosted me onto the countertop. I yelped when I landed on the cold tile.

"Too heavy for you?" I guessed, wiggling a bit until it no longer felt like I was sitting on ice.

"Nope. Just needed free hands for this." He tore open the condom package and rolled it into place. "And for this." He reached out and cupped my breasts in his palms, rolling over my aching nipples with his thumbs.

I reached out to kiss him, then wrapped my fingers around him. "That's a mighty fine rig you have there, Mr. March."

He moaned, pushing against me. "Rachel, I won't be able to go slow. Not this time."

I grinned against his mouth. "As long as you have more condoms, I have all the time in the world."

And with that, he stepped up, lit the fuse, and we experienced the fireworks together.

Later that afternoon, I padded around Luke's kitchen in my underwear and one of his oversized T-shirts . . . and felt like I belonged there. As we cooked up some bacon and eggs for an early dinner, he took every opportunity to drop kisses on my neck, until I finally gave up trying to stir the scrambled eggs and just draped my arms around his neck.

"Are you still sure?" I asked, unable to believe even after an incredible afternoon—Venus-free, I might add—that my Prince Charming was real after all.

"Positive," he murmured into the neckline of my T-shirt, which was dipping—or being pushed—precariously low on my chest. "Even more positive than before, which was pretty damn positive."

He nibbled at a spot an inch away from my nipple, until I was ready to explode again.

"Luke," I nudged him up, really needing to talk to him. "I . . . be serious a minute."

"I've never been more serious in my life," he said. And I knew he was telling the truth.

So would I.

"I'm serious, too," I started, suddenly very aware of what I was committing to. "I've never . . . I mean, I think . . ."

"You love me, too?" he ventured with a grin that could have seduced a PMSing woman into giving up chocolate.

I nodded. Very slowly.

His eyes darkened. And, his thumb found my nipple again. "Then why was it we decided to leave a perfectly good bed to make dinner?"

"Because we need more sustenance. The last sustenance wore off," I said, huskily, more than a little grateful that he hadn't made me pour my whole heart out all at once. The tightrope I was walking was precarious.

"I think I was wrong about that," he said, pressing me up against the counter—the same one we'd started on—so that I could see, or feel, how much *he* really didn't need any more sustenance to get the job done.

But I needed to say what I needed to say. Before I got any deeper into . . . whatever this was I was getting deeper into. Because I knew that once I was in all the way, I wouldn't be climbing out again . . . nor would I want to.

"Wait."

"Hmmm?" Luke trailed lazy kisses in the spot below my ear

that drove me wild. One of many spots he'd discovered in the last few hours.

"I want . . . I'm not . . ." I tried to ignore his tongue encircling my earlobe, but it was nearly impossible. I'd now had The Luke Experience, as Gwen had termed it. All the mind-blowing, toe-tingling, and, yes, multiorgasmic sex, I could want—at least for one day. I knew what he could do with that tongue, and it wasn't a useful tool for promoting concentration in a woman.

I finally pushed him away. About two inches. But that was enough to make him listen to me.

"I . . . I've made a decision," I started.

"I hope that decision involves coming back to bed with me, and remaining there for a very, very long time," Luke answered. "We still have a few condoms left."

I tried to glare, but truthfully, having a man desire you so much that he can't get enough of you even after all day in bed, isn't much conducive to anger. But, I still had to tell him of my decision.

"No. Not yet anyway," I added at the crestfallen look he gave me. "Listen. I decided I'm not going to do the last interview." I walked away from him, knowing that I really needed to say what was on my mind before I chickened out. "There's no need, really. I believe that you are who you say you are. And even if you aren't," I said, turning back around to look at Luke, hardly daring to believe he was mine if I wanted him, "I have to trust sometime. Nothing Sarah could say would influence my decision."

Luke's face morphed into a frown. He appeared deep in thought, his forehead creased. Finally, he walked over and turned off the burner on the stove. Taking my hand, he led me into the living room and planted me firmly on the couch.

Silently, and with rising panic, I watched him build up the fire again. The rain still fell in torrents outside the windows, whether from Zeus's continued temper tantrum, or just typical

Pacific Northwest weather, I couldn't tell. The smell of bacon was suddenly making me nauseous, and I hugged myself, just now noticing the chill in the room. I had no clue what was going on . . . but it couldn't be good.

Luke finished up with the fire and came over to join me on the couch. He didn't touch me, but settled sideways, facing me. If he hadn't looked so serious, I'd have been all over him again, tempting as he was in navy boxers and nothing else.

"Rachel," Luke finally said, not meeting my eyes, but staring at the pattern on the couch as if it were fascinating, "I want you to talk to Sarah."

It wasn't what I'd expected him to say. "It doesn't matter, Luke. Really. Whatever happened between you—"

"Was a long time ago. I know." He looked up at me and I could see the sadness in his eyes. "But, you asked me earlier if I'd ever done anything I regret. And . . . I regret what I did to Sarah."

THIRTY-SIX

Venus

Isn't she home yet?" Hannah bursts into the bedroom.

"No, she's not," I say, quickly shoving my Golden Girdle back into its box and slamming the dresser drawer. "Don't you knock?"

She dangles a set of keys from her fingers. "Don't need to. Why isn't she home? Has she called?"

"I don't know. And no."

Frowning, Hannah plops down in the reading chair by the window and grinds the afghan fringe between her fingers. "I've shopped every store in town, had a manicure, a pedicure, my hair done, and . . . and then shopped some more. What can they be doing that's taking so long?"

I shoot her an incredulous look. "How about exactly what we've been trying to get her to do for the last couple of months?"

"You think? God, I hope she's okay. If he hurts her—"

"I don't get you," I interrupt, turning back to filling my open suitcase. There's a better than good chance I'll be out of here tonight and I'm not leaving behind my Marc Jacobs or Versace, just because I'm going back to Goddess Land. At least I hope I am. And I am not in the mood to deal with Hannah's floundering belief in the rightness of Rachel and Luke. "This morning, you were telling her not to let him go. Sure they were going to get together. And now that they have obviously been 'getting together' all afternoon, *now* you're suddenly not sure?"

"You don't know Rachel like I do," Hannah says, testily. "She's . . . fragile."

"You didn't seem too concerned about that this morning."

"I wasn't thinking clearly. I was . . . I was surprised she was with him. Wonder what changed her mind?"

"Me."

"Yeah. I don't get that. How could you convince her to do something I haven't been able to convince her to do for two years?"

"I'm special."

"Special, my ass," she mutters. Suddenly she's standing next to me, watching me tuck my lingerie into my suitcase. "What are you doing?"

"Packing."

"You're leaving?"

"As soon as Rachel and Luke fall in love—" I snap my mouth shut before I say too much.

I glance at my watch and then back at my now nearly full suitcase. Why am I still here? That's the only question I have. I don't get it. Rachel was ready to rock with Luke when I talked to her on the phone. I know she was. I started packing right away, knowing that the minute she finally let herself go and fell in love, I'd be feeling that tingly feeling I get when it's time for me to move on.

Only it never came.

Something wasn't right.

"What do you mean you'll leave when Rachel falls in love with Luke?"

I shrug. "Nothing. Just that she won't need me once she's

got Luke." And, according to Rule #521, as soon as Rachel makes a firm commitment to her Prince Charming, I'll be free to go.

I rub hopefully at a spot on my left arm that suddenly feels tingly. But, it's just an itch.

"She didn't need you in the first place."

Sighing, I turn to face Hannah, who has her hands on her hips and looks like the fact that I'm breathing is seriously pissing her off. "Look, I know you don't like me, and that's fine, because I don't much like you, either. But, I had a job to do here . . . I mean, I came here to help Rachel out, to help her see that Luke is the right guy for her—"

"But how could you know that before you even got here?" Hannah demands. "There's something very fishy about you, Venus. And, I want to know what it is."

She's driving me crazy, I swear. "Nothing's fishy about me. I'm just . . . good at helping people fall in love. It's a gift. What can I say? When Rachel's happy, I'll be happy." Hopefully atop Mount Olympus.

"That's all well and good, but—"

Suddenly Hannah pauses and we both turn toward the sound of a key scraping in the front door lock.

Shoving her out of the way, I dash to the living room in time to greet Rachel . . . who looks like a well-satiated cat after a meal of tasty mouse. For a minute, her eyes just dance between me and Hannah, who gives me a good jab between the shoulder blades for nearly knocking her over.

"What?" Rachel asks, her dreamy look never faltering.

"Where have you been?" I snap, then grunt when I get poked again by Hannah.

"I thought you weren't worried about her," she accuses.

"I wasn't," I reply. "I just . . ." I turn back to Rachel. "You've been gone for *hours*. You should have called."

"I had shoe shopping to do." With an even bigger grin, she shoves a shopping bag into my arms.

Inside is a box with the Kenneth Cole pumps I bet her.

"But . . ."

"You were right. There *were* fireworks. Lots of them."

"But . . . I . . . I'm . . ." *Still here.*

Suddenly I need to be alone.

Ten minutes later, Rachel knocks tentatively at the bedroom door, before pushing it inward.

"You okay?"

My head involuntarily lurches back and forth as I continue tapping my newly Italian leather shod toes together like Dorothy hoping to get to Kansas.

"Something's wrong," I finally whisper, giving my toes another sharp rap, and then peering over Rachel's shoulder to make sure Hannah is gone. "Something's not right. I don't even feel the overwhelming joy that comes from owning a pair of fabulous new shoes."

Rachel's face brightens as she comes in the room and sits at the foot of the bed. Planting a hand on my feet—presumably to stop the tapping that is even beginning to annoy *me*—she bends down to catch my attention. "Everything is perfect," she says. "You were totally right about Luke." She laughs. "You'd have been so proud of me."

I open my mouth to correct her, but she just keeps going.

"Why do you think I forked out hard-earned money for those shoes, for crying out loud? There were fireworks. And then more fireworks!"

In spite of the boulder of doom resting between my shoulder blades, I smile back. "That good?"

"Soooo good. His great kissing skills are *far* surpassed by his . . . other skills."

We share a brief laugh.

And then it's time to burst her bubble. "Something's still wrong."

"It can't be—"

I jump up from the bed, kicking the pumps off. All they're

doing is reminding me that, fireworks or not, Rachel hasn't completed whatever she needs to complete in order for me to get the hell out of here. She hasn't fully committed to Luke.

"It's not," I say firmly. "Now, tell me everything."

"I'm not kissing and tell—"

"Not about the sex. Although," I add as an aside, "if you want to document that in a diary and give it to me for safe-keeping, I'm always up for more exciting reading material."

"Venus!"

"Okay, okay." It's ten paces to the door and back, and I figure if I pace and talk at the same time, the answer will come to me. "Okay. So you and Luke got it on."

Rachel cringes. "Well, not quite that crassly."

"Okay, you had sex."

"Made love," she corrects.

I stop pacing. "Did you use that word?"

"Love?"

I notice that she blinks and doesn't quite meet my eyes. *"Rachel?"*

"Luke told me he loves me," she offers. "I . . . agreed with him when he told me *I* love *him*."

"So you didn't actually say it?"

"I agreed with him. Isn't that the same thing?"

"I'm not sure." I resume pacing, mentally willing Zeus to help me out here. "This has never been a problem before. Every other Cinderella falls right into love with the chosen Prince. It's just you who seems to be a problem child."

"I don't mean to be. I told him I didn't want to interview his last ex, Sarah. That's good, right?"

"What did he say?" I wasn't aware of the Sarah story. I *was* impressed with the fact that Rachel trusted Luke enough not to have to do the final interview . . . that was a huge step for her. But if she trusted him that much, then what in Zeus's name was the holdup? Why was I still hanging out in Cameron

Creek and not on my way home . . . or at least to my next temporary home?

"He told me he wanted me to meet her anyway."

My attention snaps back to my godchild. "He what?"

"He thinks it's important I talk to her. His relationship with her was the one thing he regretted in his past. He wants us to be completely open and honest with each other."

"Honesty shmonesty!" I howl in aggravation. "Why can't you mortals just let your issues go? Why must all matter of life-waste be dragged out to examine and pick to death?"

Rachel stood up, ready to defend. "Hey. I did my part in this. And, I think Luke's right, in a way. It won't matter what Sarah says to me. I'm ready for this relationship, and . . . and I'll still trust him."

I hear the hesitation in her voice and want to pull my hair out. "Will you?"

"Yes! Venus, everything's going to be fine."

"I'll believe that when I see it." I throw myself down onto the bed in full pout mode.

"You need to be a little more optimistic . . ."

"Optimistic?" I flip over, the better to glare at her. "This from the Princess of Pessimism? I've spent the last six weeks cheerleading your sorry ass toward the love of your life and you accuse *me* of being pessimistic?"

Rachel turns away with a shake of her head and wanders over to the closet. She puts on her favorite sweater over the very wrinkled blouse she's wearing. When she turns back, she really does look happy. Happier than I've seen her before.

I feel like I'm having a nervous breakdown.

"The exes interviews were dumb. I should never have started it."

"Venus." Rachel's smile is genuine. "It wasn't that bad. It showed me that everyone sees people differently. I saw Eddie through rose-colored glasses."

I frown. "What the hell are you talking about? You don't wear glasses."

"It means that I looked at Eddie idealistically, the way I wanted him to be, not the way he really was. I pretended things were okay because I wanted them to be okay. You were right about that."

"Of course I was. I'm always right."

She ignores me and keeps going. "I've been pretending that volunteering makes me happy, too. It doesn't. Not all of it anyway. It just keeps me from seeing how unhappy I've really been. But, I'm ready to be happy now. I'm ready to go for my dreams instead of just filling my time. And, Luke's going to be part of that. The most important part."

I sag onto the bed, more depressed than ever for all her reassurances. "Then why am I still here?"

Rachel laughs and makes a face. "Maybe because you haven't left yet?" She waves a hand around the room and her gaze falls on the packed Louis Vuitton parked next to the bedroom door. She turns back to the closet and opens the door again, noticing for the first time that my clothes are gone, and hers have been returned to their rightful place. "You've packed?"

"I should be . . . gone." I swear my throat starts closing off, and I bolt up, clawing at it wildly, tugging at the Hermès scarf choking off my airway. "You don't understand, Rachel. Moving on comes fast. Cinderella falls in love with Prince Charming, they commit to life together—or at least to love-in-the-now—and *poof!* I'm gone. I'm supposed to be gone!"

"*Poof?* Without saying good-bye?"

I glance up at the hurt in Rachel's voice. "Withou— I guess I never thought of it that way, but . . . yeah."

"Oh. Okay." Rachel turns and leaves the bedroom.

My stomach knots up. What the hell?

Dashing after her, I catch her in the kitchen, where she's pulled a Diet Coke from the fridge. She looks at it and offers it to me. I give the silver can the same bewildered look and take it from her.

"Got any rum to put in it?" I ask, trying to lighten the sudden freakish tenseness.

"I thought goddesses couldn't get drunk."

"We can't, but I'll try anything once."

We share an uncomfortable smile and then head for the living room, where Rachel stands at the sliding door and looks out toward the darkened street. "Do you really leave without saying good-bye?"

"I always have before," I say, dropping the can onto the table, not really thirsty. "It's easy."

Rachel turns around. "You find it *easy* to leave people who care—"

"You don't care about me," I protest. "You've wanted me gone from day one. You only *think* you care now, because I was right."

"You *were* right. I admit it. I was wrong." Rachel shrugs. "You've changed my life, Venus. I'd have wanted to be able to say good-bye. And, thank you."

All this human emotion is like getting sucked out to sea by the tide. All smothering and . . . and very un-goddesslike.

"Well," I say, standing up with a huff. "Now you've said it and I'm *still* here. So, there's not even a need to *say* fucking good-bye, because obviously you haven't done something or aren't telling me something, and I'm still stuck here."

I make sure the bedroom door slams firmly behind me before I throw myself onto the bed again.

THIRTY-SEVEN

Rachel

If I hadn't been so deliriously happy the next morning, I'd have tried to coax Venus out of whatever this shell was that she was hiding in. She sulked all day, stared at me with suspicion, and finally slammed out of the house, claiming she needed some "creative retailing."

I didn't let her get to me. I was too happy.

I should have been exhausted. Luke had called me about ten the night before. Missing me, he said. Wishing I'd stayed. But, he'd had to head to work early on Sunday morning, so I hadn't.

We talked late into the night—early morning, actually—and when we finally hung up, I said it to him . . . the "L" word.

"I'm glad I didn't stay the night," I told him, snuggling down into the couch cushions and tugging the blankets more tightly over me. It felt almost like Luke's arms around me.

"That makes one of us."

"No, really," I encouraged. "Aren't you glad we've talked like this? I am."

"Anything that makes you glad, makes me glad."

"Ah, agreeable. The perfect man."

"For you."

I sighed. "Yeah. I think you might be right. Thanks."

Luke laughed sleepily. "For what?"

"For sticking it out. I haven't made it easy."

"You had good reasons not to trust."

"But, I do trust you . . . now." I took a deep breath and closed my eyes. "And, I . . . I love you."

"I know. I love you, too."

The thing that amazed me most the next day, was that I really meant it. I'd fallen for him . . . and not like fallen all hot and bothered for the calendar boy firefighter, but *really* fallen. For the man Luke was. The man who knew what he wanted and went for it—against all odds, in the case of wanting me. The man who tried his best to give everyone a chance—in the case of sticking with people like Harry Middleton Rogers, who made sticking with them an endeavor suited only to saints. The man who valued honesty—in the case of his regrets about Sarah and still wanting me to hear it from her, all because he knew that starting off on a dishonest foot wouldn't work. He was willing to show me who he was and had been, trusting that if it was meant to be between us, I'd understand. And, I did. We'd both done things we regretted. No matter what Sarah said, I knew if our feelings for each other were real, it wouldn't matter.

But, I had a week before meeting Sarah. She lived with her mother in Portland, Oregon, and Hannah and I had made arrangements to meet her the following Saturday. In between, I had a week of new love bliss. Except that Luke had to work Sunday through Wednesday, so we had to be satisfied with a few hasty (and sometimes hot!) phone calls for a few days. However, I was feeling so great that even that didn't dampen my spirits. In fact, I even decided it was time to break back into the family unit for Sunday dinner. My mother would probably faint from surprise when I showed up.

I'd decided, while walking the shelter dogs—out of habit

rather than desire to avoid my life for once—that since I'd undergone a successful Love Life Makeover, thanks to Venus, maybe it was time to make over the rest of my life. Step one was to rejoin my family. And, for once, I was actually looking forward to it. Maybe I'd even take the dustcover off Sally and take her out for a drive. The idea made me almost giddy. I was excited for Luke to see her. She'd be a great match for his candy-apple red truck.

But a *whole* life makeover would mean so much more than that. Not that rejoining my family wasn't important, it was just that, while walking the dogs and thinking, I realized there were a lot of things in my life that I did out of habit, not out of joy. From the car I drove, to what I did to keep myself busy. Mentally, I listed the things that were important to me, or that felt necessary, even when I wasn't trying to hide from life. Working out, for instance, may not be my favorite thing to do, but it was important for my health.

Then there was the volunteering. Walking the dogs was fun, but maybe just once a week. Serving at the soup kitchen didn't have to be done so often, either. Perhaps on holidays a few times a year. Sis-Men was a definite keeper. While my financial lectures hadn't gone over real big, the girls and I had a great time otherwise, gossiping, talking over problems. I felt good when I was with them. In fact, the more I thought about it, the more I wondered if the next step in making over my life should be going back to school. It was a huge step, but the idea of becoming a high school counselor was terrifying and thrilling at the same time. When I'd mentioned it to Luke, he was completely supportive, of course. He knew what it was like to have a career goal, and confirmed how great it felt to meet that goal and enjoy going to work every day.

I should have been mentally exhausted thinking so much after two years of hardly thinking at all, but I wasn't. Instead empowerment flowed through me. Like for once in my life I was going to make sacrifices, not to fill up empty spaces in my life, but to make sure every space in my life was filled with things that made me happy.

When I got out of the shower Sunday afternoon, Venus was slumped on the couch, staring at the television, oddly subdued for someone who had just spent the morning doing what she loved best . . . shopping.

"Did you pick up anything new?" I asked, buckling a wide belt around my waist.

Venus briefly shook her head without looking up.

"I'm on my way to my parents' house for dinner. Sure you don't want to come? We could tell them you're an old friend in town for the weekend."

There was no response from the goddess gallery.

"My nephews won't be interested in lip liner like the Sis-Men girls, but you could always tell them stories about chariot races or something . . . just leave out the fact that you've actually seen them in person, of course." I laughed.

Venus didn't. She didn't even acknowledge me.

I stepped in front of the screen. "What's got you so engrossed?"

One corner of Venus's mouth flicked up. She gestured with the remote. "That's what Mount Olympus looks like in the springtime."

The host of the documentary continued his narration on Greek seasons. Venus's eyes never left the screen.

If I didn't know better, I'd have thought . . . "You're homesick."

Venus snorted and turned off the TV before tossing the remote onto the coffee table. "Of course I'm not. Homesickness is . . . would be . . . weak."

I arched an eyebrow at her.

She did some more sputtering before kicking her feet up on the couch and lying back, trying to appear nonchalant. "It's just that home . . . Mount Olympus has better shopping than Earth. I mean, just look at today," she said waving a hand at the empty floor beside her, a floor that didn't contain any shopping bags. "I found absolutely nothing worth getting."

"You miss the *fashions*?" I asked, incredulously. "That's it?"

"Of course that's it." Venus frowned. "Don't you have somewhere to be? Off making the world happier by your presence? Rescuing lost kittens? Attending to the nutritional needs of the poverty-stricken?"

"No need to be nasty." I retrieved my purse from the table by the door before turning back to Venus. "Sure you don't want to come for dinner? You're welcome." I didn't expect a reply, and didn't get one. Fine. I wasn't going to beg. She was obviously sulking about something. "See ya."

No sooner had the door closed than I heard the soothing voice of the TV narrator again, extolling the virtues of Greece.

Not homesick, huh?

THIRTY-EIGHT

Venus

"O mm."

"Ommmm."

"OMMMMMMMM."

"OMMMM, dammit, OMMMM!"

I slam my fists into the carpet and throw myself backward.

The pebbled ceiling of Rachel's living room stares back at me unblinking, offering no help at all. Neither did the ten entire minutes of yoga I'd just attempted in order to bring myself back to some resemblance to my normally calm, cool, dishy-goddess self.

Rolling up to a sitting position, I examine my pink halter and hip-gripping black yoga pants, twisting this way and that to get a better look at every curve. My fabulous figure usually brings a smile to my face. But, today, even looking completely smashing in this outfit doesn't improve my mood.

"Grrr!!!"

Raiding the freezer produces only the dregs of some obscure store brand of ice cream. What happened to Ben & Jerry's? I thought all single, desperate, mortal women kept an emergency pint of B&J's around to suck down when they felt pathetically alone.

Oh, yeah. *Rachel's* not alone anymore, so what does *she* need with serotonin-boosting, glucose-spiking frivolities like Ben & Jerry's? I, on the other hand, am totally alone, figuratively *and* literally. And I could use some fucking Chunky Monkey!

A few bangs of my forehead on the now closed freezer door do nothing but aggravate the headache I've been nursing all week. Since Rachel and Luke hooked up, in fact.

Since they hooked up, and I didn't *poof* away to my next travel destination.

I'm obviously completely losing it. Not *liking* my job as a fairy godmother certainly doesn't mean I'm not good at it. I am, dammit! It's like following a recipe. Take one stupendously fantastic fairy godmother (me!), mix together a willing (or eventually willing, in Rachel's case) Cinderella and a to-die-for Prince Charming (what could be hotter than a calendar model?), preheat to the combustion point, then step back and watch the body parts rise. I did *all* of that, but instead of having a perfectly baked relationship cake to offer my father as proof of my skill and dedication—okay, my *resignation*—to fulfill the terms of my punishment, my cake has been rejected. That's the only explanation. After two thousand plus years, suddenly, my efforts are being ignored. I've done everything exactly the way I'm supposed to.

Or have I? Maybe I'm missing something. Something really, really important.

Maybe I need to reread the Fairy Godmother Rule Book.

Rachel and Hannah went to Portland today to meet Luke's original ex, Sarah. They should have just left well enough alone. I blame Luke. If he wasn't so damned honest—

The soft, leather-bound rule book is tucked beneath my Golden Girdle. I haven't looked at it in years. There's never been a need to. It's like driving for thirty years and then suddenly deciding to read the driver's training manual. You already know the rules, and if you don't, all those unfollowed rules are now ingrained habits, so what's the point in torturing yourself with your errors?

However, desperation calls for desperate acts. I have to figure out why I'm still stuck on Planet Boring.

I skim down the rules with a fingernail—painted with Amazing Apricot, my favorite color, which usually makes me smile, but today does nothing at all to cheer me up. The answer has to be here.

I'm pretty sure the hang-up isn't Rule #521, the one about Rachel needing to make a dedicated and firm commitment to Luke. I watched her all week, and her commitment seems pretty firm. She's happier than any time since I arrived, and when Luke dropped her off this morning, after she spent the night at his house, she tried again to get him to let her off the hook about meeting with Sarah.

Luke was unyielding. "Not wanting to talk to her proves you're still afraid she'll say something that'll change your mind about me."

Rachel and I both opened our mouths to protest at the same time, but I snapped mine shut and made myself scarce after she glared at me. Not that that stopped me from listening (and peeking) from just around the corner.

"She can't say anything that would make me stop loving you," Rachel said firmly, stroking her hands across his nicely formed pecs, probably to try to distract him. It was working for me. "I haven't come this far to break my own heart."

"Then go," Luke said, removing her hands from his person. Apparently he was more distracted than he looked. "Prove it to both of us."

"Now you don't trust *me*?"

I'd have been indignant *for* her, except that she hadn't trusted me, either, in the beginning, so, you know, *turnabout* . . .

"We can go around and around about this all you want," he

replied. "It's not going to change my mind. Nothing's going to stand between us. And this would be a spark just waiting to flare up during our first argument."

"I think this *is* our first argument," Rachel grumbled, but by the sound of it, she was cut off mid grumble by a lip-lock.

After that, she climbed into the Subaru with Hannah, like a good little girl, with no further argument. And, even though it showed she was committed to making—and keeping—things right between the two of them, I couldn't help but feel . . . I don't know . . . concerned? Worried? Twitchy.

Not really wanting to be alone, I'd invited Luke in for a distraction, er, for coffee. He had other plans.

I sulked, then tried yoga, and now I'm skimming the stupid Rule Book in search of answers.

So, anyway, #521 isn't the problem. There are other rules about how much interference can be used to effect the end result. I feel that I did an exemplary job keeping my nose out of where it didn't belong. Okay, so Rachel had to banish me from listening in, but really, that was all for entertainment value, not butting in.

The last rule in the book catches my eye. I'm sure I've never read it before, because, upon Zeus, by the time you've read 635 rules, you know there can't possibly be anything else important to say. In fact, there are exactly a thousand rules, which goes to show that Zeus just likes to show off. I could have written the same book with only four rules:

1. Get in.
2. Get 'em together.
3. Get out.
4. Get divine additions to wardrobe and footwear while you're at it.

Simple, straightforward. None of this shit like Rule #1000: "A fairy godmother shall protect herself at all times from becoming emotionally involved with humans . . . or suffer the consequences."

As *if*.

Dropping onto the bed, I lob the book onto the top of the dresser and finger the Golden Girdle instead. It's unbelievable that Zeus would even waste breath and paper devising stupid rules like that. Like I'd ever lower myself to caring about humans.

It looks like the gold is flaking off the girdle. After two thousand years, I suppose it makes sense that it's getting shabby. What wouldn't? At home, of course, nothing deteriorates, nothing ages. Not girdles *or* goddesses. A shudder ripples through me. If I don't get out of here soon, maybe *I'll* start aging. I'll be the one flaking and falling apart.

What if it's *already* happening?! I dash over to the full-length mirror in the corner of the bedroom, adjusting it to eliminate any distortion. Everything looks okay . . . I think. I turn around and examine my thighs for cellulite. Clear. I hold up my arms at right angles and do a chicken flap, checking for underarm wing flab. Clear.

On close examination, my eyes appear to be free of crow's-feet . . . Zeus forbid!

I'm hot. I'm still hot.

I will *forever* be hot.

But telling myself I'm hot, and having a *man* tell me I'm hot are two entirely different things. Seriously. I can stare into this mirror like Snow Damn White, 24/7, and listen to the imaginary voice (that sounds suspiciously like my own) telling me I'm gorgeous, desirable, and sexy, and it comes nowhere near hearing it from a real, live, in-the-flesh male. God or mortal . . . it doesn't even matter. At this point, I'm not picky. It just can't be me!

That's what the problem is! (Well, not *the* Problem, because *the* Problem is that I'm still here and shouldn't be.) But the problem with *me* is that I simply haven't been getting enough attention lately. It was okay when Rachel wasn't getting any action either. But now that Rachel and Luke are getting busy, I'm just . . . well, jealous. *I* want some action.

Even just a little.

Like a kiss.

Or a cuddle.

I pick up the girdle from the bed and slip it on, turning from side to side to admire it in the mirror. It really does flatter my narrow waist. Which in turn flatters my still-pert breasts. Which accentuates my perfectly contoured hips. Which then highlights my . . . well, you get the picture.

Heph really *did* outdo himself with this gift. The little gold fibers running through it had once worked magic. They'd still work magic if I—

I bit down on my lower lip and frowned at my reflection. But only briefly. Not long enough to cause any wrinkles.

All isn't lost, really, as long as I have the girdle. I *could* put it to good use. Just enough to pick up my spirits, of course. Drastic measures aren't required. I mean, there's nothing to feel guilty about because *I* won't be doing any seducing. Right? The girdle would be doing all the work, and . . . well, two thousand years is a long time to go without being paid the proper attention!

Before I change my mind, I whip off the girdle and put on my favorite siren dress. The red one cut down to *here*. With the barely there straps and the sequins.

A pair of fuck-me black stilettos, a slash of red lipstick, and another look in the mirror, and I'm almost there.

The girdle goes back on and I almost feel like me again. Like Venus, Goddess of Beauty, Love, and Fertility. Like Aphrodite! Like the deity I'm supposed to be.

Almost. But not quite.

I still need the Man. Rachel won't be back for hours. It won't hurt her. But it'll sure as hell help me.

I go in search of the phone.

THIRTY-NINE

Rachel

You okay?" Hannah asked warily from the passenger seat.

I smiled. "I'm okay. I'm really okay."

At first, after meeting Sarah and talking to her, I admit I wavered. Luke had left her at the altar.

Okay, not at the altar exactly, but close. Three days before the wedding.

She was still furious with him. Moving on—even fifteen years later—obviously wasn't an option for her. Admittedly, I'd not moved on for two years after Eddie and, without Venus's prompting, I might not be moved on now. It was eye-opening.

But listening to someone bad-mouth Luke—someone who wasn't so obviously self-centered as Harry Rogers—was really hard. My breath grabbed in my throat as Sarah worked herself into tears, replaying the humiliation of having to tell her family the wedding was off. Recounting how much they'd been in love and how she didn't understand why Luke called things off. She cascaded into near hysterics before her mother came into the room and gently removed her from our wide-eyed stares. When she returned, we half expected Mrs. Henderson to call the cops to throw us out for harassing her daughter. Instead she offered us soft drinks and sat at the kitchen table with us and explained what had happened.

"The whole situation was so sad," I told Hannah now, as we headed up I-5 toward home. Toward the rest of my life, which would definitely not be wasted on bad memories. Unlike the rest of *Sarah's* life. "But once her mother explained about the emotional problems Sarah had even before Luke left her . . ."

Beside me, Hannah nodded. "He did what was best under the circumstances. Even Sarah's mom agreed, so no worries. Fire Boy is definitely not dumping you at the altar. Hell, I'm surprised he hasn't already dragged you *to* the nearest altar."

I laughed. "We haven't even discussed that."

The arch of Hannah's dark brows told me that she didn't believe that for a second.

"We haven't! Okay, he mentioned that that was his ultimate goal, but—"

"Ha! And we all know that when Luke Stanton sets his mind to something, he always gets it."

I opened my mouth to protest and then clamped it shut and just giggled. There was no use denying that Luke wasn't sidetracked real easily. Chasing me—the Queen of Relationship Rejections—for so many months, and ultimately catching me, proved Luke was unrelenting even in the face of inevitable failure.

Okay, so failure hadn't been exactly inevitable. I'd caved, I admit it. And I was so glad I had. I'd even agreed that maybe, probably, I was willing to take the leap of faith sooner than later. I'd never been so sure of anything in my life, and there was no use postponing it just in case I changed my mind. There would be no mind-changing. Luke was more than Mr. March to me. He was Mr. March and every month in between. He was the guy who saw the holes in my armor and got out the blowtorch to open up those holes until I could see more clearly through them. He was the one who wanted to hold my hand while I made over my entire life, *following* my dreams this time instead of shoving them out of sight and trying to forget them.

And, it wasn't only Luke who should get credit for my transformation. Venus deserved a medal. Or maybe a party. That was it! I'd throw her a party in thanks. It wouldn't be a big party, because it wasn't like she had a huge social group, but even with a small party, if she was the center of attention, she'd be happy. It would be a great way to say good-bye, too.

Good-bye.

I suddenly remembered the conversation we'd had last weekend, when I'd come home after my first day with Luke. Venus had said it would be swift . . . her leaving. When things were settled, when I was committed to Luke and had truly found my True Love, she'd be gone.

"Hey!" Hannah latched onto my upper arm. "Wanna cool it with the lead foot?"

I eased up on the accelerator I'd unconsciously pressed harder, as I realized that when I got back to my apartment . . . Venus might not be there.

I took my cell phone from my purse and handed it to Hannah. "Dial my number."

"Why?" she asked, even as she did as I requested.

"I'm worried about Venus. She was . . . not feeling good when I left this morning."

"She seemed fine when I was there. She certainly felt well enough to bitch about the fact that *she* didn't think I should have these particular Jimmy Choos if she couldn't have a pair, too."

I would have smiled but I was too busy worrying.

Hannah handed me the phone and I listened to it ring. And ring. And ring some more.

Venus never answered.

Shit.

I hung up and put a little more weight behind the accelerator.

FORTY

Venus

The room flickers in waves of warm candlelight. The drawn drapes give the illusion of evening . . . because romance in the daylight isn't as romantic as it is in the darkness with only the shimmer of flames to light our little haven.

A deep, rich voice croons from the CD speakers, wrapping around the two of us like a cashmere blanket, as I wind my arms around his neck, and he pulls me closer. Our bodies nearly melt into one with only our clothing and a thin strip of gold between us. Our rhythms perfectly align as we sway to the melody of the love song that sets the mood. I could stay like this for eternity.

It's been so long since I've done this. Felt this. Too long. I *deserve* this.

I know it's make-believe.

To me anyway, because *he* doesn't realize that this love isn't real. To him, his adoration—his worship—of me is as real as if the Golden Girdle around my waist doesn't exist. In his eyes, I am the only woman in the heavens, and I cling to that belief because, right now, it's all I have.

I know it's only pretend.

And I don't care.

Because sometimes . . . *sometimes* this feeling is more important than breathing.

As our faces linger a breath apart, I feel whole again. Like I used to be. I feel, not like Venus, the rebellious daughter, the fairy godmother under duress, always doing for others, but like myself. Like *Aphrodite*. Goddess of Love. Goddess of Beauty.

I'm loved like Rachel is loved. Just for this moment *I* have the prince. After more than two thousand years without love, I want this.

I *need* this.

As we float through the room, reality fades, and time doesn't exist. I'm me again. I'm adored. Loved. Like I should be.

This man's moon orbits my sun.

What Rachel never finds out can't hurt her.

FORTY-ONE

Rachel

Is that Barry White?" Hannah leaned toward my front door, straining to hear the music coming from behind it, as I searched my purse for my house key.

I paused and flashed a startled glance at the door, which wasn't completely muffling the unmistakable voice of Barry White.

And if Venus was listening to Barry White—

"That girl's lost it," Hannah complained. "She may have fashion sense, but mixing Barry White and Prada is like parking a mobile home in the middle of Rodeo Drive. She's nuts."

Or depressed.

If Venus was still here, even though I was absolutely, 100 percent sure of my love for Luke and his love for me . . . something *was* wrong. She'd been telling me that all week. But, I'd thought maybe seeing Sarah would change that. Solidify my feelings for Luke. Make them so unmistakable that Zeus would know she'd succeeded in making me over. I'd forgotten that until we were driving home, and I'd sped all the way here—sure that Venus would be gone from the apartment by the time I got here.

But, she apparently wasn't, if she was inside listening to a

Barry White CD . . . which she would have had to go out and specially purchase because I don't *own* a Barry White CD.

Maybe Zeus had gone back on his word. Maybe he wasn't counting Venus's Love Life Makeovers anymore and she was stuck here. She'd kind of grown on me, and I'd gladly help her after all she'd done for me.

But she'd be devastated.

"She probably just playing a joke on us," I said holding up the found key in triumph. "She knew we were going to be home about now, so playing awful music is probably payback for not letting her go with us this morning."

I shoved the key in the lock and pushed the door open. The entryway was dark, as was the rest of the apartment, it appeared, except for a kind of glow. Hannah and I cast each other bewildered looks. Leaving the front door open, we stepped around the corner into the living room.

It took me a minute to process what I was seeing. And then it was like a slow-motion thing, like a car wreck, where you see what's happening, but your brain and your eyes aren't quite in sync. My eyes saw the candles, the bottle of wine, and two glasses on the coffee table. They registered the couple slow dancing in the center of the room, indeed to Barry White. They recorded that the woman was Venus, but it took my brain several seconds to focus on the fact that the man in her arms . . . was Luke. And as we watched, Venus lifted her head to accept Luke's kiss.

The sound that came from my throat was half-gasp, half-cry. Hannah took my shoulders and righted me when I pitched backward, away from what I couldn't believe I was seeing.

Venus's head jerked toward me and our eyes met.

Did it take as long as it seemed for *her* brain to connect that I was home and she was caught? Or did the slow dawning in her eyes just mean she didn't care that she'd been caught?

I didn't wait to see what Luke's reaction would be.

I just ran.

FORTY-TWO

Venus

Noooo!"

This can't be happening!

I shove Luke away from me, and he barely reacts, continuing to stare at me like he wants to consume me with his eyes.

"Stop it," I snap. "Just stop. It's not real."

"You *bitch*." Hannah looks like she's ready to rip my heart out through my throat.

At this point, I'd gladly do it for her. But I don't have time. I have to find Rachel.

Luke reaches for me again, wanting to get back to our dance.

"No! *Argggh!*" Tearing off the girdle I fling it away from me across the room and dash for the door.

Hannah snatches at me on the way by, snagging an arm and whipping me around and almost off my feet. "Leave her alone. Haven't you done enough? What is this, a fucking game to you?"

"No," I say, as I start panting. I'm going to hyperventilate. Then, I'll pass out. I can't pass out. "No. You don't understand. It's not real."

"Looked pretty damn real to me." She turns a cold glare toward Luke who's standing in the middle of the room, rubbing his eyes, trying to wake up from the dream he's been in. "I can't believe you'd do that to her."

"Let me go!" I wrench my arm out of Hannah's grip. "It's not what you think. I have to find her. I have to explain."

I barely hear Hannah's snort of disgust, as I tear out the door and down the stairs. Luke's on his own. At this point, I don't care. But I do care about Rachel.

Only she's gone.

FORTY-THREE

Rachel

When I found out Eddie had betrayed me, anger exploded out of me. This time the anger felt like it was pulling me inside out, compacting me, pressing in on me from all sides and squeezing the life I'd learned to live in the past two months into a tiny package that would eventually disappear inside of me, to be forgotten.

Or not.

I didn't know who I hated more. Venus for being the antithesis of the Disney fairy godmother every little girl once dreamed of coming to her rescue. Or, Luke for digging until he unearthed my heart and then kicking it back into the hole at the first opportunity.

Didn't matter.

Nothing mattered anymore.

I sat on the end of the pier and stared out into the Sound. Sailboats floated in the distance, blowing silently across the water, their occupants enjoying the unexpectedly warm October sun. A sun I was too cold to feel.

Silent tears burned tracks down my cheeks and inflamed my eyeballs. Thank God no one was here to witness. I needed time alone. Time to figure out what to do. Time to figure out how to get rid of Venus. Quotas be damned, there was no way she was spending one more day in my apartment. Or one more second in my life.

A rhythmic vibration pounded through the boards of the dock as someone ran along it somewhere behind me. I didn't turn to see who it was. Hannah would have followed me, wanting to know I was okay. I'd just tell her I wanted to be alone.

"R-Rachel?"

I turned slowly to face not Hannah, but Venus, not bothering to hide my anger and pain. She didn't deserve to be protected.

"I need to explain."

She looked like she'd just had sex. Her hair was sticking out every which way like she just got out of bed. Her outfit was askew like she'd tugged it on in haste.

"You don't have to explain anything," I said, then turned back to the water.

"It was a mistake. I swear."

"Of course it was a mistake. You got caught. I'm sure that wasn't your intention."

"No, really. I just . . ."

I heard her take a big gulping breath and I turned again, squinting at her in the bright light. She looked like she was crying.

"Oh, my God. You are such an actress. What? You think you can come down here and cry big crocodile tears and make me believe that you really didn't *mean* to do it? That you *accidentally* convinced me that you were here to help me and haven't been planning all along to give me a little taste of happiness and then rip it away from me? Save your sob story for someone who doesn't know you that well."

She just kept shaking her head. "You have it wrong. I swear."

"Swear all you want. I'll never believe anything you say to me again." I shut my eyes against the pain. "Shouldn't have believed you in the first place."

"It wasn't . . . it wasn't real. I don't want Luke."

"Of course you don't. You just wanted to see if you could *get* him. Now that you've answered that burning question, you have no reason to want him anymore."

"*No.*" Venus wrapped her arms around her middle and swayed almost like she hurt as much as I did. If she was a member of SAG, she'd be accepting her Oscar about now. "Luke is meant for you, Rachel. I don't feel—"

I jumped up so fast, Venus backed up a few paces, obviously scared I'd push her in the water. Only my ignorance about whether demoted goddess bitches could swim kept me from doing just that. My life may have been in ruins, but I still had enough sense not to add a murder conviction to the rubble.

"You're right. You *don't* feel. You don't feel anything at all." A sickening laugh escaped me. "Do you know that I actually envy you? I wish I had no feelings. I wish I could walk away and forget all about this. About Luke. About *you.*"

"You don't mean that," Venus said, leaning toward me as if to touch my arm.

I lurched out of her way. "No wonder your father banished you," I growled, my voice rising with each word. "You deserved it, if you were screwing with lives there like you have been here. If I could, I'd banish you, too!"

Her eyes widened just a fraction.

It was enough that I knew I had my answer.

I'd banished her from listening in on the interviews with the exes. I'd banished her from spying on Luke and me. There *was* a magic word. I could get rid of her permanently.

My voice was strangely strong and calm as I squared my shoulders and issued my edict. "I *banish* you from my life, Venus Cronus. I never want to see you again."

The sound that came from Venus's throat was the exact combination of choke and sob that she'd made in front of Starbucks the day I'd complimented her handbag.

Venus

Zeus knew what he was talking about when he warned against a goddess . . . er, fairy godmother, getting emotionally involved with humans.

Only I don't think even he had any idea of the depth of the consequences.

Rachel

Venus was right about revenge not being the top priority with a true broken heart. Revenge took too much emotional energy, something I sorely lacked when it was all over with.

I'd say, all things considered, that my life *was* better than it had been pre-backstab. I discovered that, unlike with the anger and embarrassment after a phony broken heart, a true broken heart requires a healing power present only in the maternal gene. Mom knew just what to say—or not to say, more importantly. Mom brewed the best hot cocoa—made medicinal by generous splashes of peppermint schnapps. And, of course, she gave the best hugs.

My family, who knew nothing about Luke, still knew with one look, that my emotional fragility was way more serious than with my breakup with Eddie, and they absorbed me into their love and their lives as if I'd never left. So even though my heart still hitched every time I saw my brother rub his wife's pregnant belly or my sister kiss her fiancé, I pushed those feelings aside and remembered that it wasn't important who I loved in my life, but that I loved at all.

They did their best to make it easy for me. Connie loaned

me the twins for "auntie time," during which it's impossible to remember your woes, as two mischievous toddlers entertain you with SpongeBob impressions and armpit farts.

Joe found me one day standing in the garage staring at Sally—dustcover-free—and offered to help me polish her up so I could drive her. Even though the future medical student in him would much rather have assisted in surgery than wax a car, he knew I needed it. I'd decided that, though I was alone—probably permanently—I didn't have any less life-living to do. Selling the Subaru and driving a car I adored was the first step I was taking in not worrying about loving someone else and just loving myself.

Roxanne was surprised when I offered to help out with her wedding plans, but once she realized I wouldn't lose it when she talked about invitation fonts and wedding cake flavors, she relaxed and we began bonding again, sister to sister.

Even Hannah was part of my healing. We started up our Saturday morning coffee dates again. Even though she had every right to say "I told you so"—because she had—she didn't, and was just there for me when I wanted company, distracting me with her humor, and never mentioning Luke or Venus, which was just the way I wanted it.

The reminders were there anyway, without them being brought to my attention. Out there on the pier that day, I don't know what I'd expected when I banished Venus. An instantaneous disappearance? A puff of smoke like a magician's trick? Instead she'd just turned slowly away and walked off the dock, leaving me feeling oddly hollow. I knew that once she found her next victim, she'd be fine. I wasn't sure when I'd ever be fine.

When I finally went home that night, she was gone. Physically anyway. Her spirit, however, clung to my apartment like the plague, refusing to be banished even after I'd thrown away the candles and the Barry White CD she'd used in her seduction scene, washed the sheets from my bed, and refilled my closets and drawers with my own items.

Still, she was everywhere. In the holes in my living room wall where the firefighter calendar—now ashes in the fire grate—had once been nailed. In the amethyst earring I found stuffed in the couch cushions. In the giant family-sized bag of M&M's still in my kitchen cupboard. Every time I thought I'd exterminated the final piece of her, another piece would materialize.

The most obvious piece of Venus that I couldn't eradicate from my life was the presence of Luke. Amazingly, he thought he could get away with pretending not to understand what the problem was . . . why I couldn't see him anymore. It was like he had selective amnesia about what he and Venus were doing that day. He claimed to have no idea what I was talking about.

Which just went to show I was right all along. Luke Stanton, being male, *did* have a glaring fault . . . the inability to be a man and admit that he'd screwed up. Not that that would have excused him in my eyes, but still.

After a few days of refusing his calls and taking my breaks at the precise moment he walked into the bank, he got the message and backed off. Grudgingly.

As fall slowly morphed into winter, I slowly morphed into the new Rachel. I still volunteered but with focus now, instead of maniacally, as I had before, trying to stuff activity into every crevice of my life. I gave up Habitat for Humanity, promising to come back next summer when I had more time, but I kept walking the shelter dogs. It was good exercise and gave me time to think—something I wasn't avoiding as much these days, as I'd started thinking about the future instead of the past. Besides, the dogs were good listeners. I'd even adopted one of my own. Gracie, the mostly dignified, little curly-haired terrier mutt, became my constant companion, my closest confidante.

I also kept up with my mentoring group, and, after some initial whining when I refused to tell them why Venus wasn't around anymore, we got back to the way we used to be. Okay, not exactly. I stopped forcing finance down their throats and started listening more and lecturing less. After a few weeks, I told them of my goal to become a high school counselor and found myself with my own cheerleading squad. By mid-November I'd started researching my options for going back to school.

And I found myself smiling again.

I was going to be all right.

"I'm hurrying, Gracie. Hold your horses."

Horses were something Gracie couldn't hold. When she had to go she had to go—even if I wasn't out of bed. And she was prepared to do anything to ensure my prompt attention. Like pulling things off shelves in the living room, which I could hear her doing now. So much for dignity.

I groaned. Five A.M. was her favorite time to show how wrapped around her paw she had me, especially on the days when I *didn't* have to get out of bed for work. Like weekends. Or holidays, like today, which was Thanksgiving.

Of course, on days when I *was* up at five and tried to coax her out for a walk before I showered and got dressed for work, she'd lounge around in bed watching me through heavy-lidded eyes, preferring to get in a few more winks in the warmth of my abandoned sheets. Today, when I could have slept a couple more hours before we headed over to help my mom with the family feast, Gracie, of course, wanted to be up before dawn even thought of cracking. She'd been tearing around the apartment for five minutes like a greyhound, while I'd dragged myself out of bed. I tugged sweats on over my pj's, as Gracie continued her frantic pacing, leaping, and crashing into things, meant to clarify the urgency of her need.

"I'm going to buy you some Depends, if you have that much of a problem," I muttered, though affectionately. At least she didn't pee on the carpet. Her bladder was something that she *could* hold. Having an accident was wholly against her sensibilities, but that didn't mean she held it quietly.

"All right," I finally said, tugging on my sweatshirt and grimacing in the hall mirror as I bent to clip Gracie's lead on her collar. "Thank God, it's still dark outside. If the neighbors saw me, they'd call the cops about the unsavory character lurking around."

Gracie yanked me down the stairs and around the side of the apartment building to an area of tall dewy grass that she considered her own. She played there, exercised there, and, most importantly, pottied there. Thankfully, the chill air prevented her from wanting to linger too long this morning, and a few minutes later we headed back in. I didn't really like being outside in the dark anyway. Who knew who might be lurking around the shadowed corners of the building, waiting for unsuspecting female dog walkers. When I heard a loud diesel vehicle coming up the road, I hurried Gracie back in and locked us safely in the apartment.

"I know you'd do your best to protect me, girl," I told her as I popped open a Diet Coke—the equivalent of coffee for me most mornings—and refilled her water bowl so she could refill her bladder. Then, I needed to pick up all the stuff she'd dumped on the floor in her bid for attention this morning. "But, you're not exactly a rott—"

A sudden pounding on the front door had me clutching my heart and Gracie doing her best *imitation* of a rottweiler, trying to prove me wrong.

No one should have been knocking on my door at this hour. Maybe whoever was coming into the parking lot as Gracie and I dashed back inside had seen me, a female alone, with only a twenty-pound dog for protection.

"Rachel!"

Whoever was at the door called out my name with the next round of knocking, and Gracie and I looked at each other in bewilderment. Who in the world? My heart stopped again when I silently and stealthily looked out the peephole.

He was the last person I expected to see at my door.

I stepped back and shook my head at Gracie. "We're not here," I whispered. "I don't want to talk to him."

"Rachel, please." Luke knocked again, softer this time. "I know you're there. The peephole just went dark. Your family needs you at the hospital. Open the door."

Frowning, I whipped open the door and glared at him. "How dare you use my family to get at me! You don't even know them. They don't know you. You're just as despicable—"

"Rachel! Stop it." Luke reached in and grabbed my shoulders, which sent Gracie into a fit of rage.

She may not have been a full-sized guard dog, but by the time she got through trying to chew a hole in the leg of Luke's fire pants, I was almost convinced the terrier in her was mixed with rottweiler blood after all.

I finally disentangled her—only to avoid a lawsuit for not controlling my vicious canine—and locked her in my bedroom until I could get rid of Luke. To keep her occupied I tossed her the once pristine—now heavily chewed—Prada loafer I'd found under the bed after Venus left. My ex–fairy godmother would have had a heart attack to find out her precious Italian leather shoe had been reduced to a dog toy.

When I got back, he was in the living room, picking my cordless phone off the floor next to the couch where I must have left it last night after talking to Hannah. She was meeting me at my parents' for dinner today.

Holding it up, he gestured to the charger on the table. "Battery works better if you plug it in at night."

I blinked. "Surely you didn't come all the way over here at this ungodly hour to criticize me about my phone-charging habits."

"No, I came over here because your family is at the hospital and I thought you might want to be there."

I opened my mouth, but no sound came out as I tried to process what he'd just said.

When I just shook my head in confusion, he continued. "I was at the hospital after a call this morning when a pregnant woman came in to be admitted. I heard her give her last name as Greer, and remembered that you said your brother and his wife were expecting a baby soon. The older woman with them was using a cell phone to make some calls. She appeared to be *concerned*, when she couldn't reach someone named 'Rachel.' I introduced myself and offered to come find you."

Everything fell into place. Connie. The baby. My not "concerned," but probably *panicking* mother, who couldn't reach me because my phone battery was dead.

"Oh, my God," I finally cried, hopping into gear. "I'm supposed to be there."

I located my purse under the coffee table, where Gracie had dragged it this morning, during her why-aren't-you-walking-me-right-this-second? tirade. I scooped all the contents back into it, only to have to dump them out again on the table when I didn't come across my car keys.

After a thorough search, I *still* couldn't find my keys.

"Gracie Ellen Greer!" I hollered through the apartment. "Where are my car keys?"

"Rachel."

"I don't have time for this, Luke." I pushed past him and began searching all over, looking for Sally's keys. Since Gracie hadn't developed the ability to actually leave the apartment on her own, the keys had to be here somewhere. "I'm supposed to be at the hospital with them. I'm supposed to be in the delivery room with Connie. My brother doesn't do well with blood. Where are the damn keys?"

I crawled underneath the dining room table, found a lipstick and a used tissue, but no keys. My skull cracked on the edge of the table during my hasty exit.

"Come on, come on," I muttered, starting to really panic.

I couldn't let my family down right now. I'd done enough of that in the past and I wasn't going to do it again. Especially not when they needed me most. "Where in the world could they be?"

"Rachel." Luke's voice was very calm, which broke through my alarm. "I'll take you."

"What?"

"I'll take you to the hospital. You don't look like you're in any condition to drive, even if you did find your keys."

One look at my shaking hands and I knew he was right. But he was still dressed for work. I tried not to notice how great he looked.

"Aren't you on duty?" I waved in the direction of the uniform pants Gracie had tried to mangle.

He glanced at his watch. "I'm off in ten minutes. I cleared it with the chief to leave a few minutes early."

I didn't want to be grateful, but I was. "Thanks. Uh, I need to change real quick."

Ten minutes later we were on our way to the hospital, each of us absorbed in our own thoughts. My mind couldn't decide what to think about. Connie in the hospital, ready to bring a new baby into our family, should have been my top concern. But, being this close to Luke after two months was wreaking havoc on my brain cells. They didn't know which way to turn.

"How've you been?" Luke finally asked, keeping his eyes on the road for the most part, but I could see him darting glances in my direction every once in a while. His expression was unreadable.

"Fine," I said. "Fine."

"I'm glad to see you're spending time with your family."

The one good thing I'd gotten out of my time with Luke.

I just nodded. I didn't know what to say. My heart had healed for the most part . . . heck, it should have, considering Luke and I had only been an item for such a short time. But, it was still taking far longer than I expected it to.

Maybe that was the difference between a true broken heart and a pretend broken heart. Much as I didn't want to admit that what I'd felt for Luke was true. It hurt more than I thought possible, to have really given up my heart completely, only to have it stomped on anyway. That was what I'd been worried about in the first place. Hurting when it was all over.

Maybe Eddie had a right to hurt me. After all, I hadn't really loved him. Venus was right about that. I'd just loved the idea of him. The idea of our relationship.

But with Luke . . .

"Here we are."

I glanced up to find we'd pulled up to the entrance of the hospital already. I reached for the door handle, then remembered my manners and turned back. "Thanks. I appreciate you coming to find me. I'm sure my family does, too."

"Look, Rachel—"

I held up a hand to silence him. The look on his face was too much. He was hurting, too, I could tell. I almost reached for him, but then the truth came back to me.

"I can't do it, Luke. Betrayal is betrayal, whether you admit it or not."

Before I could cry, I got out of the truck.

Six hours later, we had a new baby girl in the Greer family. Alexa Constance joined brothers Brett and Nate, who really weren't quite sure what to think of her squirmy little self when my dad finally brought them to meet her.

The rest of us were exhausted, but thrilled. This would be the talk of many a Thanksgiving dinner in the future. "Remember the year little Alexa decided she wanted all the attention?"

Dinner wasn't going to happen today. We'd decided to postpone it until the next day, when Connie and the baby could lounge around on Mom's couch while we waited on them hand and foot.

I finally decided to head home to change clothes and let

Gracie out. I'd reached the front door of the hospital before I remembered I didn't have a way to get home. "Damn," I muttered in frustration. I'd have to call a cab.

Heading over to the information desk to ask for the number of a cab company, I found Luke hunched over in a waiting room chair. He looked up and rose as I approached.

"Hey," he said, a sad smile curving his lips. "Everything okay?"

I nodded. "It's a girl. Alexa."

His smile broadened. "That's nice."

I nodded again, really awkward. "What are you doing here?"

"Waiting for you. I thought you might need a ride home."

"You've been here the past six hours?"

"I went home and changed."

He had on a T-shirt covered loosely with the same flannel shirt he'd worn chopping wood the day I'd poured my guts out to him. Before we'd—

"I walked Gracie, too."

My eyes darted back to his face. "How'd you get in my house?"

He dropped the silver house key I'd forgotten I'd given him onto my palm. "I didn't figure you'd be able to get away to take care of her. Besides," he laughed wryly, "we had to come to an understanding after she tried to bite my leg off this morning."

I laughed in spite of myself. "Yeah, she thinks she's a lot tougher than she really is."

"We found your car keys, too." He produced those from his pocket and handed them to me. "Under the couch. I bribed her to find them with beef jerky."

I looked at the floor, unable to meet his eyes anymore. There were too many memories there. I found myself losing my anger in their deep blueness. "Thanks. For everything. You . . . you didn't have to."

"Yeah, I did."

Taking my arm, he led me out the doors and into the gray day. The parking garage was across the street from the hospital.

"Hey," I said, as we reached his big red truck. "It's Thanksgiving. Aren't you spending the day with your family?"

He shrugged. "I had more important things to do today."

He shut me into my side of the truck, and I buckled in and tried not to cry. This was too much. The emotions of witnessing childbirth . . . something I was back to suspecting I'd never experience, and now this, realizing, as much as I was angry with Luke, he could still do things—was still *willing* to do things—that reminded me how much I loved him.

Unbelievably, it was really hard to remember why I now hated him. Without Venus in the picture . . . maybe we could . . .

No. Taking him back just because Venus wasn't here as a temptation would be like playing with gasoline just because there didn't happen to be a flame in the vicinity to ignite it. I just had to hold on to the feeling I'd had when I walked in on them dancing in my living room by candlelight.

Or not, I thought, as my stomach knotted.

Looking for a distraction I checked out the textbooks piled between us on the bench seat. They hadn't been there this morning.

Not quite believing what I was seeing, I hefted the top book into my lap and flipped it open. *Greek mythology?* Had Venus told him who she was? Had she convinced Luke that she was better for him because she was, after all a *goddess*, rather than a mere mortal like me?

Oh, my God.

I'd thrown Venus out of my house, out of my life. She had nowhere to go, as far as I knew. Had she moved in with—

"What are these for?" I asked, the words bursting out a lot more forcefully than I'd intended. But the idea of Venus *living* with Luke, and Luke being here with me, being *nice,* was more than I could stand. I felt like I was going to throw up.

"My sister," Luke replied. "I told you Emma was going back to college. She's borrowing the books for one of her classes."

"Oh." As much as I didn't trust him, it sounded plausible. He *had* mentioned that to me.

I thumbed absently through the book until I got to the chapter on Aphrodite. Venus. Reading about her in black and white was strange and otherworldly. She was obviously a different person—goddess—back then. Despite what she'd say differently, she *had* become humanized during her time on Earth. During her time in my life.

A sigh escaped me. I missed her. Her fierce sense of fashion propriety. Her obsession with M&M's, eaten on everything from bagels to scrambled eggs. Her single-minded drive toward what she wanted, toward what she knew *I* really wanted. In spite of everything she'd done, in spite of hurting me in a way no one had ever hurt me before . . . I missed having Venus in my life.

Not wanting to think about it, I went back to the textbook, reading it like it wasn't about someone I'd come to think of as a friend. A rotten friend, but a friend nonetheless. In black and white, Venus was a larger than life goddess. The text mentioned her lovers, her husband, even her beloved children. Funny, I couldn't picture her as the maternal type, but the book said she was very dedicated to her children. It must have been unbearable for her to be away from them. I didn't even have kids, and I still knew how she must have felt to have been banished here, unable to contact them to tell them she was all right and still loved and cared for them. No wonder she'd been so adamant about fulfilling her quota and moving on. It was her only option if she wanted to see her family again.

I read on. It mentioned her mistakes, her trials, her troubles. With a slight chuckle, I wondered which "trouble" had caused her banishment. Even goddesses weren't perfect. And

Venus's imperfections, her mistakes, had brought her here, away from everything she loved. No wonder she'd missed home. Everything . . . every*one* she loved was there.

Here, she had no one. But me.

And, I'd treated her like crap.

I'd known she was homesick in the end. I'd seen it in the longing in her eyes when she saw Greece on television. It was apparent in her attitude when she realized that my falling in love with Luke, for some reason, hadn't moved her that next step closer to home. Something had been wrong and she knew it. Just how desperate had she been?

There was one last paragraph about Aphrodite and Hephaestus, which described the Golden Girdle he'd made for her, to show his devotion to her, only instead it made her even more irresistible to men and gods. To make up for a loveless marriage, Aphrodite, Goddess of Love, wore the girdle to charm men and gods into falling in love with her . . .

My head shot up to look at Luke's profile, even as my brain searched for a memory as to whether Venus had been wearing a golden girdle when I'd seen her with Luke. I didn't even know if she had it with her, though I knew she kept a gold box in her lingerie drawer. I'd never seen the contents, but if it was, indeed, the girdle, and Venus had really been as desperately homesick as I was beginning to think she'd been . . .

"Do you remember kissing Venus?"

Luke's head shot in my direction. He'd been pulling into my parking lot just then, and my question so startled him that he ran into the curb. He wrestled the big truck into a parking space and slammed it into park before answering me.

He was pissed. "What in the hell are you talking about?"

I flinched as my suspicion grew. I'd never point-blank asked him before. The week he'd been trying to get me to speak to him, he'd continually told me he didn't know what he'd done to make me so angry, while I told him he knew *exactly* what I was talking about.

Maybe he hadn't.

Maybe he didn't.

"You . . . you don't remember being in my living room, kissing Venus, my cousin—"

"I know who Venus is," he snapped. "I just want to know what in the heck gave you the idea I'd be kissing her, when I'd just finally managed to get *you* to kiss me? What? You think I was *collecting* women or something?"

"No, I just . . ." I dropped my gaze back down to the book. If Venus had been wearing the girdle, Luke wouldn't have been able to resist her. It wouldn't have been his fault. I'd worried about him being coerced into falling in love with me. But what if the coercion had happened later? Because Venus was lonely for affection.

Venus had tried to tell me it was a mistake. She'd said it wasn't real. I hadn't let her explain.

I felt like I was going to hyperventilate. Pressing my hand to my chest, I tried to slow my heartbeat. If I'd just let her explain . . . Maybe it didn't excuse what she'd done, but it would have let Luke off the hook. My life wouldn't have been ruined.

"Rachel?" Luke touched my shoulder and I turned to face him. He wasn't angry anymore. Only when he reached for my cheek, did I realized I was crying. "What's going on? Why would you ask me if I'd kissed Venus?"

"I made a mistake," I whispered miserably. "I thought . . ."

"Why would you think that?" He was genuinely puzzled. "God, I love you so much. I thought you finally understood that."

"I . . . I . . ." I couldn't get the words out.

Luke, knowing me better than I knew myself, understood. He stowed the books on the dash, unbuckled my seat belt, and wrapped his arm around my neck, gathering me into his arms. I dove into their comfort, their forgiveness, my whole body shaking with sobs, as I completely lost it.

* * *

I realized that I couldn't move forward with my life with Luke until I'd settled things with Venus. I couldn't just forget what had happened, and now that I understood that Luke truly didn't remember being with Venus, dancing with her, kissing her—as much as that image would haunt me for a while still—I knew that the only way to move on was to make things right with Venus. Give her a chance to explain.

The only problem was, I didn't know how to find her. I'd banished her. How did you take back a banishment?

"I un-banish you, Venus Cronus," I hollered at the chilly November sky. I'd been pacing the damp, hard-packed sand at the waterfront—the last place I'd seen her—for an hour, trying to stay warm, trying to figure out how to get her back. "You can come back anytime now. I really, really need to talk to you."

There was no answer, except for the cry of the few gulls circling around the docks looking for scraps to scavenge.

"Come on!" I called again, twirling around, spreading my plea out on the wind. "You *have* to be able to hear me!"

She *had* to hear me. I had to give her credit for getting Luke and me together. Maybe I was her last case. Maybe, if I did this one last thing, told her she was right about Luke and me—I could do that at least, even if I couldn't forgive her for what she did—then maybe, she could go home . . . to be with her family. Because of all the things she'd done for me, she'd returned me to *my* family.

That may have been more important even than giving me Luke.

Returning the favor was the least I could do.

She wasn't coming. "Ven-us!" I finally cried.

"Couldn't you have picked someplace that wasn't as hard on the shoes?"

I whirled around to find Venus picking her way through the soggy sand, around seaweed and rocks that *were* hell on snakeskin. "Couldn't you have worn more appropriate shoes?" I asked quietly, afraid of scaring her away again, but smiling so she'd know I was teasing her. Giving her a chance.

She finally came to a halt a few feet away. She looked like a different person. Not in style or appearance, but in her eyes. She looked both haughty and hurt. Angry and sad.

Been there, done that, I thought.

I got right to the point. "I'm ready for an explanation."

She raised an eyebrow. "What if I'm not ready to give you one?"

"I figure that if you're still here, you can't go anywhere until we fix things, right? Otherwise, you'd already be gone." She didn't respond, just continued to stare out at the water over my shoulder. "Luke and I made up today. I love him and I think I understand what happened. I forgave him."

Only her eyes moved as her gaze darted back to my face. They were full of fear. She was still here. I was basically telling her that True Love had prevailed, that she'd succeeded in getting us together, her latest Cinderella/Prince Charming matchup, and yet, she hadn't magically disappeared.

"Tell me what happened," I said. "Make me understand."

She opened her mouth, then clamped it closed again, frowning. "What difference does it make? You've forgiven him. That should be enough."

"Is it?" I asked. "You said I had to learn to love again. I have. My whole life is different than it was before. I have you to thank for that. But why should I be the only one to have to learn something?"

"What in the world does *that* mean?"

I laughed. "It means, did you ever think, Fairy Godmother, that maybe *you* have something to learn, too?"

"I . . . no . . . I . . ."

"Think about it."

Venus visibly sagged and then sighed. "I have thought about it. If Zeus wasn't such a stubborn—"

She was interrupted by a clap of thunder, simultaneous with a spike of lightning, which struck the ground about thirty feet away from us.

"Holy shit!" I screeched as we unwrapped our arms from around each other. "When are you going to learn? You don't taunt the prison guard!"

Our eyes met, and we finally laughed, easing the tension.

"Come on," I said, and we headed down the beach, avoiding the charred sand of Zeus's warning. "Tell me what happened."

Venus hesitated, but finally did tell me, reluctantly. "Part of my punishment is that no man can . . . remember. Kissing me, being with me. Whatever."

"Go on," I encouraged, when she paused. I sensed we had no choice but to get this all out in the open.

"I can use the girdle to get them to do whatever I want, to romance me, kiss me, sleep with me, even."

I shot her a horrified look, and she shook her head.

"Not with Luke. *Never* with the princes. Even I have *some* scruples."

Relaxing, I stepped around some slippery looking seaweed that had washed up on the beach, and then rejoined Venus. In an unusual move for her, she'd removed her stilettos and was carrying them, walking barefoot in what had to be freezing cold sand.

"You don't know what it's like," she continued, "to not be remembered. It's like . . . it's like being invisible. But sometimes—even realizing that it won't mean anything to anyone but me—it's more important to feel loved than it is to—"

"Breathe," I finished for her.

She turned to look at me, eyes glistening as she nodded. "I didn't mean it, Rachel. I swear. I totally fucked up this time. The last rule was right. *Zeus* was right." This she said to the sky, almost pleadingly, willing her father to understand. "You were right," she whispered. Then she turned back to me, laughing humorlessly. "I let my emotions get in the way of just doing my job. I was jealous."

"You were jealous of *me*?" That was laughable.

"I was jealous of *you*. You had Luke. You had a guy willing to practically stalk you for your attention. Not because he was a creepy stalker guy, but because he already loved you, even when you wouldn't give him the time of day. Even when you wanted to be invisible, he still *saw* you. *That's* what I was jealous of. I've been invisible . . . for two thousand years."

I hugged her as she sobbed, mostly because I was sobbing, too, and we were holding each other up.

Venus finally pulled away, self-consciously wiping her nose on her jacket sleeve, until she realized that suede shouldn't be used as a tissue. She produced a Kleenex and blew her nose loudly before answering. "I'm sorry, Rachel. I just needed to . . ."

"Breathe," I said again. "I get that."

"I'm sorry."

I reached out and touched her arm. "I forgive you."

An odd look came over Venus's face. She glanced quickly down at her arm, where my hand lay. She pulled away and began rubbing both arms briskly, like they were cold, or itched. Her eyes widened as she stared back at me. "I have to go."

She turned and began running toward the road, stumbling in the soft spots, stubbing her toes on wood buried in the sand.

"Venus, wait!" I ran after her. What the hell was wrong with her? What had I said?

Finally stopping near the road, Venus reached under the boardwalk and produced her Louis Vuitton suitcase from behind one of the supports.

"I forgive you, and you suddenly need your suitcase desperately?" I asked, out of breath from chasing her. "Not exactly the response I expected."

Venus swallowed hard and chewed her lower lip. "It's time," she whispered. "I'm tingling."

"What?"

She held out her arms, and I swear they were actually beginning to look translucent. "It's time to go." She darted a glance up at the sky. "Just five minutes, *please*."

"Five minutes? What are you talking about? Venus, what—"

I could see the beams of the boardwalk behind her . . . through her. Reaching out, I tried to grab her. My hand went right through her.

"Venus, wait!"

"I can't. I told you it would be fast." She looked like she was crying again, mascara tracks streaking down her face. God, of all people, you'd think she'd know about waterproof mascara, I thought, in that way our brains have of thinking stupid thoughts when they don't want to face real thoughts. But maybe she didn't know about waterproof mascara because she'd never had a need for waterproof mascara. Because I'd never seen her cry before.

Until now.

"Thank you," I finally cried, when I could hardly see her anymore, and I knew it would be my last chance. "Thank you."

And then she was gone.

Poof.

FORTY-SIX

Venus

I didn't get magically transported back to Mount Olympus. I wasn't greeted with fanfare and exuberant welcomes by my friends and family. I didn't get to go home. I guess I haven't reached the magic number yet.

After I'd become fully invisible, I heard Rachel ask in a whisper if we'd ever see each other again. I doubt it. I'll be busy with my next godchild, whom I'll handle much, much differently. To protect her.

To protect myself.

Maybe the *next* one will be my redemption.

I've landed on the coast again, though I don't think I'm in Washington anymore. And, I have no idea what time of year it is. There's a six-month gateway in time where I can be dropped. I swear Zeus punished me once by dropping me in the middle of a Midwest blizzard when I'd just left sunny Hawaii—and was wearing a bikini. Maybe this time he's not quite so mad since I seem to have left cold and dreary November in Cameron Creek, and landed someplace pleasantly warm and sunny. There are even buds on the cherry trees lining the town streets. Like it's springtime. It'll take some exploration to figure out where I am and what I'm supposed to do next.

I suppose, like falling off a horse, I should jump back on, pick my next godchild, and get riding again. But, upon Zeus, I'm tired. I feel like I've run a marathon in stilettos—not a smart thing to do—but then much of what I've done in the past two months hasn't been the smart thing to do.

But, I've been forgiven. And in being forgiven, I don't feel quite so lonely anymore. I may be invisible to all the men I've sought attention from here on Earth. But not to Rachel. She'll remember me. My Cinderellas will remember me.

I drop the shoes I'm still carrying to the ground and slip my feet into them. Adding a few inches to my height adds confidence to my spirit, and I feel a little more like my old self (and by "old," of course, I in no way mean to imply that I *look* old).

I am Venus. Hear me roar.

I am too big to ignore.

Chuckling over my own humor, I start walking. Past souvenir shops and an ice cream parlor. A shoe repair, a gallery of some sort, and a bookstore.

The bookstore window has a display of mythology books. Hey! There's one about me.

I glance up at the old-fashioned sign hanging down from the side of the building. I can't help but smile.

Maybe I'm home after all.

The sign reads: MOUNT OLYMPUS BOOKS.